Thunder

Moon

Book 2 of Kazza's Chatterre Trilogy

Copyright 2015 by Jeanne Foguth

Cataloging-in-Publication Data is on file with the Library of Congress.

ISBN: 978-0-9913338-8-2

Acknowledgments, Etc.

Many thanks to my faithful beta readers, without whom my work would have 'rogue commas' and 'renegade spelling', not to mention strange formatting anomalies, like the occasional extra space before a period. Thank you, Kensleigh, Paul, Kaj, Pauline, and Marcha Fox, I don't know what I would do without you grammar-nazis.

Thank you also to Kiara Graham for her prowess with digital design – I love the way you have incorporated the main characters as well as water and stars.

Books by Jeanne Foguth

Kazza's Sci-fi Chatterre Trilogy:

Star Bridge

Thunder Moon

Fire Island

Fantasy

Xander's Sea Purrtector Files:

Latitudes and Cattitudes (prequel to the Sea Purrtector Files)

The Red Claw

Purr-a-noia

The Vi-Purrs

Me-YEOW!

Contemporary Suspense/Romance

Deadly Rumors

Fatal Attractions

Passion's   Fire

Chapter 1

In the black nothingness of night, the wind blasted sheets of knife-like water over white-topped waves. Lightning lit the sky. Then a resounding boom shook their fragile vessel. Water began pouring into their boat.

His mother screamed and his baby-sister, Nimri, shrieked.

Again, thunder boomed and lightning streaked down, as if aiming at the boat's flapping sail and flailing ropes. The tiller his father was holding disintegrated in a blinding blue explosion and his father shouted in surprise.

Hot embers seared into Thunder's tender flesh and Nimri howled in pain. The putrid stench of burning hair assailed his nose a moment before icy sheets of rain mingled its stench with the cloying sweetness of cantaloupe. Temporarily blinded by the lightning, he clung to the course lumpy cloth, biting his tongue for fear he would scream in terror like Nimri.

The coppery taste of blood filled his mouth and he knew

nothing on Chatterre could be worse than this storm.

Panic welled, face buried against the rough, wet burlap sack, Thunder fought to overcome his terror, then like the answer to a prayer, a warm damp nose nudged his ear.

Kazza!

Thunder grouped for the cat's comforting body, then held him close enough to realize that Kazza's muscles were trembling as badly as his own. "We'll be fine," he whispered, hoping the raging storm would cover the terror in his tone, "It is only a storm. The Lost take boats into The River during storms all the time. If they can do it, so can Father and Mother." A tentative purr rumbled deep within Kazza's core and he felt a bit better. Thunder stroked Kazza's head, but then the heavens boomed, again. Simultaneously the boat slammed against something hard then rolled like a wounded beast in the wind-whipped water.

Just when he'd decided nothing could get worse, everything became still. In the ominous silence, he heard his great-grandfather's enraged voice cursing his enemies. Kazza growled deep in his throat and the fur on his back quivered. The hair on Thunder's neck stood on end in response to the cat's emotion, even as he thought, *thank goodness! Rolf will calm the heavens and save us!* Thunder raised his head above the lumpy sack of melons, but for several frantic heartbeats, the only thing in his ink-black world was the sound of his great-grandfather's angry voice speaking in the magic language.

Kazza shuddered and huddled so close that Thunder could barely breath. "It's okay, grandfather will save us." Kazza's mournful mew disputed his optimism; at least it sounded that way. Thunder petted the cat's sleek fur, his fingers tracing the contours of a soggy, tufted ear. He leaned to the side and whispered words of encouragement, but Kazza seemed focused on the magic language his great grandfather was shouting and only became more agitated.

Abruptly Rolf stopped speaking. The black began to fade to dark gray and the dark clouds seemed to be holding their breath. When Thunder looked around, he saw dark water shooting through a jagged hole in the bottom of their boat. The savage fountain was where his father had stood, Thunder tore his gaze from the broken deck and looked for his father. All that met his gaze was nearly ripped beyond recognition. His mother had her fist stuffed in her mouth and her eyes were huge with horror as she watched the shooting fountain, which was filling the boat. Already, its level had risen to Thunder's knees – and Nimri's waist. His little sister grasped their mother's thigh in a death grip, her terrified stare mutely fixed on the rising water.

The storm had taken his father and it would soon take the rest of them.

A scream surged up his throat.

Thunder scrambled on top of the rough bench seat as a huge wave crashed against the side of their small boat. He tumbled backward, colliding first with the lumpy sack, then landing face first in the rising deluge. He choked on a mouthful of brackish water before he pulled himself back onto the seat.

As if shaken from a trance, his mother lifted her arm and shook her fist at the riverbank they'd left such a short time ago.

He looked to see where she was pointing. His great grandfather, the most powerful person living on Chatterre, stood high on the bluff, clutching his staff of power. Again, hope warmed Thunder as he gazed in awe at Rolf, who obviously had seen their plight and stilled the storm. Even from this distance, he could see his great-grandfather's black eyes flashing with fury as he looked at the sinking boat. How angry he must be for the storm defying him! Thunder held his breath as Rolf raised his staff to save them and shouted something unintelligible to the heavens. Thunder's heart slammed against his ribs in anticipation of seeing a display of his great grandfather's mighty myst magic first-hand. They were saved!

"Let there be more water," his great grandfather bellowed. Thunder frowned in confusion wondering how more water would help.

The River seethed and rose.

"Grandfather!" Thunder screamed above the hulls groans. "Help us!"

Rolf tilted his head back and screamed at the churning clouds. "Wipe out the corrupt Lost." The black skies boomed. Lightning streaked. Thunder's heart hammered against his ribs as he gripped the sinking boat in helpless shock. He stared transfixed as the flood uprooted century old trees, yanking them into the churning waters as easily as his father pulled weeds from the soft soil in their garden. His great grandfather shook his staff. Lightning slashed across the black sky, the boom cracking so close that his teeth vibrated.

Thunder screamed his great grandfathers name pleading for help.

His mother grasped his arm, yanking him around to face her. "Don't." His sister clung to her other side. "He is the power behind the storm."

"No!" he said, unable to believe such an awful thing.

"When we crossed the middle of The River, we joined the Lost." Tears welled in her eyes. He stared at her, unable to believe anyone could use myst power in such an awful way. As the water boiled into their boat, she held him and Nimri tight and told them that their great grandfather must have found out about their plan to end the feud between the tribes and in retaliation he'd brewed this storm for revenge. She stared at the place where his father had been when he shook his fist in defiance. "We should have known we couldn't hide this from Grandfather. We should have known he would retaliate. We should have found another way to heal the breach." She hugged them so tight Thunder couldn't breath. "I'm so sorry. So very, very sorry." Her voice trailed off to a whisper as she stared at the water boiling into the boat, where his father had been. "If I'd known he was willing to kill us, I would have found another way. I would have. I would have." she repeated, as if assuring herself. "If I survive, I still will," she vowed. Her arms tightened around him. "Promise me that if you survive, you will find a way to end the feud." Her eyes bore into his until he gave a slight nod. As she kissed his forehead, a mammoth wave crushed the boat's flimsy side.

With an ear splitting groan, the craft slowly began to slide beneath the water. He screamed, "Mama!"

Another wave slammed against the boat. The force catapulted Thunder into the storm-tossed waves. He gasped, barely filling his lungs, before he plunged headfirst into the water. A gaping black chasm rushed toward him like a hungry mouth. Thunder kicked against the grasping tentacles of water, but the darkness kept speeding toward him. His lungs burned for air. He fought to break free of the ravenous force, but something coiled around his chest, joining the relentless current pulling him toward the murky shadows. Thunder put all his effort into one final thrust, and propelled his head above the water. He gasped for air.

"More!" his great grandfather bellowed.

"No!" screamed Thunder. Fury overwhelmed his fear, making him feel strong. "Stop the storm!" The whipping wind stilled.

An ominous black cloud rolled aside to reveal a star-studded patch of indigo blue sky. The waves calmed.

Rolf turned. His gaze locked on Thunder's face. Eyes flaming with anger, he roared with rage, "Any of the Lost who sets foot on Chosen soil must die!" His grandfather's arrogance seemed to make him grow taller and fiercer. "That means you." He pointed his long bony finger at him.

Thunder wanted to shout back that he wasn't one of the Lost, he was Chosen, but he knew his great grandfather recognized him. Knew he intended to murder him because of the peace his parents dreamed of. A lump of dread filled Thunder's throat.

"Next time, I will not spare a single donkey!" Rolf's finger didn't waver. Thunder imagined he could feel the sharp nail pressing against his chest. "You will pay for your interference." Thunder knew his great grandfather was speaking directly to him, but wasn't sure what he had done to make him so angry or why he would set all nature against them just for crossing the river, which was something the Lost did every market day.

Rolf straightened and grasped his twisted black staff, murder in his look and said something in the magic tongue.

Before Thunder could gasp, raging water surrounded him. Rolf bellowed with fury, then the water swept him downward, beyond the old man's sight.

When, the pressure eased, he saw their boat, his mother and Nimri fluttering downward, like autumn leaves falling from a tree.

His mother's stern gaze bored into him. 'Remember your vow.' He wasn't sure if she had said the words aloud or if he imagined her voice; regardless, he lowered his head in submission. When he looked back a moment later, only the shattered remains of their boat were visible.

He opened his mouth to call for his mother, but chocked on cold water.

'Live for me.' A glow appeared beneath the shattered hull. 'Live for us all.'

"I can't," he cried. Icy water poured into his mouth.

'You must.' The glow grew. Suddenly, he was thrown clear from the water. Then his stomach hit a white-topped wave and he gasped in water. Rolf bellowed with fury. Eyes stinging and lungs laden, Thunder fought against the unrelenting power of the river and screamed for his parents.

Again, a black void loomed ahead. But before he got sucked in, a hand appeared in the depths of the nothingness and beckoned to him. The slim fingers were a woman's. His mother? Grandmother? He quit fighting the current and reached downward. 'You must live for us all.' His mother's appeal echoed through his mind.

Thunder fought to move, but something restrained him. His eyes opened. Solid rock faced him.

Disoriented, he thrashed at his bindings, but they held fast. Panic seized him. Thrashing first left, then right, he fought the bindings. Sweat stung his eyes and bathed his body before he lay quietly to weigh his options.

A cool breath of pange scented air bathed his face. Thunder frowned at the familiar scent, then turned his head toward the draft, but stopped when he recognized his own bedchamber.

It had been the nightmare from his childhood.

Again.

He'd had the same nightmare each night for the past seven days.

And, as he had for the past seven days, immediately upon

waking and realizing he was no longer a child, he remembered Nimri's worried glances at Sacred Peak and her whispered admission, "Every night, when I sleep, I see hordes of ravenous celestial dragons spewing from the Star Bridge." A chill coiled around his heart.

Had his sister's worry over the Star Bridge become the catalyst for him to relive the worst day of his life in his dreams?

Why did his thoughts always switch from the nightmare that spawned his fear of water to the Star Bridge?

Did he dream because Nimri put the thought in his mind or was it a premonition?

Their world had been invaded once before. Gooseflesh rippled over Thunder's back and arms at the memory of the dragon that Nimri envisioned, when they had barely survived one?

Previously when he'd woken in panic, which made the loss of his family stay fresh as a new-cut wound, he'd been able to get up and exercise away his fears. But, this night his sweat-soaked bed linens held him captive, so he had to think about the implications. Lying there trapped by fear, dread and fabric, he knew he had to get up to escape the worry. Had to move. Had to drown the memories with exercise. All he needed was a helping hand to free him from the linen's grasp. "Gunda, Carn, come," he called before remembering they'd fled to the distant inland mountains months before. Where was his mind, if he couldn't recall such a basic thing?

The nightmare had gotten to him so badly that his heart was still pounding like a herd of stampeding horses. He lay imprisoned in linens, looking for something to focus on. Something safe. Something that wouldn't give him time to think about any deeper meaning his nightmare might have.

His attention fastened on the vacant eyes of the crystal cat skull he had found as a child. It lay on a table, in front of the window and seemed to glow with life. Though he knew it was just the way the crystal shone in moonlight, as he looked at the skull, his feeling of impending doom increased, until gooseflesh burst over him and he imagined that he was looking at death.

He tore his gaze away. The maroon hues on his bedchamber's solid rock ceiling were much more calming.

He wondered how many days it would be before someone missed him.

How many days would it be before someone made the effort to make the climb to look for him?

He should have moved closer to the rest of the Tribe after his adoptive parents passed on.

Even if he had, no one would come looking for him because they were afraid of him.

All except Nimri and Larwin.

Hope warmed him for a blessed moment. Then, he realized Nimri was too far along with breeding to climb the treacherous path to his rock-hewn home. And Larwin would not leave her side.

His bones would probably turn to dust before anyone missed him.

If anyone saw how bed linens could subdue him, they would no longer respect him.

Again, a breeze caressed his cheek. Thunder looked at the open window, in front of which, the skull glowed a sinister scarlet. Heart hammering with fear, it took a moment to realize the moon hanging over Sacred Mountain was red. Mouth dry, he realized that while he could ignore his warning dreams, he couldn't ignore this powerful omen of doom. He should have done something when Nimri first told him – anything instead of sit and wait until it was too late. If he could just get free of the linens, he'd seek Nimri and Larwin's council and do whatever they said.

No sooner had the conviction filled his mind, than the bedclothes dropped away from his body.

Thunder leaped out of bed, certain that something dreadful was about to happen … or had happened while he wrapped himself in denial. He dashed out the door of his rock-hewn home, into the small adjoining garden that overlooked the sprawling river valley, and leapt onto a stone bench. He stretched his tall, lean body to look over the pange tree's branches and then studied every detail of Sacred Mountain's face. Out of the corner of his eye, he noticed movement in the shadows beneath a nearby buddleia bush. He whirled to face the darkness, cooling sweat mingling with gooseflesh.

A deep rumpling purr of assurance came from the murky blackness, then Kazza's lithe six-hundred-pound silhouette emerged from beneath the bush. The cat's dark tufted ears twitched with interest, and the sonorous soothing vibration intensified.

Relief swept through Thunder.

Kazza's purring assurance chased away the worst of Thunder's dread with the sound of comfort. The great cat hopped onto the bench, next to him and Kazza twined his supple gold, black and white striped flanks against his thighs. The sensations of comfort overpowered the dream-induced terror. 'You are mine,' the huge cat seemed to say as he wrapped his tail around Thunder's waist, 'and I will protect you.' Warmth crept into Thunder's core; replacing the numbing cold.

Thunder sighed at the reprieve.

An affectionate, leathery nose prodded the palm of his hand. Thunder stroked Kazza's muscular spine shoulders to flanks, then fingered the smooth, silky texture of his luxuriant fur until his tail twitched. It had been nearly impossible for all their skills and resources combined to kill the lone dragon. They could not chance another beast coming through, much less an invasion of many.

The insistent need to close the Star Bridge began circling through his mind.

Thunder sat down on the bench, his arm draped around Kazza's massive shoulders. The cat sat next to him, whiskers whirling, eyes alert as if reading his thoughts and the waking worries he had taken from his vision. Together, Thunder and Kazza turned and looked past the garden's encircling stonewall to scrutinize Sacred Mountain's cloud-shrouded summit as they were both worried about another invasion.

Would Nimri and her soon-to-be-born-babe be safe from more marauding dragons?

Would any of them survive another assault by the aura-devouring beasts?

Kazza stopped purring. His ears tilted forward, one tuft moving up and down, as if in expectation. A sweet-scented breeze caressed them, then the craggy contours of the mountain's sheer rock face appeared in harsh contrast to the black moss of the star-studded night sky. While they watched, clouds scudded away from the moon, bathing the peak in a reddish hue.

Kazza shivered at the sight of the evil omen.

So did Thunder.

Some legends were true and in them, some fates could be worse than the near drowning he kept reliving in his nightmares.

As he gazed at the red rock, Thunder became even more certain that Nimri's dreams and his nightmares were omens: unless someone closed the Star Bridge's magic portal, more of the aura-consuming beasts would invade their world. Once here, the dragons would destroy everything, as they had on the old world and Chatterre would become a lifeless cinder, like Larwin described their old world to be.

There were no more magical portals to take the tribes to a new, safer world.

With no other option, they – no, he – had to make this world safe. Thunder swallowed. "Nimri's dreams are warnings of what could be," Thunder murmured. "And mine are a sign for action."

Kazza purred in agreement.

Thunder cleared his throat. Kazza tilted his head to one side, watching him with unblinking amber eyes. "I must find a way to close the way to the dragons."

Kazza purred harder and licked his hand, in agreement.

What if it was already too late to close the portal? A lump of dread formed in Thunder's stomach, then he shook his head. It couldn't be too late. "I need to talk with Larwin and GEA-4 and find out if either of them have any ideas about dealing with this. He frowned. And, I need to find out more about Nimri's dreams." Kazza's whiskers twirled, then his luminous amber gaze moved back to the ill-omened peak and his ears flattened against his head.

Thunder hand settled on Kazza's powerful shoulder as they stared at the jagged rock. "The ancients needed mystics on both worlds to open the portal. I wonder if it can be closed from one side." Kazza leaned against his thigh, but his solid support didn't encourage Thunder as it normally did. Instead, a choking lump formed in Thunder's throat. "Nimri could handle this side – she wouldn't have to climb the mountain, and I wouldn't mind going to the other side if I believed I had a chance of surviving long enough to fulfill the need, but Larwin said there was no air on the old world." And that it had taken hours to move from the surface to the portal – no one can hold their breath that long. He turned his attention to the great cat; Kazza's amber gaze appeared to blur. If he found a way to the other side, he doomed himself to death. Yet someone had to go. He had to go, thus he must find a way to survive long enough to protect the rest. Thunder's heart slammed against his ribs. He took a calming breath, but the air only made him worry how he could possibly close the breach and a certainty grew that this time he would not cheat death, though the thought gave him pause, he told himself that one life compared to the thousands he could save was insignificant.

Still, he didn't know how he could possibly complete the task destiny seemed to have given him.

But he would find a way – somehow.

Thunder hurried inside and rummaged in his clothes chest for his favorite breeches and leather vest. As he dressed, his hand touched the amulet bag his mother had made before The River swallowed her. When his fingertips brushed its intricate beadwork, he wished stories had been passed down about how his ancestors had opened the portal, but that information had been lost over the past millennium.

How ironic that the Star Bridge, which had once saved his ancestors had become the path that could doom them.

His fingers tightened around the amulet's worn leather and beads. Though he wished he could elude this fate, it seemed as if his entire life had built toward this desolate destiny. Closing The Portal would mean that he would die as he lived most of his life: alone. He swallowed and vowed, again, that if there were a way to save Chatterre from Solterre's fate, he would find it.

Despite the darkness of the night and the evil red moon, Thunder jogged down the twisting trail from his home. Near dawn, when he came to the wheel-rutted main track, he ran faster. Sweat bathed his brow and soon his panting breaths blocked out the normal night sounds. By late afternoon, exhaustion rippled over his muscles, but still he plodded toward the last place he wanted to be: The River. Since he'd nearly drowned, as a child, he'd only been this near the area when the dying dragon had fallen and its heat had turned the turbulent water into billowing masses of steam and cracking clods of once-wet muck.

His pace slowed as he neared the dragon's petrified carcass. His sister had seen the remains as an opportunity to fulfill his parent's goal of joining the tribes, so once the remains had cooled, each tribe had built an earthen ramp and twisted sturdy vines between the rigid limbs so no one would slip off the craggy belly into the rushing river below. Though Nimri and Larwin had used the new bridge many times to visit him, and many couples had followed Tansy and Otter's example of giving life-vows, which joined Chosen and Lost, this was the first time Thunder had attempted crossing the beast's long, rough belly.

Thunder stepped from the hard packed soil onto what had had once been the beast's tail then stood still, breathing deeply as he studied how the creature arced upside-down across the water. Three of the ten wingtips plunged deep in the water, causing white-capped waves to slam against their lifeless edges. All ten legs stretched toward the clear morning sky, as if trying to grasp thin rays of morning light from the sky.

As he stood staring at the bridge, a donkey towing a cart piled high with lumpy sacks clattered up the Chosen's earthen ramp. With a jounce, the wooden wheels rumbled onto the dragon's throat, and bumped onto the rough scales which covered the beast's chest. A tiny green orb eased out of one sack, fell to the ground, then rolled away. The larger boy gave chase, after what was probably a cabbage, but it fell into the water before he could grasp it. The dot disappeared for a moment, then bobbed to the surface further downstream. The boy cried out, as he slipped and fell on his bottom. Somehow, the child managed to scramble backward. Cold sweat bathed Thunder as he watched the lad inch back toward the flat center area of the throat. The kids looked the size of fleas compared to the dragon, but that didn't mean the path was safe. The boys laughed and scrambled after the donkey. Thunder watched them approach his side and wished crossing the river was as easy as they made it look. Then, he looked for the cabbage, but it had disappeared. If he didn't get past his fear of being so close to water, he could lose everything he cared for.

When the cart and laughing boys passed him, Thunder squared his shoulders and by force of will, hiked up the rest of the beast's tail. Focusing on a tall pine, on the opposite shore, he crossed the belly without looking at the vile water below, and only lost sight of the tree after he started down the scaly throat. By the time his moccasins touched the soil on the other shore, Thunder knew he could do anything.

Through the rest of the morning, he forced his fears back, and by early afternoon step by step he climbed up a path, which passed through Nimri's sprawling herbal garden. He felt proud that he'd come this far.

A thin gray tendril of smoke rose from the stone chimney until it mingled with the sequoia boughs a hundred feet above. Thunder paused for a moment and watched the way the sun's rays caressed the home, which spiraled around the tree's massive trunk.

When Rolf had exacted his revenge, all the stately trees on his side of the river had been ripped from the ground and torn to bits by the raging water. A leftover chill from his nightmare washed over him and mixed with a sense of homesickness. Thunder shook off the memories and hastened to the kitchen's thick round door. Scents of fresh-baked bread mixed with the aroma of the dried herbs. His mouth watered as he knocked. "Nimri. Larwin," he called.

The sound of hurried footfalls preceded Larwin's arrival. "Thunder! Come in!" He nearly pulled him over the threshold, his every gesture displaying happiness to see him. "What brings you here?"

"His dreams do." Nimri hugged him. "It's good to see you." Her unborn baby kicked him in the stomach.

Thunder chuckled as he kissed her ear. The babe kicked him, again. "Hugging you is getting dangerous." Then he whispered, "How do you know about my dreams?"

She tried to smile as he stepped back in time to avoid a third kick. Thunder smoothed a stray lock of ebony hair behind her ear. He'd never seen her dark hair free from the braid that hung to her knees or such a look of fear in her eyes.

Larwin clasped his shoulder. "Do me a favor. It's been a year. If another madrox was going to come, it would have by now. Convince your sister that we're safe, then maybe we can all get some sleep."

Nimri looked from her husband to him. "I think dragons go by a different sort of time."

Thunder sat down at the table. "I can't tell anyone we're safe while the star bridge remains open." Nimri looked relieved as she put a pot of water on to boil. He gestured to her swollen stomach. "Obviously, you can't climb the mountain to check it and I'm not certain that myst travel could tell us anything."

Nimri winced. "That's the last thing we want to do." Larwin gave her a questioning look. "Remember how the dragon followed our essence?"

Larwin slumped onto the bench. "I thought you were dead." He swallowed hard.

"I wish we'd finished the job instead of celebrating." Tears welled in Nimri's expressive green eyes.

"We can't change the past," Thunder said, "but perhaps we can alter the future. I know I must close the star bridge, but don't know how. Have your dreams offered a clue?"

She shook her head. "I wish they had."

"I'd hoped to fill the cave with water but…" He shrugged helplessly. "There's no water on the mountain top and no way to get enough up there."

Nimri put mugs of steaming tea on the table, then added plates. Larwin grabbed two long loaves of black bread and began slicing them. Thunder glanced around the kitchen. "Where's Bryta?"

"Helping Pearl nurse Zurgon, if you can believe that."

Thunder raised a brow. "You taught her how to heal?"

"No one can cure old age," Nimri explained. "All my life, Bryta considered Pearl her main rival, yet now, with Zurgon dying, they swear that they've been best friends since childhood."

"Perhaps Zurgon came between them." Thunder crumbled a slice of bread. "I need to close the portal, so let's figure out a way."

"The star bridge was opened when mystics from both worlds worked together, one on each end." Nimri studied the tea in her cup, as if looking for answers.

"There's no air on the old world, so obviously there isn't anyone there to work with." Larwin ran his fingers through his shoulder-length hair in frustration. "If I hadn't lost my suit-"

"The ugly black muscle one?" Nimri interrupted.

Larwin nodded. "It carried air, but not enough to sustain life indefinitely."

"When Thunder and I use myst, we don't need air." She bit her lip and looked at him. "Do you think I could spirit travel to the other end?"

"No." Thunder frowned at her. "Especially not now." No matter how many solutions she proposed, he must climb the mountain and find a way to close the portal.

"GEA-4 doesn't require air," Larwin said.

"And she can not use myst," Nimri said, effectively closing that possible option.

"Did Rolf ever say for certain how it was opened?" Thunder asked.

"Not to me." Nimri clutched her mug as if she needed its heat. "He was convinced he could keep himself alive forever, so he never made an effort to teach me anything of value."

"Sure he did." She looked at him with surprise. "He taught you he was a lying, vindictive monster." Thunder picked up a breadcrumb and rolled it between his fingers. "Sorry. I'm obviously trying to avoid the real issue by upsetting you." He cleared his throat. "I wonder if we could load the cavern with potassium nitrate, charcoal, and sulfur."

"Primitive gunpowder." Larwin's eyes gleamed. "I like that

idea. You might be able to use my laser projector to ignite it. I'll get it. And for something like that, GEA-4 would be useful." He left the room as if every second counted.

Nimri looked glum. "How could we haul enough minerals and chemicals up that treacherous trail? And worse, how could we be certain we don't blow the top of the mountain off and make it easier for the dragons to enter our world?"

Thunder winced.

"Explosives should work," GEA-4 said as she entered from the garden. The android placed a basket filled with aromatic leaves on the counter.

"So you believe that we can haul what we need up the mountain?" Thunder asked, hope warming him.

"That would be unnecessary." Thunder wondered if he would ever get used to talking to GEA-4, whose mouth didn't move and whose silvery eyes never blinked. "Onboard the Pterois Volitan, there are enough explosives to disintegrate the entire planetoid but it would be safest to set just enough off in the old world's tunnel to collapse it."

"She is correct," Larwin said, as he reentered the kitchen.

Nimri looked at Larwin in surprise.

"But I still don't see how that helps me, without the air suit," Thunder said.

"I do not need air," GEA-4 said, "and I am familiar with the weaponry aboard the Pterois Volitan."

"You want to do this?" Thunder eyed the small, silver-eyed woman, uncertain about how he felt about her volunteering to take the burden off his shoulders.

"As per Article 123, it is my duty to protect allies."

"That's what got us into this mess," Larwin muttered. Then he gave Nimri a warm look and took her hand in his. "And I'm glad I found this world." He cleared his throat and addressed the android, "How would you make certain you and Chatterre were protected from the blast-pattern?"

"Leave the torpedoes on the planetoid with a timer, then fill the cave with rocks and dirt to cushion the blast."

Larwin squinted at the android and frowned. "It could work."

"Do we have another choice?" Thunder asked.

Larwin shook his head. "Not if the problem is so bad that both of you are having nightmares."

"If GEA-4 can do this, you don't have to climb Sacred Mountain." Nimri smiled.

Thunder placed his palm over his amulet. "Yet I must go." She stared at him. He raised his hands in submission. "I don't know why, I simply know that I must."

Tears welled in her expressive green eyes. Silence stretched as they stared at each other, then she slowly nodded. "How long before you leave?"

He stood up. "The sooner I leave, the sooner we're all safe."

By the following dawn, he and the android had climbed above the tree line. GEA-4 faced the rising sun, to absorb its power. Exhausted, he sat on a cold rock, and looked at fluffy peach puffs hanging innocently between a clear blue dawn and the far off bluff, where he'd grown up. Would he ever see his home, again? Did it matter? By the time the android was ready to continue on, the burning sun had faded the clouds to white.

*C*hapter 2

Raine piloted Nambaba around the asteroid's rough outcropping, in time to see the mooncalf's tail disappear behind another large, rocky lump. "Oh, no, not this time."

Trying the same trick three times in an hour was too much. The only thing worse was that it had gotten away from her the first two times. "We are not playing ring-around-the-rock, again," she said through clenched teeth. Raine quickly calculated where she needed to be to ambush the beast and rammed Nambaba's nav-stick hard to starboard. Her ship's antiquated hull groaned.

Getting into position in time became a test between Nambaba's sluggish controls and the mooncalf's speed, so Raine pushed her ship past its limits and imagined the stubborn beast soaring through the cosmos, unsuspecting of a surprise attack.

Suddenly, a warning light pulsed crimson.

Almost immediately, a cautionary tone blared.

Raine gritted her teeth and focused on her goal. The ship was almost in position for a hypoblast that would send the mooncalf flying homeward when the nav-stick began shuddering.

"Warning," Nambaba's calm maternal voice said.

Death in this backwater asteroid field would be preferable to any punishment she would get for losing one of The Zar's herd. "Hold course," she commanded.

Oh, how she wished she could punish the beast for all the problems it had given her. The maddening adolescent had given her such a bad shift that she imagined she could taste its silica-rich blood. Raine's quivering finger tightened around the trigger in anticipation of the coming shot. "I'm a dragon officer," she growled through clenched teeth. "I must protect the mooncalf."

"Visual contact in one micron," Nambaba stated.

The mooncalf's gnarled golden nose appeared beyond the asteroid. Raine took deep breaths, while reminding herself of honor and duty as she counted off the seconds until she could see all five pairs of wings beating in harmony and the targeting program turned from red to green.

She jerked the targeting from a killing shot to a near-miss and fired.

The hydro jet exploded past the mooncalf's starboard side, as she accelerated her ship toward it, in an attempt to turn it back toward Vilecom, its home moon. The madrox's nostrils flared large enough to berth Nambaba, while its five pairs of golden wings frantically flapped as it twisted backward. A moment later, it disappeared behind a different asteroid.

Raine thrust the nav-stick forward and accelerated around the rock in the opposite direction.

"Target lost," Nambaba belatedly stated the obvious.

If she returned without the mooncalf, she'd be tortured until she begged for death.

Her antiquated spaceship turned tight around the asteroid. When a jutting beak of rock blocked her way, she eased out of the turn, but the nav-stick flopped forward like a piece of beached seaweed, and Nambaba dove toward the rocky outcrop at full speed. Raine yanked the nav-stick back. The trajectory didn't change. She moved it from starboard to port. Nothing.

Warning whistles shrieked through the cockpit. The entire console seemed to strobe scarlet. The view-screen skewed sideways toward the asteroids' surface.

"Collision alert." Nambaba serenely stated the obvious.

"Change course to avoid." The controls didn't move and the ship remained jammed on the collision course.

Raine dropped her targeting array and then punched the console with her fist. Next, she grabbed the nav-stick, but now, instead of being free, it was stuck in a dive. She clamped both hands on the nav-stick, and strained to pull it back. Sweat broke out on her brow. Her helmet's visor fogged. And for all that effort, the nav-stick only jerked backward a notch, so they were still racing toward the unforgiving rock.

More alarms joined the clamor booming throughout the control-hub.

"Collision alert," Nambaba repeated.

Raine hit the thrust-reverser. It sputtered, but didn't power up. "Illegal maneuver." As usual, Nambaba's computer generated voice sounded too calm in light of the circumstances.

Raine punched the control panel again. "This is an emergency."

Nothing happened.

Raine slammed her fist against the button a third time. "Override!"

The asteroid's craggy surface filled half the panoramic view-screen. So close she could identify rock formations. At this speed and with the rock's mass, there wasn't space to maneuver.

But she had to try.

She smashed the button a forth time.

"Collision warning." Another siren joined the din. Trust the Overlord's maintenance program to make certain that all the alarms functioned, while fundamental safety and navigation systems were barely operational.

Raine struck the thrust-reverser with all her might. A burst of pain went from knuckle to shoulder, but the course stayed the same. Raine heaved her entire one-hundred-twenty-pounds against the controls. The nav-stick jerked free. Her solar plexus' hit so hard she felt the impact from her forehead to her toes. Despite the pain, she pushed with her legs.

The stick shot forward so fast, the seat harness cut into her shoulders jerking her backward. On the view-screen, rugged rock still dominated. "If I die, so does Dalf." Raine gritted her teeth and held on.

"Command does not compute."

"Allow pilot override."

The view-screen's rocky image magnified the panorama and revealed a thin crack. As the seconds ticked by, the crack enlarged until it resembled a gigantic mouth opening to devour Nambaba, like it had the dust-covered ship that was already in the bottom of the crevasse.

ooo

Tem-aki absentmindedly fingered the embossed insignia on her spacesuit as she studied the mineral analysis of the large asteroid she had landed on. Despite its high iron content, it wasn't worth the fuel to haul the huge rock to Guerreterre. Tem-aki stretched her back by extending her legs and pointing the toes of her heavy turquoise boots, causing the insignia on her uniform to appear to flicker like burning flames.

If Guerreterre hadn't been experiencing a rare peacetime, this work bay would have been filled with enough weapons to vaporize a small moon. Fortunately for her, during peacetime, replacing the arsenal with a science lab had been a priority. Using the old warbird for research gave her more room for experiments than any other space lab she had ever been assigned to. Tem-aki closed her eyes and allowed herself a moment to bask in the luxury of getting a great ship like the Dasya Voltain and the chance to follow her brother. But if these rocks only had basic elements, which just about any world could provide, she'd need to look elsewhere and that would mean, she would lose her chance to search Larwin's last known coordinates.

Tem-aki swallowed. Despite what the official paperwork and atmosphere-free surroundings said, she refused to believe he was dead. She'd fought for this assignment after getting word of his death, so she could finally have closure, but thus far, that had alluded her. Tem-aki shook her head at her naïve belief that she could find something as small as a ship in a square light-year of space, yet she was unwilling to give up her self-imposed assignment. Her mother acted like a search was a total waste of time, but she had acted that way as long as Tem-aki could remember and she suspected it was because it was rare for a warrior to live beyond his teenage years, so her mother had probably begun to accept Larwin's death as inevitable as soon as he qualified for the military academy.

Tem-aki studied the computer's analysis. Despite the iron content being too low to interest Guerreterre's Supreme Commander, it might be high enough to interest some of the more primitive industrial worlds her planet controlled. She chewed her lower lip. Unless she found something marketable, soon, she would be reassigned.

Something thudded against the hull of her ship so hard that the screen flashed black. "What the-" Tem-aki dashed to the auxiliary control board and smacked a toggle switch. A hologram image of the Dasya Voltain inside the asteroid's deep canyon shimmered into view; semi-transparent dust and rocks rained down onto her ship's image, as the clatter of the real ones bombarding the hull echoed through her ship.

Were asteroids subject to earthquakes? She'd never heard of such a thing, but that didn't mean it was impossible.

"Computer, analyze cause of disturbance." Despite her impatience, the holograph image swirled and changed, expanding outward until it showed an odd thing undulating through the asteroid belt in pursuit of a madrox. "What the-"

"It is a scyphozoan style spacecraft," Dasya Voltain said.

"Who uses them?" Tem-aki asked, as she stared at the ungainly thing that looked more like an unraveling ball of spaghetti than a spacecraft. Surely something that cumbersome in appearance couldn't be a war ship.

"They were in service on Kalamar fifty years ago."

Tem-aki frowned. She'd heard of Kalamar, but couldn't recall where or why. "Are they an enemy?"

"Negative. A treaty was established ninety-three-years ago."

Dasya Voltain had to be wrong. Guerreterre didn't make treaties with other worlds; they simply took them over. The madrox in the hologram darted deeper into the asteroid field and the raggedy-looking spacecraft went after it. Tem-aki shook her head at the bizarre behavior. Spacecraft went into warp drive to avoid the energy-sapping dragons, they didn't follow them. She squinted at the images, certain that her tired eyes were betraying her, but the old spaceship continued to weave through the asteroid field in pursuit of the beast. If Kalamar pilots chased madrox and the beasts actually ran from them, she could understand why her world had a treaty with their world – going against crazies, who had weaponry that terrified a madrox would probably have forced the Guerreterre's forces to fight until the resources were wiped out, and the planet was probably just as worthless a project as finding useful resources in this asteroid belt.

A flicker of movement brought her attention back to the hologram image in time to see the madrox fly over the cleft she was in, again. A heartbeat later, the spaceship went over. If the dragon ever got tired of leading that nutty pilot around and started looking for other entertainment, this hole could become a trap.

"Computer, start engines and prepare for departure." Before she finished the sentence, she felt the deep rumble of the engines coming online.

She frowned at the hologram image. Had her brother died at the claws of a madrox? She shook her head. Such a primitive beast could never have brought down a Colonel in the Shadow Force. Still, the beast and the crazy pilot chasing it were the only anomalies she'd seen in the weeks she'd been prospecting the asteroid belt, so maybe she should check them out further.

As Dasya Voltain exited the cleft, Tem-aki transmitted her research file to the Mineralogy Department, while she searched for a safe place from which to observe the odd chase.

The big question was if she could get approval to change

her geological survey to a reconnaissance mission.

Chapter 3

Though Raine's muscles screamed with pain, she continued fighting for control. It seemed like an eternity before Nambaba's trajectory shifted toward another plume of suspended dust, where the mooncalf's tail had fanned the asteroid's surface.

A moment later, the antiquated ship entered the unnatural haze. Solid particles slammed against the panorama-window with such force that Raine feared it would crack. Worse, the image on her navscreen looked like a burial shroud was wrapping around her ship. Gooseflesh erupted across her skin at the thought. Abruptly, the display went black. She needed to see more than she needed extra hydro shielding. "Nambaba, purge all sensors."

Still flying blind, Raine visualized where the asteroid had been before everything had gotten clogged with dust, placed her feet against the console, kept pulling back on the nav-stick and prayed for a miracle.

Nambaba's hull moaned in agony.

Thunk! A larger rock smashed against the hull sending an echoing crash throughout the ship.

A muted, high-pitched shrieking sound began and quickly got louder and louder. She usually heard something similar during reentry through Kalamar's humid atmosphere and had learned it was caused by the ship's trailing tentacles rubbing together, but the shriek had never lasted so long or been so loud. She hoped the purge was causing the horrid noise and it would soon be over. Eyes tight shut and teeth clamped she hung on.

Suddenly a calliope of alarms began screaming warnings of doom.

"Spirit," Raine prayed, "either give me strength or instant death!" Nambaba shuddered so violently her sweat-soaked hands slipped inside her gloves. She expected the hull to collapse around her or a snagged tentacle to snatch all possibility of deliverance away.

There was a loud hiss that drowned out all other sounds, then stopped as suddenly as it had begun. "Purge complete."

Raine opened one eye and saw an open star-field. Either the Spirit had given her a miracle or she was dead. Sweat dripped from her forehead, splattered on the console, then puddled. Corpses didn't perspire, did they? Her joints ached from her ears to the souls of her feet and her right shoulder felt as if it was on fire, but she'd survived. "Thank you, Spirit!"

Releasing her death-grip on the nav-stick, Raine flexed her fingers.

"Nambaba, where is that demonic beast?"

"Command does not compute."

"Nambaba, locate the mooncalf."

"Searching." Moments later, the thin reddish line of a heat-trail materialized on the navscreen. It looked like the dragon had returned to its original heading.

"Nambaba, increase image."

"Enhancing." The image enlarged until she could see the mooncalf's wings flare as it navigated a solar current.

It was heading toward a large, black orb. What held such appeal for the heat and energy-loving beast? "What sort of power does that place have? And please don't tell me it's some sort of black hole."

"Command does not compute."

"Your programmer needs to be recycled," she growled. "Nambaba, scan the mooncalf's apparent destination."

"Sixty-two-percent likelihood that the objective is this ash-covered planetoid." The computer magnified the dark sphere in an insert box on the screen.

"What sort of energy source is attracting it?"

"Readings are inconclusive."

"Can you pinpoint the mooncalf's precise objective?"

"Negative."

What would have enough intensity to entice a mooncalf across… "Nambaba, how far have we traveled?"

"One-hundred-seventy-light-years."

Raine swallowed hard. "Which sector are we in?"

"Uncertain."

"Nambaba, explain."

"The border between Guy-N and Alif has changed many

times."

Alif's center was home to Guerreterre's Shadow Warriors. Her heart slammed against her ribs. "Does Guerreterre claim this part of Guy-N?" Mouth dry, she waited for the computer to process the information.

"We passed a Guerreterran marker buoy shortly after you ordered pilot override, therefore, it is highly likely we are in their territory."

Cold sweat bathed Raine at the thought. Some claimed that the sadistic perverts killed the inhabitants of the planets they conquered for entertainment. Others whispered that they were cannibals and ate the inhabitants. She shivered. She was inclined to believe the ones who claimed that the Shadow Warriors enslaved the people they conquered to toil in their mines. While that wasn't a much better fate, at least it was some sort of life. Regardless, whether it was fast or slow, the shadow demons destroyed every planet they conquered.

She should know, because two years before, they had ruined her family.

Had the ash-covered rock, which attracted the dragon once been a living, breathing world that Shadow Warriors had sucked the life from? Raine gulped. "Nambaba, examine everything within ten light-years of our location for heat and energy readings consistent with a masked ship." Raine scrutinized the mooncalf's destination, and thanked The Spirit that Kalamar's Overlord had the power to protect her world from such a fate.

Unfortunately, she wasn't where he could defend her.

Silence ensued while lights on the console flashed and programs whirled. Perspiration trickled down Raine's spine. "Scan negative."

"If there was a boundary buoy, there must be a ship in the vicinity to enforce their claim. Scan again."

"Scan negative," Nambaba repeated far too quickly.

Raine frowned, as she tried to make sense of the conflicting information. Perhaps Nambaba's charts were wrong or the marker had been overlooked. Since her job did not entail leaving the orbit of Vilecom, Kalamar's nursery moon, the current inter-galactic war zones probably had not been fed into Nambaba's data base. Raine took a deep breath and concluded that she had no way of knowing how close she might be to Guerreterre's space, but she certainly had a job to do and that meant she must get the mooncalf back to Vilecom.

ooo

Wheezing in the mountaintop's thin air, Thunder leaned against the jagged, freezing rock wall and marveled how the dragon's passing had made some areas smooth and slick as a pond on a windless day, while leaving other areas sharp enough to slice skin from bone.

When GEA-4, who remained full of vigor and agile as a mountain goat, finished securing the rope she'd brought, he cautiously moved closer to the portal's black, gaping maw. Looking in, he barely recognized it as the same place he had previously visited via myst. The ancient cavern had distended and reformed until neither stalactites nor stalagmites remained to mark the ancient cave. Here, the dragon's immense heat had smoothed all the stone walls so much that where the sun hit, light glinted, as if on water.

GEA-4 methodically moved down the rope until her silvery-white hair vanished in the gloom. Thunder wished he knew why he needed to be here; he simply knew he had to.

At least he'd thought he was needed here.

Several times, during the exhausting climb, he'd wondered why he had such a strong feeling about the need, when GEA-4 obviously would have made the climb faster without him. And now, when his need for air kept him from doing anything of value, it seemed like his presence was more of a problem than a benefit.

Yet, he remained convinced that he had to be here.

He turned away from the gaping hole and looked around the plateau. For over a millennium, the balata had thrived under the golden gaze of the stone guardians. Now, the only balata were growing from the seeds Larwin had planted in the center of Nimri's garden, to commemorate their victory over the dragon. He hoped the fragile purple saplings survived to spawn a new grove of promise. Hoped he was able to circumvent the coming disaster, whatever that might be.

Thunder closed his eyes against the dismal furrow of melted rock leading from the Star Bridge to the cliff overlooking their valley. Did everything the beasts touched end up barren? Nimri had once myst-traveled to the land of their ancestors. Upon returning, she'd told him the rough, barren land lay under a black sky, which held rocks instead of clouds. He shuddered at her description and the memory of her near-death experience on that lifeless land. Spirit-travel to the old world would have been an amazing experience, but Nimri was correct, it was far too dangerous.

Thunder moved away from the gaping maw and looked over the fertile valley. Dragon Bridge was no more than a thin dark smudge against the glistening water of the river. How insignificant the beast looked from here! Yet the beast's ancestors had burned the old world and it was his duty to see that it didn't happen, again.

Lungs burning for air, he hoped he survived long enough to do whatever destiny was directing him toward. GEA-4's solution had to work because if his dreams were right, as they had been before, until the Star Bridge was closed, they were all in danger. He paced alongside the slick rock, heading back to the portal. GEA-4 still hadn't returned. He slumped onto a rock, which wasn't too far from the opening, resigned to waiting, but frustrated by feeling so useless.

Beneath him, the rock shifted. They needed dirt and rocks to block the old cave, so he grasped the rock, glad to have finally found the reason why he'd come. By the time the fourth rock clattered into the old cavern, Thunder's entire body was bathed in sweat, his eyes stung, his lungs burned and he wondered why Larwin had expected little GEA-4 to do this chore by herself. Even if he kept at this for the rest of his natural life, he didn't think the project would ever get completed. He grimaced and glanced ruefully at his pack, which only held enough food and water for two more days.

By the time he'd moved a dozen rocks, his eyes and nose burned from the combined sweat and dust. He held up bleeding, a soot-covered hand. Despite the pain, the burning need to protect his world drove him to keep digging up rocks and dumping them into the old cave.

When he could do no more, Thunder sat down near his backpack, tried to wipe the grime off his hands, then retrieved his flask of water. He took a drink. If only the peak contained a convenient pond, he wouldn't need to move the stones.

But no water existed up here and wishing wouldn't create any.

He put his flask back in his pack and went back to moving rubble into the cave. As he carried a heavy rock to the opening, something tripped him. He dropped the rock, as he smashed to his knees, then staggered upright and kicked what looked like a layer of thick soot. Oddly enough, it didn't move. Thunder squinted at the heap. Had the heat transformed it? Something seemed odd, but he couldn't decide exactly what. With a shrug, he picked up the rock and hauled it to the opening.

Several rocks later, the strange soot tripped him, again. This time he remained on his knees, and studied the strange area. He rubbed a bit between his fingers. Slick, like a glaze, yet pliable as a leaf in the breeze. It held together, instead of crumble, like normal dust. He frowned. Why had this mass transformed so differently from the other surfaces? Ever the researcher, Thunder dug through the dirt and grime at the edges of the odd deposit. As he excavated around the edges, he realized the section went deeper than a hand-span. What substance had reacted like this to the dragon? If he could figure that out, perhaps one of the potters could try to duplicate the phenomena in a kiln. Thunder paused and fingered the strange substance. Even if the process could be duplicated, he couldn't imagine what use the stuff would have, but still, it was worth examining. After several minutes, his fingertips felt dried leaves, but the narrow, deep excavation he had managed to create prohibited a visual inspection. Rock chips flew, as he used Larwin's special red light to expand the hole. This time, when he peered into the crock-sized hole, torn, dirty, dry maroon balata leaves were visible at the bottom. He tweaked a leaf from beneath the odd substance. Thunder's heart hammered against his ribs with excitement, as he grasped the edge of the strange stuff and tugged, but rocks and debris still held it. He bit his lower lip and studied the substance. Nimri had often teased Larwin about his ugly, smelly suit. Larwin always chuckled his sister under her chin and joked that without that suit and the air it held, he would never have found her. Thunder bent down and sniffed the odd substance; a faint scent of sweat mixed with the vague scent of honey. This had to be the air suit. Thunder carefully cut a medium large slab of rock off it, then glanced at the gaping opening of the star bridge and began tossing everything, which covered the suit into the portal. By the time he pulled it free, he felt exhausted from the effort of unearthing the outfit. He yanked it free from its burial place. Amazingly, the filth fell away. Thunder held it up, then turned it around, but didn't see any tears. The substance's durability amazed him, as did the hawk emblem on the suit's chest. It certainly did look like his family's spirit-animal and the suit, as a whole didn't look nearly as ugly as Nimri had always claimed. Thunder held it against his chest. It looked like it would fit him. Not surprising, since he and Larwin had similar builds and size. Thunder glanced at the miserable heap of rock, which had taken him hours to dump into the hole, then looked back at the fascinating suit.

He dusted off his clothes, then stepped into the amazing outfit and flexed his shoulders. Though the front gapped open, the fabric moved with his muscles and felt comfortable. If he had the laces, gloves and shoes to go with it, maybe he could go to the old world and help GEA-4.

Thunder walked to his backpack, removed his water flask and studied the trench. Fascinating how the suit had protected the fallen leaves underneath it. Though all were dry as the surrounding dust, many had retained a hint of their lustrous magenta color, making them a pleasant sight amid the black.

He took a swig of water.

At home, when Larwin undressed, he always left everything in a heap. That should mean the other parts were close to the suit. He shrugged out of the frame-hugging uniform and began enlarging the trench. When the hollow was nearly double in size, he found a glove. It fit his left hand perfectly. Since the landslide appeared to have moved it downhill, he concentrated his efforts there. In quick succession, he unearthed both shoes.

Several breaks later, he found the second glove.

He tried on the ensemble and wished he had a clear pond to see his reflection. A quiet movement caught his attention; GEA-4 emerged from the opening, her arms filled with a large, lumpy bag.

"Have you finished setting the explosives?"

"Not completely." She placed the sack by the stone feet. "Have you found the helmet?"

"The what?"

"The head covering."

He grimaced, as he recalled Nimri's comments about Larwin's horrible bubble-hat. "No."

GEA-4 stared at the ground as if she could look through solid stone. As amazing as the odd little woman-child was, he wouldn't be surprised if she could see all the way to his distant home. "It is there." She walked far down the slope, then pointed straight down. While he blinked in surprise, she bent double, and hands moving too fast to see, dug through the rubble. A moment later, she straightened, holding something round in her hands.

Nimri had said the head covering was clear as water and round as a bowl. "How did you know it was there?"

"Everything else was packed solid and had uncomplicated chemical structures," she said. He massaged his temples, and tried to understand the information she had given him. She brought him the helmet. "Would you like me to show you how to secure the spacesuit?"

Would he? "I haven't found the laces." Thunder glanced hopefully at the mouth of the star bridge. "If you could find them, I could assist you on the old world."

Instead of immediately responding, GEA-4 turned her eerie silver stare to the helmet in her hands, then she fixed her attention back on him. He barely breathed, while he waited for her answer. Finally, satisfied by whatever her mysterious eyes could see, she gave a decisive nod. Before he was quite certain what she intended, GEA-4 began to dress him. Amazingly, she overlapped the edges of the suit and patted them in such a way that the seam disappeared, then she put on the boots and gloves. She made several odd movements that reminded him of an artisan checking their creation. Then, she put the 'helmet' on his head. A moment after she clamped it in place, she did something at his shoulders. A faint snicking sound alerted him that the suit now held him trapped inside, but there was no fresh air, as Larwin had claimed, there was only the scent of ashes long cold in a hearth. He could barely see through the grimy bubble. Couldn't breath.

"Let me out!" he bellowed as panic set in.

GEA-4 stepped back. He grabbed for her. She grasped his arm in her shockingly strong grip and tapped one of the barely visible bumps on the forearm. "I have set the oxygen at normal rate. You will now come to the Pterois Volitan and assist me determining which components will have the most salvage value." Shoulders square, she turned and went back into the star bridge.

She'd said he would have enough air in the suit. And he hadn't collapsed – yet. Thunder swallowed his fear of suffocating, then leapt into the star bridge and moved as fast as he could to get a glimpse of the fate he wanted to save Chatterre from.

Chapter 4

Raine frowned at the determined mooncalf, then studied Nambaba's scrolling data stream. What held the rogue mooncalf's attention enough to tempt it across several quadrants of space? Plutonera, or some equally volatile chemicals were the only things which she had ever heard them pursue, but, to the best of her knowledge, none had ever ventured this far away … with the possible exception of the dragon Otami's crew had lost fourteen cycles ago, and which had never been found.

Had it come this direction, too?

If so, had it been injured?

"Check for signs of a second mooncalf."

The data stream froze for a moment, then Nambaba responded, "Nothing within scanner range." The scrolling information resumed.

Raine rammed the collective forward. As her antiquated ship surpassed its design specifications, it vibrated. "Continue scanning for ships. Especially the telltale emissions from cloaked ones."

"No ships within five light years."

Raine could not position Nambaba between the mooncalf and its destination, so she set the ship's targeting sights on its objective and fired a hydro jet. Nambaba shuddered. From Raine's vantage point, it looked like the gush charged directly toward mooncalf's gleaming red eye. "Turgamatory! The Zar will have me recycled for killing the serpent!"

"Please re-state command," Nambaba said.

Raine ignored the overly polite computer and stared at the jet, willing it to miss the mooncalf.

Insolently, the creature turned its head to look back at her, then, it spotted the speeding water and desperately twisted in a backward arc. The hydro rocketed beneath its flailing forelegs and impacted the planetoid's residue-covered surface.

The tension went out of Raine's muscles and she wept with relief. "Thank you," she whispered. As a black opaque plume billowed from the surface, the mooncalf's movements became uncertain.

Yes. Raine pressed her shepherd-ship to close the gap between the beast and the desolate planetoid, then she fanned Nambaba's tentacles into a threatening halo, which had always given her control over the animals.

Instead, this mooncalf came directly toward her. "What's wrong with you? Turn back!" Loosing the dragon would be as bad as killing it.

She glanced out the panorama window, where the soot-like planetoid occupied half the view. She swiveled the ship, calibrated the targeting array, and fired at the dragon's new destination.

The beast wavered for a moment, then continued on. Its objective was either freedom or a dark spot on her screen.

Had there ever been such an obstinate creature?

She aimed a third shot.

"Warning, life-signs," Nambaba said. "Weapons lock-out."

Raine screamed with frustrated fury, then checked the view-screen, which displayed a chartreuse blinking point appeared on the facsimile of the planetoid's surface. Worse, the blip's rhythm rapidly diminished. Impossible! "What sort of thing could live on such a forsaken speck?"

"Life-signs are humanoid."

Surely a shadow warrior wouldn't have humanoid life signs. The moon calf's course never wavered. How had it known where to find the defenseless person? She looked at the walls protecting her, wondering if the calf would attack her if given the opportunity. She shuddered. Turing back to the navscreen, she felt torn between her life-sworn duty as dragon-shepherd and the desire to kill the horrid beast. A scream of frustration escaped.

"Command does not compute."

The mooncalf moved toward the blip.

Raine rammed the collective forward. Nambaba shot ahead of the mooncalf. As the ship hurled toward the surface, the flight-straps tightened across her chest. At the last moment, she flared Nambaba's tentacles. The ship landed with a jolt. Raine's head hit the headrest with a dizzying thud. Her teeth clicked together and she tasted the copper-salt flavor of blood. A black curtain appeared to cover her panorama-window and blocked out the stars. She blinked and took a quick look at the view-screen, which appeared blurry, but still revealed that the life-signs had become a slow, dim pulse. Worse, the mooncalf was still heading toward the poor humanoid. In her entire nine years as shepherd, she'd never encounter such a willful calf.

By the instinct and practice earned over years of service to The Zar, Raine locked the controls and unbuckled her restraints. "Nambaba, continue scanning for ships." Raine touched the collar of her spacesuit, which covered her golden dragon medallion. The coveted emblem, with its wave-crest design, designated her a Captain and gave her near-nobility status. Unfortunately only true aristocracy could fail at their duty and live. Die now or die later, either way, Dalf would perish.

Perhaps if she figured out what had lured the mooncalf across so many sectors of space, she could coax it to follow her home. She gave the navscreen a half-focused glance. Right now, its objective seemed to be attacking Nambaba.

She snapped her visor shut and yanked on her thick gloves, then slammed her shoulder against the air lock. The portal groaned open. She jumped blindly into a cloud of soot. Strange that the particles remained suspended.

The mooncalf's golden sheen, which hovered above, was the only contrast in the featureless fog. Raine stood still long enough to watch the obstinate beast's course. Situating herself on the same vector, Raine put her arms forward and took a cautious step forward. Eighty-three wary paces later, her toe came down on a lump and she pitched frontward. Falling in the low gravity made the world seem to slide by in slow motion. What kind of insanity had she succumbed to when she stepped outside Nambaba's security for the sake of a stranger?

Possibly even an enemy?

She grimaced and hoisted herself to her feet. As she rose, her gloved hand touched a familiar shape. Grouping along, Raine determined that she'd tripped over her quarry. A glance overhead assured her that she had time to save herself and whoever she must have injured with the last hydroblast.

Maybe she'd even succeed before the mooncalf arrived.

For the first time in the long, harrowing shift hope blossomed that something might actually go right.

Raine felt along the dust-shrouded form. Her victim seemed much smaller than her own five-foot ten-inch frame. Raine situating her hands under the unresponsive armpits and heaved the body toward the mooncalf's glow. Within two paces intense heat engulfed her as the matt-colored dust began sparkling and swirling upward. She'd been wrong, there wasn't time to save the stranger.

ooo

When the sound of thunder echoed through her ctenophore class ship, Tem-aki looked at the holograph in the corner of her lab where tiny rocks rained into the new cleft she had concealed her ship in. Each miniature iridescent speck which struck the luminous holographic hull reverberated through the actual hull until it sounded like she was in the middle of a metal stadium with thousands of spectators stomping their feet. A glance at her instruments showed the asteroid to be as stable as when she'd entered the cleft. Then, movement in her peripheral vision yanked her attention back to the hologram, and she saw another madrox, or perhaps it was the same one coming back to her research site. Tem-aki sprinted out of her lab heading toward the cockpit. By the time she'd secured the straps of the pilot's seat, commonsense kicked in and she realized starting the ship's engines was the worst thing she could possibly do.

Heart slamming against her ribs, she waited for the inevitable. But the only thing that changed was that silence returned. This beat everything her instructors had ever taught her about madrox, which supposedly attacked ships that didn't quickly go to warp. Why had the madrox hovered above her spacecraft, but made no move to touch it? What, aside from the throbbing of the propulsion system, attracted them?

Did movement triggered a dragon's predatory instincts, as it did with so many other predators?

If so, she should be safe for the moment.

What if noise attracted it? She placed her hand over her pounding heart.

Madrox didn't follow scent. Did they?

Surely scent would not be something a space-based predator followed, so it was more likely that sight or sound triggered them.

Tem-aki tiptoed back to her lab being careful not to make a sound, then she stood in front of the hologram and studied its display. Now, the other ship was making strange maneuvers, which would never get it away from the dragon. The pilot's clumsy movements made it look like the strange ship was either racing the beast to a nearby planetoid or trying to put itself in harm's way. Tem-aki leaned so close that a stray curl brushed against the hologram. She could feel the energy vibrate through it and shoved the annoying red strands behind her ear.

Everyone called madrox 'energy-loving-beasts'. What if energy attracted them? She swallowed, glad that most of her ship's systems were shut down and the frayed looking one held it's attention.

Leaning forward, again, she studied the other ship, wondering if there was a possibility that it could have had something to do with Larwin's disappearance. Her brother had vanished near this sector the year before while training an android prototype how to fly... It didn't look like this pilot knew much about flying. "Computer, identify the vessel on display."

"It is a scyphozoan style spacecraft," Dasya Voltain said.

Tem-aki sighed. "Yes, but exactly what type of spacecraft is a scyphozoan style?"

"It is a composite of five antiquated types." The system came as close to sounding superior as it was possible for a computer. Tem-aki nearly laughed since the Defense Ministry had decommissioned her ctenophore class ship over a year ago and the only reason it hadn't been recycled into razor blades was because the Science Ministry had claimed them for their exploration fleet.

"What is it's function?" Frayed as it looked, it was unlikely to be a war ship, but she'd learned not to judge things totally by appearance.

"Unknown."

Tem-aki signed. The only thing she was fairly sure about was that a ship that size was probably not a freighter.

Suddenly, the ship's shape shimmered, then it condensed into what looked like a starburst instead of a ragged comet. "What in the galaxy?"

She blinked in surprise while her computer pompously said, "It is definitely a Kalamaran design."

If its sudden shape change wasn't enough, the odd ship next moved toward the madrox as if it thought it could catch such an enormous beast with such a tiny trap. "Like a gnat trying to catch a praying mantis," she murmured as she recalled two of the insects she'd studied in entomology. Tem-aki held her breath at the daring display, expecting the madrox to devour the ship any second. Instead, it backed away as if terrified of the ship. Why was the madrox acting tame as a pet?

As she watched, the ship calmly settled onto the black surface of the planetoid. Immediately, a cloud of dust enveloped it. The dragon paused, as if undecided, then crept closer to the planetoid. "Computer, center on the ship that just landed and enlarge." Though the dragon's scales became visible, she couldn't see through the sparkling cloud. "Computer, compensate for the dust or whatever that cloud is and enhance the image."

The hologram wavered, then displayed tiny, oddly humanoid shapes lying prone between two of the tentacles.

ooo

Blood thundering, breath rasping, Raine dug in her heels, tightened her grip and tugged, again. And again. Each time she only managed to shift the strangely heavy humanoid one step toward Nambaba's hatch.

After nine pulls, sweat burned her eyes, which were useless to see in the hovering cloud of dust. Gritting her teeth, she heaved, again, and continued to wonder how the humanoid could be so heavy in an atmosphere where dust didn't succumb to gravity. That was as amazing as the fact that she'd managed to find the humanoid at all. After fifteen pulls, she let go of her unseen burden, stood and stretched a kink out of her back, then used her hand-held tracking device to verify that she was still going toward the hatch.

With only two hands, she couldn't use it and move the unseen victim at the same time. Sucking in a much needed breath, she bent back over, dug her heels into the planetoid's shifting surface and made the move again then and again and again until she felt Nambaba's hard security against her spine. Her limbs felt as if she'd swum a marathon. She paused to catch her breath and blink perspiration from her eyes before she tried to heave the victim into the hatch.

Her vision cleared slightly, and in the light from the hatch, which illuminated distorted swirling dust particles, she thought she saw her shadow lying over the silver and black form of the victim. I must be hallucinating. Raine closed her eyes and shook her head at the memory of the four-armed apparition. The instruments identified the victim as a humanoid. Humanoids only had two arms. Didn't they? The heat must be pickling her mind or the vapor steaming her visor must have altered the scene. Perhaps the thump she'd taken on the back of her head had affected her sight more than she'd initially thought.

Why was she so hot?

Knowing there was a logical reason for the heat, she looked upward and saw the wavering white glow of the dragon's immense heat overhead.

She'd been right, but she wished she'd been wrong.

She was to die on this desolate planetoid, consumed by the mooncalf she'd sworn to protect…

If she'd had a free hand, she would have shaken a fist at the hovering dragon.

Strange that it wasn't attacking.

Yet…

Odd that it wasn't leaving, either.

Yet…

Perhaps it was toying with her.

Raine scrunched her eyes closed, took a cleansing breath and looked down at the lumpy, two-headed creature, which was her burden. This wasn't a humanoid. She lost her grip, fell backward, landing hard on her bottom. Again, she thought how strange this planetoid's gravitation seemed; that soot could remain airborne for an extended time, while the two-headed entity seemed heavy beyond belief.

She slid away from whatever her sensors had proclaimed to be humanoid. Whatever it was, she did not want the thing in her ship! The stiff form didn't move a muscle. Why had she risked her life to save such a monstrosity, especially when it was probably dead?

Raine struggled to her feet, feeling hotter than she'd ever been. It seemed terribly difficult to think, let alone move. A blue flare illuminated the mangled form and she saw a beaked emblem on the other's uniform.

A two-headed Guerreterran Shadow Warrior!

She leaped backward, nearly falling, again.

Another azure flare flashed above her. She looked upward to see the mooncalf's vermilion eye watching her as it hovered overhead and tasted the dust cloud with its burning, sapphire tongue. It had approached so close that she could see how individual scales interlocked along its gnarly jaw. So close that its fiery heat overloaded her suit's cooling system. So close that she could see herself and her monstrosity of an enemy reflected in its enormous ruby eyes.

So close that she could see that two Guerreterran warriors were clinging together, instead of a two-headed monster

Raine swallowed with the realization that one must have died when her discharge impacted and that they had clung together in death.

The forked tongue inches above the entwined pair. Raine raised a clinched hand, shook it at her ward. "Go home, you miserable mooncalf."

Again, its tongue flashed toward her like blue lightning. So close that the air crackled around her. She shut her eyes, expecting to die.

"You will listen to me," a high-pitched voice said. Raine flinched. A vise clamped around her ankle. "You will carry my partner to your ship, or I will kill you."

After the brilliance of the mooncalf, it was difficult to see the warrior, who threatened her. "But-" Where the silver one's face should be there were mangled wires and gnarled metal. Her protest was lost in her scream.

"Save him." The pressure on her leg intensified until her bones ground against each other.

Rescuing a sadistic pervert, who wouldn't hesitate to murder her was asking too much. "No."

"If he dies, so do you." A small, undamaged plane of the android's metal face reflected the mooncalf's ruby-eyed stare.

Despite the heat, Raine grew cold. Her gaze moved from the torn face to the exposed wires near the android's waist, her heart beat faster at the sight of the virtual parts store of components, which would be valuable on Kalamar's black market. If she could salvage the machine, she could upgrade Nambaba and maybe even acquire a few luxuries. The android might even have priceless data in its files. Raine swallowed. If she didn't save the machine, she'd be throwing away riches, and perhaps even the title of nobility. Raine placed her hands under the android's arms.

"No," it said. "Take my partner."

"But-"

"My conduits were crushed when a hydro-blast tore out the escarpment. My program will soon terminate."

So it was confirmed, she'd somehow shot down the enemy. Was this the warrior who had killed Gornt? Had she actually taken down one of the most formidable fighters in fifty galaxies with a shepherd ship? Rumors whispered that The Zar had signed a peace treaty with the murderers. If a truce existed, it explained why she'd passed into their territory unchallenged. Trust the nobility to keep that information from the masses.

Hot and cold sensations washed over her, as did the mooncalf's seeking tongue.

"Move." The android leveled a las-gun at her. "He doesn't have much time and he can not be replaced." Sparks shot from a laceration near its left eye socket.

Raine dropped the android and grabbed the Shadow Warrior. "Can you grab hold?"

"My scanners indicate that my partner's condition is grave. You must attend him."

The android's parts were valuable beyond imagination, but she'd have to be careful how she marketed the bits and its information files – particularly if The Zar really had made a treaty and she'd shot down an ally. She looked up at the hovering mooncalf, wondering if she dared leave such wealth.

"I don't have a med-kit, much less a spare seat. If you want your partner treated, you will have to do so. Grab hold."

"I only know herbal theory from Nimri."

"Whatever you know is more than I do." Perspiration stung her eyes. Raine looked upward. The mooncalf hovered over Nambaba's hydro-shielded skin, its nostrils flared and its claws trembled.

In all the years she'd been a dragon shepherd, Raine had never seen one so close nor realized that an adolescent's snout was twice the size of her ship's hub. She concentrated on breathing normally.

The android made a sweeping motion with its arm and hurled the las-gun away, then wrapped its arms around the warrior in an oddly loving way.

ooo

Tem-aki stared at the hologram. She had to be hallucinating. "Computer, recenter and enhance on the area beneath the madrox." The facsimile flickered. When it reconfigured, a hunched, greenish form appeared to be pulling a silver and black object toward the main hub of the strange starship. "Computer focus on the humanoid forms." What had been important enough for the pilot to risk confronting a madrox to retrieve?

Tem-aki leaned so close that her skin throbbed with the energy produced by the display. Again and again the computer zoomed in until there was no doubt – the black portion displayed Guerreterre's Shadow Warrior's symbol. Larwin was the only one listed as having been lost in this sector. It had to be him. Tem-aki fell back in her chair and shivered at the realization that she had actually gotten the confirmation she had come for.

Why had the pilot risked all to retrieve him?

Wanting to see him one last time; wanting to know it was him for a fact, she had the computer focus in on the bubble-shield, but it only mirrored the madrox's sinister red glare. When he'd been lost the previous year, Larwin was testing a G.E.A. pilot prototype. "Computer, analyze the silver object wrapped around the Shadow Warrior and report."

"G.E.A. pilot test model 4."

Tears sprang to her eyes. "Larwin, what happened to you?" she whispered.

"Impossible to determine due to diminished vitals."

"That's one way to describe death," she said sarcastically.

"The warrior is injured, not dead."

Heart pounding with mixed excitement and dread, Tem-aki sat bolt upright. Surely Larwin would have run out of basics by now. "Computer, scan the warrior. Who was the suit issued to?"

"Colonel Larwin Atano." Unbelievable! Amazing! Incredible! "Vital signs are deteriorating, but stable."

Papillae bumps rushed over Tem-aki. "He should have run out of oxygen months ago."

"Twenty point seven-nine hours of oxygen remain."

How had he managed to lengthen his supply? Did that mean his ship remained intact?

Her gaze narrowed on the image. How could she get to him when a madrox guarded the other ship?

Why had that Kalamaran pilot come so far to get him?

How had they known, when her own planet didn't?

Nothing made sense – yet. "Computer, make a file copy of this situation." Tem-aki keyed in the communication network, then praying that she was doing the correct thing, she sent the file to her superior. Moments later, the halo-image changed to display the admiral's aristocratic face.

"I received your report and will send a mining team to the crevasse," Admiral Roget said. "Good work, Atano."

"Thank you, Sir." Tem-aki swallowed. "Did you have a chance to see the most recent data?"

The Admiral frowned. "Guerreterre is at peace with Kalamar. When was this file made?"

"Moments ago. I am still monitoring the madrox and ship." She discretely wet her lips. "Should I try to liberate the warrior?"

"Intervention could jeopardize our eepyllihg contract." He pulled at his goatee. "I must take this up with the warrior's Commander. For now, continue monitoring the situation." One brow arched. "Does your ship have stealth-mode capabilities?" She nodded. "Excellent. Use it, until we can determine the best way to handle the situation."

"Yes Sir." Admiral Roget's image vanished. Tem-aki ran her fingers through her wiry red curls, still stunned by the Admiral's comment about their eepyllihg contract. If they got that nearly magical fuel from Kalamar, it explained why they had a treaty and no one had investigated her brother's disappearance. Had fuel for warp engines taken precedence over saving her only sibling?

Tem-aki feared she knew the answer.

Chapter 5

After heaving her cumbersome load past the mooncalf's hot watchful gaze and into the airlock's shelter, Raine sighed with relief.

Guerreterran's greed had been a threat to planets with ancient civilizations and good resources for the past millennium, and now she was about to come face to face with one of their shadow demons.

As soon as the chamber flooded with air, she yanked her helmet off. Unfortunately, the android looked worse without a fogged faceplate. Raine ran her hand over her short, sweat-saturated blond hair.

"Help me get his helmet off," the android said.

Raine glared at the demanding machine, but knelt and yanked off the warrior's helmet. Anything to keep it happy, at least for now. Long dark hair spilled across one chiseled cheek and wrapped around his neck as though shielding the warrior. She nearly gasped at the man's unexpected appearance. Somehow, she'd assumed that anyone as savage as a Shadow Warrior would be uglier than a goatfish and mean as a sargon serpent. This fighter had smiled enough to form permanent laugh-lines. Could he be both a killer and a kind man? Perhaps he gave that impression because of the tender way the android stroked his hair out of his face. Perhaps the laugh-lines had formed when he celebrated the destruction of weaker worlds, who fought against Guerreterre's domination because they knew their only choices were to die fighting or to die in slavery. Even though the man was nearly dead, the hard planes of his face looked fierce.

It was definitely the face of a killer.

Raine sat back on her heels and studied her enemy. Was this man the same warrior who had killed her partner; the one who had shattered Dalf; the one who had destroyed her life? Or had one of his buddies done it? She sighed knowing a shadow warrior certainly wouldn't remember shooting down one solitary Kalamaran battleship, not with the thousands of vessels these savages purportedly destroyed. Not when they annihilated entire planets. Red light poured in the open view-port. Had he come back to the scene of one of his past conquests to gloat? Was that why he looked like he spent a lot of time laughing?

The android's hands fluttered over the warrior, as if he had immeasurable value.

She squinted at the exposed wires and tried to estimate how many reloons the robot might be worth. The numbers boggled her mind.

Such an irony that the war with Guerreterre had taken away Gornt and destroyed her security, and now, by a twist of fate somehow one of Guerreterre's mangled machines, which might soon provide more security than she had ever dreamed of, had come into her possession. Raine's gaze narrowed as she studied the warrior. Perhaps he could become an asset of sorts, too

She'd have to be very careful about how she disposed of the machine and the warrior; very careful about who she dealt with and what she told them for The Zar had spies everywhere.

ooo

Perspiration stung Thunder's eyes and his lungs begged for oxygen as his bleeding fingers searched for the next cleft in the sheer rock face. He willed himself to stay calm. Suddenly, green-spotted silvery tree trunks twisted around him like mating serpents. He gasped and would have taken a backward step, except the land fell away into a bottomless void.

Nightmare.

Thunder lay still and waited to wake up. Instead, the wild jumble of images increased: portal guardians; an ancient cave; Larwin's special suit; putting on the grimy headdress in order to see what his efforts were saving Chatterre from; the smell of ashes; a sense of claustrophobia. Then, after he was close to giving up following the indefatigable GEA-4, the unexpected view of a vast blackness. Before he'd had a chance to understand what he was seeing, the barren world had erupted in an angry rocky fountain; stars beyond measure in an ash black sky, GEA-4's reflection along with that of two monsters in an enormous crimson eye, and the rank scent of an old forge. The jumble switched from half-understood images to twirling orbs and strange words. Pressure on his temples mounted until his head pounded. He jerked away from the pressure and the deluge ceased.

Thunder gasped with relief, then choked on the sudden pervasive taste and smell of melted metal. He tried to roll away from the awful smell, but heavy bands held him immobile.

The bed linens had him, again.

He lay still in the pitch-black darkness, listening for the familiar sound of a night bird, trying to sense the gentlest nighttime breeze, but only heard an odd rhythmic hum. Not Nimri's waterfall, but what? Where was he? He tried to remember, but could only recall odd bits of his nightmare. Still seeking something solid to orient himself with, Thunder's fingers twitched. Then his entire hand. Odd that the linens hadn't managed to bind him from toes to chin. The strangely smooth surface where bedclothes should be felt even odder. A slight movement displaced the air near his head. Were these sensations still part of his nightmare? If so, it was certainly different from his normal one. In a way, he looked forward to finding out what came next.

Abruptly, hands clamped around his head, fingers pressured his temples and Thunder's mind flooded with a confusing tumult of mathematical equations, star charts, unexplainable words, fleeting faces and strange, fast fading vistas.

He fought to remove the grip.

"Stop fighting me," a high-pitched voice said. "You need this sub-lim data if you hope to return to Chatterre." The harsh judgment ricocheted inside his mind while rending pain shot across his forehead. Thunder groaned and pressed his thickly gloved palms to his ears, but his effort only intensified the sharp echoes and incomprehensible images.

Would this nightmare ever end?

Abruptly, the pressure on his temples ceased and the bedlam stilled. He gasped with relief, then lay still as a corpse. While he relished the serenity, the rock-hard floor pulsated against his spine. Strange. Ground only vibrated during stampedes and those horrible times, when the earth shuddered so hard that rock ripped free.

But it wasn't an ominous beat; this pulse seemed soothing. Relaxing. Barely discernible.

He must still be trapped in the strange confusing dream. Thunder clenched his hands and willed himself to awake.

Nothing changed, except after a few moments his sweat vaporized into the black silence. He shivered, as much from the chill as the fear he'd remain trapped in this strange nightmare. An intermittent draft sent wave after wave of gooseflesh across his chest, yet his lower extremities were hot.

It was the most peculiar dream he'd ever had, which said a lot because he'd had bizarre nightmares for years.

The stench of scorched metal mixed with blood. Odd. Past nightmares had contained colors, thoughts and feelings – mainly terror and pain, but never smells or periods where he simply lay there wondering if he'd ever awaken. This one held both in overwhelming quantities.

What if this was real?

The thought was too ridiculous for consideration.

If this was real, where was he?

How had he gotten to the heart of darkness?

Why did it hurt so much to think?

Why couldn't he seem to remember anything except the odd bits of dream, which seemed so real that at times he was nearly convinced they were reality?

Could he be dead?

"When a hydro blast hit the escarpment near the tunnel's entrance, we were hit by shrapnel," a shrill voice said.

"Hydro blast?"

"An archaic form of ammunition," the odd voice said, using

another incomprehensible term, as an image of water formed in his mind. "Now that you're relaxed, I can share the rest of Kalamar's language." Again, points of pressure clamped onto his temples.

"Kalamar?" he asked as an energy surge went through his head. His hair stood on end and his entire body gave a violent jerk.

"I only have time for basics." This time the high-pitched voice came from inside his mind. "My movement circuits exploded as a result of the blast and my power is failing." Whatever that meant couldn't be good, so why did the voice sound so calm? "Relax so I can download the data you'll need to survive and return to the planetoid to finish what we have begun." The tumult of confusing images and strange sounds resumed.

Black voids with dots of light; strange things that could not possibly fly yet did; creatures that tore off outer skins like cocoons and turned into humans; odd boxes, similar to Larwin's, spinning balls that Thunder somehow knew were entire worlds; tiny black marks that he suddenly recognized as words.

Nimri had told him about the mind-meld GEA-4 had done to her and how she could understand the ancient manuscripts afterward. Thunder stared at one image and gasped in wonder, as he realized the odd forms were what Larwin called 'word pictures'.

"Stop fighting me," said the inner voice. "You must have this data in order to survive."

"Where am I?" He forced out each syllable. "GEA-4 is that you? How are you speaking inside my thoughts?"

"We are in a Kalamaran ship." A crackling sound accompanied white sparks arcing in the darkness. Then, the cool, hard circular objects clutching his temples suddenly sent hot, stabbing jolts of pain all the way to his toes, but when he tried to grab them, he discovered his arms were pinned tightly against his body. "We were going to the Pterois Volitan to get the last of the supplies when the Kalamaran shot at us." She paused. "Odd that my files don't mention that they keep Madrox for pets."

Madrox! A death-like chill washed over him. He remembered its eyes; its tongue flicking at him and had thought it was a nightmare.

But this must be a dream, how could it be reality? If he'd been that close to a dragon with no protection, it would certainly have consumed his aura.

"The hull of this ship has a layer of water between its two outermost layers. It is a simple, but ingenious shielding solution. The Kalamaran's flight-suit was designed on the same principal."

"Why is it dark?" He swallowed. "Am I dead?"

"The Dragon Officer did not see fit to illuminate this area."

Dragon Officer? What was a dragon officer? Did she mean dragons had differing ranks? Larwin had once tried to explain about how each and every human from his world knew his or her rank as compared to every other one and how officers were the best. Thunder had never been able to grasp the odd concept and had never understood why it seemed so important to Larwin or why he'd looked so proud to be a colonel. Whatever those where.

This couldn't be real. He must still be home in his bed, caught in the worst nightmare of his life. He willed himself to wake.

"You are awake and in the Kalamaran ship. Why is this so difficult for you to accept?"

Were the confusing fragments true? Had he and GEA-4 scaled

Sacred Mountain's treacherous face? That portion of his memory seemed real. So did finding Larwin's special suit and trudging up the endless tunnel to help GEA-4 choose which bits from the Pterois Volitan to bring back and find out how GEA-4 intended to set the explosives from Larwin's ship so the tunnel would collapse properly. His temples hurt from remembering GEA-4's strange explanation about why the explosives needed to be set carefully so the entire planetoid didn't disintegrate and leave something called a wormhole, accessible to whatever found it. She thought Chatterre would be in more danger, that way. He hadn't understood her explanation any better then than now.

He'd told himself he could ignore his claustrophobia long enough for a look at the world from which his ancestors had fled, so he had put on Larwin's special suit and managed to endure the confinement of the horrible helmet. His last coherent memory was following GEA-4 though a long dark tunnel to get the last load of useful items from the Pterois Volitan. Specifically, the last thing he recalled was her saying. 'A madrox is approaching, so we need to hurry, but there should be enough time to get everything and still have time to seal the cavern before it makes its way to this planetoid.' Obviously, she had not been correct. Before they got back to tunnel, the old world had exploded into a geyser of ash and rock.

"We failed," he said.

"The hydro blast took down enough of the escarpment to make it very difficult for a madrox to reach the wormhole."

For the first time in his life, Thunder felt like he actually understood the words and concept behind GEA-4's words.

Cool circular objects caressed his temples. "Ah, much better, you're calm." In the next instant, the voice became internal as it began speed faster than a falling rock and he suddenly understood that the nightmare image of monstrous golden beasts swimming in a molten lake that seemed to cover an entire orb, was real. Abruptly the speed slowed and, again, GEA-4's voice was inside his thoughts. "Madrox, or as some cultures call them, golden dragons, live in the nitrogen-rich gasses of Vilecom." Looking closer, he noticed that the Madrox activity created watery ripples in the glowing surface. As he focused his attention on the strange image; a flare erupted from the gaseous surface and rocketed toward him. For a moment all thought went blank, as if the flare had burned out his memory.

A moment later a new image formed, this time a dragon flew silently through a star-studded black void. A second later the image shifted to several golden dragons attacking another sun and volatile vapor spewing toward a greenish orb. As the stream contacted the round orb, fire burned all the way around the ball. When the flames went out, the orb was cinder-black.

"You just saw an archive tape made by the Royden freight ship, Warfen," GEA-4 said. "The same flare that vaporized Latawba burned out several of the ship's controls. Guerreterran spies were fortunate to obtain this much documentation."

"R-shhh-what?"

"It does not matter. Neither freighter or planet now exist."

"Lat-awe-bah is – was – a world?"

"Correct. It was a brother world to Kalamar. Be still, I must give you more pertinent information and speech requires too much time and effort."

"But how did the world die? Did the golden dragons burn it, as they did my ancestor's home world?"

In the darkness, sparks flared. "La-taw-ba is where Vole d'Laire's brother and strongest competitor reigned as God

Head."

"Voles ruin gardens, but what is a fair ax?"

"On Chatterre a vole is a small mammal. On Kalamar, it is part of the name of the family that rules the planet and God Head is the title of the most high. We do not have time for idle talk, you must learn from the language programs and memories I gave you. "

What an incredible thought.

In the next instant, a flare lashed out across space and destroyed the colorful world. "It is estimated that ten-point-six-trillion slaves inhabited Latawba." He had the impression that GEA-4 was speaking to him, yet the sounds were so fast that there were no words. "Guerreterre's Supreme Colonel assessed that madrox were a constant threat to Kalamar. However, after seeing the madrox's docile behavior toward the Dragon Officer, it is my hypothesis that Kalamar's God Head had his Dragon Officers direct the beasts in battle and kill his own brother, but-" There was a hissing noise. Thunder smelled scorched metal. GEA-4's enunciation sounded feeble, "It is my theory that the Kalamaran strategist is incompetent because the shepherds allowed their ships to get too close to Latawba and were destroyed when the planet imploded."

GEA-4's statement didn't make sense. Worse, the stench was coming from the same area of her voice and bad smells often accompanied illness. "Are you sick?"

"Ill? No, but badly damaged. I must return to a robotics lab." A tiny spark flared. "My existence is immaterial. Your survival is my first priority."

"Is there anything I can to do help you?" Thunder asked.

"Relax and learn, so I may transfer the history of this planet as well as the two languages of Kalamar while I still have energy to do so."

"Two?"

"On Chatterre, each species has its own language. It is the same for Kalamar."

Thunder grunted in agreement, but still wondered how GEA-4 could teach the nuances of body language of another species through simple conversation. "I believe Kalamar's God Head is trying a galactic coup worthy of a Guerreterran Administrator," GEA-4 stated. Thunder frowned and wished he understood what she was trying so hard to tell him. "I base my theory on the fact he was willing to annihilate his own brother's planet and I believe he used the madrox as a weapon. In order to -" A sizzling sound sent pain whipping up his left arm and down his spine. Thunder screamed in agony.

ooo

Tem-aki gazed at the Admiral's halo-image. She hadn't eaten or slept since she'd contacted him and knew it showed, but he looked freshly rested. Worse, his expression appeared smug. It was never a good sign when a superior wore that expression. A tremor of resentment went through her, but she kept a friendly smile on her face. "The scyphozoan style, ctenophore class ship just led the madrox out of the asteroid belt." If she'd been talking to anyone except Admiral Roget, they both would have exclaimed over the amazing image of the old ship clumsily maneuvering its oddly trailing bits through the orbiting rocks with the madrox obediently following

"Have you been detected?"

"I don't believe so."

"Excellent. Once you pass the asteroid field, use stealth-mode and see where they go." Tem-aki clenched her jaws together, so she wouldn't remind him that he'd ordered her to do that on their previous communication. The Admiral smoothed his already perfect jacket. "For now, follow that ship and the madrox. Continue to record your observations, and transmit reports whenever possible." A smile stretched his mouth, but didn't reach his eyes. "Your observations will help us understand our allies. It's a very important mission and you will be rewarded."

"Yes, Sir. Thank you, Sir." Tem-aki ended the transmission, then sat staring at the blank space. If the Administration wanted to know about the planet so badly, why hadn't they sent a Shadow Warrior? Larwin had never said so directly, but it had been fairly obvious that a great part of his unit's success was their ability to infiltrate defenses and gain accurate data on the enemy. And if they could do so against an adversary, it should be twice as easy with allies. This assignment simply did not make sense, except for the fact that she was in the right place at the right time.

Or perhaps the wrong place at the wrong time. After all, who in their right mind would follow a madrox?

Tem-aki doubted if she'd ever understand her superiors. "You heard our new orders, Dasya Voltain," she said to the computer. "Follow that madrox, but don't let it spot us." She added in a whisper, "If my brother is alive, we're going to save him."

Chapter 6

"I am sorry." With each syllable, GEA-4's voice modulated from bass to soprano then plummeted back, again. "I must attempt to repair the circuit that shorted before continuing with the mind-meld."

"Is Chatterre safe?" Thunder asked. Any pain and torment were worth the price if it was.

"Our mission to destroy the wormhole was marginally successful." Her tone stabilized at a sultry pitch as she spoke the last two words. "Probables indicate that the blast, which detonated near the portal-tunnel emanated from this ship."

"But why?"

"I theorize that the dragon officer was on a training mission of some form, possibly targeting the beast for some reason." The statement ended with sparks.

After several long moments of listening to GEA-4 make more adjustments, cool spots touched Thunder's temples. "By the time we reach our destination," a shrill inner voice proclaimed, "probables indicate -" Sparks flashed. "-we will be at-" There was a hissing sound. "-enter of Gharyn Sec-tor. Probables indicate-" The voice cracked like an adolescent boy's. "Never find another wormhole back."

Thunder wished he understood why whatever GEA-4 wanted to communicate was important enough that she would torture herself to share it. He tried to rub his aching temples, but his gloved fingers were trapped. He shoved at the obstacle, but it was like trying to push away his entire head. He gasped for breath and tried to think of a different way to help himself.

"I need to mind-meld and give you the last of the information." The thin-voiced thought was accompanied by an ominous series of red sparks, and Thunder dimly made out part of a silvery-white face above him.

He could barely recognize her. It looked like Larwin's mechanical doll had been through a fire and her strange skin had melted into an awful mess of metallic bits. "I thought you were flame proof."

"But not explosion proof." The pressure on his temples increased. "Relax. Learn." A blue ball suddenly materialized in the distance and hurtled toward him. He raised his hands to catch it, but it grew larger and larger until it seemed to grow much too big to play with. And it continued to expand. Chills of apprehension coiled within him. When it appeared to be an arms length away, the ball halted in mid-air and begin to revolve. When nothing more ominous happened, Thunder studied the head-high orb rotating in front of him. The blue varied in shade and intensity from vivid azure to a strange grayish-turquoise, which had an attractive mottled pattern. As he watched, the colors rippled like water moving across a rocky shoal. Fascinating. Mesmerizing. Except for a few frothy fields of variegated green with odd fluff in areas around the edges, everything seemed to be some shade of blue. Thunder squinted at the strange areas, but the ball continued revolving. Gradually, an ugly black splotch with eight geometrically precise sides came into view. The tiny hairs on the back of his neck rose, as if he was looking as something deadly.

Thunder closed his eyes and shook his head to clear away the impression, but as he looked away from the sphere, he noticed words and symbols hovering in the air, all giving odd bits of information about water, rice production and something called pollution. No sooner had the idea formed, when the words dissolved. An odd sense of loss caused his stomach to clench. Then, his head began to ache as if ready to burst and he realized, theories about temperature and climate were softly squeaking in the back parts of his mind. He refocused on the rotating ball, needing something to calm him as GEA-4 did whatever it was that she did. As he watched the beautiful mottled shades of blue, the tiny voice became as soothing as waves lapping at the shore. Again, the black area came into sight. The water he'd nearly drowned in had been black, too. Panic built until he couldn't separate the memory from the strange turning orb. The image flickered, then the thin voice explained, "This sphere is not your river; it is a world covered in water. It is Kalamar."

He shuddered at the idea of such a nightmare place.

When only chilled skin and a drained feeling remained, the whispered tones ceased. "With your dislike for water, it is unfortunate that a Kalamaran ship rescued you." There was a crackling red glow and he smelled a strong burning stench. "I do not – have – much time – before – my over-ride shorts – out."

He placed his palm on top of the hand she had on his right temple. "I appreciate whatever you're trying to do, but I just want to get up and go home."

"That is what I've tried to tell you. You can not go home. You and I were injured by a hydro blast. You are on board a very old spaceship." There was an ominous hissing noise, then word, by word, GEA-4 continued, "We would have been consumed by a madrox if the Dragon Officer had not rescued us. The Kalamar-" GEA-4's diction slowed until it was syllable by syllable. "Are not known for benevolence. She wants something. If we _ separated." Entire words dropped. "you _ not trust _. My program _ untrustworthy _ barbari-" A fountain of sparks lit the room and static sounded like the rapid fire of a heavy rain cut GEA-4 off in mid-word.

Thunder held his breath while the silence stretched. A tiny intermittent scratching sound caught his attention and for a long period, it was his only clue that the determined android still lived.

"Guerreterre trades with them because they're the only sourc-" An ominous hissing sound sounded like a dozen angry cats. "Eepyllihg. The only fluid more valuable than water."

A starburst of sparks erupted over him. As the burst spattered to the hard floor around him, an ear-splitting shriek slashed the air and GEA-4 dropped across his chest. A jolt of agony crippled every cell of his body. A moment later, all thought and feeling vanished and he returned to the black void.

ooo

"Picking up a transmission." Nambaba's calm maternal voice flowed from the speakers in the control hub making it seem like she was everywhere yet nowhere.

Raine paused from calculating the quickest route home and

glanced at the monitor, which seemed nearly empty now that the majority of the asteroid field was behind her. There were no telltale blips to indicate ships close enough for Nambaba to pick up a communiqué from. But before Gornt had been sent to war, his crew had been warned about Guerreterre's stealth capabilities and she was in their territory. A shiver went down her spine. "Computer, display rotating views in two second intervals." Obediently, the display circled through all possible views. There had to be other explanations. Detection would be difficult with all the iron-bearing ore in the lumps of rock. Difficult, but not impossible. Her tongue flicked out to dampen her lips.

She was in Guerreterre territory. Worse, she had one of their warriors on board. That fact could be either good or bad. Good, if they did not attack their own. Bad if they thought she'd attacked him on purpose. "Can you determine location of transmission?"

"Deflection makes analysis impossible."

Raine sighed with exasperation. "You were able to track the mooncalf."

"It has a silica base; ships do not."

Big surprise. "What about the radio frequency? What can you tell me about that?"

"It is a Guerreterran frequency."

Is, not was. Raine jerked. "Translate and transmit."

Nambaba altered her speech pattern to imitate a sonorous voice. "I received your report." The tiny hairs on the back of Raine's neck quivered. "And?" a feminine voice demanded. "It was informative." Nambaba continued translating the dialogue and relating it in two voices. Either Guerreterran warriors were stupid enough to think they could camouflage their comments with chitchat about minerals, which seemed unlikely, or one of their meddlesome research vessels was nearby. The dialogue continued on about chemical analysis of various different rocks, nothing of which had anything to do with her human and android cargo. In fact, everything sounded typical of what she constantly heard in home space. Raine exhaled a breath that she hadn't realize she'd been holding. She'd personally seen two of their exploratory craft in Kalamar's territory. After the first one, The Zar had been so enraged he had offered the reward of rank and privilege to the first person who sighted another.

Otami had won and not let anyone forget his superiority. Then, his crew had lost a mooncalf and the status he'd been so arrogant about had been yanked away as abruptly as it had been given.

She had not gained as much rank as she would like, but that didn't mean she couldn't take a long fall, too. A full-blown chill rippled under her thick spacesuit.

Raine shook her head at her loss of emotional balance and told herself to focus on what to do with her unexpected cargo. Those thoughts quickly veered to guessing the value of the android's components. Soon, Raine was jotting down a list of things she wanted to overhaul and trying to estimate the expense of repairing Nambaba's obsolete circuitry.

Several moments later, the pompous voice seemed to conclude the communication with, "and will send a mining team to the crevasse."

"Did you have a chance to see the most recent data?" The woman's voice sounded as if she was trying to simultaneously placate and motivate her superior. Raine identified with her status, though couldn't imagine spending her life dealing with rocks, chemical properties, ease of extraction and the other boring space babble, which Nambaba had been relating. Not when she could herd madrox.

"When was this file made?" the pompous male said, "Guerreterre is at peace with Kalamar."

Were they talking about her being in their territory? Raine froze, mouth open. and stared at the mooncalf's knobby nose, which was visible in the corner of the oval view screen.

Since when were they at peace with the Guerreterran savages?

What data had been sent and why had it mentioned Kalamar?

Surely it couldn't be a coincidence that a research unit was in the area on the one day in her life when a misfit mooncalf had dashed millions of light-years from it's home moon and lured her into their space… the day she'd inadvertently downed one of their warriors. "Nambaba, were you able to intercept the file that they mentioned?"

"No." Nambaba said then quickly changed her tone and slipped back into translating the woman's comments, "I am still monitoring the madrox and ship."

The Guerreterrans called mooncalves, madrox. That proved someone was watching her. The question became how much they'd seen and what they intended to do about it. Raine's stomach clenched with the knowledge that she had to be the one and only dragon shepherd within a million light years.

Did the woman know the android and warrior were in her storage locker? That she's blasted the escarpment and injured them? Raine's fingers went to her dragon neckband for comfort and support.

If she'd been observed, why hadn't anyone tried to stop her? Were the Shadow Warriors organizing an attack against her or using phony mining terms to get permission to retaliate? A chill swept over her. "Nambaba, how soon until we're out of Guerreterre space?"

"We passed the buoy fifty-nine cesiums ago."

Did that mean she was safe? That they had let her go? Or were they still watching her, allowing her to know she was under surveillance … playing with her as a ghatto did its prey.

"Scan for a cloaked ship."

She'd obviously committed an act of war when she'd fired a hydro blast in their space and injured their warrior, so why hadn't the speaker retaliated and blown away her ship?

Did they adhere that closely to treaties?

If so, it went against everything she'd ever heard about the barbarians.

This had to be about eepyllihg. Were they ignorant enough to believe that monitoring her would teach them how to prepare the formula?

If so, they would not be pleased to learn that shepherds cared for the herd, but had noting to do with eepyllihg production. They could torture her for the formula, perhaps even kill her, but then she could not give information that only true nobility had.

Raine sighed and hoped they had no idea how little value The Zar placed on subservient life and prayed that they were satisfied with watching her.

But if they were as cunning as everyone whispered, that wouldn't be likely, so there had to be some other reason they hadn't challenged her for firing on their own. Raine swallowed. Perhaps their equipment was good enough to detect that the warrior lived. If he died, she'd never live long enough to find a way to save Dalf; she'd never live long enough to see another wave shimmer in the light of the twin moons; she'd never live long enough to profit by the android's parts. Perspiration stung her eyes.

"Computer, check the coordinates of the origin of this transmission." Raine shivered as she waited for Nambaba's CPU to respond and glared out the monitor at the mooncalf, which accompanied her, as obediently as a pet porpoise. "You'd better hope we get back safely," she told it. "This is all your fault, you know."

If she got back to Kalamar and managed to keep the warrior alive, would she be safe? No matter how hard she tried, she could not imagine The Zar protecting her from breaking whatever treaty he apparently had with the warmongers. She had ventured beyond the area he had assigned to his mooncalves and done so because it was her job, but that wouldn't make a difference. If Guerreterre put in an official complaint, The Zar would probably give her to the shadow demons.

Guerreterre was his biggest customer. It made sense that her planet had some sort of treaty with the savages, after all Kalamar's exclusive fuel additive allowed Guerreterre's forces to fold space. If he ever found out she had nearly killed one of their warriors, he'd probably give Guerreterre her entire family as a conciliation to keep supplying them eepyllihg.

Perhaps he would kill her, himself.

Oh, Spirit, if they made a political incident out of this, at the very least, The Zar would have her juices recycled in retribution for all the embarrassment she brought on his reign! And all for disrupting a treaty she was unaware of.

Raine frowned as she tried to figure out why the watcher had not attacked her. Would one of Guerreterre's shadow demons forfeit an opportunity to murder innocents because they wanted eepyllihg? Probably, since it gave them the ability to conquer entire worlds more than taking the life of an individual.

Or could it be because she had one of their own? She tried to imagine that the mystery ship was holding back to assure the warrior's survival, but after everything she'd heard about them, she couldn't imagine one doing anything humanitarian. Eat their own, probably, but not save a life to save one of their own.

Still, there had to be a reason why she hadn't been terminated and if there was the slightest chance it was because of her cargo, she needed to take special care. Raine cleared her throat. "Computer, scan our cargo bay and determine if our passengers are emitting any unusual energy readings: a distress signal, a tracking beacon – anything."

Why had the android demanded that she save the warrior when there was assistance nearby? Were its circuits too damaged to detect the other ship?

"Continue observing," the self-important voice said. What if they were waiting to assure themselves that she was just as alone and vulnerable as she appeared? If so, it would only be a matter of time.

"Should I liberate the warrior?" the woman asked, confirming Raine's worse fears.

Oh, Spirit, they knew! Raine shuddered.

"It would not be to our advantage," the man said,

Thank The Spirit for that! Still, she had to get out of here before he changed his mind. Without concern to plotting her optimum course, Raine grabbed the collective and prepared to ram it forward.

"Embedded identification chips detected," Nambaba said.

Chips.

Plural.

Raine paused to digest the information. Not only did they know she had the warrior, they knew about the android. Of course their warriors would be marked and the markers would be obvious to anyone with the appropriate equipment, just like everyone was on Kalamar. But how? She fingered her neck band. They'd marked the robot, too – that would make selling it very difficult, if not impossible. Her first reaction was to open the hatch and dump the evidence, but even as she had the thought, she knew it was the worst possible thing she could do. Since there was no way she could dispose of either of her problems while under surveillance, her only option was to proceed home and make it appear as if she was trying to get medical help for the victim. If she'd thought it would save her, she would land on the nearest asteroid and give her dangerous cargo to the watching ship, but the very fact that the ship remained cloaked told her there would be no chance of that.

Her only hope was saving the barbarian.

Raine prayed to The Spirit that The Zar wouldn't make her a political example, to protect his contracts and treaties.

A muffled explosion shook Nambaba's hull so hard that the nav-stick wrenched free from her grip and shot toward her stomach.

Dear Spirit, she was under attack!

Raine grabbed the stick and thrust it forward. It moved so freely that she nearly fell into the console. "Nambaba," she shouted, "run diagnostics." A high-pitched whining shriek felt as if it were knifing her head in two. She hit the containment button.

"Complying."

Wisps of acrid smoke stung her eyes. Raine yanked the nav-stick back on course, as she looked around the control-hub. Smoke boiled in all the air vents. She grabbed for her face-mask.

Dear Spirit, did that indicate an electronic meltdown?

Had she been fired on?

Had one of her supposedly injured passengers sabotaged her ship?

Had one of the out-dated components finally ruptured?

"Diagnostic complete," Nambaba calmly said.

"And?"

"The urgent repair list remains unchanged."

"Turgamatory!" Raine's fingers tightened on the collective and she stared at the attitude gauge. It indicated that the spacecraft was stable, but did she dare trust it to unbuckle her safety harness and get her breather? "What about the new damage?" She coughed. "The smoke?" Raine checked the gauges.

"Detected." The CPU whirred. "No fire." There was a longer pause. "Unable to discover smoke's source." Raine stared at the monitor's scrolling data and gritted her teeth. Unless all the instruments were malfunctioning, Nambaba could be correct; nothing appeared amiss except the smoke rolling into the control hub from every air vent.

She coughed some more. Then, with a silent, fervent prayer, she unsnapped her harness and secured her mask. When Nambaba stayed on course, Raine looked around the hazy hub. It wasn't good, but it didn't seem to be getting any worse. She switched on the lower level hallway monitor. The camera showed thicker smoke. Had the warrior tried to escape? Had he faked the extent of his injuries? Was he free in Nambaba. If only the storage locker had an interior camera or sensors so she could check! She adjusted the corridor unit to focus on the locked door and studied the surface, which should have been flat but now bulged outward. It looked like something inside the storeroom had exploded.

Or perhaps, despite the man's directive, the hidden ship had attacked Nambaba and freed her cargo. They could have simply hailed her and asked!

Oh, Spirit, had they tried to get out and failed? What could be worse than a dead warrior? … A live one that was stalking her.

The door looked bad. What if they'd expired? Would the ship, which was spying on her think she'd murdered the warrior?

Raine shivered and wished she could begin this shift all over.

"Nambaba, scan the storage locker door."

"Heat detected. Possible fire inside. Taking countermeasures." Raine started counting to ten. At seven, Nambaba reported, "Countermeasures failed. Retardant must be deployed manually." A chill rushed over her. Had the warrior died and caused the android to plan the perfect trap – a situation that mandated her response?

Raine grabbed the yellow suppressant-grenade and moved cautiously toward the hatch. What if this was an ambush? Raine paused halfway to the lower-level hatch, turned back to the monitor and studied the now convex door. She swallowed. The protrusion had to have been caused by an explosion. Obviously a small one, since the hull hadn't ruptured and only the door and surrounding wall showed damage.

She'd checked the android and warrior for arms, so there had to be something volatile about the android's construction.

Holding the small grenade in front of her, Raine gingerly made her way down the thin ladder. With every step, the smoke thickened around her. By the time her feet touched the floor the air almost looked solid. Uncertain of what to do, she looked around the corridor. "Nambaba, check for ships closing in."

"Negative contact."

Raine turned on the secondary monitor; the peaceful image seemed to coincide with the ship's CPU. She tapped it to alternate to an exterior view. The mooncalf still glided along her port side, close enough for the hull to glow with heat, just as it had been since she'd launched from the planetoid. Perhaps it had caused the problem. After all, Nambaba had not been built to sustain such intense heat for such an extended period. Worse, if the mooncalf got much closer, the hydro in Nambaba's shielding would poison it.

Perhaps the calf's presence was the reason the other vessel kept its distance. Raine shook her head at the thought of how their rolls might have temporarily switched and the juvenile delinquent of a dragon could have become her protector.

Abruptly, a calliope of alarms went off. "Heat index indicates the electrical fire is expanding. Crucial components will soon be threatened." Raine jumped. Crucial assets, like her own life and potential economic windfall – assuming the android had survived the blast and she could extract its identification chip. "Retardant must be deployed," Nambaba intoned.

"Turgamatory!" Raine lunged forward. Her hand closed over the dead bolt. The metal seared her fingers. Worse, it didn't budge. She jumped back, drew her sidearm, kicked the lock free, then jumped back, both suppressant and weapon ready.

Smoke rolled out of the cabin, like fog on an eerie dusk. Nothing else moved.

Raine took a deep breath of canned air and waited.

In the murk, flames leaped. She hit the activator button on the suppressant grenade and tossed it inside, then yanked the door closed.

A soft muffled explosion indicted that it had activated. Raine looked up and saw an odd peachy splotch above the storage locker door and started counting. At twenty-seven she realized the area looked strange because it looked hot. Get a hold of yourself. You're looking at a semitransparent section and the mooncalf is on that side. The hull isn't melting, you're just not used to being this close to your responsibilities.

She hoped.

Despite the mask, she couldn't seem to breathe. A quick glance told her that her personal tank was out of air. She attached a new container, took a deep breath and then continued the silent count. At one-hundred she said, "Nambaba, clear the air in the lower corridor and upper control-hub."

Nothing happened.

"Now!"

"Complying."

But certainly not very efficiently. Had Gornt's last moments been the sight of poisonous haze? "Verify that the fire is out, then clear the storage room."

She stayed as quiet as possible and listened for any sound, which could indicate movement.

"Countermeasures were successful. Evacuating air, now."

"Is there an ambush in the closet?" Even as she asked the question, Raine berated herself for asking the computer to do the impossible and predict the unknown. Particularly a computer who could barely clean air.

"Command does not compute."

"Nambaba, scan the closet and report your findings."

"Diminished life signs detected."

"And the android?"

"Command does not compute."

"Nambaba, what do you detect in the closet?"

"All sensors are off line." A glance at the blank monitor confirmed the bad news. What if the explosion and fire were a deception? Raine closed her eyes and tried to calm her racing heart. If it had been a trap, they would have attacked when she threw in the grenade.

Now or never. Raine squared her shoulders and tightened her fingers against the trigger. She took a step forward and whipped the door open.

Something stirred. She flattened herself against the floor, blaster ready. It took a moment to realize that wisps of smoke and chemical cloud being sucked up by the air handlers caused the movement.

She waited.

Even after everything had finally been sucked clear, she continued to wait. The hum of the vac-system shut off. She counted to one hundred, then heard the soft purr of the returning air. She moved her head slowly left, right, up and down, but could only see the android's humped back.

The face-mask provided much needed air, but made it impossible to see decent detail. She whipped it off then peered into every corner.

Nothing.

She inhaled the stench of smoke and gagged on its putrid taste. Her stomach rolled in protest at the mingled scents of burned flesh and charred electronics; tears filled her eyes and despite the absence of smoke, everything seemed to swim in mist.

Still, nothing happened and though the locker's outer wall glowed an odd orange-red, the expected attack didn't come.

Cautiously, she switched on the storage locker's light.

The Shadow Warrior lay on his back, still as death. The android, which appeared to have self-destructed at it's mid-point, sprawled across his chest, in an oddly affectionate position. Tingles rushed over her skin. They reminded Raine of a couple her brother, Preston, had told her about. They had been in a love-match between a noblewoman and a sanitation slave, the relationship had ended in a murder-suicide.

How could an enemy as unemotional as a Guerreterran Shadow Warrior possibly program feelings into a machine?

They couldn't; this was probably part of the trap.

"I've got you covered. Get up slowly."

Neither moved. Were they pretending or not? The rank smell of death and fried circuits made her suspect that her newfound riches might have caused the explosion.

Raine kept the blaster leveled at the warrior's head. When no attack came, she relaxed enough to hear his thin, rasping breathing over her own hammering heart. How had he survived the explosion and fire? But thank The Spirit he had, in case the other ship was staying back because they didn't want to harm him. The labored tone of his breathing sounded like he could expire at any moment.

Reaching over, from her crouch position, she rolled the robot aside. The warrior's gapping flight-suit revealed what had once been a well-muscled chest, but now looked like minced fish entrails. Raine gagged. "Oh, murder!" It didn't matter if he was her enemy or not; no one should suffer such injuries.

"Command does not compute," Nambaba said.

"Continue on a safe course homeward." Despite all her other problems, getting the mooncalf safely back to the nursery moon remained her priority.

The expensive circuitry in the android's mid-section had fused into a jumbled lump. What if the watcher valued the android and not the warrior? Raine covered her face and moaned.

The warrior made a faint sound. Raine looked at him. Despite his unfashionably long dark hair and battered body, he appeared to be the embodiment of manhood. How could someone, who did such cruel things, have such a kind mouth? She leaned toward him, as if drawn by some unseen power.

She lost her balance and threw her weight backward, dropping her blaster in the process. Raine froze, waiting for an attack, but none came. Carefully, she moved back to the warrior, this time, she focused on the shredded flesh revealed by the open pressure suit. She moved the sturdy fabric aside. A tiny rosy arc spurted to his ashen face. Bad sign. She winced as she leaned closer. The torn filaments from the android's mid-section had simultaneously ripped and cauterized most of the damage to his belly when it had fallen across him.

Amazing that he lived.

With each labored breath, more red blood trickled over the exposed flesh to pool in an ever-increasing puddle over his belly button.

Red blood!

She and Preston were some of the cursed few that had blood the color of Vilecom, while Shay's was the purple of royalty. Of course, Gornt and Dalf's blood oozed the honorable white of slaves.

How could a Shadow Warrior have the same color blood as she?

Raine stared at expanding red pool, shocked to discover she and the warrior shared the same color life force and wondered how to minimize the mess to her ship once the blood filled his navel.

Navel!

He had a navel?

That could only mean a mother had given birth to him.

She blinked at the shocking thought.

Somewhere out there in the stars, another mother waited for her warrior-son to return. Would the unknown woman miss her son, as she had Dalf, when he'd stowed away with Gornt? Would she have been better off not knowing what happened to Dalf or would she want him back no matter what?

Tears blurred Raine's already misty sight. She had wanted Dalf, no matter what, even when she barely recognized him because of his injuries. It hadn't mattered that she hadn't given birth to him, she had chosen him as her son. And the bond was strong, almost as strong as a biological mother's would be.

She gulped. Did that mean this warrior's mother would want him, as well? The air inside the storage locker smelled of burned flesh; the stench of the most awful day of her life, when she had identified Gornt and Dalf's bodies.

Raine took the warrior's hand and pressed it against the puncture-wound. Immediately, the injury stopped spurting, but without proper medical supplies and skill, he would surely die. She chewed her lower lip. The warrior's partner could be spying on her at this very moment, waiting to see what she would do. "If you're watching and want him saved, help me."

She stared at the warrior's mangled belly. Tears blurred her sight. The air had smelled of death and burned flesh the day she'd been ordered to appear at Defense Command Headquarters and identify Gornt and Dalf. Until then, she hadn't realized Dalf had stowed away on her partner's warship. If it hadn't been for Gornt's tattoo, she would never have believed the mangled mess they showed her used to be her beloved friend.

She stared at the seeping red blood, remembering her elation when she discovered Dalf still lived… and moments later her horror when the attendants demanded her signature on the euthanasia form. Even deaf and blind, she'd wanted her chosen son kept alive. No matter all the hardships she'd endured by hiding him, she would never believe planetary law should be allowed to dictate the definition of 'useful citizen' and have the right to exterminate all the elderly and infirm. Particularly when the definition changed with the color of the life force.

In her heart, she knew that this warrior's mother would want him saved, too. But what could she do? Saving the barbarian's life wasn't as simple as saving Dalf from the reclamation tanks. This situation required medical knowledge and skill, which meant that she needed her brother's help. Again. But would he help her save the enemy or throw him into the reclamation tanks?

The blood loss seemed as if it was slowing, but did that mean he was healing or running out of his life force?

Raine swallowed and looked away from the warrior. The android's empty eye-socket stared back at her. The parallel to poor deaf, blind Dalf nearly brought her to her knees. She closed her eyes and took a ragged breath. It wasn't easy to look at the monstrosity her son had become and it wasn't easy to love the demented shell he had turned into. But she did love him.

And out there, somewhere, there might be another mother that felt the same way about this warrior. She had to try and find a way to keep the warrior alive until she could get him real help.

She touched the golden dragon emblem on her wave-band neckpiece. Could she keep him alive until she reached Preston?

Raine squinted at the stenciled name on the silver flight-suit. Colonel Larwin Atano. Her gaze narrowed on the warrior's chiseled face. "I won't let you die." Not yet. Not until she knew if he had a mother or partner waiting for him. "I hope whoever is out there spying on us knows that." Was the woman his mother or wife?

Raine's jaw tightened. Her life had been ruined by this warrior's mercenary race. But to act as they had would make her as bad as a common killer and she was better than that. Grabbing his limp hand, she pulled off the glove, then rolled it and pressed it against the flow. Her solution seemed to work better than the finger, but she needed to find a way to continue the pressure.

Surveying the shelves revealed a depleted supply of rations, a spare WWT-98B transistor, and a remembrance cube. Raine didn't need to read the cube's inscription to know it contained the last hologram of the three of them swimming in the Wavelet Sea during the idyllic week before Gornt had been ordered to Latawba, where The Zar's brother's world was being attacked by bloodthirsty Guerreterran warriors. Raine swallowed a sudden lump in her throat and tears trickled down her cheeks. She yanked her gaze away from the translucent azure cube, but her attention centered on the warrior's lips. What was wrong with her? Jaws clamped against the confusing emotions, she turned her head away from the handsome warrior and glared at the supplies. At the back of the third shelf, she spotted an old pharmaceutical kit, which had only been singed in the blast. Snatching it, she popped open the lid and grabbed a thick, wide roll of elastic, which must have been sitting in there for the better part of a half century. Surprisingly, the stuff's adhesive still grabbed. Turning back to the warrior, she realized she'd have to pick him up in order to bind the compress in place.

"Turgamatory!" This situation kept getting worse and worse.

Settling back on her heals Raine studied the pool beneath the wadded glove. Maybe it would be better to let the butcher die, but it simply wasn't something she could do. "Colonel Atano, mother or not, before you die, you're going to understand how your greedy spirit-forsaken planet ruined my life. All you have to do is look into Dalf's face." Raine's lips compressed into a thin line. "Assuming your partner doesn't shoot us out of space before I can get you back to Kalamar, of course."

"Command does not compute," Nambaba said.

Raine glared at the hallway speaker, which was just outside the bent door. "Nambaba, is there any sign of that Guerreterre ship?"

"I have some indistinct energy readings, but no additional broadcasts or visual sightings."

That probably meant a cloaked warship was following her, and everyone knew that one of them carried enough armament to destroy an entire planet, let alone one little old space ship. Not good. "Continue scanning."

Raine bound the warrior's chest. "Can the other ship read your diminished life signs?" she whispered to him. "Will they attack if you die?"

The idea terrified her almost as much as the day she'd saved Dalf, then realized she'd have to nurse him back to some form of health.

Chapter 7

Raine blinked perspiration from her eyes, then glanced nervously at the expanding red-hotspot on the hull. The mooncalf continued to huddle close, as if seeking Nambaba's protection.

Reclamation Units were designed for being close to the incredibly hot creatures; shepherd ships were not.

Spirit, don't let me come this far, then take everything away at the last moment. "How soon before Vilecom comes into view?" When the ship did not respond, she wrote the command onto the monitor, but again, the computer ignored her question.

After what seemed like forever, Ishdoo, the frigid moon, came into sight. Would the mooncalf continue to remain docile, as they neared it? She scanned for Vilecom, but the molten moon remained hidden, so Raine stayed on course until Ishdoo's harsh frozen contours stood out in stark relief against the blackness of space.

Hoping it was not too late for her unwanted passenger, Raine eased Nambaba around Ishdoo's rugged ridges. Predictably, the differences between Kalamar's two moons made her shake her head. Vilecom radiated heat and Ishdoo emanated cold. Vilecom's surface teemed with playful dragons and Ishdoo lay barren. Vilecom brought prosperity, while Ishdoo was simply something to be avoided.

Beyond the harsh white crags, the azure arc of Kalamar's stratosphere came into view. Raine's heart warmed at the welcome site. Had her home waters ever looked so good?

"Proximity alert," Nambaba said, as if reading her thoughts. "Eighty-three cesiums."

Raine looked at the reddening wall of her control hub. "How soon before the hull liquifies?" The mooncalf was alarmingly close to Nambaba's hull.

"I have no comparative charts."

"That figures." Raine hoped 83 cesiums would be soon enough. She stared at the heated fuselage and silently willed the mooncalf to sense Vilecom and return to the nursery moon. Instead, the red tone seemed to intensify. She grabbed her helmet and snapped it in place. "Perhaps we should have chosen a different reentry path."

"Inadequate fuel for any other orbit."

Raine winced at that reminder. "Well, at least you and I should survive the worst in some way." She couldn't say the same thing for her unwanted passenger. With no time to go below and get Colonel Atano back into his space suit, she started muttering a countdown. At nineteen, she thought that the heated section looked like it might be melting.

If she hadn't fired so much hydro, the beast wouldn't get so close.

Of course, if she hadn't fired it, she might still be chasing the mooncalf.

Even when the fiery red glow of Vilecom became visible, the maddening adolescent stayed close to Nambaba. Worse, a small herd of mooncalves, which were leaping through the moon's plumes of erupting lava, headed toward her. She opened a transmission channel and hailed the team of dragon shepherds.

"Otami here," the blue team leader said. "Shift change was-"

"I know," she interrupted, well aware that she was more than nine hours overdue. "We had a runaway, and I just returned."

"Shepherd Blue-Six here, I have you on visual. Are you carrying the calf home?"

Raine sighed. "It'd be a more clever joke if I wasn't half convinced that I am. I've got a spot over my starboard rebuffer that looks like it's going to start dripping all over my panner. A little help would be appreciated."

Despite the proximity to Vilecom's comforting heat, it took three of Otami's team working in conjunction to force the stubborn beast back to the nursery moon. "Thanks Blue Team," she said.

"Any time, Gold Leader."

"Your hull looks okay, but I'd have it checked for heat fractures."

"Thanks," Raine said. "I will."

"You can stay and watch how my team handles the CRU's," Otami said.

Raine gritted her teeth at the snobbish invitation and held back reminding him that she'd trained him to handle the Reclamation Units. "Thanks, but my ship is operating on vapor."

"Your loss," Otami said.

She ignored him and altered Nambaba's trajectory to begin a landing orbit. Then, she worked the kinks out of her spine and waited for The Pinnacle to come within range. When it was close enough, she locked in a classified code and keyed in her brother's private frequency. "Preston, I need your help."

"I'm in the middle of an experiment." His tone sounded annoyed. Raine shrugged. As long as she could remember, her brother had never liked receiving calls. "Can't it wait?"

The blip indicating The Pinnacle was already inching across the view screen. "No. I need you. Right now, I'm coming down from duty and will be home by Vilecom's moonrise. Meet me at my home."

"Last time-"

"Be there and bring your med kit." If he didn't come, the warrior would die... if he hadn't already... or didn't during reentry.

Static took over the frequency. Raine clicked off the transmission, wondering if Preston would come or not. Her brother liked to control everything, so her abrupt tone could have alienated him. But then, telling him his medical talents were needed could bring him... unless he believed Dalf needed help. He'd warned her that he'd never help the 'fish-boy' again, and she believed him. Raine rubbed her aching temple. Would he help with the warrior or turn her into The Zar in the hope of gaining a promotion at her expense?

She didn't know how the warrior had clung to life this long. The hydro-blast should have killed him, ditto for the android gutting him and oxygen being sucked out to stop the resulting fire. No wonder Guerreterran Shadow warriors won so many conflicts; their bodies were nearly indestructible.

And they had red blood... Did that mean her body could withstand torture, too?

She hoped she'd never have to find out that answer.

She piloted Nambaba over the Sea of Sorrows' dark waters, then reduced speed as she neared the green expanse of the outlying marshes. A precise geometric arrangement of agricultural towers dotted the wetlands and provided navigation coordinates for the reclamation units, freighters and shepherds as they changed shift. Of course, the towers also supplied homes for the bog farmers, a distribution center for necessities, an infirmary for those worth saving from the chronic injuries they continually suffered and storage for produce. Each tower looked identical to the next, except for the position code marked on its circular top. An unseen communications beacon broadcast the code.

She verified that Nambaba had locked onto a safe course, then looked away from the simple structures, grateful that she didn't have to labor in the soggy marshes all day. Nambaba's hull groaned. Raine glanced at the sagging section of hull and hoped it could survive the stress and heat of reentry into the atmosphere.

Raine confirmed that Nambaba's speed was correct, then adjusted the trajectory to port, with the hope it would ease the pressure on the starboard side. The hexagonal shape of the Black Morass came into view. Toxic fumes from the confined sludge in the chemical dump created a hole in the ionosphere, which pilots had been quick to take advantage of. Though Raine hated the evil feel of the place and disliked how it seemed to alter communications, all shepherd and CRU ships made use of it to enter Kalamar's atmosphere rather than suffer buffeting for an extra 50 kilometers, which a direct entry demanded.

Dusk had settled over the Sea of Sorrows by the time Nambaba's tentacles fanned out across the gently rolling water outside Raine's isolated home. Raine exited the ship and jogged along the tentacle, which came closest to the docking platform attached to the front of her house. With the skill earned by decades of practice, she snatched the mooring rope and secured Nambaba. Only then did she acknowledge that Preston had ignored her plea and that if she wanted to save the warrior's life, she'd have to find a way to help him, herself.

ooo

Tem-aki studied the holographic image of Kalamar. She tapped the likeness. "Recenter and enlarge." The area rippled, then rearranged into a closer view, which showed rolling water and two round areas. Bubbles? Tem-aki tapped the largest one. "Again." The spaceship she'd followed splayed like a starburst on top of the undulating waters, but the steam rising from it's hull was quickly obscuring everything in a private cloud of fog. Only the heat-warped section of its spherical center looked familiar, but it was the first thing to vanish in the steam. "I've never heard of floating spaceships."

"Command does not compute."

"I was thinking out loud." She apologized to Dasya Voltain. The cloud shifted slightly and she saw the pilot emerge from the core and dash along one of the weird stringy bits that lay closest to the other roundish object. Tem-aki leaned forward as she tried to see better. The agile figure grabbed something out of the water, then leaped to a semi-circular area attached to the smaller sphere, leaned over and did something, then went back into the cloud of steam.

Tem-aki massaged her temples, wondering if the queasy feeling and headache, which reminded her of the motion sickness she'd been plagued by as a child could be caused by looking at water.

Tem-aki sat back and looked at the hologram as a whole. "Everything is moving," she muttered. How could anyone live on such a horrible place? And to think, she'd always imagined that finding something as incredibly valuable as a water world would be wonderful.

It wasn't.

Just looking at it made her feel awful.

Poor Larwin not only had to look at things going every which way, he had to feel it, too. She gritted her teeth and glared at the water.

For a long time, nothing changed, then a small craft approached, leaping from wave to wave. A thin green-haired entity emerged from the vehicle, its orangish-pink robes fluttered and sparkled as the person leaned over and did something similar to what the pilot had done with the spacecraft. Tem-aki squinted, but couldn't determine exactly what they had done, but suspected that they had somehow bound the structure – assuming it was a structure – to their vehicles. She tapped the holographic images of the people. "Enlarge."

The green-haired one, who was flamboyantly garbed, talked with its hands, its harsh gestures opposed the fluid elegance of its attire, which looked worthy of an emperor. The smaller blond wore a black servant-style jumpsuit and didn't look very happy.

If only she knew how to operate the computer program for verbal observation.

"Proximity alert."

The view changed to display another of the old ctenophore class ships. What had the planet lord done – bought all the old surplus ships? "Compensate."

ooo

By the time Raine secured Nambaba's tether to her home's dock, she heard the roar of an approaching boat. Preston had come. Relief flooded her.

As her brother docked his craft, he hollered, "This had better be good."

"I need your medical expertise." Raine stripped off her hydro suit, tied it to its tether, and then tossed it into the water to regenerate.

"You're sick?" Concern replaced Preston's exasperation.

"Not me. Someone I picked up." She gestured toward Nambaba's open hatch. "They're in -"

"They?"

"You'll have to see to understand." She leaped onto the tentacle and agilely moved over its rounded, water-slick surface. The tentacle's angle dipped. Good, he was following her. Raine didn't look back or say another word. But her bravado nearly failed her, when she stood in front of the warped door. Preston raised an aristocratic emerald brow at the sight and turned to her, as if expecting an explanation, but she knew him and his love of debating too well, so silently yanked open the storage locker and turned up the lights.

Blood and gore were illuminated in harsh reality. She winced and for the first time in her life, the up and down motion of Nambaba floating atop the waves made her grit her teeth at the need to vomit. Preston didn't even raise a sculpted green brow.

"Rough party?"

She shook her head and looked at the stained ceiling.

He squinted at Colonel Atano's rugged face. "He doesn't look like your type. Too normal." Preston fluidly knelt and lifted a strand of long black hair. Why hadn't she noticed the small braid and embedded feathers before? "Okay, so he's odd, but he really doesn't look like your type. I'm amazed that you'd pick him out."

She swallowed and bit her tongue. Preston narrowed his eyes at her, then looked back down at the Colonel. Raine sighed and traced a dent in the damaged wall with her finger, but studied the warrior out of the corner of her eye.

Preston glanced at the bird-like emblem embossed on the uniform, then did a double take. He hunkered down for a closer look. "Spirit, Raine!" Preston sat back on his heels. Lips flat, he looked up from the warrior and studied the damaged surfaces in the storage locker. Heartbeat by heartbeat, his expression kept getting angrier. Raine stood straighter and straighter. Posture tense, Preston looked back at the warrior. "This is a Shadow Warrior." She nodded. His voice cracked and for the first time in at least two decades, her brother lost his composure. "How- When- Where- What were you thinking to bring him here?" Preston sputtered, as he glared up at her. His pupils were surrounded with a wide halo of white.

"Can you heal him?"

"Why would I want to?"

She looked her brother in the eye. "Because I heard we had a peace treaty with Guerreterre and I don't want to violate it any more than I already have."

"You can't be suggesting that you inflicted those injuries."

She winced. "If it wasn't for me, I doubt if he would have

gotten hurt. I was only trying to do my job." She raised her chin a notch and hoped he didn't see her desperation.

Preston sputtered, then took a calming breath. "You should have told me your 'sick friend' murdered innocents." Preston's long, tapered fingers were so tight around the handle of his emergency medical kit that the skin had a bluish tinge. "What were you thinking?"

"That he had a mother out there somewhere who was worried about him."

Preston looked at her as if she'd lost her mind. "Don't you know how many of our people were killed by the monsters?" The storage closet seemed to shrink as her brother's rage escalated. "And you think we're at peace with them? Where did you get such an insane idea?"

"A transmiss-"

Preston threw his medical kit out the storage closet door. It sailed across the main corridor and hit the concave ivory-toned wall. The sound of breaking glass resonated through the ship.

Disgusted with her brother's needless destruction, Raine's patience snapped. "That did a lot of good."

"You're lucky I didn't throw you."

Raine glared at Preston. "You could have tried. In fact, you still can." He opened his mouth to make a retort, then obviously thought better of it. "He's hurt, help him," she shrieked.

"I noticed." Preston snarled.

Raine put her hands on her hips, leaned slightly forward and lowered her voice. "And he's lost so much blood it's a wonder he isn't dead."

Preston's mouth flattened. "Blood always spreads out so it looks worse than it is."

Raine looked at the warrior. Had he noticed that the warrior's blood was red? "So he's not seriously hurt?"

"I didn't say that."

Preston tried to push past her to get out of the storage locker. She ignored the fact that her younger sibling was a half head taller and grabbed his upper arm, pulling him off balance. "Help him." She enunciated every word carefully and dug her nails into his biceps.

"For Spirit's sake, why?"

Raine kept her grip on him. While, she couldn't tell him about another warrior spying on her, she had to tell him something and make it believable enough for him to want to heal the warrior. "Before I answer that, can you at least tell me if you know how to treat his physiology or if you're angry because you don't know how?"

"How dare you question my ability!" Rage broke through the fear, which had dominated Preston's cultured facade. If circumstances had been different, Raine would have gloated over the crack in his phony nobility mask. Her brother's finger shook, as he pointed at the colonel. "He's a murderer."

"That fact was never in doubt," Raine hissed. "One look at the uniform told me that Colonel Atano was a heartless butcher." She pulled her brother's arm until he looked her straight in the eye. "Some could say the same about you since you stopped treating illness and started designing germ warfare for Zar Vole d'Laire." She steeled her resolve. "And you will confirm it to me if you just stand there and let him die."

Preston looked ready to explode. Motions stiff, he yanked free from her grasp. Back rigid and movements stiff with anger, he plucked a lifting ball and levitation pin from a hidden fold in his ornate salmon and silver robe.

"Where were you going when I called? Dinner with The Zar?"

Preston sniffed. "I did that yesterday." She looked pointedly at his elegant robe. He raised a brow and touched the fabric. "This is normal attire."

Sure it was. He'd probably been miffed when she didn't comment upon his attire when he'd first arrived. "I'll get you some of Gornt's clothing. It may be normal for you, but it's way too good to get bloody."

Preston leaned over and fastened the levitation pin to the warrior then deftly manipulated the ball's red and black hexagons. The warrior rose from the storage locker's floor and hovered.

"Don't want to bend over, huh?"

"Surely you don't expect me to use this as a surgery." He touched more surfaces of the ball. The warrior floated out the door and began floating toward her home.

Raine gritted her teeth and wished she'd thought her request through to its logical conclusion: enemy blood in her home.

Preston maneuvered the warrior through the open hatch. If he was suddenly willing to help, he'd thought of an angle. "How do I know this Guerreterran warrior isn't here to spy on my tox experiments because of your loose tongue?"

"My loose tongue!" she exclaimed. "I have never said a word to anyone." To avoid another full-fledged argument, Raine began collecting the scattered items and broken bits from the battered medical kit. "If you knew everything that led up to this moment, you'd realize that theory is totally paranoid and impossible."

"That phial of tox is cracked," Preston said. "Don't touch it." Raine snatched her hand away from the innocent-looking tube. He handed her the lifting ball's control. "Hold this." She stared at the vial of liquid death while he chose a cubic plastique bottle and poured its contents over the iridescent tox-tube. Her nose wrinkled at the bitter aroma.

"You carry your bio-chemical warfare stuff in your med kit?"

"Yep." He took the lifting ball out of her hands.

"You brought something like that to my home?" As her voice rose, a frigid sensation wrapped Raine's queasy stomach in aching coils. She felt her body suddenly incline backward and a moment later she sat down hard. As darkness rolled over her senses, she put her head between her knees and gasped for breath.

"Relax, it's not that dangerous." He seemed to be shouting from a great distance. "Otherwise I wouldn't be carrying it around."

She wished the spinning darkness would stop.

"Well? Aren't you coming?" he called.

"Yes." Despite outward appearances of getting what she wanted, she knew nothing was ever simple with her brother. With an effort, she crawled toward the hatch. The sea air revived her enough to struggle to her feet, using the wall for support. She leaned against the hatch, eyes narrowed on her brother, as he sauntered along Nambaba's trailing tentacle.

The tranquil water glowed burgundy from the overhead moon. Once her head cleared, Raine thoughtfully followed Preston and the warrior. Was he going so slowly because he thought that there was no way to revive the warrior or because he was hoping to push the warrior past the revival point? Involuntarily, Raine looked up at the night sky and imagined a battalion of Shadow Warriors massing for an invasion.

She shook her head. He's probably just trying to keep his robe clean.

ooo

Tem-aki stared at the trio maneuvering over the ship's long, strange stringy part. A quick check confirmed that the identity code belonged to her brother, but his life signs were not promising. Worse, Dasya Voltain's angle made it nearly impossible to get a good look because the gaudy green-headed one kept fluttering to block her view. "Did they hurt you?" She whispered to her brother. Heart pounding, she tapped the screen, but it was impossible to determine why the two aliens were transporting Larwin with a hoverball. Perhaps he's ill from the water movement. Tem-aki's stomach constricted with sympathy. Looking at the stuff is bad enough, actually being next to it must be awful.

She closed her eyes, blocking out the nauseating hologram, for a moment, but then, fearing she would miss a clue, opened them and stared.

As they maneuvered her brother onto the flat, semi-circular surface, she got a grainy look at his face. Strange how the moonlight made him look so much darker than she remembered and how the shadows made it look like he had long black hair. A moment later, he disappeared inside the other sphere. Tem-aki bit her lower lip and stared at the closed door.

Surely they wouldn't have taken him into that place if they intended evil.

She frowned, recalling the low vital signs.

That place didn't look like any sort of medical facility, that she had ever been to.

What was that odd pair up to?

Was Larwin in danger?

The black-clad one stepped back onto the flat area and turned back toward the ctenophore class ship, then tapped its fingers at on its throat. Abruptly, the water around the circular core began bubbling, then the entire ship began sinking beneath the dark waves. Tem-aki nearly fell into the hologram. "I don't believe what I just saw."

"It was a precise representation," Dasya Voltain said.

"Have you ever heard of spaceships sinking?"

"Negative. However, sensors indicate that one was programmed to fill with water."

How bizarre. Tem-aki looked from the hologram of shifting water to the exterior window, which displayed the molten-red surface of Kalamar's magma moon. Dasya Voltain had shadowed the movement of one of their ships, until she realized it seemed to be patrolling the molten moon, Vilecom and the resident madrox, in a militaristic pattern.

Kalamar had vast wealth in water and was the only planet which sold eepyllihg, so should have appeared amazingly prosperous, yet most of the structures seemed near-poverty. The pilot she had followed, chased madrox instead of run from the energy-devouring beasts, and she wasn't the only one. In fact, since arriving, every space ship that she had seen, seemed to have something to do with the care of madrox.

Kalamar was the strangest place she'd ever heard of and she hoped they were taking good care of her brother.

Chapter 8

By the time Preston moved the pale, comatose warrior into her eating room and settled him onto her table, Raine expected a battalion of murderous Shadow Warriors to burst into her home, vaporize her and her brother, then rescue their comrade. Heart slamming against her ribs, she gazed out the open door, trying to see and hear everything. Something splashed. She shivered and held her breath. In the distance, a frog rasped a guttural serenade. Or perhaps the warriors were imitating the frog, and massing to attack.

"Guerreterran physiology is more resilient than I gave them credit for," her brother said from behind her. Raine swallowed and eased out of the doorway, where she must make a good target, then swiftly closed it and leaned against it. Preston looked over his tablecloth-clad shoulder and arched an aristocratic brow at her before turning back to his patient. His haughty behavior looked particularly ridiculous while wearing cheap plastoid cloth over his elegant robes, but Raine managed not to laugh.

Beyond him, the warrior looked white as death as he lay on his back with his feet extending several inches beyond the end of her table. Preston peeled back the warrior's environmental suit, exposing all the carnage. Spirit, but the colonel must have been a handsome man. Even in near-death, his male magnetism and raw sexual attraction amazed her.

Raine looked away from the warrior's face. Preston took his time mending the external lacerations and in the process, helped himself to several vials of tissue.

Blood and gore splattered her beige tabletop and the tablecloth her brother wore. As soon as Preston moved the warrior out of this room, she was going to throw out the cheap cloth, drench the table and floor with sanitizer and scrub the finish off everything, and then … Raine swallowed in a hopeless attempt to calm her churning stomach. No matter what, she would never eat in this chamber again. Ever. Once she got a decent night's rest, she'd talk to the fellow who had helped her find the out-of-date eepyllihg containers she had constructed her home out of and ask him to help her find a replacement for this section.

Unwilling to stay and watch the barbarous repair of the colonel's abdomen and too ill to eat, Raine scooted across the circular chamber and veered down the connecting tentacle to check on Dalf. As always, her ears popped as she descended the steep incline. Normally, she worried about landing after a space mission and then descending to about thirty feet below sea level, but today was not an ordinary day.

When she arrived at the hatch to Dalf's chamber, she held her breath and unlatched the lock. How silly could she be? First expecting a battalion of Guerreterran warriors to show up on her dock, now trying to be so quiet that she didn't disturb her deaf stepson. She pushed the hatch inward, careful not to get her feet wet as the door brushed against the water, which filled the lower half of his chamber.

Dalf curled on top of his golden air mattress, his sightless eyes staring blindly across the chamber and his favorite stuffed squid cradled in his scared arms. He looked so peaceful. Raine's eyes misted. Too bad his waking moments were such a nightmare.

She gazed at the boy until calm seeped into her core and she felt assured that whatever happened, it would be for the best. Then, she locked the door for Dalf's safety and trudged back up the corridor.

She entered her eating room as Preston applied medicated adhesive to a wound and pressed it in place. The colonel's chest looked as if her brother had pieced together a grotesque crazy quilt of flesh, but it also looked much cleaner and no blood spurted. The table still looked like it belonged in a butcher's shop and several containers contained samples of blood, hair and skin. Hair samples? Oh, yeah, her brother had found a way for this to benefit himself. She quickly looked away from the plastoid bottles. "Are you glad I asked for your help, yet?"

He looked up at her and grunted. "Hold this." Without considering the consequences, she stepped forward and grabbed the handle of the translucent pressure-instrument. When Preston loosened his hold, the warrior's skin began to shift. "Don't let it move or it won't adhere correctly."

She tightened her grip, but couldn't bring herself to look at the way the undamaged skin stretched across the lean abdomen and she refused to imagine how the warrior's stomach had looked before the disaster with the android. She glanced at the warrior's pale, pain-ridden face, then quickly looked away. "How long do I have to keep up the pressure?"

"Tally to fifty." While she began a silent count, Preston massaged his hands. If the pressure of holding one small part of a seam took this much pressure, she understood why his hands bothered him.

The warrior made a soft sound. She looked down, but he hadn't regained consciousness. Though fashionably long, his jet-black hair color hadn't been in style any time in Raine's lifetime, yet it seemed right for the colonel. The natural cut looked right for him, too. The four small braids with their tiny feathers and beads were an interesting feature. Did each feather represent a world he'd annihilated? Was that why each feather was a different color or were they some sort of award for murderous skill? And were the beads significant? Raine swallowed and looked away from the handsome warrior.

Preston made a production of sealing the tissue samples into his medkit.

Raine reached fifty and handed Preston the pressure-instrument. He tossed it into his medkit, as if the device was common as a fishhook. After making sure the bandages were in their proper place, he refastened the warrior's uniform, to help hold the repairs in place. Finally, he took off the tablecloth, wadded it up to control the mess, and then tossed it against the wall.

She cleared her throat. "Now you know how strong you'll need to make your tox." He gave her a sharp look, as if questioning her sanity. Apparently, after spending half the night trying to repair the warrior's injuries, he must have thought she wanted to save the brutal savages. Raine forced the corners of her mouth upward. "No matter what, it always comes back to making sure we can kill them effectively, doesn't it?"

He glowered at her, as if uncertain if she was being satirical or serious. "That is my job." Preston scowled at the warrior. "Amnesia is common in coma-cases."

"Then he'd believe me if I told him he was my personal slave." She studied the warrior's well-defined cheekbones and fought the urge to touch his face.

Preston's hand clamped on her shoulder, and the expression in his eyes looked like he was ready to launch into a diatribe. Then, he let go of her and stretched his back. "I'm going outside."

"Aren't you tired?"

He shrugged.

She followed him outside and gratefully inhaled the night air. "So, what are you working on now, airborne plagues?"

He ignored her and headed purposefully toward Nambaba's mooring line. With practiced ease, he punched in the code for the ship to surface.\

It was too soon, but she didn't argue with him. "What do you need? To check the tox spill?

Preston paused, then stopped. She nearly ran into him. He turned to her and patted her shoulder. She jerked away from him. He held her hands between his and began talking in a low hypnotic tone. "Relax. The spill won't hurt you." Surly he didn't expect her to believe that. He sighed. "It's toxic, but not a poison, it's a variation of a fuel derivative." He squeezed her fingers. Though he looked and sounded sincere, she didn't believe him.

Everything about them was opposite, even their fingers. Hers were short and work-hardened; his were long and patrician, just like the rest of him. No matter what she did, she'd never be tall, lissome or respected for her intellect. Those attributes had been reserved for her brother. All she could hope for was what she had: sturdy shoulders and the will to support her adopted family.

Realizing that Preston was speaking, Raine shook away her thoughts and listened.

"Actually, it was a variation of the eepyllihg additive. Ironic, don't you think? We'll allow our enemies the privilege of paying for the very thing that will destroy them." Preston chortled.

If they lost the Guerreterre market for fuel, she would probably lose her job and become useless. Then, The Zar would probably decide to reclaim the elements of all dragon shepherds. She shivered.

Preston's palm clamped against her forehead. "Spirit! You're running a fever."

Raine pushed Preston's hand away. "No I'm not." Her tongue felt furry. "You're just trying to distract me." She wrenched her hands free and stumbled over the slowly rolling deck to the vine-covered railing. Her rubbery knees barely made it. Raine curled her fingers around the smooth railing and breathed in moist air.

She drank in several gulps of oxygen before her heart rate stabilized. Straightening her spine and squaring her shoulders, Raine turned back to Preston. "Did you treat the Guerreterran so you could use him to carry a plague back to his world?" Though his back stiffened and he seemed to be watching her out of the corner of his eye, he didn't look back at her. Score one for intuition. She silently stared at him, willing him to confirm her suspicions in another way.

Finally, he turned to her. "You saw an enemy ship, shot it down, investigated the crash-site, found a survivor, dragged him to your ship, then hauled him across half the galaxy and now you want me to save him. Is that about it?" Raine gave a slight shrug, deciding that his change of subject and confrontation was all the proof she needed. Preston tossed his thick emerald mane. "While I can't figure out the how's and why's that would inspire you to fire on such a foe, I am impressed with your daring." He shook his head. "To think that you actually shot down a Shadow Warrior."

Raine still hadn't figured that one out how she'd accomplished that.

"What I don't understand is why you haven't given him to the God Head."

Raine blinked. She'd never thought of offering the warrior to The Zar.

"A gift like this would surely elevate you to nobility status and you could move from this leaky string of rubbish to the Pinnacle." Preston gestured toward the entrance of her home. A look of revulsion flitted across his face.

Yes, it would elevate her status, but it would also bring unwanted attention to her and her life. If they discovered that Dalf still lived, they would murder him. Of course, they would use positive words like reclaim elements, but no matter what they called it, she called it murder.

Raine focused her attention on the tentacle, which was secured to her front deck. "My home is not a leaky string of rubbish."

"The reclamation unit never scraps anything unless it's worthless. I know those old tanks leak, especially the one you keep Dalf in."

"It is meant to. He is a creature of the sea." She changed the topic. "I could never live at The Pinnacle." To do so would sign Dalf's euthanasia warrant.

"Since when do you love Shadow Warriors?"

"I don't even like them."

"Really?" One of Preston's shapely green eyebrows arched. "You incapacitate one, capture him and bring him home, then demand that I heal him and every time you look at him, your face softens." He chuckled, but his eyes glittered with malice. "Yet you claim you don't like them." He gave her a leering grin. "Your warrior does have a nice physique." He flexed his reed-thin biceps. "I'd forgotten how muscle-bound Gornt was."

He made it sound like preferring Gornt's healthy, sturdy frame to his fashionably emaciated one was physical. Raine felt tears spring to her eyes and nearly choked on the hostile words clogging her throat. Whirling away, she leaped onto Nambaba's trailing tentacle. Her boot slipped on the wet, rolling surface. She compensated for the rhythm of the waves and hurried to her ship. While her home might not meet her brother's exalted standards, she and Gornt had collected the five canisters themselves, made them habitable, and then connected them to the spare tentacle with the help of his best friend. While it might not look fancy and certainly didn't have all the creature comforts that The Pinnacle boasted, it was the home she and Gornt had built with their own sweat, blood and vision. It was the one place where they had been free. Her bother would never understand the wonderful feeling freedom gave her, because he'd never known anything but phony pride and arrogance. She wouldn't have known freedom, either, if it hadn't been for Gornt.

How she missed her dear friend.

Halfway between her home and the ship's core, she slipped on the slick surface, again. Raine stopped, closed her eyes and focused her energy on adapting her inner rhythms to the undulations of her home sea. Within a few moments, the peaceful cadence calmed her. Opening her eyes, she looked at the other tentacles radiating out from Nambaba forming a silvery starburst on the dark water. The magenta rays from Vilecom made her ship appear beautiful, instead of somewhat shabby.

A sinewy hand closed on her shoulder. "He's not alone, is he?" Preston leaned down and whispered into her ear. "You're being forced, aren't you? Where are the rest hiding?" Every syllable burst against her flesh with a puff of hot, stale breath.

She'd tried to find out the answer to that question the whole journey back. All she was certain of were occasional odd energy readings and bits of transmissions. She had no proof that she'd been followed. No proof that, if she didn't get the warrior's help, reprisals would be made. But she felt as if she was being watched and didn't need any proof. "The man and 'droid are it," Raine snapped. She shook off Preston's grip and faced him. "Who do you plan to kill with those germs you're brewing?" Abruptly, he jerked away from her and stalked toward Nambaba. "Slaves? Nobility? Vole d'Laires?" He stopped, back stiff, then slowly turned to stare at her. His look indicated that he thought she'd gone lunar. She swallowed. "Or do you plan to kill Shadow Warriors? If so, it seems to me that I handed you a once in a lifetime opportunity to study their DNA." Her gaze narrowed on his eyes before she asked, "Prior to treating him, did you realize they had red blood, like ours? That whatever would kill them, might also kill us?"

His pupils widened.

No, he had not thought of that, but hopefully, he would, now.

A silence grew between them, and his eyes kept glancing toward Nambaba. "What do you want in my ship, if it's not to clean up that tox spill?" Raine looked up at Vilecom, before her own indigo orbs revealed how revolting she found her sibling's work. No one, not even a Guerreterran should have to be subjected to the experiments The Zar demanded of his scientists.

His eyes began to glitter. "I want the droid."

Chapter 9

"I don't recall offering it to you," Raine could barely speak through her gritted teeth, "but if I had, how would you explain it at The Pinnacle?"

"Why would I have to explain it?"

Was he so accustomed to living with hundreds that he felt invisible? So audacious that he truly believed he could make the rules? Or just greedy? "Don't you think someone would ask where you got it?" She pressed her point. "I can bring something into my home without a hundred eyes watching. You can't."

Water sloshing was the only sound during several moments of tense silence.

"I'd like to study its design." Preston glanced back over his shoulder toward Nambaba.

"You can do that here, but not now." A yawn threatened. "Now, you need to help me move the warrior and then, I need to sleep. So do you." She turned back to her home. "You can either stay here or go back to your posh silk sheets." Slight undulations beneath her feet indicated that Preston was following her. Raine vaulted back onto the mooring deck. The fancy porpoise-boat tied up to her makeshift dock made her simple home look as shabby as the refuse she and Gornt had used to make it. Tears stung her eyes as she checked the tether line's tension.

Preston landed on the deck. She steeled herself for an argument, but to her surprise, he gently touched her. She gestured toward the sleek golden porpoise-boat. "I don't know what you told The Zar, but it had to be a whopper if he let you take one of his beloved transports instead of the skimmer you usually use."

He chuckled and his fingers began caressing her knuckles. A glance at his lean face told her that Preston's thoughts were focused on something else. Looking in the same direction, she only saw peaceful dark water. Preston exhaled. "Since Gornt's death, you don't even like sunrises and their promise of a new day." He looked at her home. She squinted at the horizon, trying to determine how long it would be until dawn. "The warrior is handsome," he said softly. "Did you want me to save him for you so he could replace Gornt or save him so I can perfect the death of his race?"

"No one could replace Gornt."

"That's good, because it would never work." His expression took on a wry look. "Not that I ever figured out how anything worked with Gornt."

"He was my friend and we cared for each other."

"So? There's a lot more to a union than friendship. Bakufus are egg layers; you're a mammal. That relationship should never have happened." She glared at him. Preston got the message and shut up.

"You shouldn't underrate friendship." Again, she squinted in the horizon. Her brother would never understand, because he was too self-centered to be a friend to anyone. "I think it's interesting that you find beauty in that savage. Especially since you've devoted the last few years to brewing up concoctions to wipe out him and all his kind."

"And one of these days I'll succeed." His chuckle sounded ominous in the dark. "Especially now that I have a live specimen to exper-"

"I told you, he's mine."

"What do you need him for?"

Insurance that no retaliatory measures were made. "None of your business."

"You expect me to waste time saving his life and not get a lab toy."

Raine's teeth ground together. "You got plenty of samples for your efforts. More than you could ever have hoped for." Inspiration struck. "Besides, he's going to be my slave." Raine almost spoiled her ridiculous declaration by laughing at his stupefied expression.

"You're not nobility," he sputtered. "You can't own slaves. Spirit! Near-nobility is a meaningless title, you know that as well as I do." He gesticulated helplessly.

Raine glared up at her brother, who lived in the shadow of The Zar's smile and had such a posh life that he couldn't understand her own struggle to survive. "You're only near-nobility, too, Doctor High-and-Mighty. You always forget that, because you live at The Pinnacle, but you and I are equal." He shook his head. She nodded. "I work directly for the Vole d'Laires, too." She made a sweeping gesture, which encompassed the entire world and included the setting arc of Vilecom. "In some way, everyone works for him. You just get more luxurious perks."

He shook his head and opened his mouth to argue.

She held up a hand for silence. "The only real difference is that you don't have a transponder code for an address."

Preston pointed toward the porpoise-boat.

Raine gestured toward Nambaba, which rode the pre-dawn tides on a halo of tentacles and impressive compared to the small, sleek porpoise-boat. Once the sun rose, Nambaba would begin to look more serviceable than elegant, but for now, she was in the ideal lighting for Raine to make her point.

Her brother's mouth flattened.

"In fact, in some ways," she added, "I have more freedom than you do." He opened his mouth to argue. She cut him off with a threatening look. "I cook and eat what I wish. You are subject to the chef's whims. So what if I don't drive a porpoise-boat? Every day at work, the view I have is awesome. You are stuck in a windowless hole. And when I'm off work, I can swim or paddle my reed boat."

"I like my life." His tone sounded stiff as his posture.

"Of course you do. You have a good life and you have lots of things I could never imagine. But they are just things and things are not really that important." She paused, then made her point, "I have family and love." Preston rolled his eyes skyward. She felt a muscle twitch, but held her temper. "Most of us have three options: swim, ride the ferry-gliders or, if we're not too busy working for The Zar, we can weave boats." But who had time for anything except working and trying to keep the house together?

"What's your point?" he asked.

"Other than the fact that you put too high a value on possessions? A reality check for both of us, I guess." Tears threatened. "I'm so tired, so unbelievably tired." She closed her eyes and fought for control.

His arms wrapped around her. "It's hard for everyone. It has been for a while, now." He cleared his throat. "The Zar got harsher since Guerreterre destroyed Latawba. He lost his famil-"

"He only lost a brother, who he rarely saw." She gave Preston a significant look. "I lost Gornt and everything that was good about Dalf." Her jaw tightened as she looked toward the water, which covered the deeper levels of her home and hid her secret from the world. "For all purposes and standards, I lost Dalf, too. Now, all I have is you and it is rare to see you. The Zar still has Brock and Annya and his niece, Marsha, too. They all live with him, so he sees them whenever he wants, so, don't you dare try to tell me about The Zar's loss. There's no comparison."

Preston studied her face. "Caring for Dalf is too much for you. Eventually will you let me recl-"

"Never," she said. She would never allow him to hide the fact he'd done one decent thing in his miserable self-centered life. They'd saved Dalf and she would care for him as long as she lived.

As Preston hugged her; his thin arms felt like thin ropes and failed to give the security Gornt's strong embraces had. "You're exhausted because caring for him takes too much."

Raine pushed away from him. "I know he's not really my son. I know he's more animal than anything, but he's all I have."

"What about Shay?"

Coldness gripped her heart. "What about her?"

"Whenever I see her, she complains that you-"

"Marsha's maid is not my little sister." She was merely the orphan their parents had taken in.

"Sure looks like her to me."

"The eyes and face are the same." Unwilling to get into this discussion for the hundredth time, she turned her back on him.

"Raine-" Preston choked back whatever else he'd intended to say.

Since Shay had entered into Marsha's service at the Pinnacle, their adopted sister had changed from an adorable, sweet girl into an egotistical dolt, who acted worse than Preston. If that wasn't bad enough, she'd fallen in love with Brock Vole d'Laire and was making such a fool of herself over him that Raine had heard pilots making jokes about her.

Shay was even naïve enough to believed the future planetary lord cared for her in return. Raine's mouth flattened. Shay would be lucky if Brock recognized her after he finished satisfying his carnal desires. Within two years, he would bond with his cousin, Marsha, and thus assure the strength of the imperial bloodline, as had all the generations before him. If Shay was lucky, she'd be banished to live out the remainder of her life toiling the marshes in disgrace; but more likely her nutrients would be recycled to fertilize the crops, so that no evidence remained of Brock's dalliance with a servant.

How she despised the Reclamation Unit! The memory of the day her mother retired slammed into Raine's memory. The Vole d'Laires squeezed every drop of value out of a worker; if the individual wasn't worked to death by their fortieth birthday, when the person's good years were past, then, on that day, their useful elements were salvaged and the remains were turned into fish food.

Their word: retirement.

Her word: murder.

How could Shay be so stupid about her choices and delusions?

Eyes closed, Preston sighed and seemed focused on his breathing. Was he remembering the day they lost their mother, too? She watched his fisted hands unclench. Raising her gaze, she noticed that the tiny wrinkles next to his eyes appeared smoother. This wasn't her brother, this was The Zar's physician, the man the Vole d'Laires counted on.

As if sensing her watching him, he raised his head and locked his gaze on her. "You truly believe Shay is courting disaster?"

Good pun. Too bad he didn't get it. Raine held in the harsh laugh. "You're there, watching it. Can't you see it?"

"It's her life," he said. "Shay is old enough to choose. If she makes the wrong choices, she will be the one to pay." He shrugged.

"How typical," Raine spat. "Let your kid sister do whatever she wants as long as you don't have to pay for her mistakes."

He looked at her as if she was one of his lab experiments. "I don't think you ever forgave Shay for endearing mother and moving in."

"What's that supposed to mean?"

"You liked being the pampered one."

"Oh, for the lov-"

"Of course, you eventually learned to care for the kid, too, but then she grew up and followed me to The Pinnacle, instead of you into the void."

"That's ridiculous." As ridiculous as the thought that being last-born was a pampered position. Raine clenched her teeth, unwilling to respond to the bait.

"Is it?" Preston's smile was icy. "I don't think she ever forgave you for bonding below-"

"Gornt was not a lesser being. He had ten times your strength. And twenty times your compassion."

"I think Shay's infatuation with Brock has its roots in the embarrassment over you and your beloved bakufus."

"Stuff kelp in it." Though she kept her tone surly, she shifted uneasily at the idea that Shay's fatal fixation on the future overlord could have been caused by her actions. The one thing she had never understood was why Marsha seemed to ignore the obvious attraction.

"Only if you take a strong look at what you've done and your motives. Why did you bond with Gornt? Surely you weren't that desperate for a mate."

"Gornt was intelligent and good company." He had been her best friend. Her only true friend.

"Which can explain a friendship, but a bonding?"

"He'd lost his mate and needed help raising Dalf. Plus, Gornt was the best mechanic I've ever known and he kept Nambaba in perfect operating order."

"You like being needed," he said. "Is that why you brought home an injured enemy? Is that why you expect me to be happy over this 'wonderful opportunity'?" Preston's tone was laced with phony sympathy. His expression hardened. "Is that why you insisted on saving the kid? So you would be needed by something?"

Raine stared at him, wondering why he kept pushing her after she'd told him how tired she was. "Go throw yourself in the

Sea of Doom, but only after you move the warrior off my table." He reached into the folds of his ornate robe, brought out the lifting ball and tossed it to her. She turned and took a step toward her front door.

"The levitation pin is with his clothes. You can return them to me, later."

"Thanks." She turned away from him and went toward her home. "I'll go nurse my new slave." Raine felt a slight undulation under her feet. She didn't need to look back to know his long-legged stride was catching up to her.

"Come back here and-"

"You and Shay live in The Pinnacle's luxury where high-placed maids have assistants." Her jaw clenched at the memory of her last visit and how inferior her home seemed afterward. She squared her shoulders. "You delude yourselves with visions of power and prestige. Those kinds of misconceptions always carry the price of death." That truth was the only thing that helped her get through the days after experiencing such pampering.

"I think you're jealous."

Raine paused and looked back at him. His face was bathed in the ominous red glow of Vilecom's setting light. A shiver rushed over her. "In a way I am." Rained turned to look at him in time to see his look of surprise at her easy agreement. "You take your life for granted and have freedom and privilege the rest of us can't even imagine. But I do not want your life or to live in a place where fifty strangers constantly watch my every move." Raine focused on a throbbing portion, which was visible under his wave-crest neck-collar, with its golden healer insignia. She gestured toward it, "You criticize me because I want to help others, yet that was the reason you originally chose medicine." His fingers touched the emblem, as if surprised it heralded his primary function. "You amaze me. You decide to go for glory and finding new ways to end life, yet you still wear the healer insignia."

"I earned this."

She tightened her fingers around her own wave collar. "And I earned this." Even though she hated it and everything it stood for. She especially hated the Vole d'Laires. "The Zar must think we're all fools for being taken in by baubles. All these bands are good for is to tell us that we are special slaves." But only those special enough to live at The Pinnacle benefited. "These collars give him the right to demand more from us."

Preston nodded. "Longer hours, but more interesting work, better food and silks." He caressed his robe.

"Responsibilities that if not completed to his satisfaction mean death." Her brother winced. "It doesn't matter what made the task impossible, he'll call any explanation an excuse and then point the way to the recycling chamber."

"He's not that bad."

"Are you certain?" He opened his mouth to say something, but no sounds came out. Raine pressed her point. "Think about how you got your illustrious position."

"What do you mean?" he asked.

"What did your promotion cost D'nor and his family?" Raine watched his eyes shift as he thought about the circumstances, which had taken his superior's life and given him the position he felt so arrogant about. "Was his life worth that gaudy robe?"

Preston chewed his lower lip as if eating unsaid words.

Raine relented a bit. "So maybe, we'll get a second or two extra if … no make that, when, The Zar decides we're no longer useful." She looked him in the eye. "The only ones who die of old age are the Vole d'Laires and maybe the bakufus who disappear into the wild seas." Deaf and blind Dalf would never have that chance at pure freedom. She clamped her jaws together, lest the lump in her throat reveal itself.

"I know you haven't liked the Winslow Vole d'Laire or his family since losing Gornt." Preston's tone was placating. Raine crossed her arms over her chest. "But he's a good man."

Her fury boiled. "The Zar gives us emblems so we'll work ten times harder than we did before, but we don't get the things we really want." Again, she clamped her jaws shut and tried to calm her thundering heart. "Have you ever known anyone to actually achieve nobility status or gain their freedom?"

Preston's eyes widened. "No."

"That's because no one ever has and no one ever will." Raine snapped her mouth shut before she could blurt out more seditious thoughts, which if whispered in the right ear, would mean instant death.

Preston tilted his head to look at her. "Is freedom so important to you?" His incredulous tone surprised her.

"Everyone should be free." It was the main thing, which had first attracted her to Gornt.

He pulled at his ear. "Would any of us know what to do without someone to test our skills and abilities, then direct us how to study?"

"Wouldn't you have liked the opportunity to find your path by yourself?

He shook his head. "The Vole d'Laires perfected their sorting methods over a millennium and know what is best."

"Before they came, our ancestors were free," Raine said.

"And starving," he shot back. She looked away from him. "You can't look back at the past and only acknowledge the parts you approve of. You have to see the whole. Before the Vole d'Laires came here to rule, Kalamar was a frozen world inhabited by illiterate masses."

"Twaddle. I'll grant you that the ice caps were huge, but the bakufus who lived in the oceans were not stupid."

Preston's lips thinned. "The Vole d'Laires promised warmth and food in return for allegiance. Are you saying they haven't lived up to their part of the bargain?"

She shook her head. "Perhaps it was a fair trade a millennium ago, but can you honestly say you still believe it is?" Would her ancestors have made the pledge if they'd known all future generations would be born into bondage?

"What are you really upset about?"

If he didn't understand, he never would. "Everything," she said. As he waited for her to clarify her statement, silence began to stretch like the reflection of Vilecom's final vermilion rays. Strange how it looked more sinister from her home water than in space. Raine shivered and tried to rub circulation back into her arms, but with every heartbeat, the blood red seemed to cover more of her world. The moon seemed to become a menacing face.

"I came when you called," Preston softly said. "And I tended your new 'slave'."

"Yes, you did."

"And even though you didn't tell me why you needed me, I came."

"I'm sorry for what I said," Raine said. "I really am happy that you've been so successful."

"All three of us have come farther than we ever believed we

would."

"Are you angry because I've put you in jeopardy?"

"What do you mean?"

Raine gestured to her home, which held the warrior and Dalf within, then to Nambaba, with its droid cargo. "First you helped me save Dalf, now the warrior. If any Vole d'Laire finds out, we'll be executed."

"Not if the tox works." He sounded impossibly confident.

Spirit, was her brother that dumb? "If the tox works, you are dead. Winslow Vole d'Laire will not share glory with a slave." Preston's distressed look made her wish she'd stayed quiet.

"Winslow might claim the formula, but he won't kill me." Preston's voice lacked conviction.

She looked him in the eye. "Think back to the exact chain of events that lead up to D'nor's disappearance. Did they ever find his body?" she asked.

Preston swallowed and refused to meet her gaze as he shook his head.

"Did you find any proof that he'd really moved off planet, as Winslow Vole d'Laire claimed?" Preston took a step away. Raine grabbed his arm. "Don't you find it interesting that a few days after he vanished, Vole d'Laire, our all-powerful and capable Zar, went to his own lab and discovered xamahas? I personally found Yeeehoohaaaa interesting, especially since I knew D'nor had spent decades trying to find just the right gas to use as a vehicle for air-borne toxins." Raine hated to make him relive his panic over the loss of his beloved mentor. Preston fought to maintain a neutral expression, but the tic next to his eye gave him away. "Don't you realize that you're dealing with a far worse dragon than I am?" she asked softly.

"You think working in my lab is worse than herding dragons?"

"They don't kill us, we kill them." His shocked expression was comical. "Only when necessary, of course. Some will not be tamed, so we have to kill them. You don't need to look so surprised. We don't make the choice. The Zar makes it. His philosophy is that if they can't be controlled, they shall be killed – they and any offspring."

"But the eepyllihg!" He glanced at Vilecom. Its red glow stained his face.

"He can afford to lose some mooncalves, but not to another moon or sun, where someone might learn the secret formula and go into competition against him." Raine shrugged. "Besides, when there's less eepyllihg to sell, he charges more per unit. Believe me, it doesn't cost him anything. Life – all life, except his own – is irrelevant to him." She silently watched her brother's expression while her meaning clarified. He shook his head, as if he'd just come to the surface after a very deep dive.

"How do you learn these things?"

"I watch and listen."

He looked around their isolated location. She decided not to point out that several people, particularly nobles, seemed to assume radio transmissions were private.

"Do you have a plan to overthrow his dynasty?" Preston's voice cracked. "Something to do with that warrior?"

Where had that idea come from? It was so ludicrous that she nearly laughed in his face. "Why bother? We're all going to die within this generation anyway."

"What do you mean by that?"

Raine pointed to Vilecom's setting arc. "Ever since the first

Vole d'Laire brought that moon to this system, it's been spiraling closer and closer to our planet. The rate it is falling is increasing. If something isn't done about it, it will soon be close enough to be caught in our gravitational pull and we will all die."

"How would you know?"

"I've been up there every day for most of my life. I know what I'm seeing on my instruments."

"And you never told anyone?"

"I told my superiors," Raine said.

"You should have told me."

She nearly laughed. "Why? I was told that our all-powerful Zar would take care of it." She took a deep, calming breath. "He hasn't." She didn't believe he would if he could. "When he finishes milking our planet of everything possible, he'll abandon us to face our death while he finds a new world to rule."

"That's outrageous," he said.

"Perhaps." She shrugged. "But it's also true."

"You have no proof."

"Don't I?" She asked. Preston shook his head. She nodded. A confused look crossed his normally taciturn features. "Answer this question: why did Winslow Vole d'Laire begin storing his excess wealth off planet a decade ago?"

"How would you know where his wealth is?" Preston demanded.

Raine raised an eyebrow. "Pilots talk." She smiled. "And we overhear lots of interesting things." Preston rubbed his forehead. "Think about it, if you spent half your time up there," she pointed, "with dragons, which have been taught their place and routine for a millennium, don't you think you'd try to find ways to relieve the tedium?"

"By spying on Winslow Vole d'Laire?"

"By watching patterns."

He blinked, as if assimilating what she'd told him. "Do you have some sort of plan to save our family?" His eyes widened and he glanced at her home. "Is that why you captured the warrior?"

No, but she needed to now that he'd brought up the idea. She shrugged nonchalantly. "Maybe."

"Oh, Spirit! What is it?" She shook her head. His eyes widened. "Do you plan to tell him our battle strategies and release him?" he asked. She raised a brow. "Granted that would get even with Winslow for declaring war and ruining you life, but-"

"I hadn't thought of that possibility, but now that you mention it-" Raine's voice trailed off as she silently watched Preston's expression tighten into a death mask, then she innocently asked, "How would I get access to war documents?"

"But-"

"You keep making more of this than it is," she lied. "Plain and simple, I want a slave."

"Why?"

"I'm always at Vole d'Laire's beck and call; I want to be in charge of something." Raine bit her tongue until the unholy inclination to laugh at Preston's shocked expression passed.

"It's to help with Dalf, isn't it?"

She shrugged, as if trying to deal with the child didn't take all her spare time and energy. "Now that you've done as much as you can for the warrior, I will find a use for him and making him care for Dalf, sounds like the right sort of justice. After all, his kind robbed him of his hearing and sight."

"Let me have him," Preston said. "It's too dangerous for you."

"If I get tired of him, you can have him for your experiments." Preston crossed his spindly arms over his chest and studied her as if she was a laboratory experiment giving him unexpected results. It was time to tell another part of the truth, but which part? She didn't dare tell him that she thought another Shadow Warrior was monitoring them and was trying to figure out a way to escape Kalamar before Vilecom wiped out everything as they knew it. The truth sounded like she was either delusional or paranoid. Raine cleared her throat. "You know how much I cared for Gornt." Preston nodded. She continued, "And how I vowed to avenge his death? Well, I've finally been given an opportunity to keep that vow."

"By saving a Guerreterran's life so he can be a plague carrier?"

"Not exactly."

The tresses of his luxurious green hair turned a sickly brown in the waning moonlight.

"I like your new hair color. It reminds me of the sea at dawn." Preston glared at her. Raine ran her fingers through her own short, unruly saffron tresses and wondered what she could say, without revealing her half-formed plan. Raine studied Preston's expression and recalled the mud-splattered boy, who had declared that one day he would overthrow the Vole d'Laires and free all slaves.

How had he become one of the dynasty's fiercest supporters?

As the silence lengthened, Vilecom's last rays receded from the still, black water. Bumps rose on Raine's arms, she rubbed them for warmth. Even at a half-million miles away, that red dwarf had the explosive power to wipe out everything.

"I don't know how you stand working so close to that and herding those beasts." Preston scowled.

Raine knew his tactics and wasn't lulled into believing he would truly change the subject, yet. "You get used to it," Raine muttered. Though she often sensed the moon's malevolence, she always told herself it was ridiculous to believe depravity could be localized in a place.

"I've never understood why the Vole d'Laire ancestors captured that piece of star when it exploded."

"Probably to warm this world. I doubt that they imagined the dragons, which infested it, would ever be more than an annoying parasite, or if they did, they probably figured that they would be safe from them on a water world." She squinted at Preston wondering how he managed to look so calm, when he was probably still trying to find a way to talk her into recycling Dalf and giving him both android and warrior.

Preston gazed at the thin red haze left by Vilecom. "When I finish the tox experiments, I want to develop a process to synthetically manufacture eepyllihg. Once we have a synthetic, we can move the moon away from our system." He sounded more confident than he looked.

"You have that technology?"

"It's in The Zar's personal archives." He shrugged. "I figure we can use the same method used to bring it here, just in reverse." He turned a sober face to her. "We must move it before it goes pulsar."

Her heart skipped a beat. While she'd mentioned the deteriorating orbit, she'd never mentioned her calculations or her conclusions. "How long have you known?"

"A few years. Most of the pinnacle's mathematicians have been working on computing a safe trajectory to boost it to a farther orbit, or at least reverse the current spiral. But what worries me is that most scientists can't agree on how much time we have left or what will happen to this planet once it's gone." He sighed. "Some say the moon should have crashed a decade ago, but the majority predict about three more solar orbits." He gave her an affectionate look. "I bet none of them realizes that it's bad enough for everyday pilots to notice."

"Why didn't you say something before?" She studied him, wondering if she'd ever known her brother. He shrugged. "How long have you known it would eventually explode?" He shrugged, a second time. "And you never thought to warn me."

"If it happens, it won't make any difference where you are. Here." He gestured to the water. "Or there." He pointed to the sky.

When she opened her mouth to argue, Preston held up his hand. "If it goes, they predict that it will have a speed of a thousand miles per second," he said. "Being close to its core will snuff you before you can scream. Everything on Kalamar will be annihilated a few seconds of terror later."

Raine shivered and rubbed her arms. "Why doesn't The Zar move it immediately?"

"He doesn't think it's a problem."

Her brother's contemptuous tone surprised her. "I thought you idolized him."

"It is beneficial for him to believe that. Do you remember Dad's philosophy or were you too young when he died?" Raine raised a brow. "'Keep your friends close and your enemies closer'," he quoted.

"Yes." Raine lowered her voice, "Are you saying The Zar is your enemy?" Or was he telling her what he thought she wanted to hear because he viewed her as his enemy?

"He's everyone's enemy. And don't tell anyone I said that."

"I didn't intend to." Raine shifted her feet.

"Are you going to tell me why you want the Guerreterran?"

"I avenge Gornt one for one, if I killed him." She tilted her head at the main body of her ship, and made certain not to look him in the eye, where he could read her deception, "But if I save him, I can increase the odds."

Preston leaned close enough for Raine to see that his eyes were shining. Hope rose within her. "And the android?"

"Initially I planned to dismantle it so I could sell its parts to finance Nambaba's repairs, but since it melted down, its practically worthless."

Abruptly, Preston walked purposefully toward Nambaba. "I'm going to take a good look at what I earned."

"How are you going to sneak it into your quarters? You live right under the God Head's nose."

"So I'll keep it here," he said.

"Why do you want the droid?" she asked.

"If I can figure out its construction, we could build some to sell."

Raine snorted. "The Vole d'Laires are the only ones who could afford them, and if they found out a slave had them, they'd just confiscate what they wanted."

When Preston looked back at her, his face molded into such a sinister smile, that shivers raced up and down her spine. "I know."

The hint of evil in his expression chilled more than her backbone. Raine wondered if she'd misjudged her brother's loyalty to their avaricious dictator, or if Preston merely wanted her to believe it was so. Prudence kept her silent.

He purposefully stepped into Nambaba. She was left wondering what the future held and if there was any way to survive it.

Chapter 10

As Raine walked Preston to his porpoise-boat, Ishdoo hovered, cold and pale in the morning sky.

Raine put her hand on the weather-beaten railing around her docking deck. "I don't know how the robot's arm got welded to the floor." The weathered wood moved beneath her palm.

He stared at Nambaba. "Next time I bring your supplies, I'll bring tools and more sedative."

The railing had needed stabilizing for a solar orbit, but Preston hadn't noticed, previously. Why did males go out of their way to pursue projects, like repairing the android and offered to get special tools to get it out of Nambaba, and at the same time, ignore repairs, which they already had tools and supplies to accomplish? Perhaps afterward, he'd help her with the repairs that would make her home safer.

He cleared his throat. "Promise me that you'll give the warrior the injections."

"I said I would, but I don't know why you think they are so important. After all, you said he'd be too weak to do anything. Why must I make certain he stays unconscious?" He shrugged and red tinges his neck. Embarrassment? Could this mean he was concerned about her safety? What a novel concept. She glanced at the gleaming porpoise-boat. "Be careful that Winslow doesn't toss you to the sharks for taking his toy."

Preston exuded overconfidence as he caressed the hull. "He can't afford to lose me." He chuckled. "My research is far too valuable to him."

"Only until you perfect your formula. Then, you'll disappear like D'nor."

He stiffened and his expression hardened. "What do you know of Reed D'nor?" A tic next to his eye betrayed his tension. "What do Dragon shepherds know of science?" His ridicule sounded like a pathetic attempt at denial.

Raine sighed. "Just be careful, okay? You're the only brother I have." His green brows arched. "I don't want you to disappear like D'nor."

Preston looked skyward and shook his head. The early morning breeze raised gooseflesh on her arms. When he left, she watched the wake merge back into smooth sea and rubbed her chilblains.

Raine breathed in the humid air, wishing it would revive her, instead, all she wanted was to crawl into her bed and sleep for ten rotations. But, she couldn't. Dalf and the warrior needed attention and she needed a bath.

ooo

Thunder woke from his nightmare of pain to agony. He tried to separate fact from nightmare, but it was impossible to move.

Impossible to inhale a complete breath. Impossible to open his eyes.

He lay still. His last coherent memory was of GEA-4 mind-speaking about the bizarre history of a water world, which was too horrible of a place to imagine. He shuddered. The story must have been the sort that people told around open fires on dark nights, wherever GEA-4 came from. Bad as the thought of all that water was, an entire planet would never work for the good of one person without a word of disagreement and an entire society couldn't possibly base their economy to one product. He breathed a bit easier.

Strange though, how real the images had seemed. The odd cadence of the language, with its peculiar clicks and whistles echoed in his subconscious. Thunder hummed and remembered the lyrics of a song, the clicks and whistles were as soothing as a lullaby.

Something cool and soothing caressed his face. "You're so hot," the gentle whistling voice said. A cool, hard object was placed against his lips. "Drink," the voice coaxed. But he couldn't.

Though he knew it was impossible for anyone to know the song, someone began singing the words. Her voice was so beautiful that it brought tears to his eyes. He stopped humming so he could listen, but the only sound was water lapping against something solid. The next thing he knew, his lips were pried apart and something soft as a kiss touched him. A shudder of ecstasy rippled over him, then, cool, life-giving liquid tricked into his mouth. When he involuntarily swallowed, the touch vanished.

There was a sound of satisfaction. "You see, Dalf, I did learn something from nursing you."

Again and again the woman repeated the sensual process of

filling his mouth with the liquid. But by the time he felt strong enough to force his eyes open, the only thing he could see was a strange dark space.

He closed his eyes and slept.

The black void of sleep became tinged with a golden glimmer on one edge. Thunder sucked in his breath, and waited to see what new torment his vision held. Within three heartbeats, the other side of the emptiness began to mirror the glow. Entranced, he watched light delicately churned and the amber glow drew nearer.

A familiar amber-gold eye. A tingle of recognition went down his spine, and he exhaled. Kazza had found him. His lips curved into a smile as he tried to lift his hand to scratch the cat's silken ears.

The cat's eye drew back until the entire face of the huge gold, white and black striped cat was studying him with an expression of concern. Kazza's black-tufted ears jutted forward, his gaze intent, as if he was making a mental list of all his injuries.

When the great cat's gaze rose to meet him, Thunder knew that it was a miracle that he was still alive. The background lightened into the grassy clearing next to Nimri's herb garden. In the background, sequoia branches swayed in the breeze.

Home.

Larwin and Nimri appeared on either side of Kazza, their hands on his powerful shoulders. The regal cat raised his paw, then locked his gaze with Thunder. A comforting rumble enfolded space; time stood still and three revolving orbs seemed to dance weightless in his dream. As he watched the mesmerizing balls, then the great cat's presence overwhelmed his senses.

Pressure covered his stomach and the purr receded. Without

looking away from Kazza's mesmerizing stare, Thunder lifted his hand and felt the cat's gigantic paw. He'd thought it would be impossible for the pain to be worse, but as he placed his own hand over Kazza's paw, it felt as if his entire abdomen was being torn apart and reconfigured on the cellular level. Thunder gasped, then the comfort of shadows covered him, like a warm, healing fur and Kazza's deep rumbling purr turned the agony into warmth and friendship.

"The point of confrontation draws near," Kazza's deep male voice rumbled.

Though Thunder knew that on some level the great cat was continuing to heal his body, he focused on the orange ball, which began to gyrate like an out of control top and spin toward the big, pretty blue ball and the small, grayish white one. With a crash and hiss, they all collided and the image burst into sparks and steam.

As the embers died, black returned.

Then, a golden speck appeared at the center of the dark void. The speck zigzagged back and forth, and then it was joined by another glowing speck. Soon, hundreds of random flecks dotted the darkness, like stars in the nighttime sky. Then, one in the center grew larger, until Thunder recognized a golden dragon, which flew away. As he watched, all the milling specks transformed into dragons and followed the first one.

"It begins with the termination of Kalamar," The deep voice intoned. "With the portal open, Chatterre will soon attract the energy suckers. We will not be able to repel them. You must complete your mission."

Thunder gasped as a profound sense of misery engulfed him.

"The portal must be closed," the now distant voice said.

"Yes," he gasped. He blinked tears from his eyes and peered at the shadowed contours of a strange rounded enclosure. He held his breath and tried to figure out where he was or if he was still locked in the nightmare.

The chamber felt cool and dank; nothing like his comfortable rock-hewn home. Dim light reflected from the walls, which were smooth and rounded as the inside of a glazed bowl, but the platform he was lying on seemed to be swaying like a bough in the breeze. Thunder opened both eyes, then sat up and stared around him.

He was on one of two strange mats that appeared to be made of thick bubbles, which were floating on a pool that took up the entire bottom of the room. There didn't appear to be windows or doors to escape from the flood.

Panic grew, as the memory of the deluge that had torn his life apart threatened to overwhelm him.

Thunder closed his eyes, hoping the room would go away.

It didn't.

The water near him rippled as if something large was underneath the surface. Moments later, the smooth back of a huge dark fish surfaced. It glided across the placid water to the other mat, then gripped the bubbles with webbed fingers and hoisted itself onto it. The action sent ripples of movement through the area.

Thunder gagged as nausea threatened.

The sturgeon-like creature sprawled on the mat, displaying the webbing between its arms and body, which reminded him of a bat. Though it had a mouth, the rest of its cone-shaped head was a mass of scars.

What sort of vision was this?

Thunder studied the odd apparition that appeared part human, part sea-monster. The face's disfigured flesh was crisscrossed with white scars. Thunder squinted through the gloom. Ivory on the front, charcoal on the back, the smooth hairless creature must have fallen into a vat of dye.

It made odd guttural noises as it wriggled on the mat. The filmy flap of skin connected its arm from wrist to waist flopped in oddly iridescent folds.

"Were those visions supposed to be a message?" he muttered. His voice echoed through the odd chamber, as if mocking him.

He put his hands to his face, but was surprised to see that all but his fingers were swathed in strange blue fabric. He turned his hands this way then that, then began clawing at the looser knot, on his left hand until it broke. He unwound the long strip of slick fabric and let it drift on the water. Thunder flexed his fingers, and remembered the vision of torn flesh coupled with horrible pain. Though his hand felt stiff, it looked healed.

Had Kazza folded space to aid him, or had the injuries been the illusion?

The mangled face rose and sniffed the air, like a yeti scanning the wind for the scent of prey. As it turned its face toward him, it emitted a blood-curdling howl and launched its body toward him.

Reflexively, Thunder defended himself from the beast and knocked it backward into the water, as he fell backward onto the mat.

The creature paused for a moment, then lunged back to the surface and emitted a horrendous howl of mingled anger and despair.

He shuddered.

As the beast beat the water, a circle of light appeared in the bubble's side and a woman stood silhouetted against the pale yellow light. The scent of sunlight came with her.

The creature thrashed in the water, shrieking, as if it was being maimed. The woman leaped into the water, which only came to her waist and went to the creature. Crooning softly, she wrapped her arms around its sleek cylindrical body and rocked the screeching thing as if it was a beloved babe.

"What did you do to him?" the woman demanded.

Thunder closed his eyes and gritted his teeth against the movement of the undulating mat.

"Talk to me or I'll kill you."

No dream had never demanded a response before. As his sickness escalated, he wished she would either follow through on her threat to kill him or help him wake from this nightmare.

When she continued to create waves by rocking the creature, he lurched off the mat and into the dreadful water. He hurried through the cloying stuff to the round hole, then scrambled up its strange soft surface toward the light.

"Come back here."

Never, he thought as he hurried toward the smell of fresh air.

Chapter 11

Raine stared after the warrior in amazement. Preston had assured her that his injuries would incapacitate him for several moon cycles and she'd certainly given him the injections on schedule. If she'd had any idea he could sit up, much less leap off the cot and dash out of Dalf's compartment, she would have brought her blaster.

Dalf, accustomed to having all of her attention when she came to his chamber, whimpered and rubbed against her.

It took a moment to realize that the warrior was escaping. With that insight came action and Raine sprinted up the connector-corridor after him. By the time he barreled through the exterior hatch and stagger-sprinted onto the deck, she was only two paces behind him.

The reeds undulated under his weight and he fell against a vine-covered railing, nearly collapsing it. Knuckles white, and eyes shut, he gulped in deep breaths.

Was this a ruse?

Now that he was on his feet he seemed twice as big as she'd imagined. Muscles corded in his arms and across his shoulders.

Confident that he didn't intend to leap into the sea and either swim away or dive down to where Nambaba lay on the sea floor, soaking in hydro, Raine slipped back into her home and grabbed her blaster.

When she returned, he was on his knees and had his forehead pressed against the railing. The burst of energy seemed to have sapped him. As she stood in the hatchway, uncertain of what to do, next, Dalf bumbled past her and lurched onto the woven reed decking.

"Spirit, what's next?" she said. Raine grabbed Dalf before he could hurt himself. He jumped at her touch, then seized her as if she was life itself. "What did you do to him?"

The warrior didn't respond.

Dalf plucked at the neckline of her jumpsuit. "M-m-m-mmmmm," he intoned. This is the closest thing to speech she'd heard from his lips since she and Preston had saved him from the reclamation unit. Raine wrapped her arms around him and burst into tears. "M-m-m-m-mmmm-mm," he continued, as he snuggled against her.

"I love you, too." Tears spilled down her cheeks.

She stared over the top of Dalf's head at the warrior. Bringing a comatose victim to her home was one thing; this was a whole new gamble. Her brow furrowed, as she tried to decide what to do, her wrist alarm chimed. As if sensing the summons, which would take her away from him, Dalf shrieked. Raine covered her ears and punched the message button.

Why were they telling her to report back on duty so early? As she stared at the unprecedented message, a shadow covered the screen. Raine froze and looked up at the warrior. Though he looked white and frail as a cloud, he towered over her and with Dalf clinging to her, there was no way to fight him. She put her hands up in surrender.

He reached over her and touched Dalf's shoulder. Though the contact didn't appear hostile, he went limp in her arms. A quick touch verified that he was still alive.

She stared at the warrior, wondering what would happen next. Her beeper chirped, demanded a response.

The warrior lifted Dalf from her grasp; his touch unexpectedly tender, as he lowered him belly-up on the woven reeds then straightened his flipper-arms at his sides. Once the warrior seemed satisfied with Dalf's orientation, he maneuvered his hands over Dalf, as if he was seeing through his fingertips.

Raine gripped her blaster in one hand and her bleating beeper in the other, then, without turning her attention from the warrior, transmitted a confirmation code. Still, watching the warrior and expecting a trick, she keyed in Nambaba's rise code, then inched backward across the deck to the tether and, never taking her attention from the unlikely pair, she began to untie the knot. The water above her vessel began to ripple, each swell larger then the next; each one making the deck rock harder.

The warrior sat down hard and clutched his stomach. Though he looked sicker than any live person had the right to, and though Dalf lay still between them, she knew there was only one thing she could do.

Raine leveled her blaster at him. He ignored her, and began ripping at the bandages Preston had wrapped over his wounds. With her free hand, she got the syringe out of her pocket and flicked the protective cap off. He ripped at the bandages, which were crusted with dried blood. If he bled to death, it would be his own fault. She risked a quick look over her shoulder. Nambaba was just starting to emerge from her saturation bath.

The Guerreterre ripped off the last layer of cloth as she dashed toward him and embedded the syringe in his biceps. His head jerked up and he swatted at the needle, as if it was a mosquito. She hit his hand away and jumped out of his reach. Bindings flew across the deck and he groaned as he slumped over unconscious. She winced and looked at his abdomen, expecting to see blood. Though dried brown flakes dusted his exposed flesh, his lean, muscular abdomen looked unblemished. Raine stared in shock.

The tips of Nambaba's tentacles began bursting onto the surface and bobbed erratically, yanking the pinion a new direction with each emergence. Raine threw the syringe into the water, as the main portion of Nambaba surfaces, then yanked the tether-line free, leaped onto the tentacle and dashed the close button. As the opening slammed shut, she glimpsed the warrior, sitting on his knees, at the center of her deck, staring after her as if he'd never seen an enemy get away.

Once she entered orbit, guilt over leaving Dalf in the barbarian's clutches gripped her, but she didn't have time to dwell on her actions, because the monitor flared orange. Raine gulped. This was only the third time in her entire service that the code had been this severe. She entered her code and retrieved the encrypted message.

Hagva 39:67: Guerreterre transmission detected. Source: Ishdoo.

Monitor waveband 923995 for possible triangulation, but do not

- repeat, do not -

alter normal activity.

ooo

Tem-aki studied the holographic image of Kalamar and its two moons as she sent her daily report to Admiral Roget. When the transmission was complete, the computer resumed reciting Kalamar's history, "The Vole d'Laire dynasty has ruled Kalamar for over nine hundred years. Prior to that Kalamar was a frozen back-world inhabited by illiterate masses that could barely subsist. In return for back-breaking labor and life-long allegiance, the Vole d'Laires provide a lifetime of care for their populace."

The monologue, which had been giving her a history of Kalamar and the importance of eepyllihg, as it related to their treaty, paused and the holographic image turned into a face. "Eighty-nine years ago, Zar Hokku Vole d'Laire developed the eepyllihg additive, which quadruples the fuel efficiency of our fighters.

"The formula for this substance is a closely guarded secret. Many have died trying to obtain the information." A new holographic face appeared. "Winslow Vole d'Laire, the current Zar, is rumored to be as gifted a chemical engineer as he is a ruthless politician. Due to the rumor that he and his scientists are developing an encodable toxin, which could be spread through fuel vapors, unnecessary space travel has been banned."

Tem-aki jerked her head up and stared at the image. So that was why the Admiral had virtually grounded the Shadow Force and turned the unused warbirds over to the scientists, who used a fraction of the fuel the warriors required.

The next image was of a beautiful young girl, but a young man's image quickly followed. "Annya Vole d'Laire and Brock Vole d'Laire are the only living prodigy of Winslow and

Tapanni Vole d'Laire." The image of another female popped up. "Marsha Vole d'Laire is the only one left alive from Winslow's brother's line and it is rumored that The Pharanx places great importance on her council. All family members died when a solar flare vaporized Latawba."

Tem-aki stared at their faces, wondering how one family of such regular-looking people managed to control such a major commodity and had enough power to keep Guerreterre as a paying customer and even ground their fleet at the whisper of a rumor. Why would they want to develop a toxin that could wipe out their customers? Surely that was the worst commercial plan she had ever heard of. But obviously, Guerreterre's administrators took the threat so seriously that they had grounded the majority of their peacekeeping force instead of continue their normal practice of taking over mis-managed worlds and their resources.

At least that made her job more important. Assuming she could find the necessary elements, that was.

Gradually a nightmare image of monstrous golden beasts swimming in the gasses of a blue star replaced Winslow's head. Tem-aki frowned in confusion and waited for the monologue to explain. In the ensuing silence, Madrox activity began creating sunspot-type ripples in the gas. Alien planets, which looked like jewels replaced Brock and Marsha's heads. She leaned forward, concentrating and trying to understand the unspoken message. Suddenly, a solar flare erupted from the gaseous surface and rocketed toward the green jewel planet. Tem-aki jerked backward so quickly that she nearly fell out of her chair.

Heart hammering, she stared at the soundless video clip. After the flare died, the planet looked dead as the burned out planetoid where the strange pilot had met Larwin. Tem-aki frowned in concentration and studied the unfolding information until the menacing, burning orb with its leaping madrox had devoured everything. For several long moments, flames dominated, then the image abruptly went blank.

Heart pounding, Tem-aki watched zigzags of energy, then just as suddenly as the hologram had quit, several scyphozoan style spacecraft and ctenophore class ships, similar to the one which had played with the madrox in the asteroid field, appeared from the far side of the blue star. As if in response to the arrival of the small fleet, madrox undulated up from the molten surface in a golden wave, as if to flee from the approaching fleet.

Tem-aki blinked. If she could discover the answer to why cyphozoan style spacecraft and ctenophore class ships repelled the destructive beasts, surely she could earn a huge profit. As the madrox veered away, the fleet increased speed and pursued them, much as the pilot she had encountered had done. However, with seven ships working together, they soon were guiding the madrox back to the hot, unstable-looking orb.

The hologram abruptly shimmered in all the shades of golden fire, then disintegrated like fireworks winking out in a night sky.

The room became dark, except the tiny lights on the control panel. "You just saw an archive tape made by the Royden freight ship, Warfen, covering the destruction of planet Latawba, which was ruled by Arvord Vole d'Laire, Winslow's brother. Ripples from the sub-thermal blast burned out several of the Warfen's controls. We were fortunate to salvage this much documentation.

"It is estimated that ten-point-six-trillion slaves inhabited Latawba. The Vole d'Laire family, with the exception of Winslow, Brock, Annya and Marsha, had assembled on Latawba for a family reunion, so they are the only surviving members."

Tem-aki frowned and wondered why the computer mentioned that fact when thousands of other nameless families had been wiped out.

"Prior to seeing this evidence of madrox's docile behavior toward the Kalamaran Dragon Officers," the computer continued, "the dragons were presumed to be a danger to Kalamar. Now, The Joint Council believes Winslow Vole d'Laire may have used these beasts as a weapon of war in some sort of coup against his own family."

She shivered at the thought of anyone being that inhumane to strangers, let alone his own blood.

The cabin lights came on and the holographic display dissipated. For a long time, Tem-aki stared at the empty space and wondered if the computer analysis was correct or a crazy assumption, then she moved over to the monitor which displayed a crescent of the molten moon. Madrox activity seemed to have increased to a fevered pitch and the number of scyphozoan style spacecraft and ctenophore class ships seemed to have doubled. Or else it looked like there were twice as many because they were zipping around like swarming bees.

As she watched, one of the Kalamaran vessels splayed it's tentacles wide, as the one in the asteroid field had, and seemed to be trying to keep one of the madrox between the molten moon's surface and the swarming ships.

After making four unsuccessful attempts to get past the ship, the madrox turned and dove headlong into the burning gases. A burst of molten-red gushed out from the spot where it disappeared.

In quick succession, several more dragons dove toward the same area. A digital numerical display in the corner of her monitor changed. "Computer, please explain what this distance reading refers to."

"The reading calculates the distance between the surface of the molten moon and the planet surface. After all the impacts, the moon's orbit moved slightly away from the planet's surface."

Fascinating that the movement of the beasts could affect the orbit of the moon. She wondered if the change was intentional or not.

With nothing more interesting to hold her attention, Tem-aki returned to the coordinates where her brother was last seen and keyed in magnification. As the resolution cleared, she saw the old ship lifting off from the waters near the odd round building. Two humanoids were visible on the flat surface by the round bubble-type structure, but before she could confirm if one was or was not Larwin, they moved out of sight, into the round structure.

Tem-aki glanced back at the molten moon. The ships were regaining control over the dragons and had begun herding them toward Vilecom.

No matter how many videos and holographic displays she watched or how many audio lectures she listened to, she suspected that she would never understand how Kalamar functioned, much less why.

Chapter 12

"Glad you could make it, Gold Leader." The transmission seemed to amplify Otami's syrupy tones.

Raine scowled at the monitor and wondered which ship was his. "What is the emergency?" she asked her second in command, as she watched the strange patterns of movement on the screen and tried to figure out why the entire herd seemed like it was congregated in one area, instead of spread over Vilecom.

"The mooncows swarmed, but we have them back under control." As if to defy the statement, three calves broke away from the herd and slipped past the shepherds. Strangely, their destination seemed to be Kalamar. Raine frowned and wondered why the hydro-phobic beasts were acting out of character.

Even if they weren't, Otami would claim they were. The

covetous rank-climber would do anything to make her look incompetent and feel unneeded. "How many tried to leave the system?" she asked.

"None." He paused. Raine gritted her teeth. "They were headed for The Sea of Sorrows."

In all her years of herding, Raine had never heard of anything so bizarre. But then, she'd never seen anything as bizarre as the mooncalf's behavior in the asteroid field or the way it had stayed close to her ship once the warrior was aboard, either. She angled Nambaba so she could see her home sea and Vilecom in relation to each other and was not surprised when she confirmed that the herd was clustered in line with her home. Did the warrior's presence attract them? She frowned.

She shuddered and tried to focus on the real problem, instead of flights of her imagination.

But were the coincidences actually her imagination or was she trying to ignore facts? She wished Gornt were alive so she could ask him.

"Their behavior has been erratic ever since you returned with the renegade," Otami said, confirming her unvoiced suspicion. Unwilling to fall into his all too obvious attempt to make her appear guilty of something she had no control over, she stayed silent. "Initially, they attacked Haranga's ship, then they tried to migrate to Ishdoo. The last two attempts can be described as nothing short of suicidal dives toward the atmosphere."

Raine entered orbit around Vilecom and scrutinized her monitor. As some dragons broke the surface, molten orange waves rippled across the moon's surface, then, as they dove back, small geysers of heated gas temporarily marked their passage. Aside from the fact that they were all in a tight herd, the dragons seemed to be following their normal pattern and the shepherds' orbits looked evenly spaced. In fact, nothing appeared to corroborate Otami's complaints. "They appear quiet."

Obviously, Otami was transmitting his complaints to explain the call for reinforcements due to the intercepted transmission.

It stood to reason, that if they were monitoring the hidden shadow fighter, he or she was also observing them. Raine shivered and wondered for the hundredth time how to alert the shepherds to the threat without them learning about her involvement.

ooo

Tem-aki massaged the tired muscles in her neck while studying the eepyllihg refinery. Every time her hiding place on Ishdoo orbited over the industrial plant, she tried to collect a bit more information. This revolution, azure dots peppered the dark waters surrounding the refinery. Unless they had been submerged, like the pilot had done with the spaceship, the odd structures had not been there, previously. Squinting, she studied the computer's readout and tried to understand what she was seeing.

Abruptly, one dot seemed to rise, then all the other ones followed in an oddly structured pattern. As she watched the unprecedented activity, the dots began spiraling outward from the planet, Tem-aki keyed in the code to add the strange craft to the next file she planned to transmit.

She chose one dot and magnified it. In less time than it took to blink, the featureless azure dot changed into shaggy blimp with bulges. She had never seen such a strange craft, nor did she have a clue what its function could be. She magnified the image, again, and was able to read CRU-28 beneath a strange open framework on the starboard side. No matter how clear and close the image appeared, she could not figure out what all the bladders and ducts could be for. "Whatever it is, it must have something to do with refining eepyllihg," she muttered.

"Command does not compute," Dasya Voltain said.

"Continue recording." She closed her eyes and continued to massage the tight muscles in her neck. When she opened her eyes, she noticed a dark speck undulating on Vilecom's surface, so keyed in a code to split the screen and record both events. The ripples expanded in a slow halo, as a madrox eased itself out of the fiery core and seemed to have a trajectory which would take it to the strange azure ships.

By the time the first madrox had completely broken free, converging corrugated waves covered Vilecom's entire surface as more and more madrox began moving toward the strange ships.

Without being told, Dasya Voltain added a small, square partition, which displayed the anticipated flight paths of the ships and dragons. It hadn't been her imagination, the madrox and strange ships were on a collision course. Worse, if they didn't stray from their current paths, they would converge practically on top of her hiding place.

Tem-aki chewed her upper lip, torn between fascination and fear. Several madrox had tried to converge on the old meteor crater soon after she had landed, but, like the ship in the asteroid field, some ancient ctenophore class ships had herded them back to the molten moon. In an odd sort of way, the old ships' behavior reminded her of rustic shepherds on some of the primitive worlds, which supplied Guerreterre with protein.

As they got closer, only one of the old ctenophore class ships altered course. "This is Blue-10. I've got a problem."

Tem-aki turned up the radio's volume. "Dasya Voltain, add audio file to video file recording."

"Complying."

"This is Gold Leader, state the nature of your problem, Ten."

"I've got an adolescent heading toward the Sea of Storms."

Adolescent? Sea of Storms? Were these codes for something, a specific location, or what? Tem-aki keyed in the code to expand the small square convergence screen and chewed her lip, as she studied the flight patterns in close detail to see if Dasya Voltain's presence had been detected.

If she fired up the engines, the power surge would probably be noticed, as it seemed to have been the previous day, when she'd fired the retro boosters to soften her landing in the crater. Then, too, the madrox and the old ctenophore class ships had altered course and seemed to converge near her location, but since then, there had been too many ships in the vicinity for her to out maneuver, so she'd shut down all unnecessary systems, filed her daily report and hoped for the best.

She'd been lucky so far, Tem-aki hoped her luck would hold, so, for the second time in as many days, she put on her helmet and activated her suit's environmental system, then turned off everything except the cloaking and monitoring systems. As the lights went out and the monitor went black, she prayed that she was doing the right thing for herself as well as her brother.

Then, Tem-aki watched the control panel and waited to see if the proximity light came on.

When her suit's oxygen supply was half gone, she turned on the monitor. The azure dots were now in positions around Vilecom, and a madrox, as depicted by a red dot, was near all but one. Since there was no eminent danger, she quietly keyed the ship's life support back on and resumed her surveillance.

Why did all Kalamaran ships seem to go out of their way to be close to madrox?

And why did they all seem to adhere to a pattern? Was this

some strange form of team sport? The only anomaly to the pattern was one red dot near a white dot, which the computer used to differentiate the old ctenophore class ships from the strange ones like CRU-28. They were at the closest point between the moon and the planet, and as close to the atmosphere as they could get without actually beginning a landing pattern. In fact, the old ctenophore ship seemed to be trying to stay between the planet and madrox as if protecting it.

Bizarre!

ooo

Thunder stared at the endless expanse of undulating water and his stomach constricted. He had never imaged being imprisoned by water.

But he was.

He tried to tell himself this was a nightmare, but the surging surface beneath his feet made denial impossible.

As nausea threatened to overwhelm him, he closed his eyes and placed his hand over the amulet at his neck, then he controlled his breathing. As the stress eased, he focused on his present circumstances, which were impossible to understand.

Again, the threat of nausea worsened.

Eyes tight shut, he concentrated within instead of on the inexplicable water horror he had somehow landed in. As his stomach settled, he focused on Kazza's advice and reached across the darkness in the hope of understanding the great cat's warning.

Gradually, bright points of white light pricked the darkness, then, a golden glimmer tinged one area of the black nothingness. Thunder waited, his anticipation growing as the light started churning. An amber-gold cat eye emerged. Soon, Kazza's semi-transparent form faced him over a carpet of stars.

The great cat seemed to smile. "Destiny is being fulfilled."

"Everything is water."

Kazza's whiskers twirled. "Past turning points in your life involved water."

Those had not been pleasant times.

In fact, they were the stuff of nightmares.

The great cat's eyes glistened with amusement as if he knew the enormous extent of his discomfort. Thunder raised his palms in supplication. "I thought my destiny was to close the Star Bridge."

"And so you shall, if destiny allows it." A reassuring purr accompanied the thought.

If! "I must do this or Chatterre will be consumed by the monsters."

Kazza raised his paw and flexed his claws. Several points of light converged into a blue-gray ball with two smaller ones near it; one blood-red, one pale gray.

"The point of confrontation draws near," Kazza said. Golden specks danced across the red orb's surface and it began to wobble.

ooo

A wave of magma undulated across Vilecom's surface, then another and another. The radio crackled with static. "This is Gold-Five. I've got trouble."

Raine tapped the transmit button. "This is Gold-Leader. State the nature of your problem."

"I've got an adolescent heading toward the planet."

A pack of mooncalves and their dams moved away from the moon in a starburst of golden flashes, then, before they got near

Nambaba, made a graceful curve and arched toward Kalamar's surface.

"Where are you, Five?"

"Zeda 94.7 and Romdan 43.8."

Raine looked at the view-screen and ran the calculation. He was the one at the closest point between the moon and the planet. And it looked like the entire pack was heading toward him. In all her years of service as a shepherd, she'd never seen mooncalves swarm toward the surface. She studied Kalamar; the point of convergence was the center of the Sea of Storms.

Her home.

She rammed the collective forward. "On my way." But before she reached the convergence point, the mooncalves altered course toward Ishdoo. Spirit, they act like one mind is governing them! Raine banked to port so she could thwart the new threat.

"Picking up Guerreterran band transmission," Nambaba said.

"Translate and transmit."

"Are you getting this?" The voice sounded like the woman in the asteroid field.

"You are on a restricted waveband," a second voice said.

"Admiral Roget ordered me to transmit this data-stream and Administrator Fitzminor."

"If you do not cease and desist, your transmission will be forcibly ended." With that, a piercing shriek emanated from the speakers.

"Shut off that waveband," Raine ordered.

The sudden silence felt like the slap of an icy wave, when a warm sea had been expected. One look at the view screen confirmed that the dragons were now moving back toward Vilecom. Raine expanded her view-screen and marked the spot, which had attracted the dragons. "Expand image." Nambaba complied and the screen displayed a large crater filled with ancient boulders and shadows. "Again." Still nothing. "Do you detect a ship in this quadrant?"

"Negative."

Raine should have known it wouldn't be easy. "Save images and all transmission data."

Chapter 13

Inside Dasya Voltain's two-man control hub, Tem-aki stretched her stiff muscles as she gazed at the pattern of white and red dots which surrounded the molten moon. So far, the crater seemed relatively safe, unfortunately, it also felt quite exposed and longterm exposure of the hull to the high lime content would not be good.

Abruptly, there was a flurry of activity among the red dots, which the white dots quickly responded to. She had been watching this type of scene for more than a day, but so far, all she had managed to determine was that the Kalamarans appeared to use the ships, depicted by white dots, in a similar way to how primitive sheep herders used their trained dogs. Why they herded madrox remained a mystery and though she had not put her speculation in any of her reports, she privately wondered if Kalamar's entire culture was mentally stable.

Three white dots, which she had begun to think of as 'shepherd ships' moved into a triangular pattern where the molten moon was closest to the planet's surface. Almost as if on cue, several madrox appeared to swarm toward them. Tem-aki was reminded of a video clip she'd seen about locusts attacking crops on a primitive agricultural world. Tem-aki leaned forward with interest and watched the shepherd-ships efficiently intercept the swarm of madrox before they touched the atmosphere.

Suddenly, the communication network chimed and the halo-image changed to Admiral Starm's face. He had been her brother's superior. She gulped, then said, "Admiral Starm." Hearing the squeak in her tone, a blush began to creep up her neck.

"Adjutant Atano." He dipped his head, which was not necessary for her rank. She wet her lips. "Are you still monitoring Kalamar?"

"Yes, Sir. I'm preparing a dispatch to send to Admiral Roget and Administrator Fitzminor the data I have collected during the last cycle." Hoping that he could see how nervous she was, Tem-aki forced a calm smile. "Would you like me to send you a copy, as well?"

He gave a quick nod. "For the moment, give me a synopsis."

Tem-aki swallowed and clasped her hands together to hide the tremor. "Moments ago, madrox swarmed out of Vilecom, which is the Kalamaran name for their molten moon. The madrox were apparently intent about entering the planet's atmosphere." She cleared her throat. "Three of their antiquated ctenophore class ships quickly moved to thwart a possible attack." She paused, then added. "The move appeared well practiced, as did the maneuvering of the other type of ships, which they seem to use with the madrox."

"Roget said you had a theory about the Kalamarans using them for a purpose."

"It is the only thing that makes sense – the way the ships move is very similar to the patterns I've seen used by the keepers of protein breeders, like sheep."

"Interesting."

"While the most recent break appeared to be the most violent, the dragons have displayed this type of activity since I entered this system." She closed her mouth before she started to babble.

"Is your position secure?"

"I believe so."

He gave a decisive nod. "Good. Continue monitoring."

"Yes, Sir."

"Have you detected their eepyllihg production facility?"

"Perhaps, but if you require positive evidence, I will need to come out of hiding." She took a deep breath, and reminded herself that even though Admiral Starm's brutal reputation was well known, he was several quadrants away and in no position to harm her. At least, not at this moment, and to keep it that way, it was wise to answer his questions as fully as possible. She wet her lips, then added, "All activity that I've observed seems to be divided between two areas: the madrox, which infest Vilecom and agricultural pursuits in the swampy areas of the Kalamar's surface. Scans indicate the principle crops are reeds and rice. Their space patrols are the only evidence of high tech capability and these activities center on Vilecom." She was babbling, Tem-aki clamped her jaws together, before she antagonized him.

"The manufacturing facility must be under water."

"That is a distinct possibility." She touched a few keys and sent copies of her previous reports to Admiral Starm. "In the report I just sent, there is a segment where I monitored one of their antiquated ships slipped beneath the waves. A short while ago, it reemerged and is engaging in activity with the madrox. I've dubbed the behavior of this type 'shepherd-ships' because they appear to use these to control the madrox's movements." He raised a brow. Her pay-grade wasn't high enough for her to make that sort of analytical statement. Tem-aki swallowed hard and tried not to blab out any more opinions. "Should I remain here and observe or try to get on planet to try and confirm anything?" What was wrong with her? Had she actually volunteered to try and sneak onto the planet and spy? She was a geologist, neither a warrior nor a spy. The only reason she had managed to gather so much information thus far was due to pure luck and Dasya Voltain's stealth capabilities.

The last thing she wanted to do was figure out a way to land on Kalamar; unfortunately, it looked like Admiral Starm was considering her comment. Shiver! Guerreterre had no water, therefore it was something which terrified her when she saw a lot of it. Just watching Kalamar's constantly shifting surface made her queasy.

"For the moment remain in your current position so we can find out how to produce eepyllihg. Once we have that technology, we will no longer have to suffer greedy parasites like Zar Vole d'Laire."

"I will do my best, Sir."

With a nod, he cut the transmission. The screen returned to display the movements of the white and red dots. With a sigh of relief, Tem-aki's spine collapsed into the command chair. Why hadn't she thought of the consequences before sending a copy of the bizarre behavior she'd witnessed in the asteroid field to her superior? But she knew that she would do the same thing, again, if she thought she might be able to find out what had happened to Larwin.

ooo

As Thunder moved cautiously down the shaky, curved corridor, he paused to look through the open door into a circular chamber. No fish-boy. Odd as the guy was – at least Thunder had the impression that it was male – he was the only other individual he had met, aside from his captor. He wanted answers. The woman wasn't here, so there was only one source for the answers he needed. Thunder continued down the corridor, searching for the only one in the vicinity who might have the answers he needed.

Why had he been brought here?

What had they done to him?

What did they want from him?

Why did nightmare images of a water world haunt him?

Who was the pretty little yellow-haired woman?

And how had she managed to capture him?

Worse, why did she wish to leave Chatterre vulnerable to dragons?

Would Chatterre be safe until he returned?

Had he died and gone to the realm of Hades that some of the dark fairytales spoke of?

Abruptly, the passageway jerked so sharply that Thunder was thrown against the odd wall, which gave slightly when his shoulder slammed against it, but popped back to smooth when he straightened. Curious, he pressed his hand against the strange surface, which was more like a taunt fabric than the rock and wood walls he was accustomed to. Again, the tube shuddered. He fought to remain on his feet and wondered what had caused the sudden instability.

The orb closest to the floating dock had contained a strange table, which was also made out of a something smooth and white. In fact, it seemed like just about everything in this odd place looked as if it was made from the same basic stuff. The only things that looked at all familiar were the large upside-down woven-reed baskets, which seemed to function as seats. And thus far, he had only seen those in the semi-understandable area, with the table.

Keeping one hand against the rounded wall, he ventured a few more steps down the sloped tube.

The next chamber had a gigantic flat pillow at its center and a vividly colored fish mural all over its walls. One of the fish moved. Curious, he stepped into the chamber and looked around its circular walls. Seeing more movement, he took another step into the room. Bright red finger-sized streaks burst away. Thunder stopped and stared. Nothing happened. He took a third step forward, and noticed movement from an airy plum-toned fan, that appeared to be rooted to a rocky landscape. What a strange thing to paint. A silvery cloud swept by in the distance. What sort of magic had been added to this paint? Thunder ventured farther into the circular chamber, and caressed the mural. A cool, smooth surface, which felt the same as the other wall surfaces met his fingertips.

He stepped back, caught his foot on a soft lump and landed with a thud on the huge central cushion. The smell of sunshine and fresh air greeted him as he lay on his back and stared upward at the domed ceiling. This room seemed like being in a room-size version of the clear head covering of Larwin's suit.

Movement to the right caught his attention. He turned his head and watched a swirling school of silvery fish move by. Thunder swallowed. The next moment, the dark shadow of a much larger fish passed over. What kind of evil magic did these horrid walls possess?

He stumbled toward the entryway. The floor seemed to rise and fall beneath his feet. Stomach rolling with misery, he closed his eyes tight shut, gripped the doorway and gasped for breath.

Slowly, the threatening bile resettled. Though he wanted to flee back to the exterior platform, he knew that it held no answers to his questions and his stomach wouldn't be better up there, so he might just as well find out where fish-boy was and get the answers that he needed. Squaring his shoulders, Thunder headed further down the peculiar tunnel.

ooo

Tem-aki studied the rough, white rock escarpment surrounding Dasya Voltain's observation port, then raised her gaze to compare the rough limestone to the distant arc of the molten moon. She didn't know what it was about the hot, red moon, but the closer it got the more papillae bumps popped up on her skin. She shivered and turned her attention to the holo-image of what she had concluded was a reclamation unit harvesting some sort of chemicals.

"Computer, please transmit this to Admiral Roget and Administrator Fitzminor."

"Complying."

After s few moments, a slightly static voice said, "You are on a restricted waveband. This is your second warning."

"Administrator Fitzminor requested that this data be sent to Admiral Roget."

The pompous voice said, "If you do not cease and desist, your transmission will be forcibly ended."

Tem-aki sighed. "This is Adjutant Atano. Admiral Fitz-" With a screech, the transceiver relays were back-fed, causing an overload and an alarm began shrilling. The next second, she smelled hot metal. "Computer, cease transmission."

"Complying." She snapped the cover off the radio. Inside, the board had several tiny molten puddles where the most fragile joints had been. "I don't believe the idiot did that!" What hadn't he understood about the information being requested? When the admiral found out why the data they wanted had been cut off, she hated to think what would happen to the 'by-the-book-fool'.

She looked out the window at the rising arc of what she was starting to think of as the demon moon and shivered, as she felt more alone than she had ever been in all her life.

ooo

A high-pitched keening raised the small hairs on Thunder's arms. Muscles tensed to flee, he cautiously moved forward until he was near the opening from which the awful sound was coming. He took a deep breath, then blew it out and peered around the door jam. It was the water-infested room and the black and gray creature was huddled on top of a floating mat on the far side of the chamber. Previously, the fish-boy had seemed oblivious to the water surrounding it, yet now, it seemed to cringe away, so that probably meant that it wanted to stay clear of him. Therefore, he needed to wade in, to question it.

Thunder looked back up the long corridor, where a patch of sky was still visible. He turned back to the crying creature, which seemed to be his only source for information. The water appeared to be the same depth as before and that hadn't killed him. Thunder looked back at the beckoning sunlight, then gritted his teeth and half-stepped, half-fell into the waist-deep pool.

Ripples of disturbed water caressed the mat and the fish-boy huddled, whirled toward the door, sniffed, and then threw its hideous head back and howled like a baying wolf.

"Easy, kid, I only want some answers." This assumed the creature could communicate, as a barton or cat could.

"M-m-m-m-mmmm," the thing shrieked.

Thunder focused on the whimpering animal and tried to ignore the fact that he was standing in hip-high water, in a space, which had a strange type of door, that he did not know how to operate "Relax." He grabbed the mat, which he had previously been on, pulled it close, then shoved it into the doorway and hoped the bubbles were sturdy enough to jam the door open, because there was no way he was going to get locked in this dreadful room.

Cautiously, he maneuvered across the pool, then he tentatively put out his hand and gently caressed the fish-boy's cool leathery hide.

"M-m-m-m-mmmm-mm. Ccccccccc. M-mmmmm-mm," it screamed.

"Its okay, I won't hurt you." He continued stroking the creature, as he would a yeti.

"Ccccccccc. M-mmmmm-mm."

"Like to talk, do you?"

"Ccccccccccc-ca."

Thunder looked at the tempting ray of sunlight on the floor of the dry corridor, and steeled his resolve. Hand, gentle on the fish-boy's black back, Thunder inspected the creature's pale, distorted face. A network of thick white slashes crisscrossed its features from where the hairline would have been, if the creature had hair down to where it's waist would have been, if he had a waist. As its ear-cringing howls calmed, Thunder studied the opaque white orbs, which should have been eyes. What horrible accident had befallen it?

He gently touched its face, feeling for signs of where the nose and ears might have been. While he didn't find any indication that any had ever been in the conventional areas, he discovered that he could understand it better than a Yeti and confirmed that it was male.

"Mmmmmmmmm-mmmmm-mm cccccc."

Thunder put his hands on either side of its head and looked within. Torn cartilage and scarring spoke of a terrible trauma in the past.

Compassion filled him.

As his senses probed the interior of the animal, he realized that the breathing apparatus was at the back of its head, but its form of hearing remained a mystery, unless it involved the smashed cartilage where its forehead would traditionally be.

ooo

Raine leaned toward her monitor and verified that everything was in order before she turned her attention to the starboard window, where a mooncow approach the closest Crystalline Reclamation Unit. From her vantage point, the CRU's mirrored surface made it look as if the giant beast was approaching an oddly shaped juvenile. As soon as the mooncow was in the correct position, the CRU's automated harness disappeared beneath the beast's burning heat. Raine held her breath in anticipation of the first glimpse of brilliant azure liquid, which supported Kalamar's entire culture.

Nambaba's warning system beeped. Raine jerked her attention to her monitor. A tiny white speck was moving from the center to the bottom, where a blue arc indicated Kalamar's moisture-laden atmosphere. A kelp-colored dot broke out of formation and began zigzagging in front of the white one. Situation in control, she turned her attention back to the majestic view of dragon milking.

ooo

Warmth and power surged through Thunder's back as he sensed Kazza's presence. He allowed the great cat to see the fish-boy through his eyes, then merged his myst power with Kazza's and together, they willed the creature's torn fragments to realign in their proper place.

ooo

"Gold Leader, Eleven here, I need help."

Raine looked back at her monitor, where one kelp-colored dot was frantically zig-zagging toward the Sea of Sorrows and four tiny white specks were moving to intercept it. "I'm on my way."

"Thanks, Gold Leader."

As she maneuvered Nambaba out of position, the radio crackled. "This is Gold-Twenty-Three, I've got two runaways." Twenty-Three 's tone was tense. "Heading for The Sea of Storms."

"This is Gold-Seven. Mine are turning, too. Same vector."

"Thirty-Nine, here. Ditto."

Raine's view-screen showed dragons converging on Eleven's position. "Maelstrom!" She keyed in Headquarters' frequency. Cold sweat bathed her body. "Has someone turned on an energy beacon in the Sea of Storms?"

"Negative," Headquarters relied. "What's going on up there?"

"I don't know. We're trying to contain it, but may need

reinforcements." Raine rammed Nambaba's stick forward and swooped between a dragon and the rim of Kalamar's atmosphere, then flared the tentacles. The dragon veered away.

"Bravo, Gold Leader," Eleven said. "That took guts."

"Thanks." Raine glanced at her instruments and her stomach churned. Would she have made the move if she'd realized how close to the atmosphere she was? She tapped the configuration code and held her breath.

"CRU-Four here. Our mooncow refuses to tether."

"Hold off reclamation until we get the dragons quiet," Raine said.

"Confirm order."

On her monitor, white fractals and greenish pixels performed a well-known dance above the rim of Kalamar's atmospheric layer. Occasionally the greenish pixels splayed into a starburst. The only motionless white fractals were next to the azure cigar-shapes. Obviously, she'd overreacted when she gave her unprecedented order. Just then, a white squiggle twisted and the azure cylinder spun away.

"Order confirmed. Hold off reclamation until mooncows are under control."

ooo

Bit by bit, Thunder and Kazza repaired torn cartilage using the energy channels of the creature's body to reassemble and mend the damage. Slowly, working from the center outward, the scarring melted away and the middle auditory chamber reformed in its proper position.

When Kazza eased the pressure on his back, Thunder realized how stiff he was and that there was water all around him. He sensed a purr of promise from the great cat, then Kazza's presence dissipated as the tide of space and time restored the distance between them. Thunder succumbed to total exhaustion and fell asleep.

ooo

Inside Dasya Voltain 's science lab, Tem-aki divided her attention between repairing the damaged radio and studying the strange holographic image of the way madrox seemed to almost mate with the strange ships.

Then, most of the madrox seemed to decide to head toward the planet's surface, as they had twice before. As she fused a damaged connection, fragments of the Kalamar transmissions resonated, "--- got Reclamation 8 in sight." Though it wasn't clear, she could understand the words and hear the stress, so maybe the behavior was not typical. "It's not good. The dragon is still attached and heading for home."

"Vydian, cut the harness." Though Tem-aki couldn't be positive, she was ninety-percent sure that this voice was the pilot she'd encountered in the asteroid field.

"Emergency eject, not responding."

"Keep trying."

Tem-aki admired the pilot's calm, professional tone, then laughed and wondered what else she should expect from a culture that seemed to have madrox as some sort of pet.

"It's too late," a new voice said. "It's too frigging late! The dragon just dove." Tem-aki stared at the holo-image, where a large orange molten wave expanded across the face of Vilecom. Obviously they had not anticipated what had just happened, even though it seemed like the logical conclusion. What insanity made the Kalamarans tie their ships to madrox?

"Control to shepherd One," a deep, authoritative voice said. "Report to Central Command and be prepared to give a full account of today's incident." Tem-aki bit her lower lip and looked out the portal, to see which ship broke formation. As she'd expected, it was the one with the slightly deformed starboard side, which she had encountered in the asteroid field.

"Now?"

"At shift end."

Well, she could now state with some certainty that the one known as either Gold Leader or shepherd One was the one who had captured her brother. And that was the ship she intended to keep track of. "Computer, monitor this ship at all times." She tapped the screen.

"Complying."

ooo

In the blink of an eye, the agitated dragons became docile. Raine stared at the monitor and wondered if this was some sort of test.

"Gold Leader, we're behind schedule."

"Resume pumping." She maneuvered Nambaba back into position, and watched as CRU-34 finished harvesting its dragon. Through the semi-transparent dome, it felt as if she was close enough to see the supports feather out and mechanically release the mooncow. Within minutes, the second one was being harnessed.

A melodious tone hummed through Nambaba's speakers; Raine keyed in her private com-code. "Gold Leader, I have trouble." She recognized the quiet voice of CRU-18's Communication's Officer.

"State it."

"The dragon we are harvesting is restless."

"How close is it to-"

"Oh Spirit, it's jerking the harness!"

"Free it!"

"That's against reg-"

"Just do it." Raine held her breath and stared at the monitor, which showed a coupled mooncow and reclamation ship tied in a violent wrestling match.

Something loud clanged, then static took over the channel.

Raine stared at the monitor, counting ships. Three of the eight Crystalline Reclamation Units were attached to madrox, and two were hastily separating from their mooncows, but the third pairing was slashing around in a violently erratic pattern. Raine swallowed hard and watched the madrox's savage, quicksilver movements, which looked like a frenzied shark fight.

"I don't frigging believe it," an overly excited voice said over the primary dragon frequency.

Raine swatted transmit. "This is a private waveband, please change fr-"

"This is CRU-91" The agitated person interrupted. "The cow wiped its frigging tail and sliced right through 27's hull! They didn't have a chance!"

"Please clarify." But she didn't need clarification; the monitor showed an azure cylinder spinning out of position. Eyes wide, throat dry, she helplessly watched it vanish from view behind Vilecom.

"Eighteen was off our port when it went. I don't frigging believe-"

Raine hit her override switch. "Confine all transmissions to data. All Reclamation Units, release madrox, now.

Acknowledge."

A chorus of voices shouted, "Will-co."

"Nine here, we're trying, but this old girl is fighting us."

"Cut it loose if you have to."

"Thirty-Nine here. They're breaking for the surface, again."

Raine rammed the collective forward and dove toward Kalamar's surface, again.

"Control to Gold Leader. Report to Central Command and be prepared to give a full account of today's incident."

Unbelievable! "As soon as I can."

"Now."

Raine looked at the monitor. Dragons were beginning to swarm toward the same point in the Sea of Storms. What could possibly be attracting them to such a deadly place? At least if she returned to planet, she could get to her home and assure herself that Dalf was alive.

But first, she had to answer for her decisions, which protected her crew as well as the reclamation units, to an idiot that blindly followed protocol and had never left the planet's surface, so didn't have a clue about how to do the job.

Despite the stupidity of the summons, Raine knew that if she did not report as soon as possible, she would face either demotion or death. She slammed the nav-stick to port and began her landing pattern.

ooo

Raine sat on the hard plastoid bench, back straight, eyes focused on the opposite wall where a mossy spot resembled a flying swan. When she half closed her eyes; the peeling paint became drab yellow clouds skewering a gray sky and the green bird's flight took on an ominous feeling. Gooseflesh crawled over her arms, so Raine closed her eyes and wondered why the building was not being properly maintained.

She understood why Nambaba wasn't in the best repair, when the ship had been issued to her, it had been understood that its repairs came out of her pay. And that had not been a problem as long as Gornt was alive.

But why weren't the offices in decent repair?

The sound of rustling papyrus was punctuated by the faint murmur of voices. Her home sounded more alive. Even a shift aboard Nambaba, with the beautiful contrast between the chilly lifelessness of Ishdoo and the heat of Vilecom and the continual radio chatter between pilots was more lively. A distant door closed and the soft sound of footfalls approached. She opened her eyes and resumed staring at the mossy spot, until her peripheral vision detected movement.

Shoulders square and head high, Otami strutted toward her, but he ignored her so completely that he did not even give her a nod of acknowledgement as he swaggered past.

He might as well have proclaimed that she had been ordered here based on his complaints. Raine gritted her teeth and tried not to show how impatient or angry she felt at being treated like a disobedient child and facing the possibility of punishment because of the actions of some demented mooncalves.

The worst part was that, except for the beast that had left the sector, all the odd behavior had begun on Otami's shift, not hers. Of course, it would be just like him to have her ordered to fly the extra shift just so he could blame her for everything.

Raine gritted her teeth and prepared to be subjected to another one of Otami's one-upmanship tales. His continual jealousy and status-climbing explained why she had been ordered to leave space early. And if her pompous rival had known she was waiting out here to be questioned, he would have droned on, just to make her wait. She risked a frigid glance at Otami's departing backside.

Of course, she could be numbing her backside because the Fleet Overlord was nobility and he was making her wait so she would feel every inch of her inferiority. Her molars gritted with the loathing that she could not show.

With a whoosh, a door opened. "Thank you for understanding." The unctuous voice sounded a lot like her brother. It took all Raine's willpower not to look at the speaker.

"Any time." There was the sound of heels clicking in respect, then the purposeful reverberation of departing footfalls.

Another door opened and someone with long waves of brilliant purple, which curled down over a long gauzy pink jacket with iridescent pearl buttons pranced toward her. "The Fleet Overlord will see you now. Please follow me." Raine stood up and turned toward the pimply-faced, purple haired adjutant. He – at least she thought it was a he – made a precision turn, goose-stepped to the open doorway and then stood at attention, as if he thought he needed to guard the entrance.

Raine stepped past him, and entered the High Colonel's sanctuary. She inhaled deeply and caught the scent of myrrh, her brother's favored scent. She frowned. Preston wouldn't have any reason to be in this room. Would he? Her gaze darted around the room's thick tapestries, which all focused on the theme of dragons and their care, as she approached the huge slab of polished lava that had been turned into a desk.

She snapped to attention in front of the man who held her destiny in the palm of his pudgy hand. Instead of acknowledging her, the fat man's attention stayed on his monitor's scrolling data. Raine stood ramrod straight and focused on the frolicking dragons in the tapestry behind him instead of his gaudy gold tunic and perfectly dyed emerald coiffeur, which she suspected was a wig.

"Do you know what percentage was harvested during your shift?" he asked without looking up.

"No, Sir." Her neck and spine ached as if the weight of the world was balanced on top of her head.

"Six point seven percent." His tone was so censorious that his jowls quivered.

"In light of the cost in lives and ships, I though it was prudent."

That got his attention. "Did you order all Reclamation Units to cease production?" He glared at her. Her mouth went dry and she nodded. "On whose authority?"

"The situation warranted it. If you would like to view the tapes -" She reached into her carry-bag.

"You work for me," he cut in. "I tell the fleet what to do. Not you."

"I understand that, Sir. I believe you or any other responsible shepherd would have done the same, if they had been in my position."

"You'd better hope the video-logs bear out your claims."

"It will." At least it would unless Otami had found a way to change the data logs.

The Fleet Overlord returned his attention to the data-stream. "Until my investigation is complete, you're on leave." He made a swishing motion as if shooing away a pesky insect.

"But Sir, the dragons have been acting-"

"Without pay," he barked.

"We need every herd-"

He surged to his feet and leaned across his desk. "I gave you an order." Spittle sprayed her face. She fought her inclination to shove him backward.

"Yes, Sir. B-"

"Leave!"

Her molars ached from gritting together and tears blinded her, but she kept her chin high and her pace steady, as she walked out of the office.

With each step, she became more certain that Otami had set up this humiliation.

With every step, she assured herself that Otami's lies would catch up with him.

As she left the building, sunlight bathed her face and her jaw trembled. A second later, a hand clamped around her arm and yanked her into the shadows. She gasped.

"Shhh. You need to come with me."

"Preston, what are you doing here?" She twisted to stare at him. "Why are you here?"

"Never mind. You need to come with me."

"But Dalf-"

"You can't go home. Not now. Not ever."

A chill washed over her. "What do you mean?"

"Didn't Rufurt tell you?"

"Tell me what?"

"That your punishment for disobedience was that everything you possessed was condemned."

"No, they can't! Dalf-"

"Should have been recycled long ago." He shook her arm. "Think of it this way, you're being freed of the anchors you've tied yourself down with, now you can-"

"How dare you talk like Dalf is nothing! He is a living being. And what about the warrior? Have you realized that you'll lose your DNA bank?"

He paled. "What about the android?"

"It's still aboard Nambaba." She gestured to the mooring area.

Preston squinted at the docks then glared at her. "So I've lost that, too."

Raine looked at the maze of empty wharfs and realized that to a physician they would appear as if their only function was a tidal barrier. From the sky, submerged ships were visible and the broken concentric rings were obviously docks. Nambaba was merely one of many shepherd-ships absorbing hydro beneath the surf.

Preston grabbed her arm and began dragging her toward the public ferry dock. "We need to get you to The Pinnacle." She tried to pull free. "No one will look for you there, so its your best chance at staying alive." Her blood ran cold as the significance of his meaning sank in.

"What do they know?"

"Who gave them my name?" he snarled.

"If anyone did, my guess would be Otami."

"I can not afford to have anyone investigate me or my activities," Preston said.

Who could? No matter how innocent actions were, people like Otami twisted situations and events into sinister plots, which cast the blame on others and left him looking superior. He was especially good at that when he was the guilty one.

How typical that the mooncows' aberrant activity had begun during his shift, but he had found a way to blame her for everything.

Chapter 14

Thunder woke from a dreamless sleep and stretched, the world moved. He stiffened. The curved gray ceiling loomed above him and the dank air seemed to suffocate him. To his left, water rippled and the strange creature snuggled against his right side. He closed his eyes and willed himself to wake from this nightmare.

"Me-Casa-D," the thing hissed and clicked.

It took Thunder a moment to realize it had spoken. Tentatively, he touched the cool leathery hide. "I'm Thunder." It shivered at the sound of his name.

"Th-under ease dan-ger. Storm come."

He chuckled. "True. My little sister couldn't pronounce my actual name, and started calling me Thunder, then soon, everyone called me that. So, the nickname stuck."

"Hear N speak. This good."

He could imagine. "I need your help." Dalf eagerly made an agreeable sound. "I need to go home."

"Where we?"

"Cal-mar." If GEA-4 was correct.

Dalf made several excited-sounding clicks. "You Pal- dare N play name trick. How soon eyes work?" The vacant sockets turned toward him.

"I'm Thunder. A woman brought me here."

"Shay?"

"Raine."

"Mudder no bring stray-ger here." Dalf's webbed hands fluttered.

His mother! He must have misunderstood the pain-shrouded memory. "The one who has a Ghilly dragon for a pet."

Dalf's sharp whistle startled him. It took him a few moments to realize the creature was laughing. Before Thunder could analyze what was so funny, the chamber jerked, as if caught; then the room whipped from side to side, as if it was being shaken in gigantic jaws or being toyed with by an earthquake. He fell, shoulder first, into the water.

ooo

Tem-aki stared at the holographic image, where a gigantic sky-hook hovered over the structure where her brother had last been seen. Three cables had already been lowered and as the last one was secured to the white globe portion, the sky-hook began gaining altitude.

What were they doing?

Within moments, the entire sphere had risen above the gentle waves, while the top portion was white, the lower was a shaggy green. Tem-aki chewed her lower lip as she tried to figure out why the skyhook was reeling the sphere out of the water. Was this the way they cleaned their buildings? Since Guerreterre is a waterless world, she had no idea how a water-based culture would live, let alone clean off the obviously dirty portion, which had been under water. As the skyhook continued to climb, a thin, white straggly section, that looked a lot like the stringy parts of the old ctenophore class ship, appeared. Before she could mull the unexpected sight over, another globe began to emerge from the water. Tem-aki blinked in surprise.

As the third sphere came into view, Dasya Voltain began displaying Larwin's transponder code. By the time the skyhook began to move away from the area with seven globes suspended below it, Larwin's code was strong. She studied the odd structure, which reminded her of a cluster of grapes she had seen harvested on Latawba before the planet was incinerated.

She watched with morbid fascination as she tried to understand this new development and what it might mean to her and her brother. Whatever it meant, she vowed she would not lose contact with Larwin's transponder code, if she could help it.

ooo

With the brazen arrogance worthy of a noble, Preston hustled her toward a porpoise-boat, which was tied at the ferry dock and forcing a large loon-ship to hold off docking. Raine kept her head down and hoped that none of the workers, lining the railing to see what was causing the delay, recognized her or her brother.

She leaped aboard the porpoise-boat as Preston untied the line. As she sank into the soft cushions, the ease and aroma of wealth surrounded her. "I'm honored that you'd allow a condemned person in your vehicle."

"Cut the sarcasm!" Preston slammed the hatch shut. "Do you know how furious The Zar is?" He piloted the boat away from the dock at top speed, leaving a wave in the no -wake zone.

Raine inched lower and pulled hair over her face. "I'll wager you've appointed yourself to tell me."

"Vole d'Laire counts on the eepyllihg profits to run this world." Everyone knew that. "One more glitch in the production will send you to Reclamation."

Tempting as it was to glare at him, saving her reputation was more crucial, so she clenched her teeth and tried to calculate how long it would take before they were past the ferry. Preston used her silence as an opportunity to rant about the trouble she was in, but Raine doubted if he'd shed a tear if they recycled her body minerals and suspected that he was covering emotions about Dalf and the warrior's potential discovery with his outburst.

"You can sit up," he said.

She looked back at their wide wake. "Let me guess, you're doing this because you're afraid I'd be interrogated and Vole d'Laire will learn that his star toxin inventor did something decent like treating injuries." Preston stared at her. "Don't worry, I'll never tell the Guards that you treated either of them."

He smirked as he pressed the submerge button on the console. "You don't know anything about me." As the boat dove beneath the waves, she wished he were right.

ooo

Thunder crawled out of the wildly rocking room, and began climbing up the equally chaotic corridor. "Does this happen often?" he asked through gritted teeth.

"Never," Dalf wailed. "Are de Guerreterre attacking?"

"I don't know." Thunder lost his grip as the floor became the wall and tumbled into the mural room, where the fish in the pictures on the walls had previously looked like fish were darting in the leafy grass. Unfortunately, now, the mural was a moving between water and half sky, which mirrored the violent motion he was feeling. He clutched his stomach as his shoulder slammed against the large cushion, which was now on a wall. With a rush, the images of fish were completely replaced by amber sky over water. He groaned as the round room gently moved back and forth like a bobber on a fishing line. He moaned as he clutched his stomach.

A loud whoop-whoop sound made his ears cringe, then the room stabilized and the murals appeared to soar like a bird over the water.

What a horrible place.

What an incredible wall.

As the chamber swung, like being inside a pendulum, Thunder was flung onto his back. He looked up; three huge ivory-colored balls, which were connected to the pale green tube, all of which seemed to be in the clutches of a mammoth ruby-throated dragonfly. Somehow, he knew that magical painting didn't surround the room; it was some sort of incredible window. Nausea forgotten, he touched the cool, smooth surface and marveled.

A sharp whistle broke over the whoop-whoop-whoop beat of the dragonfly's wings. Dalf's face appeared in the open doorway. Thunder hadn't thought the fish-boy's complexion could get any whiter, but he'd been wrong. "Are you looking for me?"

With rapid clicks of happiness, the creature tumbled into the room and landed on top of him. If only the kid could see and tell him what was happening.

"Relax. Sleep, if you can. I'm going to touch your face and try to help your eyes."

Dalf trustingly snuggled against him. Thunder took a deep, cleansing breath and hoped he could rebuild the missing tissue.

ooo

Tem-aki stared at the magnified view of the skyhook as it proceeded on a ENE heading, the grape-cluster-structure now stable below, as it moved across the otherwise desolate sea. Abruptly, one of the sensors chimed and she checked the view-screen. The madrox were swarming between Vilecom and Kalamar's atmospheric layer, again. The only difference was that this time the point the beasts were congregating at was farther northeast.

She blinked and thought back to the previous points of congregation, and was fairly certain that it had also been in line with the odd grape-cluster-home.

What is it about that structure that attracted them like filings to a magnet?

ooo

As the porpoise boat popped back above water, Raine glared at Preston. "Nambaba is my personal property."

He rammed the stick all the way forward. The porpoise-boat leaped through the waves.

"You weren't serious about everything being confiscated, were you?"

"Every time the dragons targeted the Sea of Storms, they pinpointed your home." Raine gasped and shook her head. Preston glanced at her, his expression grim. "Winslow doesn't know that and he won't learn about it."

"You can't be serious."

"A certain individual owes me a life-favor."

"Why are you doing this?"

"Who says I'm not doing it for myself?"

Raine, who had always thought Preston did everything for his own benefit, even though he always claimed to be doing favors for others, didn't know what to say. They passed a channel marker warning: Preston reduced speed and adjusted the altitude. By the time he swung the boat into a shipping lane, the porpoise boat was skipping over the wave crests. He quickly overtook a large, fast-moving swan-ferry and several slower flattop freighters

Within minutes, a yellow warning buoy announced the end of deepwater. Preston slowed the craft as they swept past outlying bubble homes and cut back even more as marsh encroached on the channel. Here, the small houses were woven of the reeds that surrounded them and easily destroyed by storms and insect infestations, but for once, Preston was going a respectful speed and obeying the no-wake warnings. Gray birds swooped to catch the clouds of biting insects that plagued the area. Raine shuddered to think of living in the shadow of The Pinnacle and enduring the hardships for the privilege of serving the Vole d'Laires.

"Does anyone ever own anything? Actually own it?" Preston's question startled her.

"I own Nambaba and my hous-"

"Do you?"

Raine bit her upper lip. She had until Vole d'Laire blamed her for the mooncow problems.

Preston began maneuvering past a massive swan ferry. As the porpoise-boat eased into its shadow, a crowd of hydro-farmers hooted from the rail above them. Suddenly something hit the windscreen. Preston casually flipped a switch and rinsed it away.

"What was that?"

"Kelp leaf."

"I hope whoever lost their lunch-"

"They didn't drop it, they threw it." Preston's expression was angry. "You live in solitude and rarely come here. You have no idea what public sentiment is like. Since the war ended, public opinion has turned to rage against the Vole d'Laires."

Raine's jaw dropped and she shook her head.

Preston nodded. "A revolution has been brewing ever since Winslow took over, but it's been worse since the war. You only see your loss. I don't think a single family was spared the pain of loss and they all blame Winslow." The porpoise boat passed out of the ferry's shadow. "You asked why I saved you. I saved you so we could save each other and Shay. We need to collect supplies and make a plan to flee off planet before Vilecom crashes."

"What about Dalf? He needs the oceans, they're his heritage."

Preston made a dismissive gesture. "When you chased the dragon and found the warrior, did you see a habitable planet?"

She shook her head. "It would be better to move the moon than find another habitable planet. Dalf-"

"Forget him. He's already gone." They moved past a crush of destitute-looking huts anchored amongst a sea of saw grass. She stared at the markings of each residence and wondered how her brother could ignore so many innocent souls.

"Dalf can't be gone."

Preston's lips flattened. He flicked a switch and a whale song filled the boat.

ooo

Thunder guided a torn ligament along the atrophied optic muscle toward old scar tissue. When it arrived where it belonged, the old wound shimmered and glowed as it transformed into a glowing liquid, which secured the ligament in place. And then, the light expanded until the vacant eye socket filled with radiance.

Cell by cell the first damaged eye was restored, but before Thunder could finish the second eye, he was thrown across the room. He landed face first.

Pain radiated through his head. Dalf shrieked. He heard several more thuds and bangs as the rest of the room's contents tumbled across the room. Then, all became quiet except for the base whomp-whomp-whomp, which he'd been ignoring.

It took all his willpower to roll onto his back.

The monstrous dragonfly was hovering above him. Were they safer here or outside this strange place? A thin strip fell from the dragonfly, above and seemed to be coming toward him. Thunder put his arm across his eyes. It landed with a loud whack that made the room shudder. When he opened his eyes, the line lying across the clear wall looked thick as his waist. His mouth went dry.

Thus far, this place had provided one amazement after another. What would happen next?

"No," Dalf whistled. "Not Doom Sea."

Thunder turned toward him and was amazed to see that his attention was on the black ooze underfoot and not on the giant insect, which had grasped the structure they were in. A loud snapping sound brought his attention to the area near the big pillow, where Dalf had been thrown. The crack near the fish-boy looked like a break in ice. As he watched, the break widened along with a horrible stench.

Dalf wrenched back his webbed hand, as if he'd touched embers. The fish-boy screamed as he scrambled to his webbed feet and rushed out the door.

Thunder looked down. More back tar-like stuff oozed through the damaged area. He gasped and choked on the acrid stench. Ignoring his pain, he rolled onto his feet and hobbled after the panicked boy.

ooo

Tem-aki sat inside Dasya Voltain's science lab, her attention torn between the holographic image of the grape-cluster-structure and the madrox activity on the view-screen. As the skyhook neared a vile, black octagonal area, the madrox became disorganized and the ctenophore class ships begin to regain control.

With that worry for her brother's safety dissolving, Tem-aki magnified the sky-hook's image until she could see the pilot's expression. He looked like he knew that the demons of hell are after him. Tem-aki frowned and glanced at the larger picture, which showed the skyhook hovering over the edge of the huge octagonal area containing a black substance. "Computer, do a chemical analysis of the contained substance." She tapped the contents of the manufactured containment area.

"Complying." A few minutes later, a chemical readout appeared on the view-screen.

"That's a chemical dump," she exclaimed as the skyhook dropped the tether lines and the grape-cluster-structure, which held Larwin, fell toward the toxic brew.

ooo

Preston slowed the porpoise-boat to a crawl as he approached The Pinnacle's floating wharf, which was a beehive of frantic activity. The few times when she'd been here before, everything had been spotless and people had moved with the dignity befitting nobility. Now, things appeared as untended as the Control Center Office had, and what was worse, everyone seemed to be sprinting from one place to the next, tunics flying like gossamer comet tails. The scene looked as unusual as the lone rocky protrusion in the water-world on which it was taking place.

Raine frowned and asked Preston, "Why is everyone in a panic?"

"I don't know." Preston touched a recessed area and the window slid away. Screams and sirens filled the air as everyone fled toward the already jammed doorways, which were hewn into The Pinnacle's solid rock face.

What was going on?

Complexion pale, Preston nosed the porpoise-boat into a mooring clamp, which wrapped around the boat, then raised it to wharf-level. Raine stepped onto the floating reed wharf and continued to gape at the frantic activity. "We won't find out what's going on by standing here." Preston grabbed her upper arm and pulled her along with him.

When her feet left the wharf, she stumbled on the solid surface of rock. Despite her misery, The Pinnacle's grandeur permeated her with a sense of awe. Her right foot touched the quartz walkway. When it remained stable, she fell against her brother. Preston effortlessly took her arm and steadied her. Another step later and a different siren roared to ear-splitting life. Raine's heart missed a beat. People screamed in terror.

Two attendants plunged past them and ran for the palace, as if the hounds of hades were in hot pursuit.

"Spirit, save us! Preston, what's going on?"

"I don't know." His fingers tightened around her upper arm. "The same thing happened earlier today. Hold onto me and try to get to that door." He gestured to a barely visible panel set into the wall.

She gripped his arm and tried to adapt her pace to the unbending rock, even then she tripped and fell against him. "Sorry. I'd forgotten how hard walking on something solid was."

He put a supportive arm around her waist. "If I don't get away from this island every few days, I forget how to walk on surge-swells."

Though Raine would have liked to talk about the unprecedented revelation that he periodically left the center of power, she wisely focused on her footing. Still, it seemed to take forever to reach the safety of the doorway and she felt as ungainly as a seacow. Preston tightened his grip around her waist and hauled her toward an oval recess in the rough rock wall. He punched a protrusion, which pivoted to expose a hidden keypad. He paused long enough to hit a series of symbols, then the cleft closed and a slab soundlessly moved aside to reveal a dark chamber.

The hair on the back of her neck shuddered as he yanked her forward.

ooo

Tem-aki stared, unblinking at the transmitter signal, as it pulsed in the structure's holo-image. Her eyes felt dry, but she was afraid to blink for fear the signal would be cut off. Panic clutched her chest. Against all odds, she had found her brother alive in the asteroid field, and been able to follow him this far. Now, she needed to rescue him from the Kalamaran's chemical dump.

She keyed in a code and the holo-view changed to include the madrox, many of which were still milling around between her and her brother. There was no way she could fire Dasya Voltain's engines, or get past the beasts undetected. And even if by some miracle, she did manage to somehow enter the planet's atmosphere, and actually rescue her brother, it would be impossible to escape from the planet.

Helplessly, she watched the grape-cluster-structure swing closer and closer to the lethal black sludge. The house's exterior seemed to be warping where black crud splashed on it. This was not good. If only there was a way she could help.

"If only the designers made ships you can keep in stealth mode even when you enter atmospheres!"

"Command does not compute."

"Can you determine if Colonel Atano is safe?"

"Negative. My sensors are only capable of monitoring the transmitter in his uniform. There is no guarantee he is wearing it."

Tem-aki digested that information, trying to decide if it was good news or bad. "Get a close-visual on the transponder's location."

"Complying."

ooo

The deck was tilted precariously close to the fetid black ooze and the vines, which had entwined the area looked dead. Either the fumes from black stuff were as deadly as they smelled or he'd spent days, instead of hours, healing Dalf.

Despite the fact that in the past, he had lost track of time's passing, when on a myst journey, Thunder didn't think the healing had taken days.

Dalf stared at the scene, his wide mouth open and revealing pointed teeth. "What happen?"

"I hoped you could tell me."

"Sneak on faddur ship. See world no wadder."

"How do we get there?"

Dalf looked at him as if he was deranged. "Gone."

The deck tilted toward the dead leaves. Thunder gritted his teeth against his raging stomach and looked at the vile black liquid surrounding the dock. "I have to get to land."

The boy looked at him as if he was absurd. When the deck tilted, again, he plopped down on the reed flooring and looked as if he were waiting for death.

Thunder stared out across the putrid panorama and began to look at the details. Though it pulsated, the crust near him appeared to have a rigidness similar to ice. Thunder picked up an odd yellow rectangle and hurled it. It cut through the crust, as if it was an eggshell. So much for walking away.

A breeze wafted in, lifting the hair off his neck and bringing the scent of fresh water.

"Kid, we've got to get out of here."

His head drooped. "Everyone come here die."

oOo

When the door closed, the room was pitch-black. The tiny hairs on Raine's arms shivered to attention, then Preston snapped his fingers and blazing light flooded the strange square room. She jerked and then blinked, as her eyes adjusted to the brightness.

A young orderly scrambled off the elegant maroon floor cushion and tried to stand at attention despite his eyes being shut tight and rimmed with the telltales of sleep. He smoothed down his frothy tunic with one hand and awkwardly saluted empty space with the other. Preston cleared his throat. The boy's face reddened and he pivoted toward the sound. The kid would never make it as a dragon shepherd. When he got past his temporary blindness, he saluted Preston a second time and gave her a half bow, half courtesy. Supreme in his dignity, her brother returned the boy's salutation, then cocked a thumb at her.

The boy's expression was tremulous. "Officer Bakufu, Sir! I'm to escort you to The Zar."

So Preston's concern was a sham. Raine took a deep breath and inclined her head. "Lead the way, but slowly, please. My gait has not adjusted to solid floors, yet."

"Understood. You may place your hand on my shoulder, if that will help." The boy gave Preston a nervous look, then twirled. Cobwebby lavender material billowed out to reveal a silver bodysuit. "Let us go, Sir."

Under other circumstances, she would have been amused by the boy's sense of pomp and circumstance. Instead, she straightened her spine and marshaled all her dignity as she tried to march with dignity. It was difficult enough, in the isolation of the room, then the lad opened an ornate door onto a hallway teeming with people wearing tights and dressed in flimsy fabric, who rushed in every direction. Raine tried to breath, but it felt like the crowded hall had sucked the air out of her lungs. Still, she strove for dignity, since it was the only thing she had.

Head high, Raine tried to ignore the wrinkles in the thick fabric of her serviceable khakis. She followed her pigeon-stepping guide toward her fate and wished that she'd at least had time to wash her face.

Her heavy space boots clumped against the paving stones and her heavyweight tan shirt and pants, which were what her crew favored, seemed horribly out of place amid the diaphanous, pastel trailing fabrics, sparkling tights and dainty dancing shoes that everyone else wore within these stone walls.

A particularly wispy tunic caught her attention. If someone had intended her to feel as out of place as possible, they'd succeeded. Of course, if she'd had time to wash and change into something that gauzy, she would have felt the fool, so perhaps this was best.

As she looked away from one outfit that was mostly bare skin, she realized she was being taken to the Council Chamber instead of The Reclamation Center. Why did they have to torture her with a phony hearing when they obviously planned to salvage her minerals? "So much for blending into the crowd," she muttered.

"Beg pardon, Sir?"

Raine hitched her chin up a notch. "I said is there always such a big crowd?"

"Yes, Sir."

For a moment, Raine was tempted to kick the boy's fluff-shrouded behind, but his inability to determine her gender was the least of her worries.

The lad led her to a massive door. The last time she'd entered the twenty-five-foot-tall monstrosity, she'd been informed that Gornt's minerals had already been reclaimed and been invited to view the recovery of Dalf's elements. The ornate gold plated carvings, which covered the door's surface, seemed to leer at her. Despite the door's enormous size and obvious weight, the boy effortlessly pushed it open. As it swung inward, she involuntarily sucked in her breath at the sheer magnificence.

The lad made a sweeping motion with his arm, as if entering was an honor instead of day of reckoning.

Head high, she forced her feet to move forward. A dual line of Vole d'Laire ancestors looked down on her from the semi-translucent columns, which immortalized them. Raine walked toward her fate, steps still unsteady, it felt like every etched eye condemned her clumsiness.

Strange how a dozen generations of Vole d'Laires felt more intimidating than misbehaving dragons. Spirit, what was wrong with her? The columns were only carved stone; a memorial to the past generations. They didn't have eyes that could see or tongues that could condemn. But the officials seated at the massive conference table, where she was being led all had their attention on her.

Bells jingled. "Sorry I'm late, Uncle," a sweet, high-pitched voice said. Raine paused. Someone skipped to a halt next to the distant throne, silvery chiffon layers floating around the slender form, making Raine feel even worse about her rumpled uniform. The five officials seated at the conference table half-rose and bowed to the newcomer.

Raine tried to walk as quietly as her boots allowed as she continued moving through the memorial stones. The final column was a detailed memorial to Winslow Vole d'Laire. Since he still lived, his face had not been added to the fully detailed body. Raine shivered. What would it be like to enter this space day after day and know that an artisan was patiently waiting for your reclamation so the memorial could be finished?

Five more strides brought her to the foot of a table large enough to seat a hundred. Raine clicked her heels together and stood at attention. Zar Vole d'Laire sat enthroned on a golden platform at the far end, wearing a purple garment with wide sleeves. His attention was focused on the twirling girl, who was wearing a sheer silvery tunic over pastel tights. In fact, every eye, except her own seemed to be captivated by the girl in the shimmering clothes.

Silence ensued, even when the girl stopped spinning and went to stand next to The Zar. Raine looked at the four men sitting on low, ornate cushions, two per side of the massive stone table; their attention mesmerized by the girl's hands, as she caressed The Zar's sleeve.

Raine lifted her gaze a notch and stared at the dragon that topped the ornate golden throne and she forced her body to stand as straight as possible. Silently, she prayed to the spirit for strength to face whatever her future held.

The diminutive girl turned and stared at her as if she was something unexpectedly nasty. She knew those judgmental eyes. Marsha. A chill rippled down her back. The Latawban princess had taken refuge at The Pinnacle, shortly before the destruction of her home world. Shay had been so enthralled with Marsha that she had tried to emulate everything the princess did.

Raine's teeth clenched with a hatred she had never understood, but had felt from the first moment she had met the beautiful girl.

Perhaps Preston was right when he theorized that she detested Marsha because Shay adored her.

Raine squared her shoulders. Marsha smiled at her. The last time she'd seen that smile, Marsha had been watching slaves being tortured. Was she anticipating that sort of entertainment, now?

"She is here, Uncle." Marsha's smile widened. For a millisecond, her eyes flashed crimson, then her gaze focused on The Zar for a lingering moment. The intensity of her posture relaxed. When she turned, her eyes were their normal ebony.

Marsha's silver-tipped fingers tightened on Winslow's forearm, in what should have been an affectionate gesture, but somehow seemed controlling. Their gazes locked and Marsha smiled. Raine's skin crawled. Heart pounding, she looked away from the child-woman.

Stature stiff, eyes vacant, Zar Winslow reminded Raine of a child's puppet. Spirit, let this be my imagination.

Marsha leaned forward, her eyes gleaming with anticipation. Winslow and the four grandfatherly men bent toward her, blank emptiness in their eyes. I must not think or show emotion. I must not blink or itch anything. I must not let them know my fear, for they will feed on it, like dragons on psychic energy.

Silence grew as her mouth dried and the hushed anticipation became baffling. Marsha shifted her feet with annoyance; Winslow Vole d'Laire's sleeve fluttered like the wing of an injured bird.

Suddenly light glared from the golden platform. Raine closed her eyes, then peeked through her lashes. Whatever it had been was gone. She focused her attention on the dragon that topped The Zar's throne and stared at its ruby eye. Motionless, she waited and hoped that whatever was going to happen would happen soon.

The smile on Marsha's face faltered and the silvery sheen of her dress dimmed. Marsha lifted her hands over her head, in a long, sensual stretch, then took several mincing steps away from Winslow. He remained still as his ancestors' statues. Raine watched the reflected scene. Marsha smirked toward the throne, then dance-stepped behind the elderly gentleman on Winslow's right and caressed his rigid spine. The control emanating from her brushed across Raine like a cold mist. She shivered.

A tremor of anticipation betrayed Marsha's thoughts.

Spirit, protect me.

With a majestic move, Marsha raised her arms. A tremor went through the five men and ten blank eyes turned toward her. Raine's mouth went dry and she prayed that whatever revenge the woman wanted would soon be over.

Silent despair welled within her until she wanted to scream. She concentrated on the dragon carved into the throne. Marsha twirled like a mad dervish. Raine focused on the throne even harder. Marsha spun faster, as if she was trying to become the center of all attention, but no matter how much pull she felt, she refused to submit to the smug look of domination in Marsha's eyes.

Raine began to sweat.

A siren blared.

Raine had never felt so hot.

Marsha fell into an unconscious heap on to the floor.

The four Elders lurched as if shocked from a deep sleep.

The Zar Winslow shuddered and looked up as if he could see what the alarm was about.

Despite the searing heat, Raine managed to stay at attention.

One elder leaped up, but tripped over Marsha; his skull cracked against the stone floor with a sickening thud.

Raine rushed to him, and felt for a pulse. There wasn't one.

With a thunderous crash, things began falling.

The floor shuddered and a fissure opened up beneath Marsha.

With a boom, jagged tears radiated from her comatose form.

Then, the floor rippled beneath her; Raine fell sideways, landing on all fours. Horrid groaning tore the burning air. Sickenly-sweet dust clogged her nostrils.

The commemorative columns were swaying and the ceiling had been shattered and was falling.

"Spirit!" Raine grabbed for her face-mask, as she scrambled to her feet, but it wasn't there.

The Zar Winslow stared at his commemorative column as cracks splintered the ceiling above it.

"Run!" Raine screamed.

With the sound of thunder, a fracture split the featureless, carved face.

Winslow stared, transfixed.

Raine jumped over the fissure, where Marsha and the Elder had disappeared and dashed to the throne. She grabbed Zar Winslow's rigid arm.

A deep groan drowned out the siren. The pillar began its final fall. She yanked him off his seat. "Move!" She shoved him. Surprise surged across his features. "Now!" He sprinted toward the small door where Marsha had entered. Raine dashed after him.

There was a mind-numbing groan behind her. Then a boom. A gray cloud of suffocating dust rolled over her. Something hit her in the back, knocking her forward. She fell against The Zar, propelling him through the doorway. A moment later, she hit the floor. Her body exploded with pain. The dragon's ruby eye skittered past her, the only thing with color in the gray world.

Another boom, then merciful blackness closed over her.

Chapter 15

As the black crust-covered ooze edged higher, Thunder climbed on top of the railing. Acidic fumes made him dizzy, but he crawled upward, then crawled onto the top of the adjacent round room.

"You play game?" Dalf asked.

"I need to see."

Dalf visibly shrank at his tone.

"We here do die."

Thunder glared down at the fish-boy, who was willing to wait for death, then looked for an alternative. The air was fresher up here. Beyond the orb's top, the greenish tube and four more spheres lay in the black crud. Beyond them the black ooze abruptly stopped and pale blue water began. "Fine. Sit there and die. I intend to save myself." If it was possible. It had to be possible. Thunder slid down the curved roof and landed on the tube, then sprinted along it. Several feet of putrid crust separated its end from the clear water. Thunder leaped.

His left foot landed in the crust and plummeted through. Searing pain encompassed it. He yanked it free and dove toward the water. Cold, suffocating wetness closed over him and he thrashed toward the surface.

Suddenly, something grabbed his hair and hauled him upward.

Thunder gasped for air.

Dalf clicked with delight. "Sea smell good."

The kid was insane. "We need to get someplace safe."

"We in sea. We fine."

"Maybe you are, Kid, but I haven't swum in over twenty years." And the last time he had, he'd nearly drowned.

"I no kid." The boy let go of him and with a sleek move, disappeared beneath the gentle waves. Thunder desperately tried to tread water. Suddenly, Dalf popped up in front of him. "Dell name."

"Thunder."

"Dunder no Cal-mar name."

"I was kidnapped by a woman with a dragon." A small wave broke in his face, filling his eyes, nose and mouth with water. He choked. When he caught his breath, he added. "We must get out of here so I can get home."

Dalf gaped at him. "Mudder kidnap you?"

His mother? "Beats me."

"She know you heal." His eyes widened. He waved a webbed hand toward the enclosed crust. "She lose all to heal." He thumped his own chest.

Thunder doubted Dalf's theory, but it was all he could do to stay afloat.

"Where Mudder?"

Mother? His captor had been a fish-woman? "I don't know." His memories were confused with the images GEA-4 had given him, but he was nearly sure the boy was the only fish-being he had met.

"Dis wrong. Bad wrong." The boy emitted a high-pitched clicking noise and made several agitated moves, which sent water splashing in all directions. "Homes no go Doom Sea." Dalf clicked himself into a frenzy. "If mudder alive, she at work." With a deft move, he turned his back to Thunder, grasped his hands and placed them on his shoulders, then he dove into the oncoming wavelet and began swimming toward the horizon.

Thunder gasped and spit as wave after wave spattered against his face. Perhaps he should let go and allow fate to claim him.

ooo

Eyes burning and tearing, making it impossible to see; lungs screaming for air, making it feel like she was suffocating; every cell in Raine's body screamed in agony. Had her body minerals been recycled? No, that wouldn't explain the horrid stench. She gasped, but only got a mouth full of dust. If this was what the afterlife was like, there was something worse than being a slave.

Spirit, please help me understand what terrible thing I did that I would be sent to such a miserable existence.

Hours, or perhaps moments later, something cool touched her forehead. Raine frowned. This did not make sense. First, how could she feel either pain or a gentle touch without a body?

"I've never known them to beat a woman so badly," a gentle,

bass voice murmured.

"Things must be very bad. Worse than I thought," a gruff voice said.

Every sinew howling in protest, Raine forced her right eye open. Though her eyes still hurt, it wasn't as bad as it had been.

"Ah, you're awake," said the gravely voiced blur. "Don't try to move. I reset you leg, but the mortar is still setting. Can you talk? No, of course you can't. Your jaw was dislocated, and it's far too swollen. That's fine." The gentle hand patted her shoulder. "I like to talk and it's nice to have someone listen to me."

A snort came from the vicinity of her feet. She rolled her eye downward and saw a gaunt man. The dirty top of his bald head was toward her; a long fringe of filthy gray hair marred her view of his face.

"Tsk-tsk-tsk," the voice near her shoulder said. Raine rolled her head to the left. The crone, who was peering at her looked nearly identical to the old man. The only difference was that she was not bald and the tips of her grimy tresses nearly reached the dusty stone floor.

Raine blinked.

The hem of the old woman's ragged garment brushed her broken toenails, yet, as she looked upward, the woman's smile was warm and welcoming.

"Fractured lumbar rib, costal cartilage of two more torn," the old man mumbled. "Mild concussion, assorted abrasions. Winslow really should control those brutes of his. If it hadn't been for your attire, I think they would have killed you." He didn't sound like the illiterate, unwashed masses. "Are you thirsty?"

Raine managed a semblance of a nod. The woman clumsily

rose. She stared at the man and had the uneasy feeling that she knew him. But that was impossible. She closed her eye and tried to ignore the misery that was her body.

The dank, frigid silence of the ancient cellar seemed to creep up from the filthy floor and into her bones. If I'm in prison, I'm not dead. But why were there people, who were more ancient than anyone she had ever seen, here? Raine struggled into a half-prone sitting position.

"Lie down," the man commanded.

Something squeaked then scuttled away on what sounded like small, clawed feet and a shudder passed over her, as she imagined it might be a merrat, which were said to sneak into baby's bubbles and eat them alive. Not that she'd ever actually seen a merrat, but mothers told their children the story to make them behave.

"Lie down," he repeated. Raine shook her head and tried not to wince as sharp pains raced up and down her spine. "Even though you're feeling better," he frowned, "you really shouldn't move."

"Drink this." The wraith-like woman shoved a chipped cup at her. "Then you must lie down and conserve your strength." Raine shook her head. The woman glared at her. "You'll need it."

Raine sipped the liquid just to placate her. The fresh taste tingled through her. She drank again and again until the only water left was a drop on her parched lips. She licked it. "Who are you?" she whispered.

One corner of her thin mouth curved up. "Coral D'nor."

She jerked with surprise and nearly dropped the cup as she turned toward the man, who had to be Reed D'nor. "The Zar's toxin developer." He gave a rueful nod. Reed D'nor was the man Preston revered above all, save The Zar. And he was dead.

Did this mean that she was dead?

He smiled at her. Did he know Preston was continuing his research? That The Zar had taken credit for work he'd done? "I'm dead." Dear Spirit, the pain in her jaw was unbearable!

"No, you're alive and in The caverns beneath The Pinnacle," Coral said, as she refilled the cup. "When Reed realized that he'd spent ten years assuring the doom of Kalamar, just so Winslow could add more platinum to his coffers, he realized he'd sold out our people."

"I couldn't stay, not after that epiphany, but when I tried to leave, The Zar tried to have me assassinated. I have been in hiding ever since."

Raine's hands shook as she brought the cup to her lips. After a short swallow, Reed said, "Wait. Make sure your stomach can handle that, then you may have more."

Raine looked at their dirty, disheveled state and her mind went numb at the realization of how long the couple had lived in this odious place.

"Tsk-tsk-tsk," Coral said. "So quiet. I would think you'd have questions."

"She had a dislocated masseter."

"I forgot. It must be difficult to talk or drink." Raine carefully nodded. "Tsk-tsk-tsk silly me to think I'd finally have someone who liked conversation. Let us hope Reed fixed your throat correctly. It's been far too long since he worked with an actual patient. Hmmm. Let me see if I can anticipate your questions." Despite their circumstances, Coral's eyes gleamed with anticipation.

Raine tried to nod, but pain shot through her head and she saw stars.

The corners of Reed's mouth fell and he reached over to steady her. "Time to lie down and relax." He gently lowered her to the dusty floor. "When you've rested, you can move to a warmer, safer location."

Raine caught his forearm and held on with her left hand, while she pantomimed for them to talk to her. The effort exhausted her.

"How long you can expect to be down here?" Coral guessed. "And how much time do you have before they execute you?" She tilted her head as she looked at her. "Those are your two main questions, aren't they?"

Raine held up a bruised thumb.

Coral smiled as if she'd been offered gold. "Tsk-tsk-tsk. I've never seen them brutalize a woman so crudely."

She tried to sit up, but a blinding pain consumed her. "Ribs." Raine groaned. She could barely recognize her own voice.

"Yes, several are dislocated. I've bound them, but you should lie quietly. And don't talk," Reed said. "Not with your masseter, er, jaw-bone fractured, dear child."

A flood of gratitude welled inside her heart as he uttered the same endearment that her father had favored. Though she knew it was foolish, Raine felt her attachment to the man deepen.

Raine watched a sad expression flit across Reed's face and thought that time hadn't been as gentle to him as it had to Winslow Vole d'Laire, who looked half the age. Vole d'Laire is Zar and superior to mortal man, but somehow, she couldn't convince herself that she believed The Zar was a superior being. Reed rocked backward on his heels, then rose and began a shuffling pace.

Coral caressed her face. "I don't know how long we've been hiding down here, and I can't imagine how much longer we'll be here." She blinked away tears and gave Raine a shaky smile. "Perhaps the guards will eventually get past their fear of merrats and venture down here but more likely, gravity will capture Vilecom and everything will cease to exist."

Raine inhaled sharply.

Coral pointed to her wave-band neckpiece. "I thought you might have known." Raine held up her thumb. Coral studied her, then understanding dawned. "You thought it was your imagination because your superiors ignored your fears." Raine tried to nod. "Don't, dear girl." Coral placed her palm on her forehead. "Mmmm, you're hot. I'll ask Frazier for-"

"She's my patient."

Coral's mouth flattened for a moment, then she smiled. "At least you don't need to worry that the guards will execute you." Raine widened her eyes. Coral took the hint. "Your sister cares a great deal for you; she and Brock managed to bring you to us during the confusion. Shay said that you won't be missed for days, perhaps weeks." Raine widened her eyes, again. "All the columns collapsed. Brock hopes that everyone will assume that you and Marsha were both crushed when the dragons attacked." She patted her shoulder and got to her feet.

The dragons had attacked The Pinnacle? Such a thing was unheard of. Was the declining orbit driving them insane? Had the poor beast survived the atmosphere? But she couldn't ask her questions.

As Coral walked away, Reed sadly shook his head. "Thirteen years ago, Winslow began to change from patrician to oppressor," he muttered. Reed rubbed his temples. His long, elegant fingers had broken nails. "I never saw it coming. Never!" He turned toward her and knelt. Taking her hand between his own, he swore, "I would never have begun my experiments if I'd realized how much he'd changed."

"Believe," Raine managed to say.

D'nor's face crumpled. Her heart skipped a beat as tears began to stream down his furrowed cheeks. Slowly, she inched her hand toward him and touched his finger. He grasped her hand. "Thank you. I'd thought only those who knew me understood, but you, a total stranger, perceive the position I was put in." Reed D'nor gave her fingers a tiny squeeze and gave her a watery, loving look. "I've killed us all, but you forgive me."

The warm feeling evaporated. What did he mean by that?

ooo

Salt stung Thunder's eyes and each breath scorched his lungs. His muscles felt as if they'd been shredded from his bones and his legs burned from the strange kicking movement of moving through water. At least The River had a bank to swim to; the only solid thing he'd seen on this wretched world was the strange grape-cluster style house.

Enough was enough.

He let go of the odd boy's narrow shoulders, rolled onto his back and simply floated. Water arced in an iridescent liquid rainbow as Dalf flipped around and swam back to him. Odd as the kid's physiology was, he was probably some sort of water creature, which would explain why the chamber he'd been in had been half flooded. But it didn't explain why the sweet-smelling woman had kept the kid or why he insisted on referring to her as his mother. Perhaps GEA-4 had not given him a proper grasp of the language. The idea of the angelic blond woman being the creature's mother was as ludicrous as a Yeti calling him father. The kid flipped a drop of water at him. "Why you dop here?" he asked in his odd click and whistle language.

"Need rest."

"You dired?" His strange purple eyes glowed with concern. "We have long vay do go."

If this was only the beginning, he might as well give up. Misery welled inside Thunder and he imagined never seeing Nimri, again nor her soon-to-be-born babe; never knowing that they were safe from the roving dragons; never touching land again. He shivered.

"You cold? Dad why you no swim good?"

"On my world, we only get in the water to bathe." A fountain of water erupted from the back of Dalf's head. Thunder flinched in surprise. Suddenly, he was sinking. He gasped. Water filled his eyes, nose and mouth as he plummeted downward. He frantically kicked skyward, but tendrils wrapped around his trashing legs.

Dalf whistled with alarm and dove toward him. Something coiled around his chest.

Something slimy grasped his face.

Something cold slithered down his neck.

Cold and blackness claimed him.

Chapter 16

Agony washed over her and Raine groaned. "Careful," Reed D'nor admonished. "I warned you that it was too soon for you to move."

The arm holding her in a sitting position tightened. "You'll feel better when you swallow the tincture," Coral crooned.

"Boneset and cohosh's healing properties are weeds," Reed admonished.

"Frazier and her people believe in them." So had Gornt. Raine obediently swallowed more of the bitter tea.

Reed snorted. "Their physiology is more like fish than human, perhaps it does work for them."

Raine swallowed another sip and another. By the time she finished, she actually did feel better. She should have tried to find one of the bakufus' healers for Dalf.

"Feeling better, aren't you, dear?" Coral patted her forearm. Raine gave her a thumbs up. Coral gave her husband a triumphant look. "Want to walk? It would be good for the circulation."

"I already told you that she should not attempt to walk on a fractured tibia," Reed snapped. Coral gave him a superior look and helped Raine to her feet. "Her foot everted, so the malleolus -"

Pain washed over her blocking out everything else. Raine gritted her teeth and made a small hop forward. Pain radiated from her injured leg, her stomach churned, sweat broke out as the nausea threatened to overtake her and she had to fight not to cry out.

"You must sit," Reed said.

"But-" Coral began.

"Don't argue," he ordered. Raine lurched. Coral gasped and fled. Reed grabbed Raine before she fell and gently helped her sit.

"Not a very auspicious beginning for the one who is destined to be our savior," a melodious voice said. "I told you you'd need your strength."

"Annya?" D'nor asked.

A musical laugh seemed to melt the shadows and herald the woman's arrival.

Annya was a name Shay had raved about when she'd initially moved to The Pinnacle. Judging by the nobility status of her neckband and her amethyst-tinged hair, the woman had to be Annya Vole d'Laire, Brock's unpredictable twin sister.

"What took you so long to get here?" D'nor demanded.

"Half the palace was destroyed, so work crews are everywhere.

It took time, but I'm here, now." Her clothing glinted with golden threads, but it looked much more substantial than anything else Raine had seen at court.

"Did you bring any medicine?"

"Would I be here otherwise?"

D'nor shifted uncomfortably. "No. Of course not."

"Maybe I was wrong," Annya whispered. Raine's perspiration turned to ice. Slim fingers prodded and pinched at her. "Ah, but she bruises easily," Annya muttered. "Yet she is the one." She dug into her pocket and pulled out a handful of flat stones.

D'nor's hand tightened. "She was buried under debris, manhandled and thrown into this torture chamber. She didn't get these bruises from watching lotus grow."

Annya frowned at him, then balanced the stones on her palm and held them toward her. Her regal brow creased with concentration and she centered her attention on the stones, as if they held the secrets to life. "Focus on them," she commanded. Raine squinted at the matte gray stones and noticed that each had a unique symbol etched in it. Slowly, three of them turned a bright, luminous white. Raine inhaled in surprise. Annya plucked the three out of the pile and put the remainder back in her pocked. Annya gave her a smug look. "You are supposed to serve me because I was born a deity, yet you are the world's savior and so I must be your servant." With that, she prostrated herself.

Reed gasped and threw himself face-first into the dirt, too. Raine touched her neckband and frowned. She was never a slave in her dreams. What if this was not a horrible, strange dream?

She took shallow breaths as she stared at the pebbles, which had fallen from Annya's hand. They stopped short of actually lying on the gritty floor, then as their light dimmed, slowly settled into the dirt. Did they really contain magical powers?

Not if they had foretold that she would rise over a noble. How could she, a dragon shepherd, save anyone when she could barely sit straight by herself? Raine flipped dirt at the stones, but it slid off their smooth surface like oil.

Annya snatched them, but remained prostrate as she clutched them to her bosom, and treated the mysterious rocks as it they were priceless. "Oh, my darlings, she didn't mean it. She doesn't know. Doesn't know."

Reed raised his head and stared at her as if she were insane. Raine shivered and looked away. "It's going to be fine. She'll learn."

Learn what? Open-mouthed, she stared at the man who she'd always assumed was an eminent scientist.

"She doesn't know?" Annya's tone held disbelief.

"She will." Reed D'nor turned to her. "You will."

They were both insane. Slowly, Raine shook her head and inched her bottom through the grime, as she slid away from the demented pair. The small distance seemed to make the air easier to breathe. Four more scooches brought her to a wall. She looked away from Annya and Reed. An ancient archway was to her left. She worked her way over the gritty, uneven stone floor and into the dark recess, then leaned against the cold stonewall with a groan.

A strong hand grabbed her shoulder. She tried to wrench free. "How'd you manage to take down half the Palace?"

"Preston? Why are you here? Was everyone thrown down here?" Raine gasped.

His hand tightened. "We've used the ancient levels for a

decade."

"For what?" Why? Who was her brother? She looked at Reed. Hardly any time had passed since she'd told Preston her suspicions of D'Nor's death. Had he known Reed D'nor was alive and in hiding? Had he helped conceal him? Told Shay to bring her here? Was there some sort of a conspiracy?

"Isn't it obvious?" He let go of her shoulder and took a step away. Darkness shrouded everything above his knees. "Haven't you figured out what I'm working for?"

"No," she told the shadows.

"Freedom."

Probable, if he were still a boy; not likely for the man he'd become. All he'd been interested in since his voice deepened was acquiring wealth and rank. "You'll never attain nobility status. The deities can't afford to grant it, no matter how deserving you are."

"I don't want nobility. I want freedom." The idealisms of years gone by vibrated in his voice

Raine squinted at the darkness.

"You're the one who made me want it more than my next breath," Preston said. "Every day after you taught me my lessons, you'd tell me about the Green Fields and how Kalamar once was."

"I made up those stories to entertain you until Mom and Dad got home from work. It was easier to keep you quiet with a story, than clean up the messes you made with your experiments."

"See," Annya said. "She knew. Even then, she knew! But why doesn't she know now?"

Gooseflesh erupted over Raine. "Preston, what is going on?

Why is she trying to make me part of this?"

"You were always part." He half emerged from the darkness, a strange expression on his face. "You're the one who made me part of it."

"With silly stories told to a child?"

"No, with a glimpse of the past and what Kalamar should be. What it would have been, if the original Vole d'Laire had never moved Vilecom into orbit."

Raine stared up at his face, which was midway between darkness and light, and wondered if her brother was unknowingly showing her that he was torn between sanity and lunacy. The moon often seemed to derange rational minds.

But what if Preston, Annya, Coral and Reed were the sensible ones and she was unbalanced?

She shook her head; more likely, she was hallucinating this entire situation. Maybe she'd been killed or knocked unconscious by a madrox, and was merely dreaming she was alive.

Preston hunkered down, grabbed her shoulders and shook her.

The dead shouldn't feel pain. "Stop!" she gasped. He let go and she slumped downward.

In the darkness, there was a shriek.

"You've killed her!" Annya gasped.

"Quiet, both of you," Reed said.

"I'm sorry." Preston grabbed her and hugged her to him. A moment later, she felt herself levitating. A heart thundered against her ear and confusion over her brother's many masks filled her mind.

"Fraizer, get my med kit," Preston said. Raine tried to sink into soothing nothingness. "Please forgive me, I don't know what came over me." Fortunately, his apologies couldn't keep the blackness away.

When she woke, Preston, Reed and a dolphman were crouched beside Annya, their attention on three flat pebbles on her palm. Could these dull and common stones be the same ones she had chosen? "Ansur tells of an enlightening experience to come," Annya said. "It will be inspirational and a reception for her new destiny." Her long fingers caressed the pebble and she peered at Raine, as if aware she was watching. "Think first, girl. Don't do anything rash! Get advice from those that know. Ansur is aligned with Mercury, you feel it is time to start your journey."

"And save us all?" the dolphman scoffed. "She couldn't even save herself."

"But the stones say she is the one we've been waiting for," Reed said, as he leaned forward. "They've never been wrong."

The dolphman shook his head. If it hadn't been for the war, Dalf might have grown to look and act like the heathy lad, instead of the fearful entity he'd been reduced to. The thought brought a lump to Raine's throat.

Annya didn't acknowledge Reed. She lightly touched another stone. "Tir tells of her journey. She must prepare herself, because she will need all energy forms to succeed."

Were all nobility this overly dramatic?

Annya raised her head and squinted in her direction. Raine didn't move as she stared back through her eyelashes. "The last is Wyrd. The fate stone." Annya looked at Preston. "All destinies lie with your sister. If she doesn't succeed then we all fail."

Preston shivered, as if he believed every word of the nonsense. "If Wyrd lit up for her, nothing is assured."

"Nothing is ever assured," Reed said.

The dolphman gave a whistle of agreement.

A siren shrieked; everyone went still as stone. The floor gave a slight vibration. The dolphman wailed as he scrambled to his feet. Terror warped his expression as he leaped over her. His flight seemed to rouse the others.

Preston surged to his feet. "We need to get out of here."

"No," Reed said. "This is the only place within ten miles that wasn't damaged during the last attack."

Attack? Were the Guerreterrans here to rescue the warrior she'd harmed? Raine's mouth went dry.

"If more rock falls, this will be our tomb."

"It's safer than going up and steaming to death," Annya said.

"Suit yourself." Preston paused long enough to pick Raine up. With more strength and speed than she had ever imagined, he threw her over his shoulder. The wind was knocked from her as her bruised ribs collided with raw determination. Ripples of agony washed over her, rendering her mute. He ran after the dolphman as if his life depended on winning the race, his shoulder slamming into her with every step. She couldn't inhale, couldn't scream.

He leaped over something.

Raine's world turned silent and black.

Chapter 17

Waves slapped against Thunder's closed eyelids and his grasp on Dalf's slippery shoulders kept slipping. When he opened his mouth to ask the kid to slow down; water flooded in. Choking and gagging, he lost his grip. The momentum ceased. Thunder rolled onto his back, coughing and gagging, gasping for air. Thunder was too weak to continue fleeing across the unending water to some unspecified destination. Chill bands of liquid death wrapped around him like a lover's embrace and pulled him downward. Why had he hated water so long?

From a distance, Dalf whistled in alarm.

So much easier to descend into the cool, dark welcoming depths than to fight destiny. For the first time in his life, Thunder relaxed and greeted water as a long-ignored friend.

If I die, so will Kazza, Nimri, Larwin and their unborn son.

He shuddered, then used his last ounce of strength to propel himself upward toward the small spot of light, but even as he made the effort, he knew it was too little too late.

Something hit his chest with the force of an enraged Yeti. Water spewed out of his mouth like a fountain, then moisture-rich oxygen rushed in. Thunder doubled into a fetal position and coughed as if he would puke out his lungs.

Something patted his shoulder. "You be well," Dalf clicked.

He continued coughing until the last drop was out of his lungs, then kept on because his airways blazed with misery and he couldn't stop.

Let me die now and get it over with.

Someone grabbed his hair with one hand and his jaw with another and jammed a fist full of soggy leaves into his mouth. He convulsed, trying to spit them out, but his assailant held his mouth shut. Involuntarily, he inhaled some of the mess. Someone whistled a note of triumph. Thunder huddled into a fetal position, too exhausted to count his aches and pains.

"Resd. Led lurpa word," Dalf clicked, as he let go of his head.

After all he'd done to heal the kid, this was the way he paid him back? Slowly, his breathing regulated. Eventually he collected enough energy to open one eye. He immediately closed it to shut out the under water vision and concentrated on healing his abused lungs.

Somewhere behind him, Dalf clicked and whistled about their narrow escape, making it sound as if escaping from the black pit had been a wonderful adventure.

Painfully, he turned his head. The kid and a creature that could have been his unscarred twin were sprawled on the iridescent floor. Dalf was whistling and flapping his webbed hands as he told their story. His fingers hit the chamber's low ceiling and the entire roof undulated. Thunder forgot to cough, as he stared upward, expecting the congregated turtles and ocean to pour down. When they didn't, he reached up and touched the cold water. A ripple radiated outward and a drip clung to his fingertip.

Amazing that he still had visions after death.

Thunder closed his eyes and deeply inhaled the moisture-rich air. Dalf continued his exaggerated account of his heroism and the other fish-person kept whistling with appreciation. The air seemed humid as a summer day, but held a stagnant, slightly rancid aroma instead of sweet flowers. His nose wrinkled. Peeking through his lashes, he peered into the dusky regions of the strange area, but he couldn't sense how large this air-filled void was.

As he looked up, a giant turtle's beady brown eye stared back. He moved his hand to touch it, but with a swirl of water, the turtle swam away. Heart slamming against his ribs, he turned to Dalf. "Where are we?"

Dalf glared at the interruption. "Yulder ovum."

"Explain," he commanded.

Dalf gestured to the other fish-type creature. "This Yulder." So this strange place belonged to his friend.

The second fish-person nodded. "This my." Sensing Thunder's confusion, he added, "Forbidden Sea." As if that explained anything.

"He wid me," Dalf clicked excitedly.

Okay, he was not allowed here, but it was acceptable because he was with the kid. As he digested that bit of news, something moved below his elbow. Thunder looked down at the hexagon flooring. An ivory colored oval thing fluttered inside the large honey-comb-shaped area. He blinked several times and was able to see pinkish areas where eyes would develop. He squinted at the next hexagon and saw another fist-sized polliwog. Large frogspawn? "What is this, some sort of hatchery?" He squinted at the fish-boy and his friend.

Dalf tilted his head. "Brood come dree day."

This had to be either a nightmare or a vision; yet if it wasn't, egg sacks would explain why the kid wasn't quite human.

Yulder sadly bobbed his head and looked morosely up at the turtles, which were lazily patrolling the water overhead. "Then arco and tartaruca feast."

So this place was like Chatterre, whatever was on the bottom of the food-chain had an enormous number of off-spring in the hope that a few would survive to maturity. Strange, he hadn't figured on the kid being prey, though it would explain the scars.

Yulder caressed the hexagon closest to him. "Maybe better that tartaruca gather. Better die now than burn. Better die now that breathe poison water."

Dalf whistled in alarm.

"You not know?" Yulder tilted his head to one side. "Where you be? Every dolphman know dragons come. Every dolphman know all seas turn dark. Every dolphman know all die."

"Bad wader day behind done."

Yulder clicked in agreement. "But dragon poison good water."

Dalf whistled in alarm. "How?"

"Brush water with breath." Yulder sent an explosive spew from the back of his head for emphasis.

"Are you trying to tell us that someone is using madrox to destroy this place?" Thunder remembered the image of dragons attacking another sun and volatile vapor spewing toward a greenish orb. The dragons had somehow made the flare vaporize a world, just like the millennium old legend from the old world. "La-taw-ba was where Vole d'Laire 's brother and strongest competitor reigned as God Head."

The frantic whistling from the two fish-men was as undecipherable as it was ear-rending.

"Can they be stopped?" he inquired.

"Mudder herd dragons," Dalf said.

Yulder clasped Dalf in a tight embrace. "She save ovum?" When Dalf shuddered, Yulder urged, "Must leave. Must tell." Yulder shoved him toward the darkest shadow.

Dalf stumbled, then collapsed. "Mudder dead." His whistle nearly ruptured Thunder's ear. "House go Doom Sea." Yulder sat down hard and both fish-men shrilled with agony.

Thunder put his hands over his ears. Without the woman that the kid called 'mother', the only way he could get home was GEA-4 and he had no idea where to find her. The vague memory of her disintegrating in a shower of sparks made him frown.

Yulder caressed the egghex next to him. "Many dragons. Many keepers. We must find." He looked at Dalf, his webbed palm protectively on the glowing floor. "Must help. Yulder can no leave."

"And I need to leave, too. If I don't get home, everyone that I love will die."

Yulder's look was sad. "No leave. Lungs-" He pointed to Thunder's chest with one hand and fisted his other hand. "Must stay."

Thunder shook his head. "If I'm going to die, I'm going to do it on my terms." He looked up at the hovering turtles.

Yulder heaved a sad sigh, then rolled into the shadows. He was back in a moment, an odd whiskery-looking thing in his hand. He thrust it at Thunder. "Take."

Thunder didn't move. Yulder thrust it into his mouth. He tried to dislodge the foul-tasting thing, but Dalf smacked his hands. "Go up slow, breather save." The slimy whiskers caught in the stubble covering his chin. He cringed. He'd survived water twice, before; he could do it again. If this spongy, foul tasting thing would help, he'd accept it. He laced his fingers together and resisted the urge to spit it out.

As soon as he quit struggling, Yulder let go of him. "You go. Save ovum." For a shocking moment, it looked like the fish-man intended to kiss him.

ooo

Cinder and ash floated atop the water as far as Raine could see and acrid dust hung heavy in the air. She huddled against her brother and stared at the devastation, unable to believe that the dragons had attacked The Pinnacle. She leaned against her brother for support and he put a supporting arm around her waist. Frazier, the dolphman, crouched at their feet, great gasping sobs wracking his body. In the distance, a small group of people rummaged through the rubble of the collapsed Pinnacle. What could have motivated such violence? A cool breeze gusted against her aching jaw, but was gone as suddenly as it had come.

Preston's grip tightened and his jaw tensed, until he once again looked like The Zar's physician. Raine tensed and looked in the direction of his gaze. In the distance, the sea appeared to be belching fog into the sky.

Frazier pressed against her shins, nearly knocking her over with the violence of his trembling.

Would the strangeness ever end?

Another draft blew her hair into her eyes. She pushed the clinging strands aside and studied the unusual cloud. Gold glinted from the haze. She blinked. More mist scudded aside. Was that a dragon's tail sticking out of the water? It was! Raine put her hand to her neck collar and gulped. "Has Vilecom's orbit deteriorated so far that the dragons wish to kill themselves?"

Preston gave her a strange look. "Their behavior only changed when you brought the Guerreterran here."

She shook her head in denial.

He nodded. "You must get him off planet."

Obviously her brother had gone lunar.

"I thought the Sea of Doom would solve the problem, but-" He shrugged.

"What did you mean by that?" He ignored her. She grabbed his chin and forced him to look at her. "Tell me."

He raised his hands in surrender. "I had to take measures. His presence was upsetting everyone and everything I've spent the last decade working for was being ruined."

"I strongly doubt that one warrior caused the dragons to ch-"

"Then give me a better reason," he snapped.

She shook her head. "I can't. But I do know they've been swarming more and more and I would never have shot down the warrior if I hadn't been chasing a runaway."

Preston's skin took on an ashen hue. "You shot him down?" She chewed her upper lip and nodded. "The fleet -" Unable to finish the thought, he clamped his jaw shut.

"Don't ask me how. I'm really not sure how it happened. I was only trying to do my job."

"All our destinies lie with you," he whispered.

Wyrd's prophesy. She shivered. How was she supposed to save anyone when she wasn't even able to stand unaided? "All I know how to do is herd dragons." Tears stung her eyes. "It's all I've ever been good at."

"Zandor says that those rocks never lie."

"Do they say how long everyone will live afterward?"

He frowned down at her. "What do you mean?"

"For the sake of argument, let's say that I could get to Nambaba and save Kalamar from the dragons. What about the next threat?" He frowned. "Even if I could drive them away, I still can't save our world from Vilecom."

"The scientists will find a way to change the orbit." He sounded as doubtful as he looked.

Raine shook her head. The dragons were only the beginning of the end. Their planet and everything on it was doomed.

"Fine, then we must go to a new world," Frazier said.

"Where?" Raine asked.

The dolphman shuddered. " Must have water."

She sighed in agreement. "I'd like to find one without dragons and with water." How lovely it would be to never have to go into space again, to stay home, tend Dalf and fish off her deck.

"We need a place where we can be free," Preston said. He raised his hand and waved. A distant person waved back. He purposefully began moving toward the stranger and dragging her along with him.

"Where are we going?"

"To collect everyone we hold near and dear, then leave Kalamar." His tone was matter-of-fact.

He had to be lunar. "There's no escape."

"There's always Nambaba."

"You think I'm fit to fly?" The way her ribs felt, her lungs would be punctured the moment she applied G-force power.

"To do something is better than to await death."

That would have sounded good yesterday. Today, it sounded like suicide.

Frazier scrambled to his feet, as if the ridiculous thought had to be immediately acted upon. Raine blinked back tears at the idea of another dolphman dying in space.

Chapter 18

Water rushed past Thunder like knives in a tornado and his exposed flesh felt as if it was being ripped from his bones. Worse, the water kept pulling at the breather, but if he lost it, he would die. He kept his head tilted back, as Dalf had advised and clenched his jaws.

This was the third day that Dalf had been towing him through the cold, empty water. Didn't this awful world have any land? He'd settle for having the nauseating bubble-house back if it meant that he could get out of the water. Oblivious to his difficulties, Dalf rushed ahead, body undulating through the water with a look of sheer glee on his face, as if he was having the best time of his life.

All he had to do was let go of the harness and the torture would end.

Temptation coiled through his mind and tore at his willpower.

His aching hands slipped on the thick stem. It would be so easy to let go and let Dalf swim away trailing the ropey seaweed.

If he let go, he'd be alone in the water, and he'd never get home. He closed his eyes, clung to the slick stem and told himself that he would make it home in time for the birth of Nimri's babe.

Hours later, Dalf slowed. In front of them, gray water blazed with patches of muted colors that reminded him of the crazy quilts Bryta loved to make. Moments later, he realized he was seeing a sheer rock wall, which was covered with a colorful array of mushrooms. Tiny fish darted in and out the crevasses and tall, thin lavender leaves rippled in an invisible current.

Who would have believed an underwater world would be so beautiful?

Dalf slowly swam upward, then lingered in front of a vibrant blue moss-like surface. Thunder moved toward the boy, tapped his arm and gestured toward the surface. The kid emitted a sound that equated to 'no'. Thunder emphatically pointed upward. Again, Dalf refused. Thunder dropped the seaweed strap and kicked upward. Dalf grabbed his leg and held him down.

What was the kid's problem? Didn't he realize that lives were at stake?

They glared at each other for several minutes, then Dalf shoved the seaweed strap back in and gave a small kick; they rose a few feet. Again, the kid held him back and pantomimed pain and agony if they rose too fast. Despite his eagerness to get out of the water, Thunder figured the fish-boy must know what to do in his own element. Thunder nodded and turned to look at the rock wall, where a beautiful patch of asters nodded in the gentle current. Who would have thought such things grew underwater?

An iridescent school of minnows fluttered along the rock. Some individuals paused to nibble on the colorful lichens and moss. Another nibbled at the fragile petals of a crimson blossom. It seemed such a shame for the fish to spoil such a beautiful flower. He raised his hand to wave it away, but before he could, the petals snapped round the fish, like jaws and then, flower, fish, and all vanished down the hollow stem. Thunder lurched backward and the remaining fish scattered in a silver burst. Dalf tittered. Thunder choked on a mouthful of salty water. Now even more amused, Dalf thumped him on the back. Thunder stared at the hollow stem. Animals were supposed to eat plants, not vice versa.

What kind of twisted world was this?

It took two more pauses before they reached a rocky underwater plateau. Here, the fish were larger and less colorful. Now, Dalf moved slower, with frequent pauses to peer into the distance.

Abruptly, the rocks ended and an expanse of underwater grass stretched into the distance. Dalf plowed ahead, until he came to where the lavender lawn gave way to barren sand. The kid paused, as if terrified to leave the security of the high pasture. The sunny pastoral scene seemed unreal after days beneath the dark waters. He looked upward and saw peach clouds drifting in a lilac sky. If he lifted his hand, he might be able to touch the surface.

Anticipation throbbed through him.

Dalf emitted a low, warble of worry, then cautiously went forward five feet and paused, as if sniffing the water. When nothing happened, he moved ahead another ten feet. Then twenty. After several more spurts, a forest of swaying green trunks and shadows materialized in the barren expanse in front of them.

Would trees eat them, as the flower had eaten the fish?

Dalf hovered in the shallow water, as if wondering the same thing. Suddenly, harsh sounds filled the water.

Thunder peered around, too, but didn't see anything more dangerous than a long, flat, pink creature that moved like a snake through the water. He stared at it, ready to evade an attack, until he noticed that Dalf was ignoring the beast and staring intently at the distant forest of sequoia-sized trunks. Vile as the serpent-like thing appeared, it must be safe, while the ocean floor and vegetation represented true danger. He should have realized this when he'd watched the carnivorous flower.

He hung onto the seaweed harness, uncertain whether or not he'd recognize danger when he saw it. If he hadn't needed the terrible-tasting breather, he would have asked Dalf if his conclusion about the bestiality of plants was correct.

Dalf sped into the shadows surrounding the trunks and came to an abrupt halt next to one. Heart pounding, Thunder hung onto the tether; the boy huddled against the short green fur for protection. He squinted through the shadows and water. Indeed, the furry mass attested to an animal versus plant origin. This must be the creature that had eaten all the tall grass. Dalf huddled against the thing for several moments, eyes darting at the darkness, as if expecting an attack at any moment, so Thunder looked for vicious plants, too.

When nothing happened, he began to relax. As his heartbeat slowed, he heard loud thumping noises and blaring tones. Thunder looked up. The waterline was tantalizingly close, and the dark shape of a huge body was above them. Obviously, this was the leg of a huge, gentle herbivore.

Dalf's gaze darted around the shadows of the beast's underbelly, but he never moved from the leg's safety. Thunder moved next to the kid, back to the gently throbbing leg. The soft fur stroked his spine, as he stared outward, looking for whatever danger the fish-boy seemed to sense. Dalf stiffened and stared at a light area next to the giant's body. Far above, a long, bright light moved above the peachy-toned clouds. A tremor went through the large leg. What horror could terrify something this size? As the light got brighter and bigger, the water between him and the sinister shape frothed, as if it, too, could feel fear.

Thunder tensed, certain that he knew that shape from somewhere, but the object vanished above the giant beast's body before it became identifiable. As a second strangely familiar shape undulated past, he forgot to breath. As a third blindingly bright body passed low over the sea, he winced and looked down at the ocean's bottom. The silhouette of a Ghilly dragon moved across the muck.

Ghilly dragons could devour entire planets. No wonder the massive creature above them was cowering in the water.

He could see several more colossal legs in the shadows. The leviathan must be some sort of centipede.

Would fate cause him to die here, without ever seeing the sun rise over the rugged mountains, again? Would he ever smell the heady fragrance of a buddelia, again? Or taste a pange? Would he ever get to stroke Kazza's silky fur or hold Nimri's newborn babe?

Would he die here, in the element he despised and at the killing breath of the very dragons that he'd tried to protect his home world from? If he hadn't been so curious to see Solterre, he would be safe at home and so would everyone else who was relying on him.

He had to get home and protect his world from the dragons.

As if in answer to his need, the outline of a polliwog appeared to creep over the rippled sand. Thunder squinted through the water, certain that his eyes were deceiving him, as the shadow of the tiny tadpole went straight toward the nose of the dragon. The dragon reared back, as if frightened by the polliwog.

Suddenly, the polliwog flared into a huge spider. Thunder gasped and immediately choked, so he quickly readjusted the hairy mess. The dragon twisted away from the attack and sped toward safety.

Dalf squealed and darted deeper into the giant centipede's protective shadow, then huddled against another massive leg.

Thunder's ears felt as if they were filled with air. He tried, unsuccessfully to readjust them. The leg shuddered, then a thundering boom nearly pulverized his bones. Dalf shrieked. Salty water surged into his nose. Thunder choked and coughed.

Abruptly, the blaring noise stopped.

Dalf cautiously motioned for him to follow, as he moved deeper into the shadows of the centipede's belly. After several minutes, they arrived at a solid expanse of long fur. This monstrous creature was as different from Chatterre's creatures as the madrox had been. Dalf cautiously moved upward.

It felt wonderful to get the breather out of his mouth and inhale real air. He massaged circulation back into his stiff jaw.

"Dis Cendral Command." Dalf touched the charcoal-colored wall. "Mudder work here. Herd dragon."

"You mean she uses the spider thing?"

Dalf looked as confused as he felt. "Pie-dur?"

"Never mind. Let's find her." He looked around and sighted a ladder leading from the water to the floor above. Certain that the kid's mother wasn't in the water, and had to be overhead, he kicked off toward it.

Dalf grabbed his leg and hauled him back. "Forbidden. Go dead." His frantic whistles and clicks nearly made him incoherent.

The boy must be daft. If they couldn't contact the woman, why had they spent the better part of three days under water, trying to get here? "We came here to see her. Not for you to show me the structure."

"No word building. Fly Nambaba."

Thunder rubbed his aching forehead and noticed that the skin on his arms was white and puckered. "Look, kid, you might be at home in the water, but I'm not. I have to get out of it while I still have skin." As it was, he looked like a moldy prune.

There was a distant splash, as if something big as a sequoia had fallen into the water. Dalf jolted. "Noooo," he moaned. He inched backward until his spine was flush against the wall.

Thunder squinted at the shadows, but still couldn't see any danger. So what if he didn't understand the dangers of this world, being snapped up by a flower was better than waiting in fear for an unseen enemy to attack. He swam toward the sound of the splash. Dalf tried to catch his ankle, but he shook the kid off.

Several minutes later, he arrived where the shadows met the blue-green sunlit water. The reek of burnt fish oil was so strong that it almost overpowered the salty sea-scent.. The stench seemed to be emanating from the odd silvery trunk, which was floating on the water. A thin leafless vine connected the thing to the floor overhead. Since its master had to tie it, obviously, the thing was either a vicious creature or so extraordinarily large that it needed restrictions.

Was this the thing the kid was afraid of?

As he contemplated the bizarre pet, its round mouth opened and a human sprinted out. When the person was halfway along the trunk, air whooshed out from beneath the thing's round head in a wild surge of bubbles and it began sinking beneath the waves. The person ran faster and leaped onto a floating rug.

The ship disappeared beneath the waves, as the silver and blue clad individual calmly walked on the magical mat toward the structure above him.

Something grabbed him with an invisible hold and dragged him downward.

A whistle of fear ripped through the water.

Thunder barely had a chance to stuff the breather into his mouth before the beast pulled him under. Thunder flailed for something solid to fight, but only hit water. The unseen force pulled at his breather. He clamped his jaws tight and pretended to go limp.

A moment later, he bounced on the sandy bottom. He peered through the silt-laden water, but still didn't see the monster that had grabbed him. He hung lifeless and looked for the source of the assault, but the only thing he saw was more muddy water around the huge silver spider.

Strong hands grasped his shoulders. The breather was knocked out of his mouth and he was yanked backward into the shadows. Behind the pillar, the water was calm and clear as a stagnant pool. Wailing and shrilling, Dalf hugged him. Thunder gagged. Dalf shrieked then thrust him to the surface.

Lungs burning, Thunder gasped for air. "What was that?"

"Herd ship must hydro."

The kid's answer was as confusing as the situation. He squinted up at the sun and wondered if he would ever see his world and those he loved again.

"Skin bad." Dalf splashed the water with fright.

Thunder looked at his swollen, festering arm, then at the other, which was equally bloated. He could only imagine what the rest of his body must look like. He climbed onto an odd floating mat. A warm, gentle breeze fanned his sodden clothes and felt like claws on his face. He held up his arm. "This is from being in the water so long." Dalf clattered with worry. "Relax, kid, I can fix it. It's just that my element is land. I could never live on this world any more than you and yours could live on mine." With that, he shut his eyes and focused on healing his flesh.

When his senses returned to the outer world, noise was blaring and people were running on the high platform, shouting with fear. In the distance, water began boiling. A person dashed toward it, apparently running on top of the water. Then, the strange silvery thing popped up and the human sprinted toward the large bubble. The mouth opened, yet the person ran forward, straight into the gaping maw.

Thunder gasped.

The beast lifted up off the water, brought its massive legs together with a fearful snap and shot straight up into the air. He shuddered.

Dalf clapped with delight. "Love shepherd." He pointed at a distant glowing cloud. Thunder squinted and saw a familiar undulating speck of gold.

"What is everyone screaming about?"

"Dragon."

His suspicions were confirmed. "But how can it hurt your world when the water will kill them?"

"Shepherd proceed dragon from wader." Dalf gave him a toothy smile. "Wand be shepherd, like mudder and faddur."

"A worthy goal."

"No under-dand why dragon come."

"No one ever does." There was silence overhead. If they were going to sneak up and find the kid's mother, now was the time to do it. He stood up. The floating matt tilted. He compensated, leaped to the stable part of the inclined platform and sprinted to the top. He threw himself on the decking and inched up the last few feet. Three people huddled on a bench, heads close as they chatted and waved their arms. Two were human, one looked like Dalf. The boy eased up next to him. "What's your mother's name?" he whispered to keep the kid from whistling in alarm and disclosing them.

"Captain Raine Bakufu." He struggled over the last name.

"Has a lot of names, doesn't she?"

Dalf softly shrilled in agreement. "Lasd here. Greadesd momend my life." The kid looked desolate.

"Why the best?"

"Wand grow, like faddur." In the distance a group of people ran across the high platform, their feet perfectly synchronized, as if running was a dance. "Wand see dragons." The boy frowned at the platform. "Dis no same." He rolled onto his side and put his fist at the center of his chest-area. "Feel dif-rend. War bedder."

He'd heard about war from Larwin. "Did you like war?"

Dalf emitted a high-pitched whistle. "World die. Faddur die." He touched his face where the worst scars had been. "My end."

Thunder inhaled. "And you think war is better than what's going on now."

Dalf clicked in agreement.

This was not good. Neither was doing nothing while waiting

for a disastrous end. Thunder lunged to his feet and leaped to the floating dock. He stagger-stepped until he got to the solid section, then he sprinted upward.

He paused when he reached the top of the ramp. The enormous, flat maze-like surface made from the same strange substance the bubble chambers had been. Not a centipede.

Dalf whimpered as he tried to hide behind a thin railing. What danger did the kid see? Or didn't he want the individuals to see him? Thunder squinted. There didn't seem to be other fish-folk here. Perhaps the kid didn't like to leave the sea. That could explain why there had been water inside the house.

As Dalf softy keened, Thunder tried to figure out what to do next. Should he stop one of the people that was running alone or speak to the group that kept giving the clouds nervous looks?

A cluster of people appeared in the distance. This group stood out from the others because the members were obviously ill or injured. A tall, frail, green haired creature and a shorter, sturdy-looking, dark haired apparition supported either side of a pitiful woman with honey-colored hair, who didn't look as if she could stand without assistance. A pair of pale, white haired ancients helped each other, while an amethyst-haired pair dragged a struggling fish-boy forward.

Yulder or another? Thunder squinted, but he couldn't be certain. The fish-boys were like trout, they all looked alike.

The injured woman stumbled, but the tall green one caught her and swooped her into his arms, like a babe and walked purposefully forward.

From behind him, Dalf screeched loud enough to break eardrums. "Mudder!" His high-pitched whistles rent the air. Thunder doubled over. "Mudder!" The fish-boy barreled past him as he clumsily sprinted toward the group.

He lurched to his feet and hobbled after the boy.

The rag-tag group halted. Dalf dashed straight into the tall man holding the woman. "Mudder!" They all fell into an ungainly heap.

Everyone's attention was on Dalf, their expressions proclaiming that they'd seen the dead rise. He studied the small group, trying to gauge their willingness to take him home and decided they were his best choice.

His only choice.

Chapter 19

Dalf.

Alive.

Healed.

For a moment, Raine stared, transfixed as she watched the dolphman running toward her, an expression of sheer bliss on his scarless face. She pushed away from Preston and Shay, who still seemed to be rooted to the dock. Her spine ached, but she stood straight and opened her arms wide to embrace the wonderful dream.

Dalf squealed with delight and hit her hard. The wind was knocked out of her as she pitched backward, landing against Preston and Shay. Dalf's slender arms wrapped around her in suffocating bands. A whistle of delight shrieked directly into her ear, just as everyone began to fall backward. Something hit the deck with the sound of a melon breaking. Raine hit the lumpy ground, hard. Someone screamed. Dalf's cry ended in a puff, as he landed on top of, driving the air out of her lungs.

She blacked out.

As she revived, hard restraints still encircled her waist. Dalf blubbered against her cheek and it seemed that everyone around her was either bawling or hysterical. She eased Dalf's arms loose, then rolled to her side and disentangled her aching leg from Preston. Beyond his shoulder, dragons danced among the clouds, their heat creating a rainbow of colors in the fluffy mist.

This was a very odd dream.

Dalf clung to her, as if he couldn't stand to be separated. The shrieks and screams from Annya and Coral were a perfect accompaniment to this bizarre vision. Preston appeared dazed, while Brock and Reed knelt next to Shay, his fingers feeling for a pulse. When Reed sat back on his heels, his hands in a helpless gesture, grief etched Brock's features.

Raine shook her head to clear her sight, but everyone was still there and the dragons still cavorted in the clouds.

Impossible. Dragons never entered Kalamar's atmosphere, it was too humid.

Preston had said, 'Forget him. He's already gone.' She knew he meant that he'd given into his fear of being discovered and had Dalf recycled. If she was seeing Dalf alive and well, perhaps she was dead, too. Perhaps they all were dead. Even, the warrior, who was standing behind Dalf, his posture protective, yet uncertain, looked perfectly healed. That, too, was impossible.

The only possibility was that the Guerreterre, who'd watched her save the warrior had somehow rescued and healed him and for some reason they'd saved and healed Dalf, too.

The intent to save and heal would explain why the shadow warrior she'd sensed following her had not attacked her, but that would make everything she had ever heard about Guerreterre and their culture a lie.

Despite aching temples, she tried to focus on the timeline. She'd been called back for extra duty, leaving the warrior alone when the mooncalves swarmed. She gritted her teeth. Had the entire mess that ended with the destruction of CRU-18 been a distraction to cover his rescue?

Why would they save Dalf, much less keep him?

Or maybe they were both dead. If so, why was she with Preston in the after life?

This was too unreal for explanation, but it felt good to hold Dalf's slick, sea salt embedded body, and hear him muttering intelligible sounds, instead of screaming with fear-based rage.

Even if Dalf had somehow been miraculously healed, this restricted area was the last place he'd come.

A warm breeze caressed her cheek.

"Mudder, you help Yulder ovum. I promised." A tiny bit of oxygen made it into her lungs. Hand trembling, she touched Dalf's sleek back. She knew she should be thrilled to hear his voice, after so many months, but why couldn't he pronounce T's?

The deep ocean scent of his skin mixed with salty shallows and heavy water. "Yulder?" She should be happy for this opportunity to touch him, but somehow this glimpse of the boy he should have been choked her with tears.

"Friend. He say dragons ruin world. Soon all wader like Doom Sea."

She closed her eyes tight against the threatening tears. Weren't things supposed to be perfect in the after life? Weren't they supposed to make sense? She caressed Dalf's sleek, scarless face. He felt completely healed. She opened her eyes. He looked whole, too.

Why was the warrior watching her as if everything depended upon her? He monitored her hands as if he wished they were moving over him. Heat surged through her and her hands stilled. She blinked away the thought, but the warrior was still there, large as life and desirable as freedom. Dalf burrowed tighter. She looked away from the mesmerizing warrior. Preston stared slack-jawed from Shay, who was lying motionless on the dock, to Dalf, to the warrior and back again, his expression looking as helpless and dumbstruck as she felt.

Why was she dreaming of Dalf as he should have been? Why was Annya weeping on Coral's shoulder? Why was Shay lying motionless as death, while Preston, Brock and Reed sat beside her doing nothing? The Guerreterran knelt and tenderly touched Shay's neck and closed his eyes. Preston raised his head, stared dumbfounded, then roared with rage and threw a punch at the warrior.

A near-by siren emitted a mind-numbing shriek. The tableau before her halted in mid-motion, except for the dragons, which had left their cloud games and were flying toward them.

Suddenly, everyone was running toward Command Headquarters' entrance. Brock picked up Shay and raced toward the mob. As the mob all tried to fit through the entrance at the same time, shoulders and bellies jammed and the throng became a heaving, vicious mass of terror.

Brock's steps faltered.

Annya looked like the only calm person as she surveyed the area. She grabbed Preston's wrist. "This way!" She dragged Preston toward the building's shaded wall. Reed clutched

Frazier's shoulder for support and lurched after them. Coral trailed her husband.

Dalf looked over his shoulder, screamed and fled.

The warrior looked at the herd of dragons, then grabbed her waist, tossed her over his shoulder and sprinted after everyone.

As if by magic, a slab of wall opened beneath Annya's palm. Dalf was the first one inside the building's dubious safety. The warrior's ground-eating pace halted a step inside the doorway. She slid to the ground while he stared at the walls as if he'd never seen a formed building before.

His attention was so complete, that if his protective arm had not been around her, she would have thought he'd forgotten her.

Brock brushed past them, Shay cradled in his arms, as if she was a sleeping babe instead of – Raine looked away and swallowed. She should never have been so judgmental.

Never would have been so judgmental, if she'd known how much Brock obviously cared.

Never would have been so judgmental if she'd know how little time any of them had.

She felt tears welling and averted her gaze. Preston was glaring at the warrior. Fists clenched he took a step forward, as if he wanted to commit murder. She stiffened and tilted her head up, but the warrior's attention was on Shay. Preston paused uncertainly.

Heat gushed through the open door. She looked out. The sky was golden with dragons, but now, instead of charging straight at the building, they were aimlessly soaring in circles over the misty waves. Raine shivered. The warrior hugged her closer. One mooncalf, wings spread wide, dipped low and swooped toward them.

Annya's palm hit a depression in the wall and the gap closed. "Let's get below the waterline."

The warrior readjusted his hold, cradling her as Brock did Shay. With long, purposeful strides, Annya led them to another hidden door.

"You know this building," Raine said.

Annya snorted. "I should." For a moment, there was only the sound of metal clanking with each footfall as she led them down a long winding staircase. With each step, the air seemed to grow more stagnant and cold. "Before all the problems, I was training to oversee eepyllihg production. Then, Marsha was sent here and started telling father stories. Soon after that, Latawba was attacked and we all basically became prisoners at The Pinnacle." Antagonism tinged her tone.

"Nowhere is safe from the dragons." The warrior's base tones rumbled against her ear.

"Or from Guerreterre," Preston snarled.

Annya paused and looked back. "Don't tell me you believe Marsha's stories!"

Preston frowned. "Don't you?" Doubt filled his voice.

Annya shrugged. "I guess that it was lucky for her that she was spending the year with us."

"No one could have survived the solar flare," the warrior said.

"What flare?" Annya asked.

"The one that burned Latawba. That is what you speak of, is it not?"

"Guerreterre's Shadow Warriors attacked my uncle's world. Where did you hear that it was a solar phenomena?"

"He's a Guerreterran," Preston growled.

Dalf's jaw flopped open. Frazier squealed with alarm. Startled, Annya stared at the warrior's face, then with a chuckle, she shook her head. "Good one, Doc." Dalf gave Preston a disgusted look.

"You don't believe me." Her brother looked astonished.

With a laugh, Annya shook her head and continued down the endless stairs. Raine gazed at her back for several steps, then looked up at the one person who had refused to leave her behind on the dock. What had Annya seen in him that made her think he was other than what he was?

The flight of steps finally ended at a door. When Annya wrenched the handle, it swung outward amid a chorus of wailing hinges. She stepped into the darkness with confidence. With a sweep of her hand, the lights came on. Ornate tapestries covered the walls with a vibrant pictorial history of how dragons had brought change to the frozen world, starting with the exploding sun, through how the fragment had been caught in Kalamar's orbit. Other tapestries showed the world changing from ice to water. And others showed the various stages of technology of eepyllihg production, which had brought not only heat, but unimaginable wealth. As Annya and Brock walked across the room the sound of their steps were lost in the thick, plush carpet.

The warrior stepped into the room and looked around with interest. Preston, Coral and Reed crowded the doorway, their expressions stunned.

"Well, are you coming or not?" Annya asked.

Pace hesitant, Coral entered the opulent room. When Preston and Reed entered, Dalf and Frazier squealed in amazement, then reverently closed the door behind themselves. Though the side facing the stairway had been worn metal, the interior was of costly wood, which had been carved and polished until it was a valuable work of art.

"Whose home is this?" Reed asked.

"No one's," Annya said. "It's just a place my family keeps in case of emergency and I figure that the situation above got as close to that as it can get."

Reed stared at the deep, soft crimson cushions, which sprinkled the golden carpet. Coral gripped his hand, as if she couldn't believe what she was seeing.

Neither could Raine. The lavish room made her bubble home look like the recycled refuse that it was, but the comparison between this hidden place and the dank dungeon-like place where Reed and Coral had been hiding was beyond words. If Annya knew about this sanctuary, why hadn't she let Coral and Reed D'nor hide here? Raine's molars ground together so tightly that her jaw ached. She looked away from Annya, who obviously didn't care about how old bones could ache in the damp and stared at a wall-hanging, which depicted the first Vole d'Laire using the power of the dragons to nudge Vilecom into orbit around the ice-covered world.

Preston sidled by the warrior and went to Brock, who looked too dazed to think. He gently helped him to lay Shay on a cushion. Her blue-black hair cascaded over the crimson cloth like a dark halo. As if no longer able to stand without her in his arms, Brock knelt next to her and wept. Tears clogged Raine's throat, too. The warrior seemed to sense her despair and placed her next to her sister. Preston got out of striking distance and kept a distrustful eye on the warrior.

Dalf crowded past the warrior and snuggled next to her. She hugged him with one arm and caressed Shay's cold cheek with the other. He twittered softly, as he shared her grief. Raine lost her fight for dignity and began crying. He embraced her. "I sorry for you, Mudder."

Sorry for her? Shay was the dead one. And Brock was the one whose world seemed to have ended. Shay had been right, he truly loved her. To have someone care for you like that was a miracle.

A touch, warm and gentle as a summer shower moved down her spine. It stopped at the small of her back. The heat expanded until it encompassed her and soothing sensations rippled through her core. At last, the strange dream was over and a new one had begun.

*C*hapter 20

Thunder tried not to jolt the woman, who was his key to returning home, as he allowed his healing touch to melt into her. He closed his eyes, senses stretched to discover her injuries. The cartilage and ribs were easily mended, but it was time consuming. The fractured jawbone had begun healing wrong, so it was trickier. Her legs had suffered the worst damage, but for some reason, no healing had begun. As he tried to reconstruct her torn thigh muscle, a torn tendon whipped free from his will. He grasped it, again, but it snapped free a second time.

He focused on inner peace before he tried a third time.

Gradually, an intense heat of affection suffused his being. He greeted Kazza, grateful that the great cat had come. He joined his power with the Kazza's, his fatigue falling away. The tendon slithered into place and adhered to its torn end. The abused cells were restored and the poisons in her system were nullified.

"Hurry home." Kazza's plea rumbled through his conscious. "Time is short."

Thunder shuddered awake, only to realize that the floor was shaking. He opened his eyes to darkness populated by the ghostly shapes of dragons and far away worlds.

ooo

Raine gasped as icy water replaced the loving heat. Spirit, she was still in the impossible room and the warrior was looking at her as if she was the most important person in the world. A wall-rattling discharge shook the darkened room; more water spurted into her face. She rolled aside and faced a glowing dragon wearing an ancient reclamation array.

Someone screamed. Dalf wailed.

"What was that?" Preston screamed.

"The defense blaster." Annya sounded worried.

"Will you take me home?" The warrior's soft, tender voice presented a bizarre contrast to the wet chaos surrounding them.

"Because time is short?" Raine asked, then frowned, wondering where that question had come from.

Abruptly, the room ceased shaking and the lights turned on. She swiped water out of her eyes and blinked at the lingering phosphorescent glow of the dragon on the tapestry. Slowly, she turned to the warrior and silently dared him to explain the insistent, large and impossibly furry thing she had sensed humming inside her. When he didn't speak, she demanded, "What did you do to me?"

"If you hurt her, I'll murder you," Preston blustered.

The warrior glanced at her brother as if he was as insignificant as a grain of rice, then turned to her. "I need you. You are the only one who can help me."

What a ludicrous statement. "You don't need me. You need my ship."

He put his palms upward in a curiously helpless gesture. "I would not know what to do."

"And I can't even walk." She raised her injured leg, as she made the statement, then when there was no pain, she ripped aside the tattered fabric of her uniform to display undamaged flesh. Her jaw dropped.

He raised a curiously sensual brow, daring her to deny the cure. Raine shook her head, as she tried to clear it of this bizarre dream. Dalf cuddled against her side in an effort to sooth her. She looked from his healed face to the warrior's perfect abs. This was impossible, but real. "You're a murderer," she whispered.

Confusion marred his handsome features. "I am a healer. I only kill when there is no other choice."

His attire branded him as a mass murderer, but his actions identified him as a miracle worker. She waved her hands with perplexity.

Annya cleared her throat, then apparently not knowing what to say, remained quiet.

"Colonel Atano-" Raine pinched her healed leg and then touched Dalf's face. The warrior/physician tilted his head to the side, waiting for her to continue. "Your uniform-" A drop of water fell.

Annya looked at the ceiling above them. "This bunker was designed to withstand everything, even global annihilation," she shook her head, "but our own defenses are ruining it." She turned to the warrior/physician. "You aren't from Guerreterre, as the doctor claims." He shook his head. "Then where?"

"Chatterre."

Annya frowned. "Do we ship eepyhillg there?"

"I do not know this word." The building shuddered and groaned, then everything was quiet. Gooseflesh rippled over her skin as she looked around the ornate room and wondered what bothered her. She glanced around. Water was oozing into the room around the door jam and the door seemed to be bowing into the chamber. She gulped. This room would be her final resting place. A lump formed in her throat.

"Chatterre?" Annya asked. "Where is that?"

He looked stupefied, then pointed past her shoulder to a tapestry, which depicted a crimson comet flying away from a molten-red asteroid field. If she ignored the colors, it did appear to be where she had found him.

Coral clasped her hands and stared at the warrior, as if she was looking at a god. "The Ancient sorcerers wore the feathers of the bird of glory in their hair to mark them." A trembling finger rose to hover a foot away from one of his thin, intricate braids, with its cluster of tiny feathers. "It was said that they all died for their irreverence and disbelief in science."

"We've always known some survived," Reed said, as he put a supportive arm around his wife. "The Vole d'Laire line has always had a similar, but lesser ability. This helped them hold the seat of power for centuries."

"How did you know?" Annya asked. Reed shrugged. "That was supposed to be a secret."

"Marsha never took any pains to hide it," Reed said. "And once I realized how she manipulated others, everything fell into place."

Annya frowned. "I always thought her spells were my imagination." Reed shook his head. Annya's expression suggested barely contained murderous rage. It was lucky that Marsha had died in the attack.

"If you aren't Colonel Atano, who are you?" Raine whispered.

"Thunder."

"Thunder." He seemed more like the powerful boom before the sky split than someone who lurked in the shadows. The name fit. "I am Raine."

"Will you take me home?"

She looked down. The water was at least two inches deep and rising. She touched her ribs, intending to explain how her injuries prevented her, but they felt fine. Raine inhaled deeply. No pain. She inhaled, again, then shook her head.

Annya lightly touched his forearm. "Please, can you help us?" Raine looked at the visibly bulging door and blinked back tears, as she realized that Annya didn't yet understand that she had led them to their death. Annya continued looking at Thunder as if he held the answers and that for him, raising the dead was nothing.

He raised a brow. "This chamber not meant to hold water?"

Annya blinked with confusion, then gestured to Brock, who was holding Shay's dead hand as if it was a lifeline. "Can you help her?"

"She's dead. No one can help her," Preston snarled.

Raine winced.

"Even The Zar couldn't raise the dead," Preston sneered. Her brother had always used anger as a cloak to hide his fear.

Thunder barely spared her sister a glance. "There is still a thread of life."

Sure there was.

Preston snorted, Brock kept his face averted, but his shoulders began to shake. Raine shook her head. "Even if we could get out of here and I could get to my ship and get airborne, I couldn't abandon my duty. Especially now." Her voice seemed loud in the silence.

He grimaced. "You must save your world, as I must save mine."

She thought of the barren ash-covered planetoid and shivered. Even Kalamar, with its moon of doom and doubtful possibilities of survival was better than that miserable cinder.

"Please?"

"Kalamar is much better than that barren ruin of a world where I found you."

He sighed and shrugged. "Solterre is only the portal." Thunder sighed. "If I hadn't given into the temptation of seeing the destruction the dragons did to the old world." He frowned as he shook his head.

She blinked. "Mooncalves don't destroy worlds, you Guerreterrans do." Did he expect her, of all people, to believe such nonsense? "Now, I grant you, they might damage leaky freighters, but they've never destroyed-"

"Yes, they have. A millennium ago, they attacked Solterre's sun and the flares scorched all living things on it. More recently, they attacked Latawba and it, too, burned."

"That's a lie! The Guerreterrans destroyed it."

He crossed his arms over his chest and shook his head.

"You're a Guerreterran, of course you're willing to lie for your people."

He shook his head. "I do not lie. A Royden freight ship watched the dragons attack Latawba's sun and made a memory of the flares that burned that world. It was like seeing what my ancestors went through." He shook his head, as if forcing himself to focus on the present instead of a happy memory.

She stared at him, unwilling to believe his story, because if she did, it meant that The Zar had willfully murdered Gornt and maimed Dalf. She glanced at Annya and Brock. How much did they know?

"So there is proof of the duplicity." Reed's tone was grave.

"You believe him?" Raine demanded.

"At the time, there were rumors." His mouth flattened. "But they were quickly silenced." He sighed. "I always harbored suspicions, especially when I heard how many bakufus were recruited for the mission, and knew that none had returned."

"Dalf returned." She gestured to him, as he crouched in the now shin-deep water and quietly whistled and clicked with Frazier.

Annya stared at Reed. "I was responsible for procuring uniforms for the bakufus." Her face paled. "Until the battle for Latawba, they had never gone into space and our standard uniforms would not adapt to their physiology." She looked at Dalf and Frazier as if seeing them for the first time. "I never knew. I just accepted father's word that they were the workers that we could afford to send, but what if he meant that-" She put her hand to her mouth.

Reed eyed Dalf. "He couldn't have gone, he's too young." Reed's mouth flattened. "Besides, any that returned were recycled."

Raine scrambled off the cushion, glared Reed straight in the eye and hitched up her chin. "Unless they had a guardian who heard about the planned euthanasia, faked the paperwork and snatched the victim."

"You?" Reed asked. Raine gave a short nod and watched Annya out of the corner of her eye. Reed gasped. "But how?"

"You make a habit of abducting injured people," Thunder said.

"I do not," she snapped. He raised a brow and grinned at her. Raine's mind went to mush and her attention focused on his lips. His smile widened. Did he know how he affected her? She squared her shoulders. "Would you rather that I had left you there to die?" He winced. "Besides, your robot forced me to take you at gunpoint."

"What robot?" Annya blinked than turned on Thunder. "Who are you?"

"What gun?" Preston stared at Raine.

"You jeopardized your life to save an egg-layer?" Reed stared at her in shock.

"Dalf is more than a label." She glared at Reed, but watched her brother out of the corner of her eye. His rigid stance melted, he took a step toward her and gently, then more firmly felt her ribs. His fingers began to shake, making it difficult to win the staring battle with Reed.

Abruptly, Preston plummeted to his knees and water splashed to her thighs. "What's wrong?" Coral asked. Preston tried to answer, but only managed a 't-t-t-t' sound. Unsteadily he pointed at her. Coral swatted Reed on the arm. "Quit acting childish. She's hurt; she needs rest, not a gawking contest with you."

"I'm fine," Raine assured her. She stood up, stretched and then pirouetted to prove her point. Dear, Spirit, she really was fine!

Coral, Annya, Preston and Reed all appeared to have had the same revelation, because they were looking at Thunder, with saucer-wide eyes. He was looking back at them as if he wanted to escape.

With a high-pitched screech, the door crashed inward and a wave of water surged over them. It swept everything out of its path and slammed her back against the far wall. After a moment, the water rushed back toward the stairwell, Raine dropped to her knees, gasping for breath. Thunder knelt next to Shay, feeling her floating body, as if seeing with his fingers. Everyone else either appeared stunned or was fighting their way free of cushions and tapestries.

As the water lunged back and forth, searching for its level, Thunder calmly placed his hands on Shay's head and closed his eyes.

Brock struggled to his feet, saw Thunder, and roared with rage and staggered toward him. The warrior ignored the coming attack. Raine pushed away from the wall and tackled Brock. He fought her. She hit him in the solar plexus, then pinned him. As she straddled his abdomen and held down his arms, she put her face inches above his. "If you love my sister, let him alone."

He shook his head and fought like a man possessed.

"Stop it!" Annya said. Brock still thrashed in the deepening water. If he didn't settle down, so she could let him up, it would soon cover his face. Annya shoved her aside. When her twin started to get up, she kicked him back down. "I said, stop it." Her furious tone got his attention.

Brock blinked up at her, as if seeing through a thick fog. "He's touching her."

"Unless I miss my guess, he's one of the ancient line. Give him a chance to heal her."

"T-t-th-the ancient l-line?" Preston asked.

Raine stared down at her perfectly healed body and her throat went dry. Then, she looked at Brock, realized she'd attacked a Vole d'Laire and felt faint.

While the water leveled out, everyone silently watched healthy color seep back into Shay's cheeks.

With a rumbling boom, the ceiling split open in an evil smile. "Don't those fools realize what the defense blaster is doing to the building?" Annya grabbed Brock's arm and moved as fast as possible, in the rising water, toward the stairwell.

Preston, Coral, Reed, Dalf and Frazier were close behind her.

The ceiling groaned, as if a giant was waking from a long slumber, but only dust drizzled from the gaping crack. Raine stared upward for a mind-numbing moment, then looked at Shay and Thunder, who were oblivious to the impending doom, and at the gaping maw, where the rest had fled. If she could get out of here, she could help her team control the dragons. Or she could stay here and hope that Thunder saved her sister before the building collapsed and crushed them all.

"Follow me to Nambaba."

Raine ran toward the stairwell. When she got out of the sucking grip of the water, she took the stairs three at a time, but the building shuddered from another blast, nearly knocking her down.

Chapter 21

Thunder soothed away the angry swelling at the base of the female's skull. Then, he willed the broken fragments of bone back into place. He paused, waiting to feel Kazza's presence, but all he sensed was water. It was the main thing he'd perceived since coming to this wet place. He shivered, then focused on the gray conduits and injured portions of the girl's mind. Though her physiology was closer to that of his Tribe than Dalf's had been, there were several unfamiliar parts. It would have been better if Kazza did this, but Thunder took a deep breath and persevered.

A wet chill felt as if the water was engulfing him. This would have panicked him, if not for the past three days, which made it seem irrelevant. He pushed away the sensation and began repairing the damaged blood vessels. Then, still ignoring the sense of saturation, Thunder meticulously restored each cell, pausing as he contemplated the complex structure at the base of her skull, where her anatomy was unfamiliar. Raine claimed this girl as her sister and while they shared some outward attributes, their circulatory and nerve patterns had many differences. The term sister must mean psychological bonding, instead of shared parents.

As he contemplated Shay's nerve system, a loud groan made the floor beneath his feet shudder. He jerked free from his healing trance. Water was waist deep and rising to engulf spray from cracks in the walls. The ceiling moaned like the voice of doom and began to buckle. He grasped Shay around her mid-section and hastened toward the gaping doorway. Something heavy splashed behind him. A surge hit his back and slammed him against the cold metal stairs. He threw Shay over his shoulder and sprinted upward.

A resounding crash filled the circular stairwell with mist-laden dust. The staircase shuddered, as if it was a tree about to fall. He tightened his grasp on Shay and took the steps three at a time.

He dashed outside. Within two paces, scalding, humid mist enveloped him and brought him to his knees. Shay slithered from his shoulder and sprawled over the hard, broken surface. He doubled over. Face to fractured flooring he fought for breath. It got easier when he put his arm over his nose, but it took all his willpower to push himself up and look around the broken landscape. The dragons swarming in the clouds probably accounted for the heat, but what had shattered everything?

If the dragons had touched the land, it would be scorched.

In the distance small clusters of people congregated just outside the edge of an impenetrable fog layer. The unpredictable climate of this wet world was beyond belief, Raine had to take him home. He touched Shay's sweat-soaked cheek and willed her to awaken. When her strange lash-less eyes opened, he mustered every ounce of willpower and struggled to his feet.

"What happened?" she said. "Where am I?"

"You fell." He held out a hand to her. "We must find the others." Even after she was on her feet, she held his hand. Her webbed hand felt small and fragile in his grasp. "Do you know which way we should go? They'd spoken of going to Nambaba."

"I never thought Brock would run."

Thunder arched a brow, but Shay ignored his confusion and pulled him toward a dense patch of haze. Though he'd expected it to be cooler in the cloud, it was hot as steam. "What happened here?" she gasped.

"This isn't normal?"

She shook her head, then plowed deeper into the dense shroud until only the purplish blur of her hair was visible. For what seemed like an eternity, the only constants in the murky haze were the steady pull of Shay's grip and his escalating sense of doom, Then suddenly they'd rejoined the group and she shook free of him and hurtled toward one of the taller lavender haired ones, but it was impossible to tell male from female in the mist. "I thought you'd left planet without me."

"Shay? It can't be." His voice reached a pitch that rivaled the chorus of shrill delight emitted by Yulder.

"Shay?" Reed's white hair was nearly invisible in the cloying mist. His thin, pale hands reached toward her, as Brock, who'd previously been the most attentive one shrank away. She swatted Reed's hands away. "How dare you leave me alone!" She didn't take her gaze off Brock, as she walked toward him.

"But, but, but I thought you were dead."

"Dead? How do you expect to rule a planet when you can't tell a faint from death?" Shay demanded.

"He's right," Preston said. "You smashed the back of your head when you fell." He reached out and touched her nape. "I don't understand."

"Did he heal you?" Raine asked as she emerged from the gloom.

"I don't know." Shay peered back at him. "Could you do such a thing?"

"It isn't difficult," Thunder said as he stepped forward. He touched Raine's hand. "I have given you back what you wanted. Now, will you return me to my home?"

Claw-like fingers gripped his bicep. "You can't take him. I must study him." D'nor's sparse white hair hung in dripping tendrils around his shoulders.

Thunder plucked away the man's hand. "This is not about what you want. I must leave."

"We all need to leave," Raine said. "The orbit of Vilecom has deteriorated and it's only a matter of hours before it enters the atmosphere and everything is vaporized."

"Then you will come home with me?" The idea pleased him.

"No!" Dalf shrilled.

"Don't argue," Raine said. "Come with me."

"No. I stay," Dalf said.

"You can't," she said.

"You drive dragons." Dalf made a sweeping motion with his arm. "Save ovum. Save world."

If only it were that simple. Raine opened her mouth to explain the situation to him, but the complete trust in his miraculously restored eyes made it impossible to tell him that Thunder had saved him only to watch this world he loved die.

"This is my home world," Dalf said. "I not leave."

Frazier squared his narrow shoulders. "Nor will I."

The two bakufus looked at each other, as if each expected the other to speak for the pair.

Then the male with the lavender hair reached toward Shay. "You haven't been returned to me to simply die, again. I will leave." He turned to the dolphman. "If there is any way to save this world for you, I will find it."

The green one grabbed the arms of the two old ones. "We will take the alien with us. Reed, you will have all the time you wish to study him." He turned to Raine. "How much longer before Nambaba surfaces and we can leave?"

She tilted her head. "Listen." It sounded like a huge caldron was boiling just beyond the dense fog layer. "Follow me." Single file, seven of them trouped down the inclined ramp.

"Aren't you coming, Annya?" Shay asked the amethyst haired woman.

"No. I will stay here and try to get back to The Pinnacle. It is where I should be."

Shay gave her a quick hard hug. "Be safe."

She nodded. "Take care of Brock. And remember me."

"If there's any way-" Shay was unable to finish the thought, but Annya seemed to understand. They clung together for a final embrace.

Thunder turned away from the emotional scene and followed Raine. When they jumped from the solid surface to a slick rounded log-like form, he teetered, then caught his balance and jogged after her. Something dark, like the opening of a cave, appeared in the distance. She didn't slow as she sprinted toward it. Four paces later, he entered the chilled shadows. Gooseflesh covered him. He gasped with mixed shock and relief.

"At least the heat hasn't saturated the water completely," Raine said. "Of course, the long delay only prolongs the inevitable."

"You knew it was coming," Preston said.

Raine nodded in agreement.

"Statistically, this shouldn't have happened for four more years," the old, pale man said.

"Reed kept telling me this would happen," Coral babbled, "but until we actually came out and saw it-" She ended her statement with a shudder.

"Everyone, find a secure spot." Raine touched a bumpy panel and a set of thick doors thumped shut behind them. Suddenly it was pitch-black. Coral shrieked. "Sorry about that," Raine said. The walls began to glow. "I forget that I'm the only one who is used to walking around here in the dark."

"Oh, thank you, dear," Coral said. "I really don't know why the dark should scare me, not after spending so many months in the tunnels, but it does. My, it's cold in here." Reed put his arm around her, and guided her toward an oddly bent door.

Shay took his hand. "Come. I'll show you my favorite place to stow away." She winked at Raine. "Take off is like magic." With him in one hand and Brock in her other, she ushered them down a dark narrow corridor until she arrived at an area filled with misty light. "We have to brace ourselves." She sat down with her back against one wall.

Brock hurried to sit next to her, but Thunder was more interested in the wall's odd material. It seemed to be the same as that of the bed chamber, only in these walls, swirling mist was the artist's topic.

"Sit," Shay said. "We'll catapult off any minute."

Brock pushed his back against the wall and pressed his feet against the opposite wall, in what could be some sort of attack position. Thunder sat down facing them; hand casually draped over his bent knee.

"Copy Brock." Shay thrust her feet against the opposite wall just as the entire tube began to shake.

Thunder did just that. A moment later the area was yanked upward. A heartbeat after that, it moved down and sideways.

"Isn't this a charge?" Shay's eyes gleamed with delight.

Thunder's stomach declared that he'd found something worse than boats.

The incredible movement continued. Worse, the speed increased. He'd never encountered anything like it, not even when he controlled the weather or did a spirit journey. He shut his eyes, against the pressure, but that only made it worse. When he opened them, again, the clouds were beneath them and they were moving faster than any bird alive across a panorama of clouds and water. Icy perspiration trickled into his eyes.

"Yeeehoohaaaa!" Shay screamed. "Here come the echo marshes." Beneath them, waving vegetation replaced the waves. "Oh, I hate this part." No sooner had solid blackness replaced the green, but the path turned straight up and the speed increased as if the thing they were in had been released from its tether. The force relentlessly moved them downward, until he became certain they would end up in a mass of crushed cells. Then, just as suddenly, the pressure was gone.

Shay giggled and floated upward. She rolled onto her stomach and grinned down at them. "What are you waiting for?" She somersaulted backward and shrieked with glee.

Brock drifted upward, as if people flying were an every day occurrence, instead of something the Chose learned to do in a spirit journey.

Thunder gulped. Perhaps he was in a deep trance and only believed this was real.

"Oh!" Shay clasped her hands over her heart. "This is my favorite part." Brock soared to her side and they gazed at something beyond the barrier. "So beautiful. So deadly." They clasped hands.

It was just like the molten orb that GEA-4 had shown him, and several of the weavings had depicted only now, it was perilously close to the blue and white orb. "Why was it moved?" Thunder asked. "There are safer ways to control the weather."

Brock swiveled toward him. "The orbit decayed, but it shouldn't have happened this soon."

"I heard that when the dragons started drawing close to the surface, they altered the balance."

Thunder frowned. "Dalf told me his mother was a dragon shepherd. Are we here to watch as she herds them back to the moon and they push it back on course?"

Shay laughed. "I doubt it. I mean she's good, but no one could do that."

"Too bad we can't because if they hit perfectly, it could work," Brock said.

"If herding them won't work, perhaps you could bait them," Thunder offered. Even as he said it, he shuddered at the memory of the dragon, which had invaded Chatterre, and what Nimri had endured after she'd volunteered to lure the beast into their impossibly inadequate trap. There had to be a better way. His insides quaked at the thought of attempting anything like what she'd done. But she'd done it for the entire Tribe and hadn't thought of her own sacrifice. He clamped his jaws together. Or had she?

He would never know.

"I wonder why she's staying in orbit," Brock said.

"Are you complaining about this gorgeous scenery?" Shay asked.

"When the moon crashes, this won't be safe."

"So all will be lost and this world of yours will die like Latawba and Solterre." Thunder stared at the other pair. "And you will do nothing to prevent it."

"I would if I could." Brock's tone was defensive.

"But you do not bother to look for a way." Thunder had never met such an indifferent man. "You would allow your sister and everyone else that you love to die while you save yourself."

Brock hugged Shay close, as if proclaiming that he'd saved her, when in fact, he'd left her behind.

Shay leaned away from him and stared at Thunder. "Could you do something?" He doubted it. She sighed and said, "Someone should at least try to force the dragons to bump the moon back."

She looked at the stationary view. "Perhaps that's why we've stopped. Maybe D'nor would know how to do it."

"We have a chance. We must save ourselves while we can." With that, Brock propelled himself up the odd corridor in a swimming motion. Shay and Thunder followed.

Chapter 22

As Nambaba orbited Kalamar, Raine listened to the garbled transmissions from Otami's blue unit. The screen reflected her face as she watched their attempts to maneuver the frantically moving beasts meet with defeat. It didn't look like they were trying hard. She sighed; they know all is lost. She shook her head, and realized the thought was as much for herself as it was for Otami.

The radio's talk was as useless for finding a way to save Dalf as the argument Preston and Reed were having about ways to save their loved ones trapped on the planet's heating surface. A glance at Brock's bored expression made her wonder if the Vole d'Laires cared for any of the people, or only for their profits. Even the way Shay's hand was clenched looked resigned. Raine knew that if she were Godhead and had the power to put her profits into saving the people, she would. She didn't realize she'd spoken the thought aloud until a pained look flickered across Brock's face.

"If I could do something, I would. But our best scientists have been working on this since I reached puberty and with all that time and all their intelligence, they haven't found a way." He sighed. Shay patted his hand. "If a way could have been bought, it would have been."

Shay nodded. "Marsha once confided in me that the treasury's assets were being invested off-planet so that the funds would be safe for something like this." Her slender hand gestured to the monitor. "But I think they all expected to have enough time to arrange transportation off-planet."

Raine believed the story despite the way Brock rolled his gaze upward.

"Did anyone ever look for a new planet? One where all three of our species could live?" Shay's eyes widened and her jaw dropped. She slowly shook her head. "Just as I thought," Raine said. Some situations simply were destined for disaster and she needed to learn to accept tragedy.

"It was an untruth meant to stop the people from worrying," Brock said. "If workers are distracted, production goes down."

"It really goes down when they're dead," Raine snapped.

Pure static hissed from the radio. A glance showed that Nambaba's flight path was over Headquarters. Were Dalf and Frazier still there, confident that their world would be saved? She tried to swallow the lump of tears in her throat.

Preston turned away from Reed, and glared at her. Red spots on his pale face and shiny eyes made him look ill. "Is there some reason why we're still in orbit?"

"She's trying to think of a way to stop this disaster," Reed said, as he patted Preston's shoulder. "Let her alone. You can run and save yourself later." Preston shook off Reed's calming touch.

"That may be too late," Coral said. "Please, dear, can we at least get behind Ishdoo? Surely it would provide a shield when Vilecom crashes. Don't you think that would be a good idea, dear?" she asked Reed.

"Once Vilecom enters the atmosphere, nowhere in the galaxy will be safe."

Not even in a bakufus' sacred nursery under the waves.

"If I'd known the orbit would decay so quickly," Reed said, "I would have insisted that The Zar make the calculations for nudging it a priority."

"What good would that do when we've lost the technology to do it?" Preston asked.

"It can't be that difficult," Reed said. "Look at the antiquated technology they used to move it here."

Coral patted her mate's arm, while she addressed Preston. "Don't bother arguing with him, dear boy. He's believed that the technology to move the moon was a simple thing as long as I've known him." She glared at Preston's scoffing expression. "How often have you known him to be wrong?"

"I should have done something years ago." Reed looked ready to cry.

"You weren't assigned to that team," Brock said. "If you'd tried to assist, father would have been unhappy."

Raine muted the radio's static garble and focused on their conversation. "Don't blame yourself. The moon was brought here a thousand years ago. That's when the problem started. The scientists back then should have foreseen and altered the orbit while they still had the skill."

"I doubt if they had technology to calculate so many years into the future. And there's no way they could have foreseen the results." Reed's face was getting alarmingly red. "They viewed this world as a temporary refuge while they scouted for a more hospitable world to settle. They couldn't have envisioned that the moon they captured to warm the ice would be more than a temporary refuge."

"There, there, dear." Coral rubbed Reed's back. "What is done is done. We must deal with today's choices, not what may or may not have been a choice a millennium ago."

Raine nodded. "That's right."

"But the choices should have been made then," Reed bellowed.

"They weren't," Coral said. "Is there anything we can do now?"

"Maybe," Brock said. Thunder stood behind him and nodded. How long had he been standing there?

Raine's heart skipped a beat and a kernel of hope sprouted.

"I gave my word to help Yulder save his ovum," Thunder said. He didn't look very happy about that.

Preston's face went red with rage. "You can't save the embryos any more than we could save the bakufus, themselves." He spun to face her, his expression threatening. "At least we're saving ourselves, or we would if my sister would do her job and get out of here before everything explodes."

Her brother had been a factor of her life since she was four, but for the first time, she understood why she'd had to force herself to care for him. "You've never cared for anyone but yourself, have you?"

He looked ready to hit her.

"She's right," Shay said. "Getting me the job with Marsha was about yourself and showing everyone your influence. It wasn't about what I wanted or finding me a position that would make me happy."

"Are you trying to tell me you didn't like it?" Preston demanded.

"I didn't at first. I thought – never mind. This isn't about the past, like Coral says, it's about the choices we make now."

Preston glared at her. "Is that what you think? That I only care about myself? If that was true why did I endanger my life for that spawn of Gornt's?"

"I don't know," Raine said. "But I doubt if your personal goal was saving Dalf from recycling." Since he'd helped her, he'd acted like he owned her.

He glared at her.

Shay shook her head. "Don't lie to yourself. Everything you do is for yourself or your advancement. That makes you a pitiful person. Dalf is a hundred times better than you." She turned to Raine. "Thunder thinks that if the shepherds controlled the dragons, they could push the moon back on course."

"I asked if that was why you were staying here," Thunder said. "Is such a thing possible?"

"Why would you think it would work?" Reed looked intrigued.

"Because I explained that the dragons suicidal attraction for the surface had nudged the moon off orbit ahead of schedule," Brock said.

Reed's look turned inward. Everyone became quiet as they watched him think. Slowly, he nodded. "It could work."

"But it's too dangerous to stay here," Preston said.

"And it's 100% fatal for those we left behind if we do nothing," Reed said. "As long as there is a chance-"

"You would kill us all for a chance to save some worthless bakufus?" Preston bellowed.

"My father and sister are down there, too," Brock said.

"But how are we supposed to herd the dragons if they're in the atmosphere?" Raine asked. "I can't take Nambaba in and out of the vapor layers as if it's some sort of sailfish."

"Won't they follow you?" Thunder frowned as he wondered where that bizarre idea had come from.

Raine swallowed. "That's only happened to me once. How could you have possibly known about it?"

He stared at her intense expression and shrugged. "It is how farmers lure cows."

"What's a k-ow?"

"This is irrelevant," Preston said. "And since there's no real way to get the dragons back up here, let alone push the moon, we need to decide where we'll seek sanctuary."

Unless Reed had a plan, her brother had a point.

"They are beasts used for milk, meat and leather," Thunder said. "But some like to play a game with the young ones and shake a table-covering in front of them. This makes them charge. Later, they use the technique to bring them home from the fields."

K-ows? Fields? The man was desirable as a dream and silly as a hum-dum fish.

"That could work," Reed exclaimed. He grabbed the arm of Raine's captain's chair and gazed at her control panel. "What do you use to lure them?"

She blinked. In her entire career, she'd never considered such a thing, yet she'd seen it done every shift for the past twenty years. "Shepherds don't call them; the CRUs do." Could the Crystalline Reclamation Units save them? A kernel of hope sprouted within her.

"Myst lures dragons," Thunder said. He looked as if he'd lost his best friend along with his mind.

"So that's why the dragons are lured to the sea!" Shay's expression looked as if she'd had a revelation. "But if they're already so close to so much mist, how do we get them away?"

Thunder shook his head. "The mist you speak of is fog. I speak of the essence." He cleared his throat. "Dragons consume a person's spirit."

"How dare you insinuate that you know more about dragons than I do! Do you have dragons on your world?" He shook his head. Rage continued to grow within Raine. "I've tended them since I was a child, and you have only been here for a few days, yet you claim to know how to handle them and what they eat."

"One attacked our world," Thunder said.

Raine held up a single finger. "One." She gestured toward the planet below them, which was a mass of swirling mist and golden flashes. "One?" She raised her brow.

He nodded, apparently unconcerned by her sarcasm.

Reed stepped between her and Thunder. "Be still and listen to the sorcerer. His kind are experts on this sort of thing."

Preston roared with rage. "Quit talking, turn this ship around and get us out of here." He lunged toward her. "Before the moon crashes."

"You will live or die with the rest of us," Raine said

Preston leaped at his sister. Brock grabbed him before he could strike her, then shifted his grip to resemble one a mother cat took with her kits. Though Preston seemed helpless, the expression in his eyes screamed of fear, rage, and death to anyone who came between him and escape.

Then, Thunder casually touched his neck and Preston crumpled to the floor. Though the way he'd touched Preston's neck had seemed gentle, her brother looked dead.

"You killed him!"

Thunder shook his head. "I merely calmed him."

"If you say so," Raine snapped. If he could heal Dalf and Shay, and calm her brother with a mere touch, the least she could do was listen. "Tell me what you think we should do."

They all looked at Thunder as if he was about to tell them the secrets of the universe.

How had he suddenly become the expert on dragons? They were the ones that kept the monsters for pets. "If I try to move the beasts, will you take me home?"

"If you are successful in moving the moon." Raine gave him a challenging look.

Assuming he managed to survive, he was going to live to regret this.

Thunder inclined his head. "So be it, but I need another person with me to release the myst. Are you willing?" He looked Raine in the eye, expecting her to back out, but she held his gaze and inclined her head in agreement.

Chapter 23

Having people staring at them with a mixture of hope and fear distracted them from focusing their concentration enough to succeed, so Thunder and Raine returned to the area Shay loved best. Raine swiveled to face him and appeared unruffled by the fact that they were hovering in space even before releasing their myst.

"Why did you choose me?" she asked.

"You are used to the dragons and know their ways. You are also calm." His answer seemed to satisfy her. "We begin by creating a circle with our arms and clearing our minds of worry." He showed her the traditional grip. A jolt of desire passed over him. She looked from their joined hands to his face, her expression unfathomable. Had she felt it, too? He cleared his throat. "Next, we clear our minds of conscious thought." Her trusting look never left his face. Desire to take her into his arms and kiss her nearly overwhelmed him.

Awful as her world was, it was tempting to stay, just for the chance to look at her and imagine kissing her lush lips.

If I am to get home, I must get past the attraction I feel for this woman.

He closed his eyes and began humming a hypnotic tone.

For several moments, he sensed Raine watching his face, then she, too closed her eyes and began to hum the ritual tone. Gradually, he shed his desires, concerns and fears. Then, the myst separated and he soared free of his cumbersome human form. He opened his eyes and looked toward the planet. The dragons were beginning to stop their aimless movements and some were returning to the heavens.

Raine's myst began its faltering separation.

"You are doing well," he assured her. The only one who could compare to her for first time skill was Nimri.

"This feels strange, more like a dream than reality."

"Dreams bring us close." Her myst detached from her physical form. "Are you ready?"

Eyes wide she shook her head and stared past him. "What is that?" Thunder looked over his shoulder.

Alert amber eyes peered at them from under thick black ear tufts. Kazza hovered outside their chamber, the tip of his tail tapping with impatience. "This is my dear friend, Kazza. He is the one with true healing powers," Thunder said.

The great cat rolled his whiskers and showed his enormous pointed teeth. Raine gasped. Kazza looked around, pausing for a moment to stare at the nearby rocky surface of the other moon, then, he tilted his head toward Kalamar's surface.

"We must go," Thunder said.

Raine held back. "Are you certain that beast is safe?"

"He's been with our family since he was a cub." Thunder rose toward Kazza, but Raine pulled him back.

"The airlock is this way."

"Our myst does not have the same needs as our bodies do." With that, Thunder allowed his form to pass through the frigid safety of the water-filled barrier.

Despite her dubious look, she put her hands up as if to dive through the barrier. "Wow, this feels strange. Cold and hard, yet not," Raine said. She spread her arms wide and twirled around. "What an incredible leap of consciousness and form."

"Don't forget why we're here." They looked at Kalamar's surface. Molten gold flecks swarmed like bees among the shrouding mist. Blue lightning shot upward. The flared nostrils of the nose and huge red eyes charged out of the steamy layer.

"Oh, look they're already coming." Her tone brimmed with excitement.

"And they're as deadly to you in this form as if you tried to touch one with your physical hand," he warned. "Remember we are the bait. They come so they can consume your essence."

She swallowed. "Why did you pick me for this?"

"Because we have the most chance of success." Kazza slapped Thunder's shin with his tail. He glared at the cat. There was no way that he was going to tell this woman that he was attracted to her. Kazza twirled his whiskers, then soared toward Vilecom. "Come. Follow Kazza."

"You're joking."

Thunder shook his head. "Reed trusts me because of my

lineage. Kazza's ancestry is far grater than mine will ever be."

ooo

Being without a body provided a freedom she'd never imagined. Giddiness nearly overwhelmed Raine as she and Thunder followed Kazza toward Vilecom. The closer they got, the more debilitating the heat grew. Yet she had no skin to blister or lungs to breathe. The heat cannot hurt me. It's all in my mind. She kept repeating the thought, each time forming the belief with more certainty. Slowly the oppressiveness melted away to insignificance. As it did, the shear joy of the experience welled. The urge to laugh and sing grew. "This is even better than being nobility."

Thunder gave her a confused look. "This will be the most dangerous thing you've ever done in your life."

Craziest, maybe. Bizarre, definitely. But how could something so liberating be dangerous? "What do we have to do to get the dragons to push the moon?" And how could something liquid be pushed? For that matter, how did it stay in its round form?

"I do not know."

She stopped. "What do you mean, 'you don't know'? You're the ancient one. You're supposed to know everything."

"That is what Reed believes. But if it is to be done, we must follow Kazza's lead."

They headed toward the creature, who appeared to be sprawled near the base of a building lunar flare, ears forward, as it intently watched the planet below them. The flare streamed past them, then billowed out in space. The orbit had decayed so badly that it nearly hit the atmosphere. Except during landings and takeoffs, the oxygen shroud had never seemed so close. "What happens if a flare hits the air?"

"Nothing good." He looked into the distance. "They come. It is time for us to join Kazza. He has fought a dragon before."

Though ominous looking, the creature was no match for a dragon, not even a new-born mooncalf. "I'm surprised he survived the conflict." What was she saying? She and Thunder combined didn't equal the animal. He was right, this wasn't a party.

"I was surprised, too."

"How did he do it?"

Thunder gave her a bleak look. "Don't ask."

Her stomach tightened and her heart sped. "This is so strange. In one way it's exciting." But as the dragons approached without Nambaba's shell to protect her, it became impossible to breathe. She laughed. He looked at her as if she'd lost her mind. "Even though I left my body behind, I still feel the sensations from it."

He nodded in understanding. "We become accustomed to them, so even myst uses the familiar feelings to alert us to danger." He settled next to the cat and began to stroke its spine. A deep rumble came from the creature. It was a nice, soothing sound. Raine stopped near them. "Would you like to pet him?"

"May I?"

He placed her hand on the animal's broad back. "If you calm your attitude, you will be safer."

There was a deep vibration beneath the soft outer covering. "Mmmm. Your Kazza feels nice."

"Kazza doesn't belong to me." Love tinged his tone. It would be nice to hear him say her name that way. "If anything, I belong to him." Thunder tickled the animal's ears. The base rumble of happiness intensified.

"You're serious."

He nodded. "Why aren't you afraid?"

"I'm terrified," she admitted.

"Oh."

"Why?" she asked. "Did you think my laughter meant that I didn't understand the danger?" His shrug and shamed expression confirmed her suspicion. "You seem calm, but then you've done this separation thing before."

"Not with these odds."

She snorted. "You win, you go home. You lose, we all lose. It seems simple to me."

He shook his head. "Nimri has been having complications with her pregnancy. If I don't return to my planet, she could bleed to death while giving birth."

"Nimri." She bet the woman who had his heart was as beautiful as a noble.

He nodded. "I didn't finish closing the Star Bridge." He cleared his throat. "After the moon crashes, any surviving dragons will destroy my world."

"Surely you're overstating the issue." He gave her a stern look. "Okay, so you aren't. But why should they go all the way to the Alpha Quadrant?"

"Myst." He rubbed his temples. "Our myst alerts us to unfamiliar situations. Sometimes there is valid danger. Other times our intellect recognizes that it is safe, but something has activated our warning system. It's strongest when we're in this mode, but in any form, it lures the dragons like nothing else."

"So we really are in danger," Raine said.

He sighed. "I've only faced death this closely twice before."

"What happened?"

"The first time was when I was young and my parents took me in a boat. There was a terrible storm and it capsized. I nearly drowned." Kazza turned his head toward Thunder and slightly puffed his cheeks. "My parents did drown. Until you brought me to your world, I hated water." Kazza's deep, contented vibration ended and he lunged to his feet.

"And the second?"

He gestured to something behind her. She turned. A mooncalf was approaching them at incredible speed, its gossamer wings stretched wide to catch the solar current. Her throat went dry. "What do I do?"

"Copy Kazza, if you feel that you're about to die, tell yourself to wake. This will send your myst back to your body." For the first time since she'd met him, he wouldn't look her in the eye.

What wasn't he telling her? "That seems too simple."

Instead of answering her unspoken question, he moved beside Kazza and waited. He'd said that there needed to be two for this out of body experience. If the dragons consumed one of their spirits or they were in danger of dying and 'woke' what happened to the other one? She was afraid she knew the answer. Death to one would mean death to both. "I'll do my best to stay alive. You do the same."

He gave a stiff nod. "I want to return home."

He wanted to save his world from the dragons, just as she wanted to save Kalamar from the moon. "I'm sorry. If it hadn't been for me-"

"I would have lived my life in fear of water. I should thank you for that. But I must return so I can close the portal between our worlds and keep my planet safe from the dragons." Kazza's tail wrapped around Thunder in friendship. He caressed the animal's broad back.

"How can he be here by himself, when it takes both of us?"

"Nimri."

Her, again.

The mooncalf closed the distance between them, a hundred more following close behind it. It was now or never. Kazza reared onto his back legs and bared lethal-looking claws. He would have made an awesome sight if he hadn't been the size of the horn-like protrusion on the mooncalf's shimmering nose. The mooncalf's tongue darted toward them like a bolt of blue lightning. An instant later, the molecules around her shimmered. Spirit! The dragons were worse than any storm she'd ever heard of.

"Stay away from their tongues," Thunder said. "There's something about them that saps your energy and will to survive."

Raine braced herself for the collision. Again, the tongue raced toward them and the wall of sound swept over them. Again, it fell short. But if the mooncalf's speed remained constant, it would get them next time. She glanced at Thunder, who seemed incredibly calm. Kazza exuded expectancy.

As the tongue retracted, Kazza sprang toward the mooncalf's face in a mighty leap that landed on the edge of its flared nostril. Raine and Thunder jumped after him. She leaped so high that she landed against one of the three thick ridges on its forehead and began to slide down. Beneath her, Thunder came to rest spread-eagled against the dragon's eye. The mooncalf's lower lids began to move upward.

She swiveled and straddled the center ridge, bracing her feet in the Vs, which formed where the three ridges joined. Now what to do?

Thunder rode the lid toward her. She reached for him. As he

stepped onto the ridge next to her, the beast entered Vilecom's magma surface. Though she sensed the intense heat, it was bearable. The dragon bored deeper into the molten core. Water got darker the deeper it got; Vilecom got oranger.

"How can we tell if it's on target?"

He shrugged. "I'm hoping that Kazza has some way to control it."

How could Kazza understand their plan, when he hadn't been told? Suddenly, they were out of the molten rock and into dark space, but they were heading for a disabled Crystalline Reclamation Unit that appeared to be lodged next to a shimmering, transparent ship in Ishdoo's largest crater. She blinked at the odd way the damage appeared, then looked back at Vilecom. She imaged that she could see it lurch a millimeter closer to Kalamar's atmosphere. Wow, this spirit journeying certainly had some strange effects on vision. Another dragon emerged from the moon, then a second, and within moments, a dozen surfaced. Now, she was certain that it wasn't just her imagination. The gap between magma and atmosphere was noticeably narrower.

"Did the ship call them?" Thunder asked. Couldn't he see that the ship was damaged and some sort of strange energy had billowed out the slashed side? "Dalf told me that the ships stop evenly around the moon, before they call the mooncows."

"That's it! We need to herd the dragons into the magma, then position the Reclamation Units in the direction we need them to go and call them! All that transparent stuff should make a great lure."

"Can you do this?"

"I can try."

He gripped both of her hands. "Wake."

Chapter 24

Raine heaved her cumbersome body upright and lurched toward the Control Hub. "Where are you going?" Thunder called.

She pointed a leaden arm at the end of the tentacle. "Must get to the radio." Footfalls sounded behind her. By the time she reached the connecting door to the main hub, Thunder had caught up with her, and she felt as if she'd swum the distance during a raging storm.

"Is it always this bad then the essence returns?" Thunder nodded and placed a supportive arm around her. Tingles of relief rippled over her. "Thanks. I need to get to the communications center and contact the shepherd and reclamation fleets."

"This is necessary?"

She inclined her head. "We must organize the ships in the

direction we want the moon pushed."

"That will be dangerous."

"Not as much as letting the moon fall."

All attention centered on them when they entered Nambaba's core. Reed, turned from the nav-panel, his accusing expression cut her to the core. "Gauges disclose that the moon is closer."

Raine nodded. "The dragons became mesmerized by the derelict CRU on Ishdoo." Some were still milling around it, as they had HQ. She tapped the screen.

"Otami got a report about an odd transmission just before the herd emerged from the moon," Brock said. "The good news is that all the dragons have left the planet's surface. The bad news is that massive damage was done to shepherd Headquarters and The Pinnacle."

Raine settled the com-link over her mouth and ear, then keyed in Blue Team's radio frequency.

"Rice crops are ruined and several hundred thousand died when fire rages through Sector Ninety-seven," Shay added.

"What of Yulder's ovum?" Thunder asked.

"They have no way of knowing," Shay said. "The Bakufus Sea is sacred to them and they don't share this sort of information with us 'non-water-breathers'."

"Blue Leader, this is Gold Leader," Raine said. "I have a plan to move Vilecom back into place, but I need everyone's help."

"Did you forget that you've been put on leave?" Otami asked.

"I don't think that matters any more."

"Go home. Tend your fish-boy."

Her molars ground together, but her tone remained professional. "If the moon goes down, we all lose everything."

"Don't make the situation more melodramatic than it is."

"Reed D'nor believes it. He says we need to herd the dragons to these coordinates." She pressed the transmit button to send the information to the fleet.

"Are you so desperate to lead that you invent guidance from the dead?" His mocking tone reeked with disdain.

"We must get all available CRU ships to this area." She transmitted a second set of coordinates. "Once all ships are in place and the dragons are at the entry point, the CRU ships need to send out their-"

"Get off the air and let me do my job."

Brock snatched the com-link off her head. "Blue Leader, this is Brock Vole d'Laire. Drop the attitude and follow Gold Leader's Directions." He thrust the com-link back at her.

"Who was that?" Otami demanded.

"He identified himself," Raine said.

"First you invent guidance from the dead, now nobility!" His mocking tone reeked with disdain.

"No, that's the sort of thing you do," Raine calmly replied. "My control hub is standing room only. Since I can help this situation better if I do my normal job, I'm going to put Reed on to explain his request." She handed the com-link to him and began maneuvering Nambaba toward the massive herd milling over the derelict CRU ship near Ishdoo.

Reed spoke softly.

Otami made a loud, vulgar comment.

Reed's jaw dropped. Brock grabbed the unit, again. "Do you recognize my voice?"

"Oh, this is rich." Otami snorted. "Go short-circuit your radio and get off this frequency, so my team can control the situation."

Brock nudged her away from the control panel and typed in 193092830X. "Blue Leader, you are relieved of duty." Mouth flat with anger, he pressed transmit. "Blue Team and all CRU units, verify this order on your com-links, and follow Gold Leader."

"Don't listen to him," Otami ordered. "A bakufu is impersonating him." Otami continued haranguing his crew.

Brock typed in a second code, 19304678 then glanced at her. "Is this jerk Blue-1?" Raine nodded. He added 791. Otami was cut off in mid-sentence. "I never thought I'd have to use that command code," Brock said. He stepped back and motioned for Raine to take her seat in the captain's chair. "Please, do whatever you can to save them."

"What if it doesn't work?" Raine asked.

"Then we will be no worse off than we are now." He squeezed her shoulder.

The radio crackled. "Blue seventeen here. What should I do?"

"How is your water supply?"

"Enough to protect the ship, not enough for a hydroblast," Seventeen said.

"What about the rest of you?" As the crew logged in, it became apparent that they were all in the same situation as Seventeen. Landing and reabsorbing hydro would take too long. "Hopefully we won't need our blasters." She took a deep breath and assessed the screen. "Five, nine and twenty three, secure the dragons in alpha sector and herd them toward the coordinates I provided. The rest of you form up on me." She pushed the nav-stick forward and dove toward the derelict ship.

"What are you doing?" Brock asked.

"The ship seems to be a lure, so I intend to place the bait in a more advantageous place."

He nodded. Coral clutched Reed's hand, her eyes wide with hope and fear.

Nambaba plunged toward Ishdoo's craggy surface. As the CRU ship filled her view screen, Raine slammed the nav-stick backward. It caught for an agonizing second, then held. She breathed a sigh of relief, then counted 5, 4, 3, 2, 1. She hit the magnetizer for the tentacles. There was a massive jolt. Shay screamed and all but Brock, who was clutching the back of her chair fell. With agonizing slowness, Nambaba began to pick up speed and tow the ship toward Vilecom. "Reed, I need both hands. Can you input the coordinates into the autopilot?"

He staggered upright and hobbled to the console.

"Sorry about that. I should have warned you."

He made a dismissive motion with his hand, then quickly typed in the code. "Now what?"

Before she could respond, Brock punched on the autopilot. The controls in her hands went slack and the ship veered toward Vilecom. Spirit, please let the autopilot release when needed.

Chapter 25

Obviously there was more than one way to be bait. Thunder looked around the strange room and tried to gauge how the rest of them felt about their fate. Preston's complexion looked green as his hair and Shay chewed her lower lip, but the rest were focused on the peculiar glossy area with its moving dots. The green dot, which was joined to the blue cylinder had to be them. That meant the white dots were dragons. There were at least a hundred white dots to each green one. Worse, all the white dots seemed to be clustered around them.

Thunder peered at the cool, dismal gray walls. What was Raine's plan? Would she take the ship into the magma? He shivered with the knowledge that the hull of her ship would never survive the heat. As he watched, she rammed a T-shaped handle toward the odd screen and he sensed that their speed had picked up.

They barreled forward toward the vivid red orb. Raine's mouth was set in flat determination and her attention didn't waver from the approaching moon. Her tension was palpable. He moved behind her and placed his hands on her shoulders. Shay joined him, then Brock, Reed and Coral, each supporting Raine, in the only way they had available.

Shay's jaw trembled. "So you're going to just throw the Reclamation ship into the moon." She swallowed. "What if there were survivors?"

"You saw the damage," Raine said. "The harness side was completely ripped out. They never had a chance."

"Think of this as a different form of recycling," Brock said.

Shay's eyes watered. "I guess it's wonderful, in a way. At least in death they have a chance to save others."

The molten moon now filled half the window. How soon would Raine release the derelict ship? How close could they safely get? It seemed like they were far too close already. A glance at the wall assured him it was still safe. He closed his eyes and imagined the Tribe gathered around a funeral fire. The chill of a moonless night crept across his back, while the heat of the flames sucked moisture from his face. He heard the deep rumble of the hummed tone that allowed the essence to go to the next realm. He turned his attention to the corpse and saw himself lying next to Raine.

Cold clutched his chest and he opened his eyes.

The evil moon took up three quarters of the window. Had the vision been an omen? Would this moon become his funeral fire?

Raine smacked his hand. He jerked away, belatedly realizing that his nails had been digging into her shoulder. "Sorry."

"Does the song you were humming have words?"

"No," he said. Her attention returned to the window.

"It was very calming."

Surely she didn't want him to intone the burial tone. He shivered.

Preston shoved him aside and grabbed Raine's arm. "You've got enough speed. Release it and get us out of here." His skin now looked greener than his hair.

Raine smacked his hand. "If you're that afraid, speak to The Spirit."

"What should I say?" Preston demanded. "Is there a request I can make to get Her to alter your mind?"

"Try this: Spirit, if this doesn't work, may our end be painless and swift."

Preston's eyes glazed with panic. "Drop it now." He appeared ready to strike Raine.

Thunder grabbed him and pulled him away from her. "If this is our destiny, so be it. It isn't my preference, either, but how often do we get a choice?"

She nodded and picked up the thing she talked into. "All shepherd fleet, fall back. I'm taking this in alone. Make certain no strays turn."

ooo

"Raine, don't listen to him," Preston begged.

"Do what you feel is the right thing to do," Thunder said.

She glanced at Brock. "If you can save the planet, do it." He hugged Shay close. Amazed that Brock's main concern was for their world Kalamar, instead of saving his own life, she looked at her sister. Eyes wet, Shay cuddled close to Brock and nodded. Reed and Coral added their support.

Preston's complexion reddened with anger and he lunged at her. Thunder appeared to clap his hand on her brother's neck and he collapsed like a sack of rice. Thunder turned toward her and gave her an encouraging nod. Raine swallowed. Until today, she'd thought defying convention by bonding with Gornt and saving Dalf had been terrifying.

She took a deep breath and turned toward the gauges. The heat index was rising rapidly. The monitor confirmed that a solar flare was building. A chill rippled down her back. Until Thunder had taught her essence-travel, she'd never been so close to the surface. Spirit, please let this work. She increased the power and dove toward the building plume. How close could she get before Nambaba began to soften?

The heat sensors passed redline and continued to climb.

Shay whimpered.

Raine glanced back to see her sister gaping wide-eyed at an orange area on the bulkhead. As they bother stared, the spot expanded and seemed to begin rippling.

She released the tether and yanked the nav-stick back.

Nothing happened.

Cold sweat bathed her. Raine rammed it forward. It wedged. She yanked back. Her gloved hands slipped and her spine slammed against her chair. Coral shrieked.

"Sorry about that."

A comforting hand closed over her shoulder. Thunder's touch seemed to say, that he supported her. Raine punched the release switch with her fist. It clicked free and the CRU bounced forward beneath Nambaba's slowing belly. The hot spot was ten times the size it had been a second ago and the plastoid was starting to melt. It was good that Preston wasn't awake to see this.

She tried to swallow the lump of fear in her throat.

Suddenly, a wing slashed down in front of the monitor. It was so close that she could see that what looked gossamer from a distance was merely heat radiating from a thickly scaled surface.

Something thumped hard against Nambaba's belly. She went down so quickly that she didn't have time to break her fall. The air gushed out of her lungs. She lay doubled up on the floor trying to inhale, fearing that the rippling gray plastoid covering the bulkhead would be the last things she saw.

Then, something else snagged a tentacle. For a moment, the ship quivered. When the anchor held, Nambaba's trajectory arched upward in a backward summersault. Raine struggled onto her knees and lunged for the nav-stick. Shay tumbled, screaming, against the console. Lack of oxygen seemed to darken her vision as Raine's second attempt connected with the nav-stick. The dark monitor showed Thunder grabbing Annya as he stumbled past. Raine pushed the nav-stick forward, but whatever was pivoting them backward, had the controls jammed. Unable to do anything else, she forced air into her aching lungs.

Dragons surged past the monitor like a tsunami. She held her breath, afraid that the next hit could reverse their spin and send them into the magma.

When the final read-out showed the last mooncalf's signature hesitated instead of blending with Vilecom's vapors, she keyed on her com-unit. "All CRU units, if you are at the coordinates I gave you, turn on the call, now." She winced, hoping that her voice didn't sound as terrified to others as it did to her.

The cooling hull looked like solidified water ripples, and though the reddish tones of burn-through had faded to gray, the structure had been compromised.

At least they were alive.

For now.

Raine checked her monitor. Nambaba's backward roll was catapulting them toward Ishdoo. A collision with its rocky surface would be just as fatal as melting in Vilecom. She kicked the console then gripped Nambaba's nav-stick and rotated it until she felt a slight movement. Carefully, she steered into the roll, then bit her lip and began stabilizing her course.

The hull shuddered like a massive quake. The clamor of ripping metal made her mouth dry. Shay shrieked.

Coral screamed for the Creator's help.

The floor heaved.

LED's popped.

A warning tone sounded.

"Fuel low," Nambaba intoned. The gauge for the aft tank read empty and the forward tank was dropping fast. There must be a rupture, but which one? She cut off the transfer from the forward tank.

The fuel level stabilized, but there wasn't enough to land.

Awkwardly, the ship returned to its normal flight configuration, she swallowed, wondering what would happen next.

Raine bit her lower lip and glanced at the others. Their attention was on the monitor, and Ishdoo's imposing crags. She nudged the nose to the left and entered a low orbit around the rugged moon.

"I'm alive!" Shay let out a howl of glee and launched herself toward Brock.

"Did it work?" Reed's whisper could barely be heard over Shay.

Raine keyed in analytic codes, but they only showed fifty-two centimeters of difference. "Yes, I think it might have."

Shay and Brock whooped with relief.

"Thank The Spirit," Coral breathed. Raine nodded in agreement, but her attention stayed on Ishdoo.

Chapter 26

The familiar sound of frying bacon joined the din of wailing whistles and straining metal. Thunder sniffed the air, but only smelled stagnant air and sweat. He looked around the odd, oval chamber. Reed and Coral clung together, as did Shay and Brock. Preston had rolled under the bulky table that was covered with lumps and buttons. He was going to be stiff and angry when he woke. If he woke. If Raine didn't do something about their direction, their ship would hit the cold moon ahead of them. Why wasn't she touching buttons? Why was she looking at the strange scrolling numbers, as if nothing was wrong? Fate. She'd decided that it was her time to die.

But it wasn't his time. He still had to close the portal and protect his home world. No matter what happened to Vilecom, that was still his priority. He took a step toward

Raine and positioned himself between her and the rolling information. "The moon is moving. It is time for you to fulfill your part of our bargain."

Raine raised her head and looked at him with unseeing eyes.

"I helped you move the beasts, now you must take me home." He touched the cool window, which showed a tiny arc of the molten moon. "It has begun to move. Unless the dragons reposition the balance, it will continue to do so." Raine nodded and gave him a faltering smile. Thunder tilted his head and studied her. "Why have you given up?"

"There is nothing more that I can do."

He shook his head. "There is always a-"

The harsh sizzling sound intensified. He clutched his ears. "...Dasya Voltain requests permis.... unauthorized for secure frequency..... Kalamaran Dragon shepherd .... Verifying author....." The searing sound ebbed. "... ship is carrying ID emitter for Colonel Larwin Atano and believe." Larwin!

Thunder swiveled to look for the spokesperson. "Where are you? How did Larwin send you?" he demanded.

"... my brother may still be alive, but captive." The voice seemed to be coming from the wall.

Raine shook herself as if wakened from a deep sleep and stared at him. "You lied to me. You really are a Guerreterran." Thunder shook his head. She glared at him, then shoved him aside and punched a button with her fist. "This is the Kalamaran vessel which has your brother hostage," she yelled. "If you ever want to see him alive again, put a tractor beam on these coordinates." She hit another button.

A moment later, the ship's headlong plunge toward the moon stopped. Thunder was knocked off his feet. As he plunged toward the floor, his temple hit the wall and everything went black.

When he came to, everyone was lined up against the wall staring at something behind him. Painfully he turned his head. A tall woman had a light-beam-cutter, like Larwin's, aimed at Brock. Thunder narrowed his eyes, and studied her high cheekbones and hair that looked like every shade of harvest's golden hues. She was a female version of his friend and could only be one person. "Tem-aki."

She visibly jolted and shot him a startled look. "Who are you? Why were you wearing my brother's uniform? Did you murder him?"

"Larwin is fine. I am Thunder. He and my sister are awaiting the birth of their first child."

"You lie." Now the pointed end of cutter was aimed at him. He flinched.

"How long have you been following my ship?" Raine asked.

"Since you kid-napped my brother," Tem-aki said.

Thunder finally understood. "I am not the brother you seek, but I am your brother." He smiled at Tem-aki. "You have the same nose." Tem-aki looked at him as if he'd lost his mind.

"Are you or are you not a Guerreterran?" Raine demanded.

"He is not," Tem-aki said. "He is a –"Her voice trailed off in uncertainty. "Why are you looking at me as if I amuse you?"

"You act like Larwin. Think like him."

"You sound as if you think of him as a friend." The thing Larwin called a las-cutter wavered. She grabbed the black thing with both hands and steadied the pale red dot on his chest. "What have you done with my brother? Where is he right now?"

Thunder shrugged. "He loaned me his air-suit and GEA-4 several days ago. He wanted to climb up to the portal with us, but it was more important for him to stay with Nimri."

Tem-aki blinked in confusion. "Explain."

Thunder sat up. The red dot now centered on his belly. "Please move the death-light before it cuts me."

"Fine, I'll kill your lady-friend if you try anything." The spot moved to Raine's forehead.

"This is beyond bizarre," Raine said. "I am not his lady friend. He's a Guerreterran. He has to be. He was wearing the envirosuit when I found him."

Tem-aki's attention centered on Raine. "Tell me everything you know."

"I'd been pursuing a juvenile dragon since the beginning of my shift, when-"

"Chases don't interest me. Tell me about him." Tem-aki tilted her head toward Thunder, but never moved her attention from Raine.

Raine held up her hands beseechingly. "When I realized

I'd entered Guerreterran space, I was desperate to turn the dragon, so I fired a hydroblast at it." Brock arched a sculpted brow.

Shay gasped in shock and gripped Raine's arm. "It's forbidden to fire on the creatures that sustain us."

Thunder frowned. How could the dragons sustain them, when they were essence-eaters and clearly diminished spirits?

"I fired in front of it, not at it. Then, when the mooncalf still continued toward the same point, I fired a second round."

"Do you customarily deploy your shielding like that?" Brock demanded. "Did you earn your rank by endangering the dragons?"

Raine shook her head. "It was a first. Mooncalves don't usually behave like that one." She looked the amethyst-haired man in the eye. "What choice did I have? I had to get out of Guerreterran space before a shadow warrior annihilated me. I had to get the mooncalf home safe. If I'd returned without the calf, The Zar would have had my minerals recycled."

Brock's chin came up and his mouth flattened in silent acknowledgement of the distasteful truth he found in her statement.

Shay blinked rapidly, but a tear still crept from the corner of her eye. "Brock?" Her tone held both question and plea.

"One dragon supports thousands," he snarled, "you know that."

"But she's my sister." He snorted. Shay swallowed and stared at Brock as if she'd never truly seen him before. Raine put her arms around Shay and hugged her. The death-light wavered.

Thunder looked at Tem-aki. Her confusion mirrored what he was feeling. Slowly, she moved her thumb across the top of the las-cutter. The light disappeared. Thunder cleared his throat. "On Chatterre, dragons are loathed because they take life, how can this world value them?" He massaged his temples and glanced at Reed and Coral for an answer. They had backed up against the wall so tightly that they appeared to have forced their spines to it, mute terror in their unblinking eyes.

He swiveled to see what held them spellbound.

The window framed fire, which grew steadily larger. Closer. "You need to move this ship." He pointed at the flame.

Raine leapt to the matte-black rod and slammed it to the right, as she thumped a yellow button. Tem-aki dropped the light-cutter and bounded to Raine's side. As she added her weight to the rod, the floor skewed sideways. Slowly, the framed scenery began edging from roiling gold toward the midnight tones of emptiness. Just when he realized that they might have escaped a fiery death, an invisible force hit the ship.

Shrieks came from all directions and half the tiny lights turned red. As the ship catapulted forward, Tem-aki grabbed for her light-cutter.

Chapter 27

Raine glanced at the monitor. Its wildly scrolling crimson message indicated a hull breach. She and Tem-aki fought the unresponsive nav-stick, slowly regaining control. "Nambaba, close all emergency hatches."

"Complying."

She gritted her teeth and whispered, "Focus." Sweat stung her eyes. "Navigate. Secure. Repair."

"You need to find out what ruptured." Tem-aki gripped the stick as if it was a matter of life or death, which it was. "I think I can hold it," she said through clenched teeth.

Thunder shoved her and Tem-aki, slapped his hand on the top of the nav-stick, and effortlessly shifted it. "Go," he said. "Do whatever is needed." She tentatively loosened her grip. His biceps rippled as he applied more pressure. "I can hold it." Raine relinquished her hold. The stick held steady.

She entered the diagnostic code.

Thunder glanced at Tem-aki. "Restore your circulation, then help Raine."

Tem-aki shook her hand and flexed her fingers. "What can I

do?"

"Go below," Raine said. "Check to make certain everything is secure." Tem-aki jumped into the open hatch and landed with an audible thud. Raine blinked away the shock of having the enemy do her bidding, then turned her attention to the analysis stream, which began scrolling across the monitor.

"What can I do?" Brock asked.

"Communicate," she snapped. Without taking her attention from the data, Raine tilted her head toward the com-unit. Spirit, she'd just ordered nobility!

Brock ignored her offense, grabbed the com-unit and input his code.

Mouth dry, Raine focused on pinpointing the damage.

It seemed like a thousand years, then abruptly the cockpit steadied and the warning lights went out. Thank you, Spirit.

Tem-aki climbed up, a relieved look on her face. Thunder's grip remained steady on the nav-stick and Brock's tone was soft as he finished transmitting their location and signed off. To think that she owed her life, and possibly the lives of everyone onboard to the enemy. Except, she could not think of Thunder as an enemy – his uniform, yes, but not the man. Raine swallowed and turned her attention to Brock.

He gave her a lop-sided smile. "Despite all odds, we're alive." Brock glanced at Shay, then down at the oxygen level gauge. "Blue ten confirms that Vilecom's orbit has altered from an inward to an outward spiral."

Raine studied his solemn expression and understood what he hadn't said. They had saved the planet, but they would die. She inhaled, imagining that she could already detect the thinness of the remaining air.

"Guerreterran marker buoy scanned," Nambaba intoned.

"This is Alif Sector." Relief tinged Tem-aki's tone.

Raine jerked. Could those be the same asteroids she had pursued the mooncalf through? A glance at Thunder's single-minded attention to piloting Nambaba through the rocks confirmed that he'd had secondary reasons for helping her control the ship. He wanted to go 'home'.

Tem-aki leaned forward, her eyes wide, her finger pointing at a large rock. I was in that crevasse establishing the mineral content of this field when you chased the madrox past me." Her face twisted into a sad smile. "My instructors told me to go to warp and get away from energy-sucking beasts. I couldn't believe anyone would actually chase one."

"Guerreterran warriors are taught to run?" Raine echoed before she contained her disbelief.

Tem-aki laughed. "I'm a geologist." She turned from the screen and studied Thunder. "How did you get my brother's envirosuit and GEA-4? That mess in the storeroom is the same android he was testing, isn't it?"

Despite Nambaba's stability, Raine felt as if reality was spinning out of control.

For the first time since he'd taken over the stick, Thunder's attention wavered from his course. He glanced at her, confusion in his expression. "GEA-4 is here? I dreamed she dissolved in a shower of fire." His expression became hopeful. "If we can return to my world, she can explain X-plow-sives and there is still hope of saving everyone."

Raine frowned. She'd made him a promise and he'd kept his part They had enough air to reach the burned husk where she'd found him, but not enough to leave him there to complete whatever his mission was and get everyone else safely home.

She looked at the others. As her mother had walked toward her reclamation, she'd made her swear to protect Shay and Preston. She'd done her best to keep that vow. She tried to swallow the lump in her throat. "If we turn back, someone can meet us halfway," Thunder's jaw clenched and he glared at her. "If I take you there, everyone else will die." Tears blurred her vision. A possibility came to mind. "Does your ship have enough oxygen for us to wait here for rescue?"

"There is air beyond the shape-shifter's portal."

"Ancient magic! "Reed's awe-filled tone sent gooseflesh rippling over her spine.

"Could we all go there?" Coral asked.

Shay bounced with frustration. "Why is everyone acting so weird? The ship is steady."

Brock hugged her. "It's the only way we can all survive." He gestured to the oxygen level. "The ventilator is damaged and our options are limited." Shay shook her head in denial; Brock hugged her tight.

Comprehension filled Thunder's expression. Raine squinted at the air numbers and made a quick mental calculation. "Can we get to this portal quickly?"

He fluttered his hand in a perhaps movement. "I am not certain which rock I was on."

It was their best chance for survival. "I can find it." Before she could change her mind, she grabbed the nav-stick and set a course for the desolate planetoid. She peeked at Brock, surprised that he was allowing her to find a solution to their dilemma, but all his attention was on comforting Shay.

"Are there more of the ancients where we're going?" Reed asked. Thunder arched a brow. Reed frowned. "Do many wear the feathers of glory in their hair?" A trembling finger rose to hover a foot away from one cluster of tiny matted feathers.

Thunder chuckled. "The right to wear the plumage of birds is a right reserved for peacekeepers." He frowned. "Though I am the only one who clings to the custom."

Reed blinked in confusion.

"Feature? Birds?" Tem-aki echoed. "On an asteroid?"

He shook his head. "It's hard to explain, but within two sun risings, you can be with Larwin."

"Dead." Tem-aki's tone mirrored Raine's worst fears.

Thunder frowned in confusion. "When he loaned me the air suit, he was very much alive." Tem-aki gasped, then yelped with delight and threw herself into Thunder's arms and kissed his cheek.

As his arms wrapped around the smaller woman, a jolt of scorching emotion burned through Raine and it was all she could do to keep from yanking Tem-aki off Thunder.

Molars clenched, Raine turned to the control panel and forced herself to focus on their course.

Chapter 28

Thunder stared at the heap of raw rock littering the matte black surface of the planetoid. It appeared even worse from inside the helmet of the borrowed enviro-suit, than it had from Nambaba's monitor. He blinked, but nothing looked the same. Granted, the scene was as desolate as the one he'd encountered when he came through the final tunnel of the Star Bridge, but nothing was the same. Where was the sheer cliff with the cave opening at its base?

He turned his back on the rubble and looked at the stars. They were in a different pattern, too. Thunder gritted his teeth and looked at the ship. Five faces were framed in the monitor, their expressions containing varying degrees of tension. If he didn't find the tunnel, they would all suffocate.

It was up to him, just as saving Chatterre had been, and still was, up to him. Perhaps if he couldn't find the tunnel, the dragons couldn't either. He swallowed the harsh laugh over such a ridiculous thought and turned back to the rock pile. In his peripheral vision, Tem-aki began moving debris aside. Had she found the opening with her magic tool?

When he started helping her move rocks aside, she stopped and gaped at him. "Why are you helping me? Is the path to that tunnel clear?"

"I hoped you would use your box to help me find the place." His gaze moved to the magic box.

"My tri-corder?" He inclined his head toward the amazing box. She plucked it from her waist and tapped a bump. The small silvery screen blazed teal, then displayed a scarlet sequence of numbers. Tem-aki gasped, moved as quickly as possible, away from the spot, where he felt the mouth of the cave should be, and then fell to her knees, her posture reverent. She swiped away a layer of black dust to reveal smooth, silvery metal. "I've found Larwin's ship." Tears filled her voice.

"Your brother is not there. He resides on the other side of the portal." Thunder glanced around the bleak site. "I cannot find the portal because of the fallen rock. If your box can find a ship…" His voice trailed off. If her magic held the answer, his world could be saved.

Tem-aki sat back on her heels, then slowly stood up. "You find the opening for Larwin's ship and I'll try to find your portal." The clear bubble surrounding her head revealed the doubt in her expression. "Is there any special mineral content?"

Hope waned. "It is only a very long empty tunnel, with fragments of old wreckage."

"It's a void instead of solid rock?" Tem-aki sounded cheered. Thunder nodded. "Great! You find the access hatch, I'll find the hole – that's your idea of a portal, huh?" He concurred.

What had she expected? That they would move through solid rock? "Strange." Tem-aki shrugged. "From what you've told me, we'll need to rig explosives to close the tunnel after we're through."

She grabbed her magic box and began tapping it with her clumsy-appearing glove, then she slowly turned in a complete circle, her attention never leaving the winking silvery face. After several moments, she began walking toward a high pile of rocks. If the tunnel was under that, they were goners. Thunder focused on revealing the sleek skin of Larwin's ship.

ooo

An hour later, exhausted and low on air, Thunder followed Tem-aki out of the decontamination room, glad that the too-small area with its inexplicable locking doors was behind him. Not that he liked the rest of Nambaba's claustrophobic chambers with their smooth, featureless curved contours that made it difficult to tell floors from walls. He looked away from the bleak rugged rock landscape as Tem-aki peeled off her helmet as if the clasps were as simple as common laces.

How did she make such frustrating closures look simple?

First the climb up Sacred Mountain, then the water world – were the Gods were doing everything in their power to make him feel clumsy and incompetent? He gritted his teeth and resisted the temptation to rip the fabric.

Within a moment, Tem-aki was free of the cumbersome helmet and headed to the main portion of the odd ship, Shay asked, "Have you found it?" Her fear-laced tone reminded him that their efforts affected many.

"We need to move a few tons of rocks..." as Tem-aki's voice receded, Thunder yanked at the fasteners. It seemed to take the ornery things forever to part.

When he joined the rest at the big window, everyone was silently staring at the huge pile of rock. Thunder squared his shoulders. "We'll need everyone's help."

Brock turned toward him, his expression solemn. "There are only five environmental suits with enough air to make it through the wormhole." He clasped Shay's hand in his, and looked deeply into her eyes, then turned to face the rest of them. "Shay and I have decided to return to Kalamar with Preston and help rebuild." He glanced at the odd lumpy table. "We believe it is the best choice."

Shay nodded. "But there is enough air in two of the suits for us to at least help move rocks for a while." She cleared her throat. "It is Brock's responsibility to lead Kalamar through this time of change." She looked up to him, and added, "And I feel it my responsibility to stand by his side."

"We will wed," Brock declared.

"But you can't," Preston gasped. "She isn't nobility."

"True, but she is the one I love." Brock looked Preston in the eye. "Without Vilecom and the dragons, everything will change. As soon as the moon moves too far away to make harvest practical, there will be no more eepyllihg and the economy will collapse."

"That won't be the only change, or the quickest," Reed said. "Without the moon's heat, the world will return to ice."

Brock nodded. "Exactly why Kalamar needs someone to help direct and organize the changes."

Raine swallowed. "Then we need everyone who is able to suit up." She bit her lip, then threw her arms around Shay. "Be safe." Her gaze went to the obnoxious green-haired man. "I'll start moving rocks. It shouldn't be too horrible in low gravity."She grabbed her helmet and gloves and sprinted toward the door.

Tem-aki, who had just sat down, sighed and got up. "I'll get the things we need out of my brother's ship." She bit her lower lip. "The planet doesn't sound like it has precision tools and GEA-4 needs repairs."

Thunder almost argued with her about not having tools, then thought of the amazing ones Larwin possessed, so remained silent. It would be good to see everyone, but he was not looking forward to Larwin's reaction about GEA-4's condition. He hoped Tem-aki could fix her and that seeing his sister would balance out Larwin's reaction over the damage....He was especially looking forward to feeling land beneath his feet, the fresh scent of pines, the heavy, sweet taste of a pange for breakfast.... In fact, he was looking forward to everything in his normal life, except living alone.

As he struggled to put his contrary helmet back on, he thought about Raine, who seemed happy to leave Preston and Shay behind. While he could understand why she would not miss the green-haired one, he couldn't help wondering if she treated all relationships lightly. His next thought was that he wished he didn't care.

Chapter 29

Preston and Raine struggled to roll aside a large, cumbersome rock, then turned back to the impossibly huge task of moving the landslide, only to see an empty, blank space, large enough for one person at a time to crawl through. "Do you think that's it?" he asked.

"Only one way to find out." With that, Raine stooped low and moved into the unknown. It was not any easy passage, but possible. When she got into the actual old mine shaft, it was huge, and she didn't waste any time telling the others that they were one step closer to their new slave-free lives.

Racing to get the supplies they needed, while saying goodbyes to loved ones and friends for what was probably the final time, made everything chaos.

Soon, the five of them were again, standing by the portal and watching Nambaba prepare to catapult away. What would

Brock, Shay and Preston find on Kalamar? Would their return make a difference? Raine could only hope it would.

She tried to shrug off her doubts and fears, as she motioned for Thunder to lead the way. When he got in front of her, she realized that he had made a harness out of old webbing and made a sling to carry the android on his back. Anger flared at the way he'd taken her property, but it quickly cooled, when she realized that she had never actually owned the machine. Besides, if he had left it, Preston would have used it for his own parasitical reasons.

Since the passageway was wide and straight, Raine increased her pace and walked next to Thunder, finally able to ask him how he had healed Dalf, and why she had found him in such a desolate place. For over an hour, as they hiked down into the bowels of the planet, the questions and answers flowed, and the deeper they got, the more they unconsciously leaned toward each other. And the happier Raine was that she had saved him as well as the android, but no matter how honest and kind Thunder seemed, Preston's final argument, for her to return with him and Shay rang in her mind. Don't you realize that with Marsha dead, and Brock willing to acknowledge Shay as his mate, that we will become nobility? Isn't that what you've always dreamed of? Why do you trust this – this person? Do you really believe a survivable world exists in the bowels of that ash heap? How do you know the warrior you trust too much isn't leading you into the bowels of hell? Do you really prefer to be dead or face the unknown?

Laughter from Reed and Coral distracted her mind from the swirling doubts. She looked back at them. Despite their ill-fitting enviro-suits, they were holding hands as they hiked down the long tunnel, and acting like they were having a great adventure as they looked at the increasing number of piles of debris, and joked about the fascinating historical finds they could be making, if only they had the time.

As they moved even deeper, the passage got narrower and dustier, and they ceased to find much debris, but she also began to see where someone had drilled explosives into the slick sides of the old mine, and she realized Preston was right about this being a one-way journey. Raine hoped she'd made the correct choice.

She glanced back at Reed and Coral, who continued to act like they were having the time of their lives. Considering the existence that they had endured since their supposed deaths, this journey probably was a wonderful adventure. Yet Tem-aki, who trailed far behind, also seemed to be dealing with demon doubts.

In a big chamber, at the entrance of a noticeably more narrow area, Thunder stopped walking, and touched the smooth, slippery-looking wall. "This is the Star Bridge." Raine touched the rock, which felt smooth as an oil slick. Thunder said, "Last year a madrox came this way, in the narrow parts, where it barely fit, the walls look like this."

Had she just been told what had happened to the dragon Otami's crew had lost? Hot as the beasts were, it could explain why some parts of the walls looked as if a vast heat had softened them, then the scales of a passing dragon had smoothed and altered them.

She cleared her throat, and said, "One disappeared about that time. We kept expecting it to return, like the herd that went missing, but it never did… it happened on Otami's shift, so I got promoted to chief dragon shepherd over him." Since her promotion, he had been hounding her and trying to make her look incompetent. Another realization hit her like a fist in the stomach: when she had returned with her own wayward mooncalf, he had manufactured evidence against her, so that she'd been called into HQ. "When I returned with the mooncalf, I guess he couldn't stand the loss of face."

Thunder stopped walking and gazed down at her, an odd look on his face. "Who was in charge when we left?"

"Otami."

Thunder's expression became even more perplexing. "Will he be held responsible for moving the red moon?"

"I don't know," she admitted, "but knowing him, if it isn't good, he will find a way to blame me for it." She started to laugh, and couldn't quit.

"What is so funny?"

"Nothing." She laughed so hard she started to cry.

Thunder held her close, as if trying to give support. "Please tell me."

"Otami spent his life trying to be the best shepherd and soon, there will be no more herd. I spent my life adopting the family I wanted to have, and now they are all either dead or far away. I was thinking how futile everything has been." Her body shuddered, as her tears of mirth became sobs of regret.

Thunder gestured to a pile of supplies, which looked suspiciously like explosives. Now, she shuddered for a new reason and Preston's doubts about her choice to follow the handsome healer became so loud in her thoughts that she could barely pay attention to anything else. *Why do you trust this – this person? Why do you trust this – this person? Why do you trust this – this person?* She didn't know the answer to that, or why the same question wouldn't stop circling in her mind.

Do you really believe a survivable world exists in the bowels of that ash heap? If this was the portal, which they had spent so much time getting to, then it didn't look positive.

How do you know the warrior you trust too much isn't leading you into the bowels of hell? She had no answer for that thought, either. An even older thought penetrated her fear and confusion. Once you've hit bottom, your only way is back up. It had been one of her mother's favorite sayings, but no thoughts had been able to keep her from the recycling chamber on her fortieth birthday.

Do you really prefer to be dead than an insignificant person in an unknown world? That was a very difficult question. One she didn't have an answer for.

While Raine fought with her thoughts, Thunder shrugged out of the harness he had made to carry the android, and began to busy himself with the suspicious pile of supplies. She noticed that Tem-aki seemed interested in the project, too, which didn't surprise her. She'd always heard Guerreterre's warriors were an evil bunch of destroyers, so why wouldn't one who proclaimed himself a healer, also be fascinated by destruction?

Hand in hand, Reed and Coral wandered deeper into the area, which the mooncalf had apparently burned through. Soon, the intensity of her doubts drowned out their voices. Raine didn't know how long Thunder and Tem-aki had been working before she realized that they were setting charges to destroy the mineshaft behind them. She leaped to her feet and grabbed Thunder's arm. "You can not bury us in this awful crypt!"

"This is not a crypt. It is the Star Bridge and I must blockade it so no more madrox come through to destroy my world."

"Whatever you want to call it, you can not blow this up with us all inside."

"If I do not, my world is not safe."

"From what?"

"Madrox."

"That is ridiculous. Do you know how far away we are from any possible mooncalf?" She threw up her hands. "It was a fluke that one got away from Otami."

"Was it?" Tem-Aki asked.

"Yes!"

Behind the shield of his helmet, Thunder's expression was sorrowful. "I wish I knew that was certain."

Tem-aki held up an instrument, which was similar to one Gornt had used to analyze problems with Nambaba. "I've been getting strange readings on this for the past hour. Do I have time to backtrack and check the old mine?"

"Why?" Raine and Thunder asked in unison.

"Because, I don't know what was mined here and whatever it was could affect the explosives."

"Be a quick as possible," Thunder said. Tem-aki nodded and started back.

When Thunder resumed setting up the charges, Raine demanded, "Didn't you hear what she said? If there is something chemically off, you could kill us all."

"Better that than everyone and everything on my world."

"I do not want this black hole to be my grave."

"Then leave." He pointed toward where Reed and Coral had disappeared. With no other option, she walked into the dark unknown.

Chapter 30

Tem-aki swatted her tricorder. Though it was programmed for her geological project, it was capable of determining other things beside mineral content and the reading for silica was very strange. Even stranger, the reading where Thunder was working showed oxygen and granite, yet two strides up the long incline, the readings changed to ones which she would expect to find in an oxygen-free salt mine.

Attention totally on her tricorder, she swiftly backtracked. The farther she went, the stronger the silica readings and the hotter she began to feel. Knowing she was exerting herself too much, and needed to conserve her oxygen, she looked up to orient herself and saw a bright golden glow in the distance. She blinked, certain that she was seeing things.

If she hadn't spent most of her waking hours watching madrox for the past few days, she would not have recognized the color or odd movement pattern. But she had been on Ishdo and realized that Thunder's worst fear was not based in paranoia; it was coming true.

"We've got to get out of here," she screamed into her mic. "There's a dragon in the tunnel."

Screaming panic reverberated through the speakers.

"Hurry," Thunder urged, "I must ignite the explosives!"

"Just go,"Tem-aki screamed, "I will do it."

"You know how?"

"Of course."

She saw a glimpse of his disappearing form, as she got back to the area of strangest readings. It only took a moment to activate the charges and she was a blink from following Thunder, when she realized the Android had been left behind. After heaving it onto her back, she was taking her second step after Thunder, when the charges exploded.

One minute, she was starting to run, the next, she was falling and bits of rock were exploding all around her.

Tem-aki put out her arms to break her fall.

Chapter 31

Thunder burst onto the high, charred cliff amid an explosion of rock. He stumbled as he veered to his right, finally finding protection behind a semi-charred boulder.

Panting for breath, and heart thundering with fear, it took several moments before he realized that the dust was settling. He stood up and looked for the others. Slowly, Raine, Coral and Reed emerged from the spots they had taken refuge. Mouth dry, he looked for Larwin's sister, but it soon became obvious that she must still be in the Star Bridge. Hoping that she had not been too close to the blast, or hit by a rock, He squared his shoulders and headed back into the cavern.

Raine followed him all the way to the solid granite wall that now closed the tunnel. She stooped than brushed some dust aside to reveal the components they had set up to organize the explosives; some portions had been damaged, but for the most part they had survived the detonation. Scowling, he looked for the android, but it had vanished along with Tem-aki.

Raine looked up at him, her eyes appearing impossibly large behind the visor screen. "Do you think she made it out?"

"I hope so." Thunder swallowed. "She must have made it this far. Otherwise there would not have been an explosion."

"I didn't see her between here and the cliff."

"Neither did I."

He wouldn't have thought her eyes could get larger, but they did. "You don't think she ran over the edge, do you?"

His blood chilled at the thought, but it was the only thing that made sense. "We'll look for her body, as we descend. At least we can do that."

Raine nodded.

"I don't know what I'll tell Larwin. I not only lost his sister, I lost GEA-4 … this is not good…"

"But at least your world is safe from dragons"

"True."

When they returned to the cliff, Coral and Reed were standing shoulder to shoulder staring in awe at the valley floor far below the sheer granite wall.

Raine gasped, "How beautiful. There is so much land and so little water. I've heard of this, but never though I'd live to see so much green."

Thunder had never thought he'd live to see a world of water, either but he had and it wasn't the horror he'd imagined. Grateful to be home, he worked the disagreeable clasps on the helmet and yanked it off. 'Do you want to rest here, or begin the descent?" he asked the others. "And I warn you, it is not easy.

"I think I need to rest," Coral said, pulling off her ill-fitting flight suit.

"My lungs are feeling the strain of the thin air," Reed said, "so I, too, need to rest and acclimate."

Raine nodded in agreement and began removing her flight suit. A moment after she took off her helmet, a wave of dizziness hit her so hard that she slumped against Thunder. He quickly grabbed her and helped her sit down.

"I should have warned you that the air up here was hard to breathe."

"Will it be better lower?" Coral asked.

Thunder nodded.

Before the sun set, they had found a safe place to sleep. When Thunder fell asleep, he dreamed of slim fingers. Were they a woman's? His mother? Grandmother? Whoever they belonged to, they were in deep water. He watched the hand for a long time, then fell into a deep, peaceful sleep.

He woke to a familiar, deep rumbling and opened one eye to see Kazza. "Hey big guy. I'm back." He hugged the mighty cat in greeting.

The cat placed one huge paw on each of Thunder's shoulders, and dropped its massive head to look him in the eye. Then, as unexpectedly as he'd reared up, the cat twirled and landed back on his paws. "Well?" Thunder demanded.

"She's all right?" Thunder asked.

Kazza purred.

"Thank goodness. Can we find her?"

"Are you speaking to that animal?" Raine asked, then released a pent-up breath that she hadn't realize she'd been holding.

Thunder put his hand on Raine's shoulder. "Yes, and Tem-aki is well."

"How?"

He shrugged.

"Where?"

He shrugged, again. "I don't know, but I will keep looking.

Raine covered his fingers with her own. "I will do anything I can to help find her."

"Thank you, but first, we need to make it down this mountain. Do you feel up to that?"

She looked across the magnificent valley, which would be her new home and nodded.

Thunder's fingers tightened around Raine's, drawing her tightly against his side. "For now, I want to eat, then I want go home." He tipped her chin up, so she looked into his eyes. "I want to find out if you'd like to share those plans with me."

She nodded.

Her heart leaped at the promise in his eyes, then her blood warmed as he lowered his lips to meet hers and seal the pledge.

THE END

I hope you enjoyed *Thunder Moon*. If so, please leave a review on the book's product page. Reviews are very important to authors, so they are greatly appreciated.

Thank you!

Fire Island sneak peak

Chapter 1

Tem-Aki slid over the slippery rock floor, which might have been easy to skate on, but was nearly impossible to navigate wearing clumsy space boots. Moving deeper into the treacherous tunnel, her attention was torn between staying upright and figuring out her tricorder's strange readings.

Until they had reached this narrow area, with its slick surface, the readings had been typical of a salt mine. Now, they went from strange silica measurements to even stranger oxide readings. Frowning, she pressed the tricorder against the side of the passage, but the odd analysis did not change.

Tem-aki closed her eyes and tried to focus on what she knew about silica. When molten silicon dioxide was rapidly cooled, it solidified as a glass, which could explain the slippery surface, but it didn't explain how or why this area of the mine had been altered from that of a normal, abandoned salt mine.

Opening her eyes, she looked around. Noticing an offshoot passageway, she moved into it, and almost immediately tripped over debris littering the rough potholed floor.

After she regained her balance, she realized that the readings in this area were consistent with an airless salt mine.

What in the world had caused such drastic changes in the chemistry of the main corridor, yet had left this area untouched?

Salt was a staple of life and if the deposit wasn't mined out, this discovery would be valuable to her superiors. Perhaps valuable enough to merit a promotion. That plus finding her brother, who everyone else had given up as dead, made this a very good day.

Of course, there was the problem of how to contact her superiors. She frowned, as she wished she had thought of this before leaving Nambaba and its antiquated communications. If Larwin was here, as Thunder claimed, why hadn't he notified anyone of his location?

Had she gotten herself into the same trap he was in?

Tem-aki glanced back down the tunnel to where Thunder knelt as he prepared the explosives, which he claimed were necessary to protect his people from a madrox invasion. Aside from the bizarre belief that madrox would venture trillions of light years across space to enter a deserted salt mine, Thunder seemed like a rational person.

Just as she was about to step back onto the slick surface of the main tunnel, Raine glided past, graceful as ballerina, not even paying attention to her footing as she talked to Reed. Tem-aki cautiously put weight on her right foot, but the turquoise-colored space-boot, which was on the shiny surface, slipped and she nearly cartwheeled into the mineshaft. Arms flailing for balance, she managed to avoid falling, but dropped her tricorder. A quick glance assured her that Raine and Reed, were so focused on their conversation, that they hadn't noticed her clumsiness. Cautiously, Tem-aki walked across the slick mineshaft. Perspiration burned her eyes and her heart hammered from the stress of moving over the treacherous ground. When she got to her tricorder, bending over to pick it up nearly had her somersaulting down the slippery slope. Somehow, she managed to grab it without falling flat on her face.

Standing upright, she put her hand against the wall, as she caught her breath and watched Raine move over the tricky floor with the ease and grace of a professional ice-dancer. How did she move like that while wearing a clumsy space suit and heavy boots? Raine was small, curvy and dainty – and graceful, even when wearing an out-dated, bulky charcoal-colored spacesuit. She was everything a woman should look like – everything Tem-aki knew she was not, even though her own custom-made suit was the most advanced design and an attractive turquoise color.

Just thinking about Raine's dexterity, made Tem-aki's knees shake and her boots slide.

"I can do this," Tem-aki vowed, as she focused her attention on her analyzer. The difference between the rock of the main tunnel and the smaller side tunnels was a geological anomaly she would have loved to examine in depth, but limited air made a thorough investigation impossible.

At least for now.

Perhaps after she rendezvoused with Larwin, they could recharge the air of both their suits, and continue researching this old mine. For now, she only needed to confirm that there was something worth further study.

Just when she started to feel confident, her feet slipped, again. She pitched sideways into another side-tunnel and fell on top of something with sharp corners. Fearing her spacesuit had been punctured, Tem-Aki rolled to her right and checked for damage.

No rips.

No obvious punctures.

She heaved a sigh of relief, then scrambled to her feet and panned her las-light to see what she'd fallen on. A perfectly preserved Artelbas IV bench sat at the side of the space. She stared in shock. How had such a rare and valuable antique gotten here?

The bench made the prospect of finding her brother alive and well seem possible.

"You all right?" Thunder asked.

Great, he'd seen her make a fool of herself. "I'm fine." Tem-aki gestured toward the bench. "Surprised at what is in here, though."

He gave the perfectly carved stone a disdainful glance. "Refuse." Her shock must have showed through her somewhat foggy face-place because he added, "Things tend to lose value when a person must chose between it and their own life."

Interesting and probably true, but it was still the single most valuable piece of furniture that she'd ever touched.

"You like the thing?" he asked. She nodded.

"It would be impossible to carry down the mountain, but easy to make one like it." After that strange statement, Thunder turned and strolled back down the tunnel.

How much farther did they have to go? It felt like they'd been walking for weeks. She glanced at her analyzer: 27.4 kilometers. She wrinkled her nose at the distance, which would have taken a blink of an eye, if she'd been riding in a shuttle; or a few moments, if she'd been standing on a fast-track. She couldn't recall a time in her entire life when she'd walked such a long way.

Suddenly a roaring sound surrounded her. Her eyes snapped to where the sound had come from and she saw a distant bright gold glow with bright red dots and a brief azure ripple. Tem-aki stood in shock for a moment, almost unable to comprehend that Thunder's fears about the dragons coming down this hostile hole were valid. Then, her survival instinct kicked in and she sprinted down the tunnel, toward Thunder. "Madrox! Run!"

He stared past her, transfixed, then looked down at the maze of switches and wires.

"Go! Now! I'll blow it when I get there."

He turned and ran.

Moments later, Tem-aki got to the cobbled-together maze of wires and hit the switch, then, she turned to run after Thunder. But saw GEA-4's damaged form slumped against the wall. She paused and threw the android's arms around her neck, then, she started to run after the others.

Abruptly, a deafening boom threw her face down.

Tem-aki screamed, as she put her hands out to cushion the fall.

Instead of hitting the floor, she plummeted into solid rock, but instead of hitting anything solid, she kept hurtling downward.

She closed her eyes and fought the need to throw up,

which could be fatal inside a space suit.

Moments turned into minutes and minutes seemed to turn into hours. Tem-aki didn't know how long she hurtled through solid stone, which shouldn't have been possible to move through. And she worried that she was hallucinating.

With a jarring halt, Tem-Aki splatted against something hard enough to knock the breath out of her, despite her spacesuit's protection. Strangely, though her momentum seemed to slow, it felt like she was still dropping.

Then, she hit something so hard that her knees buckled, she pitched forward landing hard on her face. Pain shot throughout her body..

Lungs burning, she gasped for oxygen, but it seemed impossible to inhale.

Desperate, she lay there, waiting for the glorious whiteness of eternity to envelope her.

Everything stayed shades of charcoal and black.

Unable to breath, beneath the crushing weight, she succumbed to the enveloping darkness.

~0~

Heart pounding and face bathed in sweat, Nimri's eyes shot open. It took her several minutes of gasping for breath to realize that she had fallen asleep in the hammock under the ginkgo tree and it had only been a nightmare.

But what a realistic one!

She tried to swallow the lump of fear that still choked her, but the suspicion that dreams could actually be real stayed. This nightmare had been different from the one that she had been having every night for the past half year. But she didn't know if it was a good sign that she hadn't dreamed of hordes of ravenous golden dragons spewing from the Star Bridge or not.

Shading her eyes from the bright afternoon sun, she gazed up at Sacred Mountain's peak and looked for an omen. She thought she saw a thin dark cloud rise above the balata grove, but she couldn't be sure. Gooseflesh rippled over her body and her soon-to-be-born-baby kicked.

An affectionate, leathery nose prodded her elbow. Smiling, Nimri turned her attention from the distant peak and stroked Kazza's muscular shoulders, then tickled the smooth, silky fur at the base of his ear until his tail twitched and his six-hundred-pounds of muscle leaned into her.

A distant bird screamed. Together, Nimri and Kazza turned their attention to Sacred Mountain's summit, where the small black cloud seemed to be dissipating. Was that a good omen or bad?

Did it mean that Thunder had closed the portal and the threat had dissipated?

If so, why hadn't he returned?

In the beginning of her dream, Thunder had been wearing Larwin's strange suit and he had been with four strangers wearing similar attire. Where had they come from? And why hadn't Thunder returned days ago? Worse, poor GEA-4 had been badly damaged.

Had her dream been real or imaginary?

Nimri caressed her bulging abdomen with one hand and Kazza with her other, trying to sooth them, even though she couldn't sooth herself.

If Thunder had not been able to close the star bridge,

would any of them survive another assault by the aura-devouring beasts?

About Jeanne Foguth

Though Jeanne began her career technical writing, her love of romantic-suspense, whether it be present, future or in an unknown galaxy inspired her to write the novels she wanted to find in bookstores. Since marrying, Jeanne and her husband have lived from the arctic to the tropics, as well as from yacht to off-grid mountain home. She loves using vivid colors and flowing shapes in her oil paintings as well as creating edible landscapes. She recently finished preparing previously-published novels for their digital debut, and is now working on new stories.

You can always find out what she is working on and/or contact her at:

Her blog: http://foguth.wordpress.com

Her web-home: http://www.jeannefoguth.com/

Facebook: https://www.facebook.com/jeannefoguth

OR follow on Twitter *@JeanneFoguth*

Other Books by Jeanne Foguth

Kazza's Chatterre Trilogy:

Star Bridge

Nimri, an herbal healer and Chatterer's new Keeper of the Peace, must safeguard her tribe from their bitter rivals.

Light years away, Colonel Larwin Atano, an elite Guerreterran Shadow Warrior, fights to save his intergalactic star-fighter. Despite all efforts, he crashes.

Larwin perceives Chatterre's resources as a means to gain power and prestige and views the planet's inhabitants as a minor inconvenience.

Nimri believes Larwin is a supernatural Guardian, who will protect her tribe from their rivals.

Who will survive the coming conflict?

Thunder Moon

Thunder Cartwright dreams that madrox (dragons) will invade Chatterre and destroy his world unless the star bridge is closed.

Raine, a Kalamaran Dragon Shepard, must catch a rogue mooncalf and return it to the herd or face possible death.

Who will will win and who will die?

Fire Island

Tem-aki Atano fell through a rift, when the star bridge was destroyed, and must find a way to survive on an island, which worships destructive madrox (dragons).

Cameron O'Ryan, must figure out if legend and reality have things in common or merely are stories told to children.

Meanwhile three dragon eggs are hatching... Will they destroy the island and everyone living on it? Or can they be controlled?

Xander's Sea Purrtector Files:

Latitudes and Cattitudes

~ A prequel to the Sea Purrtector Files ~

This short prequel to the Sea Purrtector Files centers on Xander de Hunter when he is a rising star on Catamondo's kick-boxing circuit, with dreams of becoming a Purrtector.

After a match in Seattle, he is asked to help find Cha-Cha, a white Norwegian beauty, who is missing.

With Merlin's assistance, they follow Cha-Cha's trail into the Puget Sound where Xander must face his biggest fear – water.

The Red Claw

Dame Esmeralda, the Purrsident's littermate, has been catnapped. Xander de Hunter, Catamondo's Sea Purrtector hurries to Jamaica to help rescue her, even though Jamaica is one of Dogdom's strongholds.

Could this be a trap?

Purr-a-noia

Catamondo and Dogdom's peace treaty is in jeopardy. In Haiti, witchcraft and voodoo seem to be involved in a plot to hex the Purrsident.

Will Xander be able to restore the peace?

The Vi-Purrs

The Daily Mews reports continued violence in the Dominican Republic Purrtectorate.

Xander discovers that the Moreau situation is still affecting the ability of Catamondo to purrtect cats. Worse, the office of the Dominican Republic's Purrtector seems to be involved.

Will Xander be able to restore peace?

Suspense/Romance:

Deadly Rumors

Kelsey MacLennan and Devlin Doran both want to make the world better, but Doran believes the rumors about the MacLennans dealing drugs, so his goal is to bring them down.

Kelsey MacLennan wants to make the world better, but her senatorial political campaign turns deadly and rumors abound, when the incumbent must win or be killed by his backers. Devlin Doran's younger sister died of an overdose, so his goal is to prosecute pushers. Rumors abound that the MacLennans are high in the local drug network and he is targeting Kelsey MacLennan.

Will they be able to separate fact from fiction or will the rumors be deadly?

Fatal Attractions

Ariel and Tempest Danner have escaped Tempest's homicidal father for the sixth time in five years. Armed with new identities and disguises, they are determined that Fairbanks, Alaska will be a sanctuary where they can live in peace.

Stone O'Banyon, their new landlord, has been divorced for three years. All his energy is focused on his job and Dolly, who would never hurt him.

The last thing Ariel needs or wants is the attraction she feels for another tall, dark man, who seems hard as the granite he is named for, but the fascination will not go away. Stone isn't any happier with his obsessive thoughts concerning Ariel.

Things seem calm, then Ariel and Tempest catch sight of the man they had hoped they would never encounter and things turn fatal...again.

Passion's Fire

Prior to the blaze that killed her husband, Jacqueline Cardew
believed her husband wrote the "fiery messages' she received.
Now she finds a new note inside her locked house. Jacqueline
suspects her faceless stalker murdered Adam and she is next.
She flees north, where she joins Link Gavallan's group on a two
week long Alaskan wilderness canoe trip. As they float down
the desolate river, she receives another message…

Instead of finding a sanctuary, has she made it easier for her
stalker to trap her?

www.ingramcontent.com/pod-product-compliance
Lightning Source LLC
Chambersburg PA
CBHW062013170626

46813CB00001B/138